“Hey there, Georgy girl, there’s another Georgy deep inside.
Bring out all the love you hide, and oh, what a change there’ll be
The world would see
A new Georgy girl.”
—Jim Dale and Tom Springfield

“He patiently gathered another heartbeat, another breath, and then told them stubbornly, emphatically, without a trace of repentance or regret, “Well, goddamnit, I was immortal till I died.”
—Jim Dodge, *Fup*

“I’d like a large order of French fries, with a side of mayo, extra ketchup, lots of tartar sauce, and a pocket map of Venezuela.”
—Tom Robbins at the La Conner Tavern

THIS IS A GENUINE RARE BIRD BOOK

Rare Bird Books
6044 North Figueroa Street
Los Angeles, California 90042
rarebirdbooks.com

FIRST TRADE PAPERBACK ORIGINAL EDITION

Cover Artwork: "Portrait of Ethel Pearl Fern as Dame Fortune"
by Stanley Turnball (1946).

Author Photo by Sz. Verka

For more information, address:
Rare Bird Books Subsidiary Rights Department
6044 North Figueroa Street
Los Angeles, California 90042

Set in Adobe Garamond
Printed in the United States

10 9 8 7 6 5 4 3 2 1

Library of Congress Cataloging-in-Publication Data available upon request

I WISH, THERE-FORE I AM

ADDITIONAL PRAISE FOR GARY LIPPMAN

"Shocking, tender, sexy, and a bit bananas. (There's even a bit about bananas. Literal bananas.) Thumb's up!"

—DANNY FIELDS

"Gary Lippman is an author of immense vision, caustic wit, and wry compassion for the human experience. His new novel is highly readable and just plain fun—an amusement park adventure with every turn of the page."

—JONATHAN SHAW

"You didn't hear it from me, but smart money has it that on the basis of his latest novel, Gary Lippman will be the recipient of the next Nobel Prize in Chemistry. *I Wish, Therefore I Am* is so good that I threw away all my other books"

—PATRICIA MARX

I WISH, THERE-FORE I AM

or, THIS HERE IS A LIST OF HUMBLE APPEALS TO DAME FORTUNE

GARY LIPPMAN

RARE BIRD
LOS ANGELES, CALIF.

For Verka,
For Marike and Istvan,
For My Three Guys—
Gabou, Billy, and Buddy,
For Cousin Pirate Jennyke,
and
For the Class of 1932—
Tommy Rotten and the H.Q.,
With Love and D. B.

(*"There must be rocks beneath this sand"*)

CONTENTS

ONE. AN ANATOMY OF WISHING

I wish I could hold the whole world in my hands, then pop it in my mouth and roll it around there like a gumball, nibbling on it, savoring its roundness. The question is whether to swallow the Earth when it loses its flavor, or to let my saliva dissolve it, or just to spit our planet out.

Perhaps as we grow older we either become our best selves or our worst selves. While I'm waiting on Dame Fortune, wishing she'd help me to become my best self, I'll try to remind myself of what the poet Mário de Andrade said before he died young: "We have two lives. And the second begins when we realize we have only one."

Another wish: that I could travel back to prehistoric times and lash myself to the sharp-spined back of a large Pterodactyl. I'd ride that sucker above the landscape which eons later will become West Orange, New Jersey, the town where I grew up.

Fortunately, this big bird I'm atop won't notice me, or at least won't feel irked by my presence; I'm probably causing a bit of physical pressure, maybe even a comforting kind, like a human hand caressing her scales—although such hands, and human wishes, are still a long way from evolving. As my Pterodactyl keeps flapping its leathery, fetid-smelling wings, circling the future Northfield Avenue, I'll gawk at one natural wonder after another and smile at all the behaviors, hostile or altruistic, of the other dinosaurs hustling around down below.

Most of all, I'll try to determine the site where my future home will be built. Then, once I locate it, I'll unlash myself and parachute down onto that spot, assuming it's not currently a pool of lava or the resting place of a predator. Finally, I'll stretch out on the rocky ground where my bed will someday be placed and have myself a good long snooze, snoring louder than any Pterodactyl's cries. Then my dead mother will walk through my door and wake me the way she always did, tugging up the Venetian blinds and singing, "*Rise and shine, / and give God your glory, glory, / children of the Lord...*"

"Life is a hospital where each patient is driven by the wish to change beds." The poet Charles Baudelaire nailed the essence of our condition with this observation: to be human is to be wistful, which is one of my favorite words—it means "having or showing a feeling of vague or regretful longing." You can know us by many things, but for certain by our wishing. We're composed of wishes as thoroughly as we're composed of water, with some wishes conscious and some not, some voiced and others silent. There are wishes that X will or will not happen in the future, and wishes that Z had or had not happened in the past. "To wish or not to wish"—could this be the true question?

What follows is a list, hardly exhaustive, of my own appeals to Dame Fortune. Many of the people, places, things, and situations here are real, while a few are hybrids of truth and fiction. Some names have been changed, others not. But rest assured that all the wishes in this list are heart-of-hearts sincere.

TWO. IMPATIENT WISHES

Being followed and surveilled and ultimately attacked by evil ninjas has been a fear of mine since my childhood, and I wish I didn't still sometimes worry that they're watching me from the shadows, standing there like "your mother" in my favorite Rolling Stones song title. I'd much prefer to be dancing to the Stones, even *shimmying*, as in the Bessie Smith song "I Wish I Could Shimmy Like My Sister Kate." Rest assured that if I had a shimmying sister, I wouldn't hesitate to ask her to give me shimmy lessons. Cakewalk lessons, too. And if I didn't have such a sister, or if she refused, I'd wish I could learn how to twirl around while I'm dancing like the Whirling Dervishes I saw once in a religious school in Istanbul. Or to dance the tango, which the critic Clive James calls "a holiday from the accidental, and a free pass into the realm where the inevitable, for once, looks good."

The poet Ezra Pound, whose antisemitism did not corrode his way with words, once said, "Music begins to atrophy when it departs too far from the dance." (He added that "Poetry begins to atrophy when it gets too far from music.") Boogie'ing on down is not just for professionals, either; as an African proverb has it, "If you can talk, you can sing, and if you can walk, you can dance."

Dancing, even so, has its limits. Watching people shake, rattle, and roll from behind soundproof glass so that you cannot hear the music they're grooving to (I once did this outside a nightclub in Chicago) makes even the best of dancers look ridiculous, just as sex, when detached from any desire, appears to involve strangely animated beings performing silly behaviors on each other's bodies. I wish I could remember just how silly those behaviors can seem whenever thoughts of sex, or of dancing, begin to preoccupy me.

Although I like when historical mysteries remain unsolved, thereby preserving our state of collective unknowing—the poet Kabir wrote that "The eye goes blind when it only wants to see '*why*'"—I wish to someday walk into a bar and find Judge Crater, Amelia Earhart, Jimmy Hoffa, D. B. Cooper, Sean Flynn, the subject of Carly Simon's song "You're So Vain" (could it be Carly speaking to herself?), Ambrose Bierce, the "Thai Silk King" Jim Thompson, the unsung singer-songwriter Connie Converse, and other infamous missing persons all carousing together.

Maybe the bar they're in will be Vesuvio's in North Beach, because didn't the author Oscar Wilde say that "Anyone who disappears is said to be seen in San Francisco"? And maybe representatives of the Ten Lost Tribes of Israel will also make the scene, as will the boxer-poet Arthur Cravan. Not only did Cravan, along with Alfred Jarry, invent surrealism before surrealism was officially invented, but he was a muleteer, a snake charmer, a gold prospector, and the bona fide nephew of Oscar Wilde.

In lieu of my coming upon all those well-known missing people, imagine the reaction of onlookers if I hire celebrity impersonators for Crater, Earhart, Hoffa, Cooper, Flynn, Simon, Fawcett, Thompson, Cravan, *et al* to cocktails at Vesuvio's.

Still loitering in this wish list's *Unsolved Mysteries Department*, I wish I knew what happened to the test missile that the Confederates fired up at the sky during the end of the American Civil War. Its inventors hoped to study the missile's flight and learn how it could help win the day, but that thing vanished from view, was never found again, and might still be up there now orbiting our gumball Earth, knowing its cause was lost and refusing to come down.

"*I regret nothing*," sang Edith Piaf, but only saints, sages, liars, couch potatoes, psychopaths, and cowards make such a claim. (Which category did Piaf fall into?) None of us, except perhaps those sages and saints, are free of desires, which are as common as our regrets. So the Czech proverb "What I don't have, I don't need," or the aphorist Jack Gardner's quip that "If it is gone and you are alive, you didn't need it," are no more realistic as principles than Piaf's assertion.

Even so, I wish I could feel fewer regrets and desires. Merely to remember some of mine causes me to wince. At least the phrases "I regret nothing" and "What I don't have, I don't need," however unrealistic they may be, are still useful as aspirational tools. As is the author Isak Dinesen's claim that she rose every morning to write "without hope and without despair." She may have even gotten that notion from William Blake, who wrote, "*Man was made for Joy and Woe / and when this we rightly know / thro the World we safely go*."

Meanwhile, the dice are always rolling.

Just so that you, my fellow wisher, know to whom this wish list is addressed, here are some facts gleaned in part from Wikipedia:

Many citizens call her "Dame Chance," while gamblers call her "Lady Luck." She's depicted as veiled or blind, holding a ship's rudder, a horn of plenty, or her famous Wheel. Some ascribe balance to her nature, saying she rewards moderation, while others call her capricious and argue that she favors bravery. And according to some accounts, she's got a brother: Fatum, or Destiny, who oversees the predetermined slices of our future with his Hand of Fate while she, according to her own program, tends to that future's unpredictable vagaries.

Ancient Romans built a cult around her, naming Jupiter as her father and linking her to the Egyptian goddess Isis. They built temples for her, with some located as far away as the land now known as Scotland, and the dedication day of those temples is June 24, Midsummer. Seneca, perhaps the wisest of ancient Romans, consoled his comrades that "She takes away nothing that she has not already given."

As for her Wheel, the *Rota Fortuna*, it characteristically shows the four stages of life. At the left is *regnabo*, or "I shall reign." On the top is *regno*, or "I reign." On the right is *regnavi*, or "I have reigned," and on the bottom is *sum sine regno*, or "I have no kingdom." Serving as the tenth card of the Tarot's Major Arcana, the Wheel represents bounty, elevation, felicity. But beware if the Wheel should turn up reversed in your next reading of that so-called "wicked pack of cards."

Farmers and sailors prayed to her. Pirates might have, as well. A twentieth century German psychoanalyst said, "Some people run after her, not realizing that she's been running after them but couldn't reach them—because they were running." (Compare this to the writer Alexander Woollcott's observation that "Many of us spend half of our time wishing for things we could have if we didn't spend half of our time wishing." And what did Woollcott propose we do instead of wishing? He said, "Take what you can get! Grab the chances as they come along! Act in hallways! Sing in doorways! Dance in cellars!")

Animal sacrifices have been made in her name. In one persona she is the pagan European earth goddess Nerthus, who embodies the arrival of springtime, but at the price of human beings' lives. Should we consider every life lost to bad fortune a credit to her program? Might she wear the same necklace of skulls worn by Kali, Hindu goddess of destruction?

Christians adopted her but weakened her, labeling her as a mere "servant of God" and calling her actions nothing but demonstrations of "divine will." Her most devout fans knew better—one has even named an asteroid after her. And they have divided her into different selves: *Victrix*, the fortune of victory in battle; *Annonaria*, the fortune of the harvest; *Brevis*, fickle fortune; *Balnearis*, the fortune of bathing; *Privata*, the fortune of the private individual; *Publica*, the fortune of the general public; *Dubia*, doubtful fortune; *Obsequens*, the fortune of indulgence; *Virilius*, the fortune of women's luck in marriage; and *Redux*, the fortune of returning safely home.

So many incarnations, so many names. But for pop culture-minded me, she is always how she's referred to in pop songs by the Holy Modal Rounders, Andy Partridge, and David Allan Coe: "Dame Fortune."

In one of his TV specials, Dick Cavett introduced his audience to a gorgeous and voluptuous young blond woman, saying, "Allow me to present Admiral Harvey Q. Beeswanger USN, master of disguise." I wish I could become adept at such methods of disguise myself, adept enough to be able to elude any pesky ninjas who might be stalking me. Shoe lifts, wigs, molding putty for my nose, false wrinkles, rubber jug ears, mouth inserts and dental plates with missing teeth, electronic voice modifiers, lessons in cross-dressing, male breast reduction surgery, a latex foreskin (because you never know)—I will be open to employ any of these techniques if needed. And my motto will be "*lavartis prodeo*": "I advance masked."

Even if disguise isn't strictly called for, I wish I could cultivate about myself an air of mystery profound enough to make even my intimates think, *He's so* shadowy. *What makes him tick*? My late friend Bob Neuwirth was proficient at this, maintaining a potent personal mystique even while he made himself accessible to the countless friends in his life. A talented painter and an equally talented songwriter, Neuwirth was also a scene-maker extraordinaire, a Master of Revels, the so-called "Boogiemeister." Perhaps you know the expression "There's always someone cooler than you are." Neuwirth was the one person for whom this expression was not true.

In her memoir *Just Kids* (and who among us doesn't often still feel like a kid, wishing away?), the rock artist Patti Smith writes that Neuwirth was "a risk taker...a catalyst for change...a trusted confidant to many of the great minds and musicians of his generation." Although no biography has been published about Neuwirth, he makes vivid appearances in countless biographies of other cultural figures, including those of his longtime friend Bob Dylan. In Dylan's own memoir, he writes, "Like Kerouac had immortalized Neal Cassady in *On the Road*, someone should have immortalized Neuwirth…If ever there was a renaissance man leaping in and out of things, he would have to be it."

Unlike a lot of renaissance people, Neuwirth was a *mensch*, and after he got sober, he devoted much of his life to helping others to get sober, too. This is how the Boogiemeister became "the Wagonmaster." Yet he never lost his sardonic edge when he told you his jokes and stories, and you always got the sense from him that, no matter how much help or enjoyment he gave you, there were depths to the man that you would never be able to plumb. Too many of these depths existed, and they were too well guarded. Which only drew you closer to him.

"It's a perfect world," Bob used to say, "but we just don't understand it yet." I'll never "understand" the man. And, despite all my curiosity about him, I wouldn't have that be any other way.

Another Neuwirth remark: "The truth is, there are only five hundred people on the planet. We just keep meeting them over and over again." This calls to mind a quip made by the rocker Captain Beefheart: "There are only forty people in the world, and five of them are hamburgers." Somewhat more plausibly, the naturalist John Muir said, "When we try to pick out anything by itself, we find it hitched to everything else in the universe." Meanwhile, in China, they believe that an invisible thread links strangers to each other for reasons they have not yet fathomed, or never will. They call this link "the Red Thread."

Those of you who have read the novel *Cat's Cradle* by Kurt Vonnegut, Jr., will be reminded here of Vonnegut's concept of the "*karass*," a group of people who keep getting entangled with each other for no logical reason. Me, I find the Red Thread idea more compelling, and my first impulse is to wish I could learn the names of those to whom I'm thusly linked. Am I connected, for example, to a Hermes Trismegistus-level alchemist who works by night in a shotgun shack on the outskirts of Salvador in Brazil? Or to a green-and-yellow uniformed short-order cook at the Nathan's Famous Hot Dogs outpost in a Connecticut shopping mall? Perhaps I can figure out my connections by myself, by wandering around and peering into each unfamiliar face I go past and silently asking, "Are you one of them?"

Hearing—or merely *sensing*—a "yes" from someone will probably prove to be gratifying. I'm not sure what would happen next, though. Would we just make awkward small talk until we continue on our paths, me on mine and you on yours while the Red Thread again stretches tautly between us?

In New Orleans they say, "If *ifs* was skiffs, we'd all be boating." I prefer how my Uncle Wolf expressed this concept to me when I was a child: "If wishes were horses, beggars would ride." The second or third time I heard Wolf say it, my imagination got fired up by the image of desires turned into thoroughbreds and mounted by grizzled yet suddenly jubilant men and women. No longer a child, I've stopped wishing that wishes could be horses, because while beggars would indeed get moving, some of them might get bucked from their steeds and break their necks or else get trampled under hooves before they'd be able to climb back in the saddle. When the going gets tough, it would be ideal for the horse-backed beggars to mutter to themselves this consolatory advice from the author Hunter S. Thompson: "Buy the ticket, take the ride."

I've heard it said that a happy marriage is the union of two forgivers. I've also heard it said that you don't marry one person, you marry three: the person you think they are, the person they actually are, and the person they're going to become after being married to you. As for our failed relationships before marriage, it might be helpful to remember that the only common denominator in all of them is/was us.

I wish I knew all the methods to make a marriage successful. I do know that selective hearing is one of them. In my favorite memoir, James Thurber's *My Life And Hard Times*, the humorist describes an eccentric aunt of his who had a burglar phobia. She managed this phobia by gathering all her shoes around her at every bedtime. Then, shouting "Hark!," she threw her shoes down her darkened hallway. As for her husband, he would be sound asleep or just pretended to be asleep, having "learned to ignore the whole situation as long ago as 1903."

Since 1903! Well, if my wife Berta's own selective hearing ever fails her, or if it falls short of the Thurber uncle's selective hearing, I hope Berta isn't ultimately driven to murder me. Being by nature patient, loving, and emotionally stable, Berta seems unlikely to go down this path. In case she does, though, I wish her the luck of Terence Bell. Who is Terence Bell, you wonder? According to my favorite reference book, *Brewer's Rogues, Villains, Eccentrics* by William Donaldson, this chap Bell was a building-society clerk from Hampshire, England who also happened to be one of the world's least successful practitioners of uxoricide, or spouse-killing.

With an insurance policy in place, one that would pay out 250,000 pounds for her accidental death, Bell put a lethal dose of mercury in the missus's strawberry flan. That mercury just rolled off the plate. So into her next meal, a cooked mackerel, he poured the rest of the mercury bottle. Mrs. Bell ate the fish with no resulting problem. A change of scene was necessary, Bell figured, so off they went to vacation in Yugoslavia where, in spite of his urgent prompting, Mrs. Bell refused to pose for a snapshot on the edge of a scenic cliff.

For attempt number four, the increasingly desperate husband started a fire outside his wife's bedroom while she lay inside, ill with chickenpox. Are you surprised that a neighbor showed up to put out the flames? Sticking with the arson enterprise, Bell started another fire that destroyed his home, but the spouse skedaddled out of there in time. Interestingly, Bell never utilized any kitchen implement as a murder weapon, being perhaps unaware of William Burroughs' remark that "Whoever holds a frying pan owns death." (Burroughs used a pistol when he accidentally killed his wife while playing their "William Tell routine," but that's a tale for a different time.)

My favorite of Bell's attempts was the sixth. In order to "test the brakes on my car," he asked his target to stand in the middle of a road so he could drive straight at her. History does not reveal how Mrs. Bell eluded this fate, but she did, after which Bell hastened down the wind to the police. He made a full confession, and only then did Mrs. Bell learn why, as she put it, "That mackerel had tasted a bit off." Her ignorance was as remarkable as her husband's failure rate.

Even harder to kill than Mrs. Bell was everybody's favorite Russian mad monk, Grigori Rasputin. During my teenage years, Rasputin fascinated me. Not only was he murder-proof, until he wasn't, but how appealing he was to the women of Saint Petersburg! *If an ugly bearded freak like him could get laid*, my thinking went, *maybe someday I can, too.* I even made a Grigori Rasputin-themed Valentine's Day card for a friend. The card showed the mad monk's glowering face saying, "*Call me Grig.*" I also thought about writing a story which saw Rasputin cheating death in Russia and making his way in disguise to silent-movie era Hollywood, where he would become a film director and resume his flamboyant ways.

I wish I had not considered it too simplistic when my elderly friend Barbara told me, "In every decision you make, you're prioritizing one of three goals: power, freedom, or love." Standing on rue Madame in Paris one afternoon last year, I listened to the sound of children who played in a nearby schoolyard. It belonged to the school my son had attended, and I remembered when my boy's voice had been a part of that sweet cacophony. Then I remembered a question I posed to Barbara, which was whether she herself had tended to prioritize one goal more frequently than the others.

Chuckling at this, Barbara told me, "Oh, yes, I do."

"You do?"

"Yes. I choose *love* every time."

If I'm wise, it seems to me, I will do like Barbara does. *Every* time.

"Ah, sweet mystery of life. What a gift, huh? Ain't you lucky you got in?" So said the *bon vivant* New York street violinist Ruby Levine. Barbara would have liked him, I think. And I wonder what they would have thought about that five-thousand-year-old male corpse who was discovered well-preserved in an Austrian glacier. As soon as the news got out that the ancient man's sperm might still be viable, women began clamoring to have his child. Which makes me wish that, if I can't stay "in" forever according to the Ruby Levine sense, then at least let my dead body be kept "on ice" this way. Not to be thawed out in the future—it would be too weird to wake up in a radically different civilization—but merely to have my genetic material turn up all those millennia down the line. (Surprise, "I'm" back!) That the prospect sounds like a fun new twist on Ruby Levine's "getting in."

I wish I could regard the world with the serenity of the pair of white marble sphinx statues who gaze out at elegant Andrassy Street from their perches on either side of the Budapest Opera House. How can you not love lion-bodied, eagle-winged, serpent-tailed, woman-headed stone creatures? They might even be cousins to the sphinx that adorns Oscar Wilde's grave at the Pere Lachaise Cemetery in Paris, not far from the singer Jim Morrison's own resting place.

My other favorite mythological creature is the phoenix. Who wouldn't want to watch a flaming resurrection? Yet if Dame Fortune ever asks me in a dream if I have a "spirit animal," I'll tell her, "Yup. It's the '*sphoenix*,' which is the fanciful hybrid of 'sphinx' and 'phoenix' invented by James Joyce. He identified it as 'a mystery with a happy ending.' Because who doesn't love a mystery? Even you, Dame Fortune, must, on occasion, enjoy a happy ending."

If you're searching for real-world animals to appreciate, how about our canine companions? As the Texan Jewish wit Kinky Friedman liked to say, "Dogs teach us loyalty, courage and unconditional love, and we teach them to sit and fetch." It's true that dog-love can go overboard; the author Edward Abbey was correct in observing that, "When a man's best friend is his dog, that dog has a problem." Still, I'm not ashamed of how close I feel to my dog Rosalita. She's not historically significant compared to the Pharoah's companion Abuwtiyuw, history's first canine with a recorded name. Or the Xoloitzcuintli favored by the Mayans and the Aztecs. Or Panhu of Irish mythology. Rosalita is not Alexander the Great's mastiff Molossus, either, or Donnchadh, which was Robert the Bruce's hound, or even Fortune, the wonderfully named pug belonging to Napoleon's first wife Josephine.

Rosalita is just a Mexican street dog, the black-and-gold-hued mixture of twenty-two different breeds who narrowly escaped execution in the Tijuana dog pound and survived a transcontinental road trip to wind up in my home. Yet in spite of her ordinariness, I wish I could behave more like her. In fact, my dog is my primary guru. Why? Because, unlike me, she's excited to wake up each morning. She appreciates the natural world and feels at home there. In fact, she seems relatively content with nearly all circumstances she finds herself in, welcoming things when they appear and not lamenting for too long when they vanish. In this, she intuitively lives by the author G. K. Chesterton's belief that "An inconvenience is an adventure wrongly considered" and "An adventure is an inconvenience rightly considered."

Like all non-human animals, my dog Rosalita has a mostly clear conscience. (The poet Wisława Szymborska: "*The rattlesnake approves of himself without reservation.*") Rosalita eats when she's hungry, sleeps when she's sleepy, and feels goodwill toward all other creatures except for squirrels. She's loyal, too (although the aphorist Karl Kraus criticized canine loyalty by noting, "A dog is loyal to men, not to other dogs"). She's curious about much, knows how to pay close attention, doesn't need to force herself to exercise, doesn't take insults personally, doesn't morbidly dwell on the concept of death. She keeps her expectations of others and of herself realistically low. She's not hung up about bodily functions and has no interest in sex, although she had some surgical help with her lack of sexual interest. Best of all, she doesn't mind going around naked in public.

Of course, it's easy for Rosalita to be Zen-like—she's in the proverbial catbird seat, not needing to work or to suffer in order to receive meals and shelter and ear-rubs. (I try to be mindful of my own state of considerable entitlement.) Still, she does have a few habits I *wouldn't* wish to follow. Chasing those squirrels into traffic is one of them. Welcoming intruders to our home as gladly as she'd welcome invited guests is another. (The Jake Thackray song about his equally friendly pooch goes, "*You're so nice / that burglars who burglar us burglar us twice*").

I fear the day when Rosalita will pick up fleas and bring them into our home, although, as the Japanese say, "A reasonable number of fleas is good for a dog. Otherwise the dog forgets he is a dog." And I'm not pleased that Rosalita regularly violates the admonition of the Cramps' song title "Don't Eat Stuff Off The Sidewalk." Then again, Rosalita is probably not a Cramps fan.

Songs! I wish I could write the script for a Broadway musical, with the score consisting of my favorite Country-and-Western songs. Many aspects of contemporary American life would be touched upon in the storyline, which will depict a couple's romance from before the beginning to after the end:

Initial loneliness: *"At the Gas Station of Love, I Got the Self-Service Pump"*;
Economic uncertainty: *"Too Much Month at the End of the Money"*;
Family dramas: *"Please, Daddy, Don't Get Drunk This Christmas," "Get Off the Stove, Grandma, You're Too Old to Ride the Range"*;
Religious complications: *"They Ain't Making Jews Like Jesus Anymore," "Jesus is My Lawyer"*;
Erotic missteps: *"I Went Back to My Fourth Wife for the Third Time and Gave Her a Second Chance to Make a First Class Fool Out of Me," "I Fell for Her, She Fell for Him, and He Fell for Me")* (this

latter song reminding me of the time in a synagogue when I made goo-goo eyes at a woman who was making goo-goo eyes at my friend Brigitte who was making goo-goo eyes at a man who was making goo-goo eyes at me);

New love in bloom: *"If I Said You Had a Beautiful Body, Would You Hold it Against Me?," "I'll Marry You Tomorrow, But Let's Honeymoon Tonight";*

"Getting to know you": *"I'd Like to Check You for Ticks," "She Never Told Me She Was a Mime," "How I Lost Thirty-One Pounds in Seventeen Days";*

Interior designs tips: *"I'm Gonna Hire a Wino to Decorate Our Home";*

Increasing estrangement: *"I Can't Love Your Body if Your Heart's Not in It," "Ever Since I Said 'I Do,' There's a Lot of Things You Don't," "I Hate Every Bone in Your Body Except Mine";*

Frustration and rage: *"You Can't Have Your Kate and Edith Too," "If I Can't Be Number One in Your Life, Then Number Two on You," "You're the Reason Our Kids are Ugly";*

Explosions of violence: *"The Next Time You Throw That Frying Pan, My Face Ain't Gonna Be There," "I've Got You on My Conscience But At Least You're off My Back";*

The drowning of sorrows: *"She's Acting Single, I'm Drinking Doubles," I'd Rather Have A Bottle In Front Of Me Than A Frontal Lobotomy"; "I OD'ed in Denver";*

Thwarted new possibilities: *"I Could Get Over Him (If I Could Get Under You)," "If You Don't Believe I Love You, Just Ask My Wife," "Velcro Arms, Teflon Heart";*

The darkest hour: *"You're Going To Be Fine and I'm Going To Hell," "I Don't Know Whether To Kill Myself Or Go Bowling";*

Declarations of independence: *"Get Your Tongue Outta My Mouth Cause I'm Kissing You Goodbye";* and, finally, "The peace that passeth all understanding": *"God is Great, Beer is Good, and People are Crazy."*

Another artistic wish of mine is that it had been I and not Joe Brainard who invented the simple yet ingenious "I Remember" form of literature in his experimental memoir of that title. "I remember the only time I ever saw my mother cry. I was eating apricot pie" goes one of Brainard's entries. Then there is "I remember my American history teacher who was always threatening to jump out of the window if we didn't quiet down. (Second floor)," and "I remember my day dreams of being a singer all alone on a big stage with no scenery, just a single spotlight on me, singing my heart out, and moving my audience to total tears of love and affection."

I could do my own "I Remember" bits, of course, even many of them with just a single humble subject. Bananas, for example. How much I enjoyed eating them with Jell-O and cottage cheese when I was a child. The unspeakable thing a friend told me he did once with a banana. Also, the afternoon in the early nineties when I walked down Yonge Street in Toronto with a banana jammed in my ear, pretending it was a cell phone. My former law professor Lamar was in on this prank, trailing me by twenty feet and speaking on his own "banana phone."

Even better for an "I Remember" treatment might be the subject of pubic hair.

* I remember accidentally seeing my mother naked and feeling puzzled that the platinum-blond hair on her head did not match the color of the hair between her legs.

* I remember standing at a urinal at the Ziegfeld Theater in Manhattan before a screening of the Who rock opera movie *Tommy* and feeling disturbed when I felt hair starting to sprout down below.

* I remember my first blow-job. The giver, whose name was Lisa, had shaved her "hairy business" into the shape of a heart, which made me feel even more louche than I already did.

Although Georges Perec and other cool authors have written their own versions of the "I Remember" form in honor of Joe Brainard—and although I borrowed Brainard's form for the eulogy I gave at my father's funeral—I will refrain from writing any additional I Remember stuff here. Even so, you can consider this wish list a kind of variation on the literary form Joe Brainard invented.

In a dream, Dame Fortune asks me, "What are your most recurrent wishes? Not that I necessarily plan to satisfy any of them, you know."

"Well," I say, noticing that I can't behold the Dame's face at all because it's obscured by a dark veil, "the predictable cluster of personal stuff, I guess. I wish I could be a 'fine figure of a man,' not too dumb for New York City or too ugly for LA, with my BMI lower, my scalp hairier, my legs longer, and my hands and my penis and my ears and my muscles all bigger. Much bigger. Plus, while we're at it, let's make my intellect keener and my charisma off the charts. Still, I realize that it's probably best for me if I don't wish for too much. Or if at least I don't focus on any unfilled desires. My chief wish, dear Dame Fortune, is that you won't regard this wish list as presumptuous. Trust me, I won't complain if few or even none my wishes are granted. I'm all about counting my blessings."

Nodding her veiled head, Dame Fortune asks, "Do you know the joke about the old woman and her young grandchild strolling on the beach in Fort Lauderdale? No? Well, along they go, but then the old woman has to watch helplessly as a tidal wave comes crashing in and sweeps the little boy out to sea. Horrified, the grandmother falls to her knees and raises her eyes to the sky and prays to me, Dame Fortune, for her grandson to be restored to her. '*Please*, Dame, give me back the boy! I'll *never* take anything for granted *again*, I'll never complain! Just send him back to me!' Sure enough, the next tidal wave to crash onto that beach brings back her grandchild, depositing him right next to her. He's drenched and coughing up water but otherwise okay. Hugging and kissing him, the grandmother feels ecstatic that she got her kid back. But then she notices something different about him, so she looks up at the sky again and shakes her fist and in an angry voice she shouts at me, '*He had a hat*!'"

"That's a good one," I say. "I promise I'll never run a 'He had a hat' routine on you."

"Promises, promises," says the Dame. "My advice is not merely to count your blessings but to fall to your knees every few minutes and thank me and all the other higher powers (if indeed we exist) for those blessings. Don't focus only on your blessings, either, but thank us as well for all the injuries and humiliations that you've knowingly or unknowingly been spared."

"I'll do that."

The Dame says, "See to it. And perhaps you ought to consider this wish list less like a variation on Joe Brainard's I Remember work and more like what ancient Greeks like Epictetus and Epicurus called a 'hypomnemata.'"

"A what?"

"A series of reflections, meditations, and self-reminders. With," she adds, concluding my dream, "the word 'wish' being the least important part of each page."

During my childhood, I wished I could travel to Japan to catch a glimpse of Godzilla, Mothra, and Rodan. So frightening were these movie monsters that they made their human victims speak in such a way that their words did not match the movement of their mouths. I also wished to visit Scotland in order to commune with the Loch Ness Monster. Then, a little later in life, it was the Pacific Northwest for an *al fresco* lunch with Bigfoot. The same wish applied to the Yeti in the Himalayas, although an *al fresco* lunch there might be subject to deep freezes and avalanches. Later still and it was extraterrestrials, whom I hoped would beam me up to their starship and probe me—but tenderly, tenderly—with their curved and shiny surgical instruments.

For a year of two in my forties, I hiked around the wild forests of Pennsylvania seeking without success to trap the wart- and mole-covered creature called a "squonk," which I first heard about in a Steely Dan song: "*Have you ever seen a squonk's tears? / Well, look at mine.*" After visiting one of my favorite places, the Museum of Jurassic Technology in Culver City, I sought out the Cameroonian Stink Ant, the Ringnot Sloth, and the "Wish Upon a Piece of Hair" I'd seen displayed. Next came my searches for a griffin and a chimera…

And I'm currently on the lookout for the only mythic creature around whom even ninjas tread lightly. She's the protagonist of Paul Dehn's poem *Alternative Endings to an Unwritten Ballad*, which begins: "*I stole through the dungeons, while everyone slept, / Till I came to the cage where the Monster was kept. / There, locked in the arms of a Giant Baboon, / Rigid and smiling, lay…MRS. RAVOON!*"

Believe it or not, I may have actually met this Mrs. Ravoon, except she was a he, or a he in drag: *Mr.* Ravoon. For two or three years in the mid-eighties, I used to bump into a remarkable-looking old man around Manhattan with disturbing frequency. I call him "remarkable-looking" because he was always dressed in black, with a shapeless long blouse hanging loosely from his slumped-forward plump frame. Mr. Ravoon's hair was dyed jet-black, too, and over his left eye he wore a black eye patch. As for the frequency of my encountering the man, I call this frequency "disturbing" because it occurred every few months, and every time at a different library, where he would be reading the same hardbound reference book: *Who's Who in America*.

The gargantuan Rose Reading Room of the New York Public Library's main branch; the Jefferson Market branch in the East Village; the front room of the private New York Society Library on the Upper

East Side—whenever I walked into one of those locations, there he would be, with the hefty *Who's Who* volume held open in front of his face. The man never seemed to notice me, but as I did my own reading, I observed him, and his one visible eye would start to flutter and then shut just before he'd sink into sleep, snoring gently.

Was this stranger a harmless New York City eccentric? Was he a warlock, a sorcerer? Was he the Hand of Fate in human form? Or was this old man the Reaper, the Angel of Death—"Stretchfoot," as death was called during the Middle Ages because he "stretched out the limbs of the dying"? Was this old man, in other words, a harbinger of my demise?

Already familiar with the poem about Mrs. Ravoon, I decided to call the old man by the same name. And each time I saw *Mr*. Ravoon, his presence freaked me out. My disquiet really soared during the summer of 1987 when I walked into the library at the Pompidou Center in Paris—I was on vacation in France for a few weeks—and found the eye patch-wearer already dozing at a table with *Who's Who in America* open and in front of him. At first I thought I was hallucinating. Had he actually followed me to Paris? It seemed so! And Mr. Ravoon was snoring louder now than I'd ever heard him snore.

Once I regained my composure, I rushed out of the Pompidou Center—not just the library on the ground level of this odd gigantic building but the building itself. Then, as I hurried through the Beaubourg neighborhood, I kept glancing anxiously behind me, trying to catch sight of Mr. Ravoon in hot pursuit. (Beaubourg, I should mention, already had quite a creepy vibe. A nearby café I'd visited, Le Tribunal, featured Satanist images on its walls and a "staged," but maybe *not* so "staged," black mass advertised for Saturday nights.)

During the next week or so in Paris, I maintained a look-out for my *bete noire*, prepared to be confronted by him again at any moment. If Mr. Ravoon could chase me across an ocean, couldn't he chase me anywhere? He surely pursued me into a few of my nightmares, and I avoided all libraries, especially the Pompidou, during the rest of my stay in France. I avoided them back in Manhattan, as well, and looked with suspicion at everyone I encountered who wore an eye patch.

Perhaps my caution worked, or perhaps I outlived Mr. Ravoon, because I never saw him again after that Paris summer day. Eventually he disappeared from my nightmares, and other eye patch-wearers no longer frightened me, either. (One of them, a Hollywood hipster at the trendy Bar Marmont on Sunset Boulevard, wore his sky-blue patch for an hour before he wearied of it and pushed it up on his forehead like a pair of sunglasses, demonstrating to everyone present that the patch had only been a pretentious unneeded accessory. As for the dark-gray eye patch worn by a sour-faced crime novelist at a bookstore's Q&A session, also in Hollywood, this was probably *not* an accessory, since the novelist exploded in rage when an audience member seated near me blithely asked him, "What's under your patch?")

Now, being much older, I wish that my curiosity about Mr. Ravoon had been greater than my fear of him, because if it had been, I could have made an effort to speak to that old man clad in black and maybe gotten to know him. What was under Mr. Ravoon's own eye patch? What had led him to Paris? Why was he always reading *Who's Who in America*? Did he ever recognize me? And will I ever, when I least expect it, see him once more?

Perhaps at the instant that I die, knocked to the ground by a sudden stroke or heart attack, Mr. Ravoon shall reappear. Yes, perhaps through the rapidly dimming light on this last day of mine, I'll look up and find him leaning over me while he clutches *Who's Who in America*. Mr. Ravoon's eye patch will be gone now, both of his sea-foam-green eyes will be fixed on mine, and he will say, in the first, and final, time I get to hear his voice, "I'm wide awake. How about you?"

"Uh...yeah," I'll answer. "You've certainly got my attention."

"Good. Rise and shine. Care to have a peek at the page I've been reading?"

I'll nod my head, too weak by this point to resist. Mr. Ravoon will place a warm hand on my shoulder, holding open that volume of *Who's Who in America* in front of my face. And just before all my light flickers out, I'll be able to read in there the long entry about him.

"I read the Bible," a child named Alison writes in a letter to God, though she might have more luck addressing Dame Fortune. "What does 'begat' mean? Nobody will tell me." This letter by Alison appears in the book *Children's Letters to God*, which was compiled by Stuart Hample and Eric Marshall. Another child, in another God-directed letter, writes, "My brother told me about being born but it doesn't sound right." I sympathize with this kid, wishing as I do that I'd had better sex education available when I was six years old in 1969 and asked my mother at our dinner table about "being born."

"Get your mind out of the gutter!" she shouted at me.

"What does 'gutter' mean, Ma?"

She scowled. "That's the place where your mind is stuck right now with all its filthy questions."

Knowing what "filthy" meant, I said, "Why is my question about babies filthy? Like a toilet bowl, you mean? And why did you say my mind has *questions* when I only asked you one question?"

On the radio in our tiny dining room that day, our shared favorite song "Georgy Girl" was playing. It was the theme tune to the 1966 film of the same title, the film which had made a star of the young English actress Lynn Redgrave. The song "Georgy Girl" had entered my life when I was five and my mother hummed it to me while we were flying to Saint Croix for a vacation. Then, whenever it blasted onto the radio (*"Hey there, Georgy girl, swingin' down the street, so fancy free, nobody you meet can ever see the loneliness there—inside you"*), my mother and I would sing along with it. Of all the pop tunes that have accompanied me through my life like loyal friends (and popular music, whether I've liked this fact or not, has mattered to me more than any other kind of music), "Georgy Girl" is the most important. It stands for me even now as a symbol of Esther Lippman and the child's love I felt for her before I reached adolescence and our lives together grew turbulent.

Once upon a time my mother had been beautiful. In fact, before rage and bitterness and shame and disappointment and then serious illness destroyed her beauty, Esther Lippman had looked like a New Jersey–born Jewish Grace Kelly. And yet, unlike that movie actress turned Princess of Monaco, my mother was a prude, and puritanical in her prudery. At movie theaters, for example. Whenever we went to see a film together and a romantic scene got cooking, she would roughly place her hands over my eyes *and* over my ears. Should a scene get especially amorous, she would complicate matters further by physically hauling me out of the theater, which I tended to resist, causing a vigorous struggle that would either amuse or enrage our fellow audience members. (I guess it depended on how much they were enjoying those sex scenes.)

Such censorship went on until I was a teenager, when I began refusing to go to movie theaters with Esther Lippman. At the age of six, though, I was still innocent enough to ask where babies "came from," and the result was that my mother ultimately dragged me out of my chair, spun my body around, bent me over, and "*potched my tushy*," which is the Yiddish term for spanking. As I recall, it was a pretty vigorous *tushy-potching*. Vigorous enough for me to get her message.

And vigorous enough for me to instead bring my baby-making question to my father. It happened one afternoon while I was eating a Dixie Cup in Warnako Park and Bernie Lippman sat beside me on a bench which had peeling green paint. The color is relevant because, on hearing my question, he turned nearly as green as that bench.

"Ask your mother," he said.

"But I asked her already, Dad! And she *potched* my *tushy* and said something I didn't understand about a gutter..."

Bernie Lippman was not as handsome as Esther Lippman had been beautiful, but he had his charm. He looked like a slightly less hip Buddy Love, the slick-haired crooner played by Jerry Lewis in the film *The Nutty Professor*. Bernie Lippman might have liked that film's song "We've Got A World That Swings"; he himself was a hard-drinking, gambling, New Jersey-bred Jewish swinger. Still, he looked positively squeamish as he took in our conversation. He might as well have been as prudish as his ex-wife was when it came to discussing sex with his only child. In the end, however, he sighed, a defeated man, feeling he had no choice but to plunge ahead.

"Well," said my father, holding his hands away from his chest with the palms directed inward to suggest the shape of large female breasts, "you know how women have these, uh…" Then, overcome by his discomfort, Bernie Lippman stopped. "Like I said, forget it. Ask your mother."

"But what if she spanks me a *second* time, Dad?"

He shrugged his shoulders. "I'm sorry. I can't help you."

Unwilling to take another chance with Esther Lippman—and more confused than ever by Bernie Lippman's citation of female breasts as the opening gambit of his brief failed sex education lecture (all these years later, it still makes me wonder)—I had no choice but to turn to my friends at school. There, at the playground and in the hallways, a lot of theories were offered to me, but none with any sense of authority. Only one explainer, a curly-haired boy with a Batman lunchbox who sat next to me in our cafeteria, seemed certain of what he had to teach. And the sole thing he wanted in return for his teaching were my cinnamon Pop-Tart and my Hostess lemon pie. My mother always packed two desserts in my lunchbox, which featured on both its sides the mournful face of her great hero, our martyred President Kennedy.

"You know your *too-too*?" the boy said as soon I handed over my desserts. At the moment, my hunger for knowledge exceeded my hunger for sugary processed baked goods. "So your dad has a *too-too*, too."

Nodding my head: "I know. I've seen it in the locker room in his country club."

"Right. So your mom, she *doesn't* have a *too-too*. She used to have one, but your dad cut it off with a steak knife."

"He *what*?"

"Then," said the boy with the Batman lunchbox, his conversational momentum carrying him past my surprise, "your dad makes your mom stand against a wall in their bedroom and she bends over and he puts this electric toy where her *too-too* used to be." He stopped to munch on my Pop-Tart. "That toy makes a noise like a washing machine when it gets going."

I stared at the boy with the Batman lunchbox, amazed. Nothing in my life to this point had stunned me as much as this scenario now being described. In its way, I found it even more disturbing than the bloody physical fights my parents had launched into in front of me.

More disturbing than my father finally saying, "I've had it" and moving out of our apartment.

More disturbing than the custody arrangement in which a judge ordained that my father was supposed to pick me up for dinner twice a week.

More disturbing than my mother sometimes thwarting that arrangement by hiding with me in our bathroom, her hand pressed over my mouth, and pretending we weren't home when my father would come to pick me up. ("Spite work," she called this maneuver, which made me feel like we were Jews hiding from Nazis.)

More disturbing than the other times when Esther Lippman would press a hot compress to my forehead to simulate fever and then would order me to go tell my father that I was too ill to go to dinner with him.

More disturbing than her smacking me whenever I accidentally said "Daddy" in her presence instead of what she'd taught me to call the man, which was "homewrecker" and "bastard" and "that monster who wants to murder us both."

By the time I had met the boy with the Batman lunchbox, I had come to accept my parents' endless war and their willingness to involve their only child in it. Esther Lippman was on the offense, Bernie

Lippman was on the defense, and I was forced to serve two roles—as their one-boy army pitted by one against the other as well as the conflict's big prize. As terrible as my parents' custody war was, it was at least familiar to me. But what the boy with the Batman lunchbox now revealed was entirely something else. Crazier than anything I'd even seen in movie theaters or on TV.

"A *steak* knife?" I said. "An electric *toy*? How do you know all this?"

"Because," the boy announced, pumped full of pride, "one Sunday morning I woke up early and I hid in my mom and dad's bedroom closet while they were sleeping and I kept the door open a little bit so that when they woke up I could watch them."

"I don't believe you," I said. Who would dare to do such a thing?

Shrugging his shoulders, the boy got to work munching on my Hostess pie. "I know what I saw. I know something else, too. What they were doing, it's called 'fuck.' That's what my mom kept saying while my dad was using the noisy electric toy on her."

Back home from school that afternoon, I decided to give my mother one last try in order to confirm my new arcane knowledge. If knowledge is indeed what it was. Deciding to start out delicately, I said, "Ma, do you know what 'fuck' is?"

The spanking she gave me this time was not a sufficient response for Esther Lippman. After *potching* my *tooshy*, she ran to our bathroom to grab a bar of Irish Spring soap and then, once she'd chased me around our house and finally cornered me in the living room, she "washed my mouth out with soap," as she called it. My mother needed to struggle for a while before she could ram that bar of Irish Spring past my clenched teeth, but the woman was nothing if not persistent.

Soap, let me assure you, my fellow wisher, tastes exactly how you imagine it does. I wish I didn't remember this taste. But not entirely, because, as the poet Yehuda Amichai has written, "*Whoever remembers his childhood best / is the winner, / if there are any winners*." And thirty-five years later, with my childhood memories still mostly intact, I took my three-year-old son Gideon for a walk, where we bumped into a friend of mine who was eight months pregnant.

"Why did you get so fat?" Gideon asked her.

She laughed and I laughed, but our laughter seemed to trouble him, so I told him, "I'll tell you tonight," hoping that by then he'd forget to repeat his question. Of course, he did not forget. In fact, he only waited five minutes before he repeated it. So I told him, "She's not fat.

She's got a baby in her stomach."

Gideon pondered this for a moment, then said, "Why would she eat a baby?"

Again I laughed, but it was time, I knew, for our first sexuality-themed father-son talk. (Actually, this would be the second such talk—we'd had our first a few weeks earlier, when I instructed Gideon to stop grabbing the ample breasts of his Brazilian nanny. "But I *like* to squeeze her stomachs!" he'd protested.) Perhaps the ghosts of my parents were observing me now as I tried to determine how I should handle the sex education of their only grandchild.

Would I order Gideon to "get his mind out of the gutter"? Of course not.

Would I hold my hands out from my chest, evoking for my son the image of female breasts, those "stomachs" he'd recently been keen on squeezing? Of course not.

After considering my options while Gideon watched me with a curiosity that was so much like my own when I was around his age, I decided to go with an all-too-familiar response.

"Ask your mother," I told him.

There are many precedents to this wish list of mine, many memorialized big yearnings such as the handwritten note left by the polymath Robert Boyle before his death in 1691. Boyle's list consisted of future innovations he hoped would benefit humankind, innovations that ranged from the mundane to the colorful: "A perpetuall Light," "The Attaining Gigantick Dimensions," "The Transmutation of Species in Mineralls, Animals, and Vegetables," "The Art of Continuing long under water."

You can count me in with Boyle on that stuff, and for other "betterment" wishes, too. Every time I read the daily news, I feel just as horrified as the next wisher by how cruelly members of our species are treating our planet and each other, with the less fortunate among us usually receiving more barbaric treatment than the rest. Which is why I wish I could be an ace crime-fighter like my childhood heroes Doc Savage, Flash Gordon, The Shadow, The Phantom, Mandrake the Magician, and Conan the Barbarian.

If my thwarting evil directly is a wish too far, then I've got a Plan B. It's my wish to visit the medieval-era Old-New Synagogue of Prague and slip a note into a crevasse on the sarcophagus of Prague's medieval Kabbalah-adept Rabbi Low. This note would implore Low's ghost to help me build a new superheroic Jew-saving Golem from the mud of the River Moldau. Once our creation is in fine shape, we would inscribe on our creation's rough forehead the letters of the Hebrew word for truth: "*aleph*," "*mem*," "*tav*." And once our Golem is up and running, or shambling, I would persuade this noble brute not only to protect Jews from their antagonists' villainy but also to protect the rest of the human race, not to mention our global environment.

The French say, "To understand all is to forgive all." Perhaps. But forgiveness does not entail allowing bad guys to cause harm or get away with any harm they've already caused. So our re-programmed Golem will have to shatter plenty of antisemitic, racist, misogynistic, homophobic skulls before we arrive at the "friendly, friendly world" that the comedian Andy Kaufman liked to sing about. It won't hurt, either, if our Golem will possess the sarcastic temperament of Bill Hicks, who was the righteous comedic yang to Kaufman's absurdist yin. (Why is it that each of them left us way too soon while the assholes live on and on?)

In the end, I hope our Golem shall promote the humanistic qualities that the philosopher Isaiah Berlin prescribed: "less Messianic ardor, more enlightened skepticism, more toleration of idiosyncrasies." And I hope, as well, that our Golem will not eventually run amok, in which case Rabbi Low's ghost and I would be forced to deactivate it by erasing the letter *aleph* on our creation's forehead, thereby turning the word "truth" into the word "dead."

Please note that I'm striving to be realistic with my Golem wish, aware as I am that Dame Fortune is probably never going to hand us a full-bore "Nirvana Now," that hippie demand. According to the Upanishads, "*Only when men shall roll up the sky like a hide will there be an end to misery*." War, for example, is like poverty—here to stay. The endless catastrophic hostilities in the Middle East, for instance, may well be a permanent condition. The nearest thing to a reconciliation there that I know of was a concert by the rock band Camper Van Beethoven in which they played a medley of Led Zeppelin's "Kashmir" and "*Hava Nagila*." And the hostilities are potentially applicable to all. As the old saw has it, "You may not be interested in war, but war is interested in you."

Is aggression coded into human nature, a brick wall against which we must keep banging our wish-stuffed heads? In a word, yes. Human nature is always what it must be and rarely what we wish it to be. As inevitable as our wars are, though, I can't help but wonder if they must always be so catastrophically *fatal.* Is it too much to ask that our conflicts be conducted how ancient Australian tribes settled their beefs? They did so not with material weapons but with old women who just shouted obscene insults at each other. And instead of bemoaning how little we can do to make peace possible, we might do well to remember the saying about the two symbolic wolves that we've got living inside us. One is vicious, the other is benevolent, and the one that wins their constant struggle is the one whom we *feed.*

Perhaps this metaphor influenced Hermann Hesse in his novel *Steppenwolf,* where reconciling our lower and higher natures will allow each of us to become "a better hand at the game." Without a doubt the "two wolves" metaphor influenced a t-shirt I saw once, a t-shirt that said, "I'VE GOT TWO WOLVES INSIDE ME—AND THEY KEEP ON FUCKING!" (Better they fuck than they endlessly fight, I guess.)

So much of life boils down to kindness, to what Abraham Lincoln meant when he said, "When I do good, I feel good, when I do bad, I feel bad, and that's my religion." What a religion to practice! And what a paradise it would be, if we did not judge and then abuse each other based on any of the usual racial, ethnic, national, sexual, cognitive, and physical yardsticks that are so often foolishly, toxically, applied! Even a little less judgment and abuse would be like Heaven on earth every day.

When he was asked to teach the entirety of the Torah while standing on one foot, the Talmudic sage Hillel said, "That which is hateful to you, do not do to your neighbor. That is the whole Torah. The rest is commentary." Lord knows the Golden Rule ain't perfect; in a letter to God, a child named Darla asks, "Did you really mean the 'Do unto others?' stuff? Because if you did then I am going to fix my brother." Still, after all these centuries, the Golden Rule remains a comprehensively useful guideline for human behavior.

Naturally enough, "Do unto others" should especially apply to the privileged. As the poet and playwright Friedrich Schiller noted, "If luxury does not inspire generosity, the luxury is undeserved." And for a hardcore twist on the Rule, meet Tokugawa Tsunayoshi. An all-powerful sixteenth century *shogun,* Tsunayoshi instituted in Japan the "Laws of Compassion" which protected all of that nation's dogs from being injured and even ignored. The penalty was death, forced ritual suicide. So how about the UN enacting modern-day Laws of Compassion for canines but also for all non-canine beings? We can dispense with the compassionless capital punishment, even though only a death sentence might impel certain folks to be kind to each other.

In the Tsunayoshi spirit, I wish that, whenever people are rude to me, I could remember how often other people have been congenial. And I wish I was enlightened enough to treat those rude people with the same warmth that I gratefully reciprocate toward those congenial ones. The writer Kevin Kelly has a wise take on this, advising us, "Don't treat people as bad as they are. Treat them as good as you are. It's thrilling to be extremely polite to rude strangers."

Even mild gossip can have a nastiness at its core, which is why the artist Yoko Ono suggested that we "try to say nothing negative about anybody for three days, for forty-five days, for three months. See what happens to your life." Does kindness have its limits, however? A certain jazz musician was renowned for saying only good things about other people, so a friend of his asked him, "How about Hitler?" After pondering for a moment, the jazzman replied, "He was the best in his field."

There have been times, I will admit, when I wished I could do like the Nick Lowe song and be "cruel to be kind." Well, not quite cruel, but a tad less kind to other people in order to be more kind to myself. Which brings to mind something my Uncle Wolf once said to me: "If you're on a ship and a person you care about is drowning, throw them a rope and stay up all night if you have to in order to pull them back onboard and rescue them. But if they're going to drag you into the water with them, thereby endangering your own life, then you must let go of that lifeline."

I like how the novelist D.B.C. Pierre characterizes a good death: "one only noticed in retrospect." (I also like that Pierre quoted the movie *Airplane!* when he accepted a literary award, saying, "Looks like I picked the wrong week to quit sniffing glue.") Our most undying wish has always been for immortality. An ancient Greek myth says it was granted to us, but boss god Zeus struck dead the god of medicine, Asclepius, because Zeus feared that that divine doctor would make all humans live forever. Maybe Olympus's big daddy did right by us, however, because immortality must be exhausting. Think of the Wandering Jew, that insulter of Jesus in a medieval European legend whom Jesus condemns to travel around this gumball planet until Jesus is ready to return to it. Now think, specifically, of all the wishes the Wandering Jew must have made along the way, with his dearest wish being that he be allowed to die as soon as possible.

Nix-nix to immortality, then. But how about a humbler wish, the no-brainer that no one should ever die young? And why not keep alive the middle-aged and moderately old among us, while we're at it? Unfortunately, old Stretchfoot, that Destroyer of Delights, is even more interested in us than war is. If only Stretchfoot, or Zeus, or Dame Fortune, or the Hand of Fate, would at least give us helpful warnings when they're in our neighborhood. One example of such a warning appears in a favorite novel of mine where the soon-to-be-slain protagonist places objects on the countertops in his home but they keep mysteriously sliding from those surfaces and falling to the floor. Who says gravity can't be poetic?

Onward to what is perhaps the least surprising personal wish of mine: that I could be young again. I know just what my friend Ray means when he says, "It feels so weird to be the same age as old people," just as I know what the poet George Oppen meant when he said of getting older, "What a strange thing to happen to a little boy." Sometimes I wish I could be like the fingernail-sized jellyfish *Turritopsis dohrnii*, which can reverse its aging process when it feels stressed, turning all of its cells into juvenile form and then growing up once more. Or maybe I should wish that I could answer this question posed by the baseball player Satchel Paige: "How old would you be if you didn't know how old you were?" Paige himself had trouble with this matter, explaining, "I don't know how old I am because a goat ate the Bible that had my birth certificate in it. That goat lived to be twenty-seven."

More utopian wishes: Whenever my father drove us in his green Eldorado past my hometown's cobalt-blue water tower, I stared at it with awe. The tower's base was a long thin filament and the top was bulbous, a word that makes me recall Captain Beefheart's song lyric "*A squid eating dough in a polyurethane bag is fast and bulbous. Get me*?" Lest this notion strike you as quirky, my fellow wisher, bear in mind that Beefheart once described New York City as "a bowl of filthy underpants." As another musical eccentric, George Clinton, said of yet another, Sun Ra, "This boy is definitely out to lunch—the same place I eat at."

I remember how crestfallen I felt the day my father explained to me that my hometown's water tower was filled with water, not with the Bosco Chocolate Syrup that I'd been wishing for. I got over my disappointment, and started wishing that in addition to water, the tower could be filled with food. Enough food and water, in fact, to quench the thirst and relieve the hunger of every thirsty and hungry living being on this gumball planet, including Captain Beefheart's squid. And I wish that this food and water would be available for no charge, which would make it like the act of wishing. This act, as far as I know, remains absolutely free.

I wish my body could boast enough muscles that I would qualify as one of the bodybuilders hanging out in the boudoir of the old-time film actress Mae West. And I wish that when West's valet told her, "Ten men are waiting for you there," and she replied, "Send one of them home, I'm a little tired tonight," I would not be that luckless guy who got sent packing. Because I fear I would be.

Like Mae West, Louis Armstrong is a national treasure, of course, and I wish I could have seen the look on the Pope's face when he asked "Satchmo" if he had any children and Satch's answer was, "No, Pappy, but me and the missus still be *rockin'*!" Grace abounding to Mr. Armstrong! As a friend once said of him, "How can you help loving a guy that makes the world smile and such a happy place like Louis does? If he couldn't blow or sing a note, he'd still be worth his weight in laughs."

Armstrong was a "*Lebenskuntsler*," which is German for "artist of life," and I wish I too could be one. I've never felt so validated, so valorized, so *championed*, as I did when I received the letter in which my college European History professor Harold Poor bestowed on me this "*Lebenskuntsler*" compliment. I wish I could believe the compliment, and wish that I hadn't lost that letter right after I received it. I also wish that Harold hadn't died of AIDS at age fifty-seven, younger than I am now. And I wish that my friends Irving and Robert and everyone else who died of AIDS were also still alive.

Another compliment I particularly cherish is my friend Jimbo's remark that I experience my life primarily as a series of stories.

Although most tales conclude with a resolution, even airtight closure, my favorites are left open, and I especially like those stories where a surprising new addition occurs years or even decades after the story has seemed to end.

During the autumn of 1991, I lived for a month at Manhattan's infamous Chelsea Hotel, and one windy Saturday afternoon when I was waiting in line to use the lobby's pay phone, I got to chatting with a perky, spiky-haired, throaty-voiced young woman named Mercy. She told me that she and her roommate lived in Bob Dylan's old suite at the Chelsea. Being a longtime Dylan fan, I told her I'd love to see the place sometime.

"How about now?" said Mercy, and before you could say "Jack Robinson," we were riding in the hotel's rickety metal elevator, where my new friend asked, "You're not staying in the room where Sid Vicious killed his girlfriend Nancy Spungen, are you?" I told her, "Not that I know of." And a few minutes later, we were stepping together into my new acquaintance's suite. There I was greeted by a surprise. It was a muscular blond young man who sat naked in bed with a comforter bunched around his ankles and the receiver of a Princess telephone pressed to his ear.

"This is Aquinas," said Mercy. "He's my roommate."

Not making any move to cover his nakedness, Aquinas waved to me with his free hand and went on speaking to whoever was on the other end of the phone line. I waved back, averting my eyes, and then Mercy showed me around. Once our brief tour was finished, she said, "I've got some homework to do, so I'll show you out," and in the doorway I thanked her for her hospitality and asked what sort of homework awaited her.

"Law stuff," she said. "I'm a paralegal. That's my *day* job, anyway."

"Hmm. Mind if I ask what your night job is?"

"Not at all. I'm a dominatrix."

The lock of surprise on my face must have been significant, because Mercy burst into a high-pitched titter that didn't match her throaty voice. Until that day, I had never met a dominatrix, much less a sex worker of any sort, yet I made a futile effort to look unfazed, worldly, cool. "Does your night work…pay well?" I asked.

"A lot better than the paralegal shit."

"I'll bet. And your roommate in there—is he, like, a dominatrix, too? Or a dominat*or*, I guess you'd say?"

"Aquinas?" Another high-pitched titter. "Are you kidding? As *if*! No, Ackie is *way* too skittish for my line of work...He's a hustler."

This threw me for a new loop. "You mean, like, a *pool* hustler?"

"Dude, I don't think he even knows how to *play* pool. I mean he's a prostitute. A call boy. A male geisha, he calls himself. He advertises under the name 'Dynasty of Light.'"

During the next few weeks, Mercy and I met for drinks a few times at a bar near the Chelsea, a bright shiny place which the following year would close down and reopen, ironically enough, as New York City's first S&M-themed restaurant. (I've always had the freak hots for theme restaurants, with my favorite being one devoted to the life and work of the author Franz Kafka. Everyone working there looked like him.) Over drinks, Mercy told me a lot about her work, and sometimes when we bumped into each other when she was on her way to meet a client, she would show me the leather dominatrix outfit under her trench coat.

Unfortunately, we didn't keep in touch. Still, at a party in the East Village in 2017, I began speaking with an obese, bald, middle-aged man. He said he lived in St. Louis and was visiting Manhattan for the first time in decades.

"When were you here last?" I asked him.

"Jesus," he said, "the mid-nineties, it was. Back then I was living with a dominatrix friend in Bob Dylan's old room at the Chelsea Hotel."

I stared at him in silence for a moment, casting my mind back to a windy afternoon at the Chelsea more than thirty-five years ago. "May I ask you something?" I said finally. "Was your roommate's name—?"

"Mercy," he said. "You knew her? Were you one of her clients?"

"No!"

"Or maybe one of mine? I advertised myself as 'Dynasty of Light.'"

I shook my head, amazed at this unexpected new chapter to the old story of Mercy and Aquinas. "I wasn't a client," I told him. "But I lived at the Chelsea in '91. You were blond in those days, right?"

Aquinas sighed—and every one of those vanished thirty-five years echoed in the sound of his sigh. "Blond," he said, "and *beautiful*."

We're not finished discussing stories. Apparently, the author Isak Dinesen promised her soul to the Devil in exchange for the Devil's quid pro quo that everything Dinesen experienced from that moment on would be rich material for tales she could tell. Did she meet him at the crossroads of Highway 49 and Highway 61, where the bluesman Robert Johnson did his own deal with the Devil? Both Johnson and Dinesen probably subscribed to the Yiddish view that "God made people because God loves stories." I know I do. I only wish that I wasn't such a sucker for reductive formulae. The kind, for example, that pertain to the nature of storytelling.

When someone told me that the archetypal tale from which we spin endless variations could be summed up as "Things are not as they seem," I thought, *Makes sense.*

Then someone else said to me that, no, the only story is, "The chickens do or do not come home to roost," and I thought, *This is maybe more accurate.*

Then someone else said that the only story is, "The galaxy, or just a family, is threatened, and then the galaxy, or just that family, gets reunited," and I thought, *More accurate still.*

Then someone else said that actually there are two core stories: "a hero goes on a quest" and "a stranger comes to town." *Even better*, I thought.

Then someone else added three more *ur*-tales to the mix: "a struggle for power," "the love between two people," and "the love between three people." *So* that's *it*, I thought.

Then someone else added "the siege of a city," "the return home," and "the sacrifice, or the self-sacrifice, of a god." *Perfect*, I thought.

Then someone else said, "There are no stories, only thirty-nine basic dramatic situations, each one being metaphorically paired to an erotic position in the *Kama Sutra*," and I thought, *How intriguing...*

Then someone else said, "Forget this Kama Sutra junk, there are indeed stories but only seven of them, seven archetypal stories, which are those of Orpheus, Achilles, Cinderella, Tristan and Isolde, Circe, Romeo and Juliet, and Faust." *At last*, I thought, *I truly get it*!

But when someone else spoke up, saying, "What about King Lear?," I realized I'd been conned.

According to the poet Andrei Codrescu, "The only paradise there ever was was a love song." "Wishing songs" are by nature pretty paradisiacal, too, and one of the best of these I know is Simon & Garfunkel's "Punky's Dilemma." In this tune, the singer wishes he could be, successively, a Kellogg's Corn Flake, an English muffin, and a first lieutenant, providing poetic motives for each wish. Not surprisingly,

The Holy Modal Rounders' afore-mentioned "Dame Fortune" is likewise a wishing song, with the singer importuning the Dame to "*throw your changes and I'll catch them. If I can I'll use them well...Pour your horn of plenty on me. Tell me secrets rare and strange...*"

Another one of my favorite wishing songs is "Eight Ball Blues" by Steve Goodman. After Goodman sings, "*They say to know the best in life, you've got to know the worst,*" he undercuts this notion with his next line, which is "*I wish that I had been the clown who thought of that one first.*"

Dying at age thirty-six of leukemia after a long battle with that affliction, Goodman certainly "knew the worst." And yet his good cheer remained unadulterated to the end. He dubbed himself "Cool Hand Leuk," wrote a song called "A Dying Cubs Fan's Last Request," and, while he was close to death, he sang at many of his concerts the oldie "When The Red, Red Robin Comes Bop-Bop-Bopping Along." Goodman made sure while singing to emphasize the song's bridge, which goes, "*Wake up, wake up, you sleepyhead, / Get up, get up, get out of bed, / Cheer up, cheer up, the sun is red, / Live, love, laugh and be happy.*"

Few lyrics, if you ask me, are as ebullient as that one, especially when delivered by an artist who was gracefully laughing in the chalk-white face of old Stretchfoot, that Terminator of Tra La La's. By crooning with such joy in this fashion, Goodman was effectively blessing himself the way the ancient poet Virgil spiritually validated the medieval poet Dante, saying, "*Te sopra te corno e mitrio*"—"I crown you and miter you over yourself." Incidentally, Virgil also knew where he stood with the Dame, having written, "*Let us follow our destiny, ebb and flow. / Whatever may happen, we master Fortune by accepting it.*"

Another great wishing song is "Down The Drain" by the band The Jazz Butcher. In each successive verse, the singer lists different places where he wishes he'd been born. First, it's "*in a bar,*" so "*I wouldn't have to walk so bloody far*". Then it's "*on the beach,*" with "*everything I want within reach.*" Then it's "*in the woods,*" where "*I don't want to be misunderstood.*" Then it's "*up a tree,*" because "*walking on the ground's just not for me.*" Then it's "*in Selangore,*" although "*I wish I'd been a tiger even more.*" And finally, it's "*down the drain,*" because "*it's where I've ended up all the same.*"

I'm glad that "Down The Drain" is easy for me to play on guitar, so I'm able to disguise how musically untalented I am. (What is "easy," though? The guitarist Joe Pass says, "When the chord changes, you should change.") I wish I hadn't rebelled against my musician mother by refusing to take music lessons at school; maybe I could have gotten proficient enough at playing guitar that I could be like Wes Montgomery, who said he never bothered to practice—he would just open his guitar case "and throw in a piece of raw meat." Or maybe I could have mastered the fiddle. Then again, the violinist Tommy Jarrell has said, "Ain't nobody mastered the fiddle. There's notes in that fiddle ain't nobody found."

At any rate, I'm content having not been born in a bar or on a beach or in a forest or up a tree or in Selangore or down any drain but in the Overlook Hospital in Summit, New Jersey, where I arrived by way of cesarian section. I suppose I'd been wishing even then for the "easy way out," despite my usually agreeing with the poet Rainier Maria Rilke that in life we ought to "hold ourselves to the difficult."

Let's keep the music playing. Sure, the Rolling Stones' guitarist Keith Richards might have been kissing all the asses of the non-musicians in his audience when he announced, "To me, the art of music is listening to it, not playing it. The real art of it is hearing it." I wish Richards actually meant this, because his words remind me of something I was told by a *merengue* master I met backstage at a nightclub in Harlem when I was dating his band's female Jewish saxophone player. After I mentioned to this kind old Dominican musician that I didn't play any instruments, he said—and he may have just been another ass-kisser—"If you can't play nothing else but you really, truly, deeply love music, then you're an 'ear man.' You're 'playing your ears.' Your ears are your instrument. *So go and play them like a maestro*."

The only problem is that I wrecked a significant part of my hearing at Madison Square Garden rock concerts in the late seventies, after each of which my ears would ring nonstop for days. By far the worst of them was not the Who or Led Zeppelin or Jethro Tull but Neil Young on his "Rust Never Sleeps" tour. As soon as Young and his band Crazy Horse began to play, I and everyone else around me began to scream in pain, with our hands pressed over our ears, fearing that the damage would be permanent. Why hadn't I thought to wear earplugs back then?

A better question is, how bad is my current hearing loss? I'm afraid to find out. The one time I met Neil Young, I asked him how his own ears were, and he said, "I've got the hearing loss of an admiral on a mid-sized destroyer." I like that answer. I also like that he once wrote about his band, "I remember Crazy Horse like Roy Orbison remembers 'Leah' and 'Blue Bayou.'" I think I know what he means here. I feel the same way about everyone to whom I've dedicated this wish list.

So much of my waking life, and a good portion of my dream life, too, has been occupied with wishing I could be other than I am. In his literary work, Jorge Luis Borges proposed the notion that one person is, in an important sense, all people (just as "the Aleph" in his story of the same name is one place which is also all places). I'm not sure I agree with Borges here, but I wouldn't mind metamorphosing into a few of his vivid characters. Not Funes the memory prodigy or the other primarily ill-fated protagonists, but someone like the Jewish playwright Jaromir Hladik, for whom God, or Dame Fortune, stops time while Hladik faces a Nazi firing squad. This divine kindness is not meant to save Hladik's life but rather to allow the playwright to complete his last project—complete it not on paper but in his mind. Once Hladik mentally finishes the last sentence and feels the satisfaction of a job well done, time resumes, and the bullets fly and find him.

For me, "wishing I could be other than I am" usually means wishing I could be "hip." Hip, I mean, in the comprehensive sense that the writer Glenn O'Brien defined the word: "Hip is a noun, a verb, and an adjective. Hiply is the adverb. Hip is a joint. When hips get together, they do the bump. They do the hip shake. When a hip gets cut off and smoked, it's a ham." You can be *too* cool for school, of course. Still, being thought of as hip, as cool, as "with it," has been a prevailing influence on my behavior for as long as I can remember. In fact, the thought of people thinking of me as *unhip* feels nearly as unbearable as the thought of a sudden, violent death or of a slow, agonizing death. And doesn't unhipness imply its own kind of death, the kind that derives from social abandonment?

"What do you care what people think of you?" asked the physicist Richard Feynman, who supposedly scribbled his formulae while he hung out in striptease bars.

The answer is, *don't*. Instead, do as Merle Haggard sang and "take a lot of pride in what you are" while "wearing your own kind of hat." And if, like the increasingly haggard Haggard, you're "always on a mountain when you fall," you can at least say that your "mama tried."

The dream of being hip, or being thought of as hip, dies hard, so I go on dropping hipster argot into my conversations—*bon mots*, I mean, like "O my stars!," "Jumping Jehosophat," "man alive," "lands' sake," "Katy bar the door," "loaded for bear," and "solid sender." That last term is mentioned in separate golden oldies by John Lee Hooker, Little Richard, and the charmingly named Sox Wilson.

What if you're not hip enough to *grok* hip lingo? I spent way too much time during my junior high school years trying to figure out the difference between "going out with" and "going with." These terms connoted two apparently different and distinct romantic relationships, and it frustrated me that I couldn't tell how they differed, although I didn't dare to ask anyone about them, not even my closest friends, lest I be thought of as unhip. Wouldn't a hipster already know the answer? Does a hipster ever have to ask?

My friend Gloria faced a similar situation in grammar school. Whenever she had to recite the Pledge of Allegiance with her class, she kept wondering who "Richard Stands" was, as in "*...and to the Republic, for Richard Stands, one nation, under God, indivisible...*" Even at age six, Gloria felt too embarrassed to ask her friends who this important-sounding Stands guy was. That fear of unhipness strikes again!

Eventually, Gloria found out the truth, just as in time I learned the difference between "going with" and "going out with." But I wish I hadn't wasted, and didn't *still* waste, so much time striving to be hip. And I wish that Richard Stands would actually exist and turn out to be some benevolent gigantic spirit who is currently sleeping like King Arthur but will awaken and then guide America into becoming a kinder, safer, more fulfilling place. In other words, the Messiah, or at least another egalitarian Golem. Mr. Stands, needless to say, will have more virtuous goals than being, or seeming, hip. Perhaps he's a she. Won't matter. May Richard Stands reveal him- or herself as soon as possible.

While walking one afternoon past Manhattan's Lipstick Building, which bears its name because of its shape and dark magenta color, I found myself wishing I could be large and strong enough to wrench this skyscraper up from its foundations, King Kong-style, wave the thing around with one hand, and then smear it across my puckered mouth.

Another cosmetic wish: If only I could powder my nose with the "wishing powder" that the author Langston Hughes bought for himself while he was visiting New Orleans. This powder was so potent that the day after buying it, Hughes wrote, "Quite unexpectedly I found myself on the way to Havana." Now that I've mentioned the Crescent City, let me add that I wouldn't mind owning a mojo hand as well as a trick bag containing goofer dust, black cat bones, gris gris satchels, boa constrictor tongues, the potent brew called "Red Fast Luck," and other items that would prove useful in a world where juju magic could be real. Although, when pressed on the matter, I would not wish that such a magic was real. Langston Hughes might dig voodoo, but I find it too frightening to dwell upon. Bad enough as it is that we've got all these ninjas running around making trouble.

As much as I enjoy Warren Zevon's song "I'll Sleep When I'm Dead," I've never felt like singing along with it because I'm a troubled sleeper. Garden-variety insomnia, itchy skin, light sensitivity, temperature sensitivity, mattress sensitivity, the frequent need to urinate, the even more frequent need to flip over my pillow whenever it feels hot against the back of my head (I'm not alone with this need—I saw my maternal grandfather David Fennel do the same pillow-flipping maneuver when he was in a hospital bed after his seventh heart attack)—these are only some of the conditions that keep me out of the arms of whatever slumber god is blood-related to Dame Fortune.

In Thomas Pynchon's novel *Mason & Dixon* you can read about Veevle, an eighteenth-century British mariner who is "legendary thro'out the Royal N. for being impossible to wake to stand Watch. Countless hundreds of Ship-mates have tried without issue to rouse the somniac Tar." The shipmates scream at him, hit the soles of his feet with rope, light matches between his toes, cram cockroaches up his nose, give him coffee enemas, whisper promises to him, even lower his body into the ocean. But "at the touch of the Waves, he but makes a snuggling motion, and begins to snore."

The sailor Veevle stirs up a memory of mine from a Rolling Stones concert in the late nineties. As I walked to my seat at Madison Square Garden a few minutes before showtime, I noticed an elderly couple who sat together with their heads resting against each other's and with both of their mouths hanging open, obviously asleep. *As soon as The Stones hit the stage*, I thought, *these folks will wake up with a jolt*. But once the concert had ended and I was leaving the arena, I noticed that the elderly couple were seated in the same physical position in their seats, their mouths still agape and their heads still touching as they leaned into one another.

Worried that they were dead, I put my hand in front of their open mouths. Good news: each elderly person, I found, was breathing. So they'd both slept through two hours of highly amplified rock'n'roll. Impressive! Even so, I didn't wish to be the one to rouse them and deliver the bad news. As a rule, I try not to be a bad news-bearer, having adopted this rule for myself after I was foolish enough to be the first person to inform my friend Becky that her brand-new tattoo, the word "RESSIST," was misspelled.

I'm not saying I wish I could be more like that deeply dozing elderly couple or like Veevle, and I don't wish for any sailors to rouse me if I do wind up behaving like that somnolent seaman. But a few nights each month of their brand of deep sleep sound utterly sublime.

Another reason for my insomnia is the medical condition of sleep apnea. I wish I could will myself free of it, and wish that a few of my close relatives did not also suffer from it decades ago, when a corrective CPAP machine was unavailable to them and might have lengthened their lives. Although doctors warn me that I must wear the CPAP's nozzle-mask over my face all night, every night, or else my lifespan will be shortened, the mask hardly makes for a sexy look, much less for primo comfort. One night some years ago, I was lucky enough to be able to welcome an attractive Londoner to my bedroom for our first time together. I thanked Dame Fortune too soon, though, because the "English Rose," as she liked calling herself, had not yet finished undressing before she caught sight of my bedside table, where my CPAP machine with its rubber hose and translucent mask quickly freaked her out. Was this a bizarre torture device I intended to use on her? She must have thought so, because she swiftly put her clothes back on and fled my home without a word beyond "I need to leave." And my impassioned cry of "But I need that thing to treat my *sleep apnea*!" only seemed to hurry her faster out the door.

A few months after I received my apnea diagnosis, I was hanging out in the central camp of Nevada's Burning Man Festival near a stout young man who lay on his back fast asleep. The man's intense snores and sudden cessation of breathing made evident to me that he was a fellow apnea sufferer. A brother victim! Just to make sure the man knew what he was dealing with, I wrote a note for him that read, "YOU SUFFER FROM A CONDITION CALLED SLEEP APNEA AND SHOULD GO TO A DOCTOR FOR HELP." As I gingerly placed this note on the man's chest, however, he awakened abruptly to the sight of a stranger setting a sheet of paper on top of him, and without reading it, the young man clawed the note aside, sat up, glared at me, and shouted, in a voice even louder than his snoring, "Why are you *touching me*? I *hate* being touched! Fucking *hate* it!" And my impassioned protest of "I'm just trying to help you with something called *sleep apnea*!" only served to intensify the man's angry confusion.

Why not take naps, you say? The reason I don't is that I can't turn off my thoughts very readily. If I could be a napper, though, I'd take my *siestas* while reclining in a baobab tree the way I saw a pride of lions do it near Tanzania's Lake Manyara when my wife and our friend Tamara and I were visiting. Eight or nine of these glorious creatures lay conked out on a single tree, draped like golden decorations on those thick branches or like the angels that William Blake claimed to see crowding together in a tree when he was a child. (Years later, Blake would remark, "A fool sees not the same tree that a wise man sees.") Eventually, one of the African lions climbed down and disappeared behind a screen of bushes before returning five minutes later and climbing back up the tree to reassume his snoozing spot.

"What was the reason for that temporary disappearing act?" I asked our safari guide. I would have tried to ask the lion itself, but I remember that the philosopher Ludwig Wittgenstein said, "Even if a lion could speak, we would not understand it."

The guide laughed at my question. "Like many of us," he explained, "lions prefer to do their business in private."

RANDOM WISHES DIRECTED TO DAME FORTUNE AT 3:48 A.M. WHILE SUFFERING FROM A TYPICAL BOUT OF INSOMNIA:

* I wish "counting sheep" worked for me. I find it way too boring, although I know that's the point. And I wish that, after an hour of sleeplessness, I would seize the initiative to go outside to watch the sunrise rather than remaining in bed and watching online videos or trawling through social media or communing with Mother Fist and Her Five Lovely Daughters (if you know what I mean by this reference, and I think you do).

* I wish I was not so prone to botching up stuff in my life and then, in trying to correct the errors, making everything worse. I might as well be the hapless editor of a newspaper, the *Dublin Penny Journal*, who apologized in print for having erroneously referred to "*His Grace, the Duchess of Dorset*" and subsequently amended it to "*Her Grace, the Duke of Dorset.*"

* We know that Dame Fortune is sister to Fatum, possessor of the Hand of Fate, but what is the Dame's relationship with old Stretchfoot, that Ruiner of Relationships? And with Mother Nature, and Father Time, and Robert Graves's top muse, the White Goddess? How freely do they all communicate with one another, if at all? Do they coordinate their treatment of us mortals? Celebrate each other's birthdays? Have sex? Engage in feuds? And do those pesky ninjas work for Dame Fortune, or are they free agents? I wish I knew…

* In the Middle Ages people believed that bear cubs are born as formless blobs and must be licked by their mothers into the familiar bear shape. In this spirit, I wish I could lick certain people into the incarnations I wish they'd have.

* I wish I could spot a UFO, or otherwise could encounter and learn about alien life forms—ideally the friendly and intelligent kind. Yet it seems reasonable to believe that while the universe likely is, or was, or will be, teeming with life, this life has never visited us in any way and probably never shall. The distances in space and in time are both too vast for interstellar travel. Besides, any sophisticated civilization out there, and *right here*, may well destroy itself as well as its home planet before it gets to visit others.

* I wish that flying drones did not exist. Why? Because in spite of all the technological benefits they offer, I predict that someday

they will be dropping bombs on the heads of civilians worldwide. And drones may not be the worst of it. My friend James George, an amiable and wise Canadian diplomat, spent much of his very long life campaigning against humanity placing mass-destruction weapons in outer space. When George first mentioned his concern to me, I thought it seemed too abstract to worry about. Now it seems all too real.

* If I ever flip my wig and turn to a life of crime—becoming a second-story man, for instance—then I wish I could join up with a colorful robber band, one that features Red Scarlach, Korolu the Singing Bandit, the courtesan Balloon Smuggler, "Death-Dodger" Vautrin, Ming the Merciless, Benya Krik (who said, "Everyone makes mistakes, even God"), and catfighting rivals Hecuba and Hungry Helen. Oh, and the zombie Bredda Gravalicious, this zombie scaring me silly when I sneaked out of bed after "lights out" one night in the autumn of 1969, defying my mother in order to watch *Creature Feature* on our TV set.

* My friend Hiroko is a charming and energetic woman in her mid-nineties. One morning when she was a teenager, she was walking to work in her hometown when the sky suddenly lit up and she got knocked unconscious. On waking up, she found her face on fire. Why? The date was August 6, 1945; Hiroko's hometown was Hiroshima; and so I wish—not just because of Hiroko but especially because of her—that nuclear energy did not exist. Or at least that we had never discovered it. As the Sun Ra song goes, "*It's a motherfucker, don't you know: / If they push that button, your ass got to go.*"

* The Hasidic sage the Baal Shem Tov said, "How can you worship the Lord who made the golden sun if first the yolk of the egg cannot make you giddy?" I wish he could have informed us which came first, the chicken or the egg. I'd also like a definitive answer as to why the proverbial chicken crossed the road. Then again, as it says on goofy t-shirts, "LET'S DREAM OF A SOCIETY WHERE A CHICKEN CAN CROSS A ROAD WITHOUT ITS MOTIVES BEING QUESTIONED."

* I wish I had a chart tabulating how frequently I've said to people, "I wish you *would*" as opposed to "I wish you *wouldn't*." I also wish that more people in my life would say to me, "Your wish is my command" and sincerely mean it. At the same time, I wish that there were less people whom I would feel obliged to obey whenever they tell me, "*My* wish is *your* command."

* I wish that the apartment building in Manhattan where the Marx Brothers grew up had not been knocked down ages ago because

it stood only one block from where I live now and I would have liked to look through their old window whenever I feel lonely and imagine them as children playing inside.

* I wish that misogynists would be forced to face the fact that in most of the areas which make our species worthwhile in spite of its flaws, women are straight-up better than men. As a law school professor of mine once observed, most of history's woes have been the result of too few jobs and too much testosterone. "Women get shit done," that's for sure. Look no further than that warrior of the heart Eleanor Roosevelt. Pretty much superior to every man whose words I quote throughout this wish list, Eleanor rightly urged all of us to try doing something that scares us every day. Sometimes I wish she hadn't, though—this advice is usually too frightening to follow.

* I wish I had attended various lectures in the past. For instance, the one at the Sorbonne where Salvador Dali sat in the audience soaking his bare right foot in a dish of milk from start to finish. Or the one Albert Einstein gave to a group which included Franz Kafka. Or the one where Sigmund Freud heard what Mark Twain had to say. Of course, Twain might have benefited by listening to Freud, Einstein might have benefitted by listening to Kafka, and they all might have benefited from listening to Dali, whom I wish I could have met in 1987 when I visited his museum in Figueras, Spain. Apparently, he was dying at the time in the upstairs living quarters.

* I wish that, if a psychiatrist had subjected me to the famous "Marshmallow Test" when I was a child, I would have passed it. Presented a marshmallow and told, "You can eat this treat now *or else* refrain from eating it for five minutes, after which, as a reward for your restraint, you'll be given a *second* marshmallow and be allowed to eat *both* of them," instant gratification-minded me would have tried to hold out, sure. But I know I would have only lasted for at most thirty seconds.

* I wish that when the Renaissance sculptor Donatello was working on his statue *Zuccone* and shouted at it, "*Speak*, damn you, *speak to me*!," the statue had answered him with the sardonic words of the artist Ad Rheinhart: "Sculpture is something you bump into when you back up to look at a painting."

* I wish I could have met a certain famous American novelist before he died so that I could have told him that, although his talent far surpassed mine (his handsomeness, too), he and I were nevertheless in one sense equals. This was because, unbeknownst to the novelist,

my father had once conducted an extramarital affair with his mother. I even sat next to the mother and son once at a Manhattan restaurant but thought better of introducing myself to them and sharing what I know of our connection.

* "I Wish That I Could Hurt That Way Again" is the title of a barroom weeper I like. But speak for yourself, masochistic singer! Being highly pain-averse, I wish to never feel anything like, say, the sting of a tarantula hawk wasp. Says the entomologist Justin O. Schmidt, this wasp sting's effect is akin to "a running hair dryer...dropped in your bubble bath." The worst pain I'd willingly allow myself to experience is an anthropoid bee sting: "Almost pleasant, like a lover just bit your earlobe a little too hard."

* According to the poet Stephane Mallarme, "The world exists to wind up in a book." I wish I could cram more of the world into the wish list of mine the way Robert Burton did with his *Anatomy of Melancholy*. Along with sections on the "black dog," "blue devils," and "noonday demons" of depression, the Burton book features, in the words of its editor Kevin Jackson, "urine and uxuriousness, bradypepsia and beavers, fauns and Frenchmen, Yorkshire and youth, eunuchs and eggs, jealousy and jugglers, onions and orators, vineyards and Venus, quinta and quotations..." At least my wish list has its own fair share of quotations.

* I wish I hadn't drifted to sleep while watching TV yesterday because while I dozed I had a nightmare about Mr. Ravoon. Remember the black-clad eye patch-wearing *Who's Who in America*-reading old man I used to see around New York and Paris? My nightmare was a scary dramatization of this verse by Paul Dehn about Mr. Ravoon's original female counterpart: "*I fled in the storm, through lightning and thunder / And there, as a flash split the darkness asunder / Chewing a rat's-tail and mumbling a rune / Mad in the moat squatted MRS. RAVOON!*"

* I wish I could remind myself more often that, in order to achieve long-term gains, one must usually make short-term sacrifices. Which can sting like motherfuckers. (Or like a tarantula hawk wasp.) And I wish I could hold two opposed ideas in my mind at the same time while retaining the ability to function, although I suspect that doing so would make my insomnia worse.

THREE. IMPERTINENT WISHES

I wish I could be invited to a raucous house party in which all the other guests are chemistry's Periodic Table of elements metamorphosized into human form. I've never been good at grasping scientific laws, but the names of the elements have always captivated me, so while the table's inventor, Dmitri Mendeleev, acts as our DJ, spinning the Jackson Five's "The Love You Save," Pizzicato's Five's "Tout Tout Pour Ma Cherie," the Ramones's "California Sun," and all my other favorite dance songs, I'll do the Watusi and the Swim with Beryllium. I'll do the Hokey Pokey with Copper and Zinc. (As a bumper sticker asks, "WHAT IF THE HOKEY POKEY REALLY *IS* 'WHAT IT'S ALL ABOUT?'") I'll do the Limbo while Argon and Cobalt hold the pole for me. Then, to the amusement of Rubidium and Yttrium, I'll perform a Twist much like the one Dick Shawn does with his bikini-clad beatnik girlfriend in the screen comedy *It's A Mad, Mad, Mad, Mad World.* And I'll follow the Twist with a dance that resembles Jonathan Winters destroying the gas station in that same comic film, which was released in the year of my birth.

During our periodic table house party, Mendeleev will be sure to spin plenty of disco music, about which I feel a mild lingering guilt, because when I was an ignorant teenager in the late seventies, I loaned my angry voice to the nationwide chorus of "Disco sucks." This attitude of mine was not consciously racist or homophobic, it was merely, obnoxiously pro-rock'n'roll. Yet it kept me from admitting, even then—and even to myself—how much I adored songs such as "Don't Leave Me This Way," "Then Came You," "When Will I See You Again," "I'll Be Around," "Doctor's Orders," "Could It Be I'm Falling In Love," "I Just Don't Want To Be Lonely," and "Year of Decision." I wish, by the way, that "Year Of Decision" would automatically start playing in my head whenever I need to make a hard personal choice.

Near dawn, when Daft Punk's stirring "Touch" spins, our party starts to wind down, although Molybdenum, Antimony, Tungsten, Bismuth, Astatine, and Seaborgium form a conga line which spills out onto Bleecker Street and proceeds north through

Greenwich Village. In the meantime, most of the other elements remain behind, either passed out cold, or necking and petting in a dark corner, or sitting with crossed legs in a loose ring around the DJ booth. Darmstadtium is yawning adorably, Mendeleev unselfconsciously wears a lampshade on his head, and the still unknown 113th element watches everyone with an enigmatic smile on her otherwise blank face as I in turn observe her, wondering just what her deal is.

My friend Michael, an ardent afficionado of esoteric lore, was born on the same day of the same year as I was. It's a pleasure to wish him "Happy Birthday" on our shared birthday, and to grow old in lockstep with Michael. Let me wish *you* a happy birthday this year, too, my fellow wisher. But I hope I won't need to select any birthday presents for anyone because my imagination, which I otherwise take pride in, does not extend to gift-giving. Quickly frustrated with the process, I usually end up buying favorite books to present to my intimates. Not a bad choice—as the film director John Waters says, "If you go home with somebody and they don't have books, don't fuck 'em." For all his bibliomania, though, Waters does not himself give books as birthday presents. Rather, he hands out pre-printed cards which read, "A GENEROUS DONATION HAS BEEN MADE IN YOUR NAME TO THE CHURCH OF SCIENTOLOGY."

Equally mischievous is the way Waters deals with snoopy guests at gatherings in his home, the breed of party guests who like to peek into his bathroom's medicine cabinet to find out what the contents are (and maybe filch them). Before a party, Waters removes all the toiletries and replaces them with hundreds of glass marbles. Hence, thanks to gravity, which is a key tool in Dame Fortune's trick-bag, as soon as those snoopers go snooping, the myriad marbles come cascading noisily out. No doubt the snoopers' faces quickly turn the color of Pepto-Bismol.

Mischief! Ever since my childhood when I would avidly watch the TV show *Candid Camera*, I've loved making it and watching it made by others. Which is why I wish that Coyote and Raven and Anansi and other Trickster figures in the world's folklore systems would truly exist. I also wish that they would permit me to attend their annual gatherings, where a team of Lakota *heyokas*, clowns who do everything in reverse, will be on hand. Maybe the Trickster gods will even initiate me into their club—without pranking me too brutally, that is—and will then support me in the humorous yet fundamentally harmless acts of mischief I'll go on to play. I say "harmless" because the best pranks are never cruel; pranker and prankee should wind up laughing together. And all the better if the mischief "expands your sense of the possible," as my late friend John Perry Barlow would have said.

A longtime mischief-related wish of mine is that I would have stolen the official-looking black jacket with the word "SECURITY" printed on the back, which I found in a men's room at a nightclub in Cleveland in 1999. I was too timid, and too moral, to lift this jacket, but now I can't stop fantasizing about what mischief I could practice while wearing it. I also wish I'd bought the formal doorman's outfit, complete with tasseled hat, that I came across in a thrift shop on Saint Mark's Place in 1983. Who cares that it wasn't my size? More mischief could've been made!

Of course, there are times when mischief is not appropriate; if you're sitting in "*God's classroom,*" the poet Hafiz noted, it's best to "*stop throwing spitballs for a while.*" Then there are the times when the tables get turned on a mischief-maker: I once got rid of some overly aggressive Christian missionaries by telling them I was a Satanist—"a Luciferian," to be exact—but I got creeped out myself when Kinky Friedman inscribed one of his books to me with the salutation "SEE YOU IN HELL." By the same token, I've enjoyed scrawling "FOR SENSUAL MASSAGE" in the memorandum section of every bank check I wrote, whether the check is meant to pay the IRS or my dentist, but then Kinky signed a different one of his books to me by writing "FOR DEPOSIT ONLY."

My favorite shelf in my personal library is devoted to what might be called "Trickster Lit," which includes such classics as Mikhail Bulgakov's *The Master and Margarita*, Joe Orton's play *What The Butler Saw*, "The Open Window" and other stories by Saki, plus, best of all, the ReSearch volume *Pranks*. And I wish I could add to this library by finding the free time (and the initiative, and the patience) to research and write a biography of the eccentric Irish prankster Horace de Vere Cole (1881-1936). I think of Cole each April Fool's Day, which in my book (and maybe Dame Fortune's) is the holiday that matters most.

How can you not love a man who threw a dinner party in which all the guests eventually discovered that they had the word "bottom" in their surnames? My favorite prank of Cole's involved the production of a new play in London. For the opening night performance, Cole bought and distributed free-of-charge tickets exclusively to bald men. Why? It was so that, once these men sat down in the theater and removed their hats, the men's placement in the same section of the audience ensured that their bald heads spelled out a word that was only visible to theatergoers in the balcony. It was the word "FUCK."

My latest mischievous wish is to be able to "astral project" so that I can secretly visit the homes of my friends and thereby satisfy my curiosity about their private habits. I'd also be tempted to visit my enemies in order to hide all their left shoes, thereby forcing them to go barefoot or else to wear two right shoes.

If astral projection is not available, I wish I could self-teleport, or "*jaunt*," like the hero of my favorite science-fiction novel, *Tyger, Tyger* by Alfred Bester. As with Vladimir Nabokov's *Lolita*, there's a hidden playful structural trick to Bester's narrative, one I'm proud to have figured out. Both of these tricks are literary pranks, I suppose, although in *Tyger, Tyger* the mischief suggests a happy ending while in *Lolita* it opens up a whole new dimension of heartbreak. And heartbreak all too often dampens the mischievous spirit.

I wish my friend Coco wouldn't whine so much about her generally fortunate life. Whenever she begins histrionically bitching about her latest gripe, I've tried repeating to her Jim Dodge's advice in his novel *Stone Junction*: "Don't snivel when you lose or gloat when you win." I've also tried quoting Ralph Waldo Emerson to Coco, saying, "Win as if you were used to it; lose as if you enjoyed it for a change." Alas, such advice usually doesn't work with my friend. So I take another tack, asking her, "Are you healthy?" Once she answers, "Yeah, I guess," I yell at her in mock outrage, "*Then shut up*!" Because just as, to quote the author Ross MacDonald, "There's nothing wrong with Southern California that a little rise in the ocean level wouldn't fix," there's also nothing wrong with someone's life that a little dose of, say, cholera wouldn't fix.

If only I could take my own advice! Unfortunately, I'm just as much of a whiner as Coco is, prone to falling into dark funks during which I brood about past wishes that Dame Fortune refused to grant. I brood about my personality flaws that make me feel unworthy of having any wishes granted. I forget or willfully ignore all the wisdom I've been setting down in this wish list. And I ignore the poet Rumi, who wrote, "*All thoughts, happy or sad, are guests. Welcome them.*" Or if you can't *welcome* the negative ones, at least don't struggle against or gratuitously indulge them. Letting the chips fall where they may is always a good strategy. So is letting the dice keep rolling.

Recently, I wasted thirty-six hours doggy-paddling through a fetid swamp of self-pity while, unbeknownst to me, a friend of mine was dying of an unexpected heart attack. Instead of being on my bummer trip, I could have been hanging out with him one last time. "Time just gets away from us," Charles Portis writes in his novel *True Grit*. Yet on occasion time just abruptly, alarmingly, *stops*. So why not be like Lee Dorsey, who sang the anti-tragic words "*Everything I do gon' be funky from now on*"? Dorsey wasn't jiving, either. As his producer Allen Toussaint said, "You could tell that Lee was very glad at all times to be at the moment where he was."

I wish that when Jesus was dying on the cross, he could have foreseen with certainty everything that would occur during the next two thousand years in his name, the bad things as well as the good things. Surely no person has ever had or will ever have their mind blown in quite so colossal a manner. I harbor a similar wish that applies to Anne Frank.

In a lighter vein, I wish I owned a print of the painting in which Jesus is throwing his head back and having himself a belly-laugh. I wish I could own a t-shirt which shows Jesus riding a skateboard and which says, "YOU *KNOW* HE WOULD HAVE." And I wish I could own a poster which shows Jesus doing some carpentry work. When carpenter Jesus accidentally strikes his thumb with his hammer, he cries out in pain, "*Elvis H. Presley*!"

And the wishes about inspiring people just keep on coming. I wish I could say "What, me worry?" with the same easy-come-easy-go insouciance of *Mad Magazine*'s Alfred E. Neuman. I wish I could sincerely join in when Popeye sings, "*I yam what I yam and that's all that I yam.*" I wish I could smell the perfume Wild Hyacinth just to find out if it makes me behave as violently as it does Curly of the

Three Stooges. And if Wild Hyacinth gets me into a street-fight, I hope I will remember this advice from a novel by John D. MacDonald: "Hit through the target and beyond, not hit at it. When you hit someone in the nose, try to smash an imaginary nose on a person standing directly behind him. That gets the back into it."

As for self-defense, how about if you follow the sumo wrestler technique of causing your testicles, if you possess them, to retract back into your body up the inquinal canal? Takes practice, I'm told. And be aware when you're overmatched. You don't want to try your luck against someone like the mass murderer Carl Panzram, whose last words before being electric-chaired were, "I wish the whole human race had one neck and I had my hands around it."

Personally, I don't have much of a tolerance for witnessing violence anymore. There's enough bad juice already dripping off my brain; even slapstick stuff in comedies can make me give a rictus grin. Still, I wish I could watch a ninja pitted against a warlock in a fifteen-round steel cage competition, because I'm truly curious who would win. And I wish I could watch Dame Fortune slap the piss out of the Hand of Fate when it tries to pinch her ass, because the Hand would richly deserve that treatment.

(Rumor has it that the Dame plays just as rough with Long Daddy Green, the god of money, whenever he tries to rip her off.)

Once upon a time, the magician Doug Henning performed for a group of Inuit people at a gathering place near the North Pole.

"Entertainment is good, but why are you doing magic?" one of the male audience members said to Henning. "The whole world is magical. It's magic that snow falls—all those little crystals completely different. *That's* magic."

Henning said, "I made a beautiful silver ball float in the air. *That's* magic."

"But there's a ball of fire floating through the sky every day," was the Inuit man's response. "It keeps us warm, gives us light. *That's* magic."

The two were at a standstill until the Inuit man went off to discuss the matter with his fellow audience members. Then he returned to Henning and said, "Now we know why you are doing what you do. It's because *your* people have forgotten the magic. You're doing what you do to *remind* them of the magic. Well done!"

The philosopher Ludwig Wittgenstein observed that "The mystical is not *how* the world is, but *that* it is." Isn't the flow of blood through our veins miraculous enough to warrant our permanent awe? And don't forget that all of those veins, and everything else in us, grew from the unconscious genius of a single cell. "People ought to be walking around all day," wrote the scientist Lewis Thomas, "all through their waking hours, calling to each other in endless wonderment, talking of nothing except that cell."

What's more, it's not just our bodies that should make us drop our jaws in wonder. The poet Mary Oliver wrote, "If you have not been so enchanted by this adventure—your life—what would do for you?" Excellent question. And since most human eggs never get fertilized, how many geniuses have not been born? How many geniuses *were* born but never received from Dame Fortune those head starts and lucky breaks that could have allowed their talents to flourish?

If you listen to Oliver's fellow poet Hafiz, even crazier stuff is happening. "*Clouds pull each other's pants down and point and laugh... Angels and flowers are playing hooky in graveyards, rolling on cool stones...And luminous fish jump out of rivers / spitting emeralds at all talk of Heaven / being anywhere else but—Right Here*!"

I wish I didn't need to be reminded of all of the above, but I do. Daily. Just as I wish I could be continually reminded of the final paragraph of the introduction to William Saroyan's story collection *The Daring Young Man on the Flying Trapeze*: "Try to learn to breathe deeply, really to taste food when you eat, and when you sleep really to sleep. When you laugh, laugh like hell. And when you get angry, get good and angry. Try to be alive. You will be dead soon enough."

My father was a plumbing supply salesman, yet I doubt he ever heard the aphorist Georg Lichtenberg say, "Everything that matters in life flows through tubes," with "generous input and unimpeded output" being the ideal state of affairs. This rushes me on to another anatomy-related wish: that I could appreciate my body more, however unhappy I usually feel about its appearance in my bathroom mirror. "Appreciate it," I mean, not only for its general good condition but also for the glorious feat of engineering any human corpus is.

Unfortunately, I don't understand nearly enough about how said engineering works, how our physiological systems dovetail with each other, how the pancreas and the kidneys and the gallbladder do what evolution has ordained they do. I've tried reading books about human anatomy but find them dull. All I remember is this admission from the above-mentioned Lewis Thomas: "I am, to face facts squarely, considerably less intelligent than my liver." So my wish here is that I could learn all these lessons by being shrunk with bleeding-edge technology to the size of a microbe, just like how the heroic team of scientists in the groovy sixties movie *Fantastic Voyage* get reduced to the same size. Then, as with that team, I'll go on my own fantastic voyage through the body of some living human volunteer. An investment banker named Thornton Pisher III, for example.

Watch me climb inside Pisher's inner ear! Thrill to how deftly I'm able to dodge Pisher's white blood cells! Applaud as I water-slide through his blood vessels, and go quiet as I pause to meditate inside his left lung, thinking, "*Breathe…*" All the while I'll be listening to anatomy lectures from the ghost of movie sex symbol Raquel Welch, who might have learned what she knows about the human body from her having co-starred in the original *Fantastic Voyage*.

I'll listen carefully to all the lectures, but during our shared lunch break in the stomach sac of volunteer Pisher, I'll remind Raquel that my wife and I once dined with her, along with our film director friend Sara, at a Greek restaurant in Montreal. Sara was directing La Welch in a film being shot there and invited us along to dinner, where the legendary film actress, then in her early seventies, proved to be intriguing company. As she picked at a few asparagus stalks, her diet-conscious main course, Raquel told us that during her teenage years she'd been a rabid fan of Elvis Presley, so I asked her if she ever met him.

"Oh, *yes*," Raquel said, "Elvis and I got to know each other when we were doing separate stage shows in Las Vegas."

In retrospect, I can't believe how cheeky I was in asking my follow-up question, but ask it I did: "Were you ever able to, uh, *consummate* your schoolgirl crush?"

Raquel's wrinkle-free face reddened, but she seemed not to take offense at my *chutzpah*. "Oh, *never*," she replied. "I was *married* at the time, and so was *Elvis*! What's more, I was friendly with Elvis's wife Priscilla!"

A few weeks later, my friend Sara mentioned that she and the movie queen had grown close on the film set in Montreal where they worked together. "Raquel told me so many great stories," Sara reported. "How she was always outsmarting producers who wanted her to shoot nude scenes. How crazy the actor Oliver Reed was. Oh, and how she and Elvis used to sneak away from their spouses in a casino in Vegas to find little hiding spots where they could fuck."

This is a naughty tale I'll remember, no doubt, when my fantastic voyage reaches our volunteer's genitals. But I won't mention it to my spectral microscopic lecturer Raquel. I'm not *that* cheeky. The naughty tale *does* remind me of a different wish of mine, which is to always be able to discern what the truth is when I'm confronted by two different versions of a story. For instance, "*We would not betray our spouses in Vegas*" versus "*We snuck away to find a hiding spot to have sex.*" Or, "*He embezzled from his employer*" versus "*It was an arithmetic mistake, not embezzlement.*" Given what I know about human nature, it's probably more accurate for me to believe the version in which people behave *less* nobly.

I wish I could dive from my childhood home's plastic treehouse into the boundless mythic Ocean of Knowledge, where I would win a swimming race with bearded Neptune in spite of frequent pokes from his trident. Then I'd claim as my spoils the right to replace my mortal eyes with pearls taken from that body of water's finest oysters.

If this wish is not granted, then I wish I could be swallowed by a whale yet survive in its belly for long enough to discover there an exact reproduction of my childhood bedroom. As always, my dogs Barney and Roxanne would be sleeping on a rug beside my bed. My mother would be asleep in her own room, dreaming dreams which are no doubt very different from my own. All my paperbacks and comic books and record albums would line the walls, and there would be no hint of the trauma that must have prompted a recurring nightmare I had in my twenties. This nightmare always started out pleasantly nostalgic, with adult me using a Super 8 camera to film my sleeping pajama-clad child self. Then child me awakened and yawned and rubbed his eyes and sat up and noticed the camera and broke into a grin and waved to adult me, waving cheerfully with both hands, this poor boy being unaware of the fresh blood that covered his little face.

"Rise and shine," indeed.

I wish that my law school classmate Hepzibah Max would have nightmares about me more often, provided that she contacts me as soon as she wakes up the next morning to tell me about these nightmares. Or maybe I should wish instead that she would have no such nightmares, only exceedingly pleasant dreams.

Let me explain. One morning during the summer of 1991 when I was living in Bennington, Vermont, I took my beige Buick station wagon for a drive on the mostly empty scenic roads north of my home. At one bend in the road, a blind spot, I nearly got into a high-speed head-on collision with a Mack truck. I no longer recall what the truck looked like, or how much I was at fault as opposed to the other driver, but I found the experience so upsetting that I may not have noticed even at the time of our near-collision anything about the truck's appearance. All I recall now is that right afterward I pulled my station wagon over to the side of the road with my entire body shaking.

Before that day I had survived a few perilous close calls, in automobiles and otherwise, yet none of these had qualified so overtly as a near-death experience. I must have been driving over eighty miles per hour, and the truck had been going fast, too, and we'd missed each other by no more than an inch. Back home, still trembling a bit and feeling emotionally wrecked, I belted down two shots of vodka, although at that time I had sworn off alcohol, then I remembered to check the voicemail on my landline. There was only one message on my machine, but it was one hell of a thing.

"Hi," said a chirpy and familiar-sounding Midwestern female voice. "It's Hepzibah, Hepzibah Max, from law school? I know this is coming out of the blue, but I need to speak to you. Right away, I mean. Please call me as *soon* as you get this, okay?"

She then provided me with both her work and home phone numbers. I stood gazing at my answering machine for a few moments, puzzled. Hepzibah and I had hardly spoken during our three years together at law school, but she'd always been a likably quirky presence. She answered her office number on the third ring and sounded glad to hear from me. After we exchanged the initial pleasantries, she got down to brass tacks, saying, "Brace yourself for something nuts. Ever since I've been a girl, I've been having these vivid dreams and nightmares. *Really* vivid dream stuff. And, like, well, there's no other way to say this: they tend to come true. Which, as you'd imagine, is a blessing *and* a curse. Most of all, it's a responsibility, because if I dream something important about someone, I've learned the hard way over the years that I need to, like, get in touch with that person and tell them right away."

Curiouser and curiouser, I thought. I wasn't the type to believe in premonitory dreams; I agreed with Oscar Wilde, who observed, "There is no such thing as an omen. Destiny does not send us heralds. She is too wise or too cruel for that." But I wanted to hear Hepzibah out. I asked if she had dreamed about me the previous night. She said she had. With the vodka by now having worked its sorcery on me, I began to smile. Was it an erotic dream? Before I could dwell on this enticing possibility, though, she blasted the smile off my face.

"It was a nightmare," Hepzibah said, "and I'm reporting it to you now to warn you. In my nightmare last night, you were driving at some point today on a lonely-looking road, going fast, and you had a head-on crash with a truck."

My entire body began to tremble again, with an icy sensation slowly ascending in the center of my back. For the first time in my life, I understood that the phrase "a cold chill racing up your spine" is not merely a cliché.

"I know this sounds crazy," Hepzibah continued. "You don't have to believe any of this, I guess. But I want you to promise me something, anyway. Promise me that you won't drive anywhere today. Not even to the local grocery store. Not even fifty feet. Tomorrow you'll be fine; it's just today you have to worry about. Will you promise me that?"

I'm not sure if I believe in premonitory dreams, not even after this experience of mine with Hepzibah, yet thanks to her, I do take them seriously. Thanks to my father, too. In early 1997, Bernie Lippman phoned me at home and said, "You're a writer—see what you can do with a weird dream I had last night. In my dream, you and I were waiting for the arrival of someone, the life-changing arrival of someone called 'the Water Man.'"

My father had never recounted one of his dreams to me before, and never would again, and I failed to grasp the meaning of his Water Man dream. Not, that is, until a year later, when my son was born under the sign of the water-bearer Aquarius.

The standard line is that our dreams are all mostly about wish fulfilment. Vacuum-packed full of wishes as I am, I wish I could remember my dreams whenever I rise in the morning. Until my early forties, I had full recall of my activities in Dreamland, which included lots of guilt trips from murder raps. Why I eventually stopped remembering such fare on awakening, I can't say. The artist Laurie Anderson has suggested that when we cannot recall our dreams, it's because we've been appearing in the dreams of other people. The Babylonian Talmud says only four kinds of dreams will be "fulfilled" for us: "a morning dream," "a dream that a friend has about us," "a dream that is interpreted in the midst of a dream," and "a dream that is repeated."

Since my phone talk with Hepzibah Max, I've often mused how fascinating it would be to have one of my own dreams come true—to have it come bursting out of my noggin and play out in my waking life. This would give that life a sweet jolt not unlike how my dog Rosalita will grab a chew toy in her jaws and shake the toy violently back and forth. My dog's goal is simply to kill its prey, whereas my dream, by becoming "real" on a monthly basis, will probably eliminate any complacency I might have with the laws of physics that imprison me. Which is probably a plus. Weirdness does tend to keep us on our toes, doesn't it?

Then again, since Dame Fortune is Queen Trickster, I fear that my first dream to come true will eventually turn into a kidney-shredding nightmare, a real whopper in which Rosalita grows to gargantuan size. Then, as payback for all the times I refused to share my meals with her, she'll take me between her jaws like that chew toy and shake me back and forth until I'm dead. And then she'll eat me.

My mother taught toddler me to salute all police officers and other uniformed officials I encountered. I remember how surprised and dismayed I was to learn how prone to corruption the people who work in our public institutions are. (Not just big institutions, either. Recently, I heard about a Hooters restaurant manager who set up a beer sales contest for his staff. This manager said he would award "a brand-new Toyota" as the grand prize, but in the end, he presented the winner not a car but a Star Wars-themed gift: a brand-new *toy Yoda*.

How crushing it is when those we are urged to trust most fail us. Which brings us back to cops, and a particular New Orleans policeman who was assisting my friend Stacy after someone had burglarized her local shop and stolen from it a cache of valuable vintage wristwatches. When Stacy asked the officer how likely it was that she would get back her merchandise, he pointed to the pricy Rolex on his wrist and said, "What do *you* think?"

Once she got the message, Stacy said, "But my wristwatches that were swiped were *ladies'* wristwatches."

The cop grinned from one big red ear to the other. "I've got a wife *and* a girlfriend," he explained, "and all three of us celebrate Christmas."

"*The rain it raineth every day / Upon the just and the unjust fella, / But chiefly on the just, because / The unjust steals the just's umbrella.*" Words from someone who must have been "once bitten, twice shy." If only corruption, and the scarcity of resources that creates it, could be eradicated. Short of that, I wish that evildoers great and small would not so often get away with their sins and their scams. And I also wish that the reason they so often get away with the evil they do would not be the fact that their victims usually simply shrug their shoulders and say, "It's not worth the time and effort and hassles for me to try to bring them to justice." Alas, I've often been that kind of shoulder-shrugger and big-crime minimizer myself.

Which catapults us back to the matter of trust, and how we ought to put less faith in the word of people we don't know well. The Russians have a proverb, "Trust, but verify." I wish I'd learned about this proverb a long time before I actually did. It goes well with the writer Rebecca West's admonition that we should believe little of what people say about each other and even less of what they say about themselves.

On the rare occasions when someone does me harm but this harm turns out to help me more than it hurts me, I wish I could swallow my pride and *thank* those harm-doers. Admittedly, this is a hard ask, but rabbinical ethicists say we need to do it anyway. And whenever we fall into the trap of believing that the evildoers among us are not "made" but rather "born that way," I wish that we'd all remind ourselves of this verse by W. H. Auden: "*I and the public know / What all schoolchildren learn / Those to whom evil is done / Do evil in return.*"

Franz Kafka never wrote about ninjas, but he might as well have. I wish I had more knowledge about these "shadow warriors," these "invisibles," especially those pesky ones who might even now be dogging my steps. (Another wish of mine is to be less prone to paranoia, Kafkaesque and otherwise.) I do know, thanks to Wikipedia, that in their heyday five hundred years ago, ninjas were regarded in their homeland of Japan as less honorable than samurai warriors. I know as well that they got recruited from working-class families. And that they were organized into guilds. And that the snug black clothing worn by ninjas may only be a literary conceit. Wouldn't their programs of murder, espionage, and sabotage better succeed if they were disguised as ordinary citizens?

To qualify as a ninja, you need to master forty-eight malevolent techniques, such as keen listening, the attachment of cotton bottoms to straw sandals in order to walk in silence, the making of other footwear designed for walking on water, the hurling of charred turtle powder into an enemy's eyes during a struggle. Also required are expertise with ropes, grappling hooks, and collapsible ladders. Ninja powers of a more ethereal nature allegedly include shape-shifting, the use of magical incantations, plus the vaunted ability to occupy more than one place at one time.

Then there are the weapons that ninjas need to be proficient with—the *nunchakus* and the *shurikens*, sure, but also blow-guns, acid-spurting tubes, and many kinds of bladed killing tools. A particularly nasty spear was used in the assassination of a local warlord who sat on his toilet unaware that an ill-intentioned ninja was scrunched up inside that toilet, waiting for this very moment. Modern historians suggest that the warlord may have died of a natural gastric crisis rather than by anus-stab, but no historian will be able to discourage me from forevermore peering suspiciously into each toilet I plan to use.

One might assume that a "Once a ninja, always a ninja" rule applies to the profession, yet some ninjas have left the game and found work as fireworks designers, pharmacists, and bandits. Were any ninja-retirees able to ascend into samurai-hood? I wish I could say. And if there are indeed dark-minded ninjas currently on my trail, I wish I could find out who hired them.

The best joke that no one except for me and my son and my friend Don finds funny concerns a guy who has a big red STOP sign instead of a head. "I found this dusty magic lamp," he explains to whoever asks about it, "and the genie I released from inside it gifted me three wishes. My first wish was for a billion dollars, tax-free. Wish granted. My second wish was for a gorgeous wife. Wish granted. But where I think I might've gone wrong, see, is when I wished I could have a big red STOP sign for a head..."

If I ever find a dusty magic lamp at the Housing Works thrift shop in lower Manhattan and rub that lamp vigorously enough, perhaps a genie trapped inside it will emerge and then, due to protocol if not gratitude, grant me three wishes. Being aware that making even a single wish with a genie might backfire on me, I decide not to wish for an infinite number of wishes. I don't want to seem greedy. So my first wish is for a mere baker's dozen of wishes while my second is to bestow a bounty of wishes to the handful of living people I most love and, perhaps more importantly, *trust*. I say "trust" because what if some of my intimates secretly resent me and wish me ill?

As for my third wish, it's one for the genie. "May you never," I'll tell him or her, "be imprisoned again in a magic lamp or in any other prison." Apart from buttering up my magical benefactor, the reason for my third wish derives from something that happened to me one summer afternoon in East Berlin in 1992. While I sat at an outdoor café with a new friend, a young woman named Manuela Mond, a bumblebee flew into my half-empty beer glass. Just for fun, I put a sheet of paper over the top of the glass, trapping the bee inside and watching it freak out. To my surprise, Manuela cursed me, slapped my hand, took away the sheet of paper, and released the bee.

"Jesus," I said. "Talk about an overreaction!"

She didn't answer. Within a minute or two, her mood lightened, and we spoke of other things. But the next day, I mentioned Manuela's behavior to a mutual friend of ours. He said, "You obviously don't know Manuela very well. As a teenager in Dresden, she joined an anti-government group, and the secret police, the *Stasi*, prosecuted her as a political dissident."

"What does this have to do with bees?"

Manuela's friend laughed again. "She was locked up for three years, and now she hates all prisons, even those as small as a beer glass."

On more than one occasion, I have been able to persuade a friend not to commit suicide, but I wish I could have had the opportunity to have a pre-self-destruction talk with the friends who did succeed in taking their lives. Some of them had understandable reasons for suicide, but others did it for the stupid old "*I'll show 'em*" reason—that old "*They'll wish they treated me nicer when I was alive*" reason. I call the reason "stupid" because it never works. Or it *does* work, but only for a day or two, and then all but your closest survivors resume their policy of not caring very much about anyone other than themselves.

Ideally, there should be other, safer ways of jettisoning the self. Sometimes I wish I would not be forced to go through life by experiencing it as a single specific individual, the as-is individual I was born to be. I'll never perceive a sunset as anyone but Gary Lippman, just as you'll never perceive it as anyone but yourself, my fellow wisher. Yet wouldn't it be cool if each of us could encounter a sunset through the sense organs of a different person? And not just a sunset but everything else that human existence offers to us, both "the bitter and the better," as my grandmother Lulu would phrase it? Which different views about being on this gumball planet would I come up with if I were not myself but a woman? Or a transsexual? Or a ninja? Or Genghis Khan's favorite general? Or the Khan's second-favorite horse? Or, for maximum experiential impact, a blade of grass that the Khan's horse trampled over while he and his marauding Mongols rode to Constantinople?

Yes, limitations suck. Yet limitations have their uses. They help to make your personal style, and can be beautiful in and of themselves, too. Think of how the meaning of life, however you perceive that meaning, is sharpened by the fact that life ends. And so, although we're not allowed to be anyone but ourselves, we can still be the best possible versions of ourselves. Which, as I've said at the start of this wish list, I wish to be.

What is one's "best self," though? Carl Jung wrote that "The meaning of my existence is that life has addressed a question to me…I myself am a question." Perhaps a piquant question to ask Jung would be why he once praised the Fascist tyrant Mussolini as "an original man with good taste in certain matters." Still, Jung's "I am a question" quip has merit, and the trick is to figure out for yourself what your personal "question" is. The *subsequent* trick is to answer this question for yourself lest anyone else, or everyone else (parents, spouses, friends, total strangers, Genghis Khan, or another tyrant), manage to answer it for you. One head start would be to remember the artist Jean Cocteau's advice to "Cultivate whatever it is that others criticize you for, because it is you." Then again, Cocteau hung out with Fascists, too.

I wish I could have been able to "light out for the Territory," Huckleberry Finn-style, and been a pioneer on the North American range so that I could say I "grew up with the country." I've loved this expression since I first heard it in Gram Parsons's lilting song "Return of the Grievous Angel." Sad to say, the pioneer life was not exactly a safe proposition. Think of all its perils. What's more, you'd have to "work as if you lived in a better nation," which is another favorite expression of mine, courtesy of the novelist Alasdair Gray.

Perhaps I ought to wish instead that I had been born in 1900 or 2000 so that I could say I "grew up with the century." This is yet another favorite expression, but again, not so safe a proposition. Think of all the bad shit the previous century had to fling at us. And think of all the worse shit this new century probably has in the works.

The dice are always rolling.

I wish I had used a different kind of blue gel-ink pen than the one I did use to write a short story by hand one sun-kissed morning in Fort Lauderdale during the winter of 2012. Why this wish? Because I slid the notebook pages on which I'd written the story into the back pocket of my Lucky Brand blue jeans, an act which unexpectedly proved to be *un*lucky. (The words "LUCKY YOU" appear inside all of Lucky Brand jeans' zippers, which reminds me of the Lucky Juice Bar I used to frequent on Houston Street in Manhattan, this tiny store's motto being "BE HAPPY, GO LUCKY—LUCKY TO BE ALIVE.")

Why was my action of putting the pages that featured my new story in my back pocket unlucky? Because I wound up visiting my family at the swimming pool of the hotel where we were staying and my intrepid goddaughter Louise, then five years old, swam into the pool's deep end and promptly, right before my eyes, began to drown.

Nearly fifty years earlier, I myself had been a child who was drowning. It was in a different hotel swimming pool, although this pool was only twenty miles south of Fort Lauderdale, and my fully clothed father had leaped into it to rescue me. Today, with my own turn to be a hero having arrived, I failed to spring into action as quickly as my father had. For a moment, I merely stood on the viewing deck beside the pool, fully dressed, and watched tiny Louise drown, thinking, *Is she just pretending? And if not, if she's for real, is there anyone else nearby—the ghost of my father, even!—who can come deal with this sudden crisis? Is it really up to* me? *Me, whose self-conception is far closer to "fuck-up" than to "heroic?"*

Heroism, I should emphasize, doesn't really become me. My one physically courageous act I can think of was the time I ran into a burning office in order to rescue my friend's computer from the flames engulfing it. Unfortunately, one minute later I was back outside, overwhelmed by the smoke and coughing for what would be the next forty minutes. Farewell to that computer. (The fire, I later learned, had been set by the office's night watchman. He too longed to be viewed as a hero, I suppose.)

An anguished scream from Louise's mother, who was also taking a dip in the pool but nowhere as near to the child as I currently was, snapped me out of my reverie. I had to move. *Now.* And without another thought (well, I *did* silently wish that I'd get full credit from all the witnesses for my heroism) I jumped into the pool and rescued Louise.

Being, as I said, intrepid, the girl went jubilantly swimming again as soon as she finished spitting up the portion of the pool that she'd swallowed. Me, I didn't fare quite as well. My blue jeans and the rest of my clothes were dripping wet. My wallet was water-logged. My cell phone was ruined, and the gel-ink with which I had written my new story on the pages in my back pocket had dissolved completely. Instead of words, there were now only powder-blue clouds. *Beautiful* powder-blue clouds, yes, but language no longer.

Later on, wearing dry clothes, I tried to rewrite my story from memory. This did not work. The new version lacked the first one's pizzazz. I gave up. Still, I'm grateful that I could save Louise (and that I didn't shout at Dame Fortune, "But the girl had a hat!"). I'm grateful that I had those dry clothes to change into, grateful that my wallet was still somewhat usable, grateful that I had the scratch to buy a new phone…And I'm grateful I got to feel close, however briefly, however strangely, to my long-gone one-time savior of a father.

Let's continue with the theme of heroism. When I was a child, I loved to watch professional wrestling matches on TV, and my favorite competitor was a "bad guy" called "Neckcracker Tommy Drake." How I wished I could meet Tommy, and thus, by proximity, partake of his power and charisma. If I could meet Tommy, I figured, I'd become cool by association. Then, when I was aged ten, I actually almost sort of did meet my villainous hero.

In the spring of 1973, my mother brought me to Phoenix for our first vacation out west, and as soon as someone in the airport mentioned Paradise Valley, referring to it as a nearby suburb, I yelped with delight. Tugging Esther Lippman's sleeve, I said, "That's where my favorite wrestler lives! His posters are on the walls in my room, remember? Whenever he gets introduced on TV before a match, the announcer says, 'From Paradise Valley, Arizona, it's 'Neckcracker *Tommy Drake*!'"

My mother smiled. "Would you like to go visit him, sweetheart?"

In the six years since she and Bernie Lippman had divorced, they had been battling in the New Jersey courts for the custody of their only child. So emotionally and morally confusing did I find their war—who loved me better? who was telling me the truth and who was lying?—that I felt the need, naturally enough, to escape into a simpler world. It was the unambiguously "good vs. evil" world of superhero comic books and professional wrestling, with wrestling, which was not actually a sport but scripted theater, playing like a live-action, more humorous version of superhero and supervillain behavior.

Eager that I be distracted from, as my mother put it, "how that homewrecker bastard is tormenting us," she encouraged my enthusiasms, buying me as many comic books as I wanted and permitting me to watch wrestling matches on television well past my bedtime. Not until our Neckcracker Tommy Drake pilgrimage, however, did I realize how far she was willing to indulge me.

The Greater Phoenix White Pages listed exactly one "Thomas Drake" in Paradise Valley. Although the number was unlisted, they provided his address. After stopping at the sleek downtown Hilton to leave off our luggage and take a nap—I was too revved-up to do anything but pretend-sleep—a taxi took us to a ritzy residential neighborhood. In front of a stucco-roofed home, Esther Lippman told the cabbie to wait for us, promising him a handsome tip, then led me up an emerald lawn on a stone path, her sweaty hand clutching mine. My other hand held a poster for Neckcracker to autograph, a desert scene that read, "ARIZONA GETS YOU *HOT!*" Better would have been an image of the man himself, but the Hilton gift shop sold no pro wrestling souvenirs.

Like his fellow "bad guys"—The Iron Sheik, Haystacks Calhoun, Andre The Giant—the 6'2", 275 lbs. Neckcracker had a gimmick, but it was thrillingly up-to-date: He was a hippie, calling opponents "brother" and sporting long bleached blond hair, bushy sideburns, psychedelic costumes, tie-dyed bandannas, funky sunglasses, and turquoise jewelry. What was the man *truly* like, though? Would he behave as villainously at his home as he did within the wrestling ring ropes? What would we do if he was cruel to me and my mother?

By the time we arrived at Neckcracker's house, I was trembling, nervous, dry-mouthed. Esther Lippman rang the bell, then fanned herself with her pocketbook. No one appeared. The sun beat down hard. Arizona was living up to its reputation. "Yoo-hoo!" my mother called, ringing the bell again—just as the door swung open and powerful air-conditioning from inside rolled over us.

On the threshold of the home stood a woman who wearing a negligee colored sea-foam green. She was in her late twenties or early thirties, slim and beautiful, with a sunburnt button nose and hair even longer and blonder and glossier than Neckcracker's hair. Precisely the kind of sexy companion I imagined he would hang out with. Even more notable to me than her beauty and negligee, though, was how she sniffled and dabbed with a Kleenex at her mascara-smeared eyes. She seemed embarrassed to weep in front of strangers, which I could understand. But what had caused her tears?

"Hello, miss," said my mother. "We've come to meet the wrestler."

The expression on the blonde's face changed from sad and embarrassed to puzzled. "Pardon me?" she said, squinting in the sunlight at the strangers on her doorstep, the polyester-pantsuit-wearing middle-aged woman and the boy in chinos and Spider-Man t-shirt.

"The wrestler who lives here." My mother motioned with her chin to the poster I was holding. "We've come a long way, and my son wants an autograph from your husband or your boyfriend or your fancy-man or *whatever* he is."

"I'm sorry," the woman told us in a soft voice which bore a hint of Southern accent, "but you must have the wrong house. There aren't any wrestlers living here."

"Baloney," said Esther Lippman, who was nothing if not, well, indefatigable. "We know for a fact that this is Jimmy Drake's residence."

"*Tommy* Drake," I corrected her.

"Anyway, it's *this* address." My mother's fingertip tapped the black numeral displayed beside the door. "The phone book said so."

I was becoming uncomfortable. This was not going at all how I'd wished for it to go. Yet I couldn't pry my gaze from the young woman. How luminous she looked as she put the tissue to her nose and blew it gently!

"Well," she said, "my husband's name *is* Tom Drake, that's true, but trust me, ma'am, he's not a wrestler. I don't think he even wrestled back in high school! He's a businessman, and he's not home now..."

"Listen, chippie," my mother cut in, "if your husband doesn't want to meet my boy, fine, but don't say he's *not* a wrestler when he *is*!"

The young woman frowned. "Wouldn't I know it if he wrestled?"

"Maybe he's living a double life!"

I winced and looked away, looked everywhere but at the woman, with my gaze eventually settling on my Keds sneakers. Not only was our pilgrimage ending in failure, but now, by raising her voice, my mother was acting pushy, foolish, *insane*, and making me appear crazy, too. Not cool but crazy—*crazy by association*. I knew Esther Lippman had brought me here to make me happy, yet the last thing I wanted now was to appear nuts in the young woman's wet eyes. And when she finally shut her door with one more sniffle and one more "Sorry," I felt as crumpled as her Kleenex. Embarrassed, humiliated—and bereft. This wasn't about Neckcracker anymore, it was about *her*. The woman's beauty, her soft voice, her vulnerability, had stirred something in me. Something deeper than a child's escapist pleasures.

"Don't worry," said my mother, putting her arm around my shoulders, as we rode back to our hotel. "You go find yourself a different favorite wrestler, and I'll get you a *dozen* autographs!"

I did find a new favorite wrestler, but soon outgrew the entire "sport." Superhero comics, too. Puberty arrived on schedule. My parents continued their war against each other. When I was in the ninth grade, my mother found a tumor in her left breast, and only with Esther Lippman's demise, soon after my high school graduation, did her custody war with her ex-husband come to an end. Now my own son is an adult, and I'm much older than my mother got to be. After telling Gideon last week about my visit to Paradise Valley—he loves to hear stories about the kooky grandmother he never knew—I became curious about Tommy Drake. Wikipedia answered most of my questions.

Drake had been a boy-preacher, then worked as a nightclub bouncer, a Golden Gloves boxer, an NFL football player, and a competitive bodybuilder. His life after pro wrestling was plagued with bad health, financial problems, and lawsuits against former promoters. At one point, he could only pay his medical bills by selling online his Wrestling Hall of Fame ring. And in his last decade before dying, he lectured against athletes' steroid use and painted wildlife pictures, art having been a hobby in his youth.

Of the many facts I learned about Neckcracker Tommy Drake, one immediately stood out. His legal name was Bainbridge Hodge. He'd only adopted the stage moniker of Tommy Drake once he started wrestling, and Hodge had never lived in Paradise Valley, either. Why that hometown was advertised as his remains beyond me. He'd spent his entire adult life in Detroit.

Discovering my childhood hero's true identity made me smile. Although my mother and I never discussed it, not even during our taxi ride back to the Phoenix Hilton, she must have suspected that we'd gone to the wrong house. I know I did. Now, nearly half a century later, we finally had our proof. At least *I* had it. And with images of an old but still fierce-looking Bainbridge Hodge filling my computer screen, I thought back to the young woman in Paradise Valley. How weird it must have been for her to find a pair of strangers on her doorstep, an annoying mother and child who called her husband a wrestler, a "Neckcracker." Closing my eyes now, I can see that woman's long blond hair again, the button nose, and hear her soft voice say "I'm sorry"...

Yet one last mystery remains: Why had she been crying?

At a Toots and the Maytals concert at the Lone Star Café in the mid-eighties, I stood in the audience near Yellowman, a Jamaican singer who cut the most impressively fearsome figure I've encountered. In fact, the memory of that sight makes me wish sometimes that citizens would pass me on the street and think, *Now* there's *a scary-looking cat*. If only they'd feel as wary of me as they would of Yellowman! Or of Neckcracker Tommy Drake, for that matter.

"What a repellently adolescent wish," Dame Fortune tells me in a dream.

"Agreed," I say. "But I can't always *choose* my wishes, can I?"

"If you really want to look like a thug, then why don't you do like the pirate Blackbeard, twisting lengths of hemp in your hair and soaking them in saltpeter and then setting them aflame in order to give your head an intimidating 'smoky' appearance?"

"Nope," I say, "can't. I've gone bald."

"Then at least make a big show of mixing gunpowder in your rum the way Blackbeard did."

"Nope, dear Dame, I can't. My body will no longer tolerate liquor, especially rum, which always used to give me blackouts, anyway."

She sighs. "So fix yourself up with the ritual 'medicine' that Crazy Horse used before battle, painting hailstones on your chest, tying a hawk to your head, and sprinkling your pony with dust."

"Can't, can't, can't. I don't own a pony, for starters."

"Hmm. I don't suppose that, in the manner of blood-soaked Aztec priests, you'd care to wear human flesh as a veil?"

"Just the thought of that makes me retch."

Behind her own dark veil, the Dame's obscured face is scowling at me. "How about having a dentist file your teeth down to sharp points and flash those fangs around until your teeth fall out one by one or need to get pulled by said dentist?"

"Nope. I like my teeth more or less the way they are."

"And tattoos? Frightening ones, I mean?"

"Nope," I say. "I've considered getting inked the simple word 'TATTOO,' or else, even better, the more Magritte-like 'THIS IS NOT A TATTOO.' And I do admire the *New Yorker* cartoon in which a person's upper back sports the inked image of an angry elderly woman shouting 'You can get a tattoo over *my dead body*' with a legend underneath this image reading, 'Rest In Peace, MOM.' But no tattoos for me. They're not a big deal anymore; as the expression goes, '*If* everyone *is cool, is* anyone *cool*?' Besides, I can easily envision a post-apocalyptic dystopian hellscape future in which all tattooed citizens are rounded up for some reason and sent to death camps."

The Dame shakes her head. "You're too Armageddon-minded. Since you mention the *New Yorker*, have you seen the cartoon where a man holds a sign reading, 'THE END IS NEAR,' and his wife stands beside him with her own sign reading, 'YOU WISH'?"

This makes me chuckle. "That," I say, "sounds just like me and my wife."

One of my favorite John Prine songs is "Please Don't Bury Me," in which Prine makes plain his wishes regarding how he'd like his body disposed of after death. Instead of being dropped "*down in that cold,*

cold ground," he says he'd "*rather have them cut me up and pass me all around. / Throw my brain in a hurricane. / The blind can have my eyes / And the deaf can have both of my ears / If they don't mind the size.*"

Much as I'd like to sketch out a similar program for disposal of my parts, I'd rather simply be cremated when it's my own turn to take the dive. There's a beauty to the thought of my ashes being sprinkled on favorite places, or distributed in miniature urns to my loved ones. On the other hand, a more primal slice of my psyche, sentimental me, wishes not to be cremated but instead to have my body stay intact and be buried in my family plot in a New Jersey cemetery. Hello again, dear relatives!

As for the epitaph on my gravestone, it will be daunting to think up better ones than the already-used "NOW I KNOW SOMETHING YOU DON'T" and "I CAME HERE WITHOUT BEING CONSULTED, AND I LEAVE WITHOUT MY CONSENT." If I were named "John Yeast," I could go with "FORGIVE ME FOR NOT RISING," which is another goodie that's been done. The actor Peter O'Toole decided what his tombstone would read when a blood-and-vomit-and-Guinness covered jacket he'd sent to a cleaning service was returned to him, still mostly befouled, with this epitaph-worthy message: "It distresses us to return work which is not perfect."

The comedian Gilda Radner died young but has a stone on her grave which reads, "I HAD A GREAT TIME." Best of all might be an epitaph idea from a different comedian, Billy Connolly: "In tiny writing on a huge stone (with) the writing so small that people would have to get up really close to read it: 'YOU'RE STANDING ON MY BALLS.'" Actually, Connolly's entire philosophy seems to be cemetery-centered. He says, "If you think you're having a bad day, the graveyard is full of people who would love to be doing what you're doing."

Have you ever written graffiti on someone's tombstone? Definitely not my thing, although I might have urinated on the grave of a man who once brutalized my mother. He nearly beat her to death, in fact. That's a tale for a different time. I will mention one further instance of philosophical tombstone vandalism, though. Beneath an engraved epitaph which reads, "*As I am now, so wilt thou be; Prepare therefore to follow me,*" some wag has scrawled in chalk, "*To follow thee we'd be content / Did we but know which way thou went.*"

Lately, I've been considering a very different kind of send-off for myself: a Viking burial. Place my corpse on a serpentine longboat, put torches to the boat, and give it a good shove into my hometown's reservoir. If the flaming vessel is too heavy to be shoved, then summon the ancient giant Hyrrokkin, who'll show up astride a jumbo wolf, using snakes for reins, because *he'll* give my ship a helpful kick. This is how they did it at the funeral of the Norse god Baldur, where Baldur's father Odin, boss god of the universe, whispered something in his dead son's ear. No one except for Odin knows what he whispered. I wish I knew, although being a father myself, I have some guesses.

We've arrived at the *Family Circle Department* of this wish list. Before my mother and my Uncle Wolf were born, my grandparents, Dave and Lily Fennel, had a child named Herbert. I wish that Dame Fortune had prevented Herbert, then aged three, from falling out of an open window when his babysitter wasn't looking. This wish is complicated, however, because had this child not perished, my grandparents might have refrained from having more children, including my mother. Had Herbert not died, I mean, I might never have been born.

One day in the early nineties in New York's SoHo district, I met an old street busker. He played a portable keyboard and said his name was Herbert. I did the mental math and realized that my dead uncle Herbert would have been the same age as this street busker. Had my dead uncle somehow escaped death? Was this him? That night I had a dream about a drowning man who tosses a pair of dice across the surface of the sea. I woke up wishing that Dame Fortune would have saved the drowned man before he sank. Maybe his name was Herbert, too.

Another family-centered wish of mine is that I could not only learn about but actually hang out with my direct descendants—if I get to have any descendants, that is. I'd also like to learn about and interact with my thousands of direct ancestors. Needless to say, Yiddish-English translators would have to be available for me and these ancestors. Better yet, I wish I could speak Yiddish myself. Hebrew, too. And Hungarian, while I'm at it, as well as the pun-rich language James Joyce invented for his novel *Finnegans Wake* and "dread talk," which is the lively Rastafarian subversion of language that changes the word "politics" to "politricks," "oppressor" to "downpressor," "library" to "truthbrary," and "understand" to "overstand."

My Uncle Wolf, a brilliant genealogist, has been able to trace a relative of ours back to the Galician town of Drohobycz in 1750, but this ancestor is pretty much a cipher. How illuminating it would be, then, for me to throw a "gene-pool party" where all of my preceding and succeeding kin can break bread and kibbitz together! Perhaps we could rent out the enormous Javits Convention Center in Manhattan for our grand affair.

Another word about ancestors: Through DNA testing, I've learned that, like everybody else, I have in my genetic code traces of Neanderthals. I wish I could spend time with these forebears of mine, who supposedly liked to place flowers in the graves of their dead loved ones. And I wish that such thoughtful people were not, except for their ghostly presence in our genes, extinct.

Now for another word about Dryhobycz, which was not just the hometown of my family but also that of the legendary Jewish author Bruno Schulz. I wish that this sensitive soul, this personally inhibited yet utterly singular literary genius, had not been shot to death by a spiteful Gestapo thug during the Nazi occupation of his, *my*, ancestral town. And I wish that Schulz's last work, the perhaps unfinished novel *Messiah*, could be found and enjoyed and studied by the world's readers. The goal of this book, according to Schulz, was to "mature into childhood," and it supposedly begins with a little boy being awakened one morning by his mother. Instead of singing to him "Rise and Shine" the way Esther Lippman used to sing to me, Schulz's fictive mother gets her child up by telling him that the Messiah has just been spotted. Where? In a village near their hometown of Drohobycz. And what was the Messiah's given name? Why not "Herbert"?

I knew I wanted to be an author, to be "a maker of sentences and a teller of stories," as the novelist John Barth puts it, when I was a child, playing with my GI Joe dolls, inventing battle scenes for them. In time, I learned to wish to write the kind of stuff I loved to read, and I learned to subscribe to a suggestion made by another novelist, Ken Kesey: "If it doesn't uplift the human heart, piss on it."

I was affirmed in my literary ambitions at a bar in Chicago one night in the late eighties, where I got speaking with a woman named Harlene. Instead of listening to her complaints about her job, my mind drifted away imagining a fictional character who'd be a good match for Harlene's distinctive name. Or a good match for the even more flavorful names "Harlette" and "Harlotta" that I soon whipped up. A similar thing happened not long after that night when I sat on a bus in Cranford, New Jersey and glanced out the window as we drove past a plumbing supply warehouse whose big front sign identified the warehouse as "Standard Nipple Works." *What a great title for a novel*, I thought. And soon enough, it occurred to me that if I cared so much about the names of warehouses and of people, then I needed to be a writer, someone who could employ such rich material. It would be a writer's life for me.

Another great "Discover Your Calling" moment occurred to my food critic friend Gael Greene. As a young journalist Gael had sex with Elvis Presley after interviewing him, then they ate egg sandwiches together in bed. Elvis was "young and hot" at the time, said Gael, "and we didn't make love, we *fucked*." But because the meal glowed brighter in her memory than did the sex, she realized that writing about food should be and would be her destiny. This was fortunate, because Gael went on to write about "the layered perfumes of a jumbo sea scallop wearing a sesame tulle chapeau afloat in a curry-scented puddle" and other rhapsodic culinary descriptions.

Although I've rarely doubted my calling as a writer, I'm mindful of something that F. Scott Fitzgerald once said: "Writers aren't people, exactly. Or if they're any good, they're a whole lot of people trying so hard to be one person." On those occasions when I did consider getting out of "the Quality Lit Game," as the author Terry Southern called it, I thought about taking on the professional title of "soldier of fortune." Given my awareness of Dame Fortune's presence in my life, that job title would fit. Or maybe I could go for something even tastier, like "licensed wet nurse," which is what it said on the business card of a woman I met once in a restaurant.

"That's the greatest job title *ever*!" I told her.

"Thanks," she said. But then, looking a bit sheepish, she lowered her voice to add, "Actually, I'm not fully licensed *just yet*, but…"

Other job titles I envy are "spellbinder," which was Auden's description of Oscar Wilde; "skip tracer," the nickname for a bail bond-person; and "rainbow hustler," which was the idealistic Tin Pan Alley lyricist Yip Harburg's self-description. I especially like the job title of Bez, the maraca-shaker for the musical group the Happy Mondays. When Bez's young son was asked by a schoolmate what job his father had, the boy ruminated on the matter before announcing, "vibe giver."

The comedian Lord Buckley realized at age thirty that he was a "lord" because, he said, whether we realize it or not, "we are *all* lords and ladies." Still, humility matters. When he retired from making art, Marcel Duchamp took his role in life down to the nitty-gritty by labeling himself "a breather." But feeling pride in your professional title matters, too. Have a look at Charles Curzon, a Scottish con man with nearly six hundred convictions to his credit. At the age of seventy-two, while partly blind and partly deaf, he took up armed robbery. Using a shotgun, he spent a decade stealing from Glasgow banks, and when someone called him an "old rogue," Curzon angrily said, "That's a stupid name. I'm a successful fucking bank robber." He's fortunate that he never encountered a particular irate bank teller in Wellesley, Massachusetts. When a local stick-up man stuck his pistol in this bank teller's face, she simply laughed, crumpled up the note he'd handed her, and told him, "I'm not giving you any money. Now get the hell out of here."

Being a jack-of-all-trades, like one Ignacz Trebitsch, might be fun. This cat's career choices included actor, oil speculator, postal worker, arms dealer, member of the British Parliament, German spy, Anglican missionary, and Buddhist monk. Surprisingly not on his resume was the humorist P. G. Wodehouse's own curious choice of second profession: "getting hit in the stomach by meteorites."

At age four, my son told me that there were not one but three professions he wished to practice when he grew up. They were "rock 'n' roll star," "champion surfer," and "a cook at a McDonalds." Instead of sharing these ambitions when I was a child, I wished that I could be a ninja. Dame Fortune declined to grant this wish, although I attended weekly judo classes taught by a man named Fuikksho Shimamoto and even bought *nunchakus*, the ninja's never-leave-home-without-it weapon. But I could never practice with my *nunchakas* without accidentally bashing my forehead with it, so I finally stashed the thing in the safety of my bedroom closet, where it vanished. Stolen, I guess, by the shadow warriors who know how to use it without hurting their foreheads.

When I was a child, I never wished to be a firefighter, much less US President, although I wouldn't mind hearing a United States Marine Band play my personal theme song—not "Hail To The Chief" but Michael Nyman's "Chasing Sheep Is Best Left To The Shepherd"—whenever I enter a room. If only this inspiring tune had been playing when I strutted into Goldman's Catering Hall for my Bar Mitzvah reception in 1976!

Sometimes I wish I'd been an investigative journalist, but while I'm interested enough in many subjects to read about them, I don't care enough about such subjects to want to research and write about them. There's a similar problem with my occasional wish to be a chef—I love to eat but would only want to cook my favorite foodstuffs. ("GOT MORE TIME FOR MISBEHAVIN' SINCE I STARTED MICROWAVIN'," says a t-shirt I own.) And even though human minds fascinate me (the more deviant, the better), I wouldn't want to be responsible for the well-being of people I dislike or feel indifferent about. Which means that my occasional wish to be a psychotherapist is off the board, too.

At other times I've wished I could be a painter, a clown who entertains seriously ill children, a radio DJ mischievously declaring the local temperature at fifty-nine degrees (no matter what the season), a Broadway actor, a film director, an architect, and a drummer. As a drummer, I would place beside my drum kit a personalized version of the sign used by the great stickman Bernard "Pretty" Purdie: "YOU DONE IT! YOU DONE HIRED THE HITMAKER GARY 'LIPS DO YER STUFF' LIPPMAN!")

Most of all, I have wished I could be an astronaut, if only so that I could smell for myself the scent of moon dust. According to the space explorer Buzz Aldrin, the "grayish-cocoa"-colored "very fine particles" of moon dust have a most distinct odor—"pungent, like gunpowder or spent cap-pistol caps." The prospect of nasally ingesting something of the moon, getting those molecules fizzing around my brain, sounds like the next best thing to being there. The best kind of lunacy.

"Now and then," wrote Mark Twain, "we had the hope that if we lived and were good, God would permit us to be pirates." During my childhood, I thrilled to Errol Flynn's movie portrayal of Rafael Sabatini's pirate character Captain Blood. I likewise noticed how much cooler than my own name were the names of Blood, Flynn, and Sabatini, and I admired a statement from Sabatini about his other swashbuckling character Scaramouche, whose name is the coolest of them all: "He was born with a gift of laughter and a sense that the world was mad."

Apart from the above wishes, I never really longed to be a pirate. A pirate's life was not for me. Still, who would reject a treasure chest filled with pieces of eight stashed away in their attic? And who wouldn't want to have witnessed a notable failed seduction in the early eighteenth century, the one that took place aboard the ship of the fearsome pirate "Calico Jack" Rackham? One of Jack's crewmen was actually a woman disguised as a man, a woman named Mary Read, and when she tried to get it on with a handsome young fellow crewman, Mary discovered that her crush was also a woman disguised as a man, a woman named Anne Bonny.

Fortunately, the two cross-dressing female pirates laughed about their situation, Scaramouche-style, finding the world mad, and they decided to be friends. The only problem was Calico Jack, who'd been sleeping with Anne Bonny. Until now, no one else onboard had known her secret. And Jack, being a typical man, grew quite jealous. Still, Bonny had the last laugh. After the pirate captain got captured by the authorities, Bonny visited him in his cell on the eve of his execution. Not to console Calico Jack, as it turned out, but to tell him, "If you had only fought more like a man, you would not be dying in the morning like a dog."

As you've noticed by now, my fellow wisher, this wish list is pretty egocentric. So be it. Like the song goes, "I've Got To Be Me." Still, as you may suspect, my boldness in writing my list only goes so far, because certain wishes feel too private for me to expose in print. A few of them I'm unable to consciously admit even to myself. So much for the "I've Got To Be Me" business, then. Rest assured, however, that I do wish I could "get naked" on the page the way my novelist friend Harry Crews advised me, writing about my life as candidly as Joe Brainard did in his *I Remember* books.

The author Annie Ernaux could get pretty candid, too. Ernaux—won the Nobel Prize, didn't she?—has said that she wrote her autobiographical novels "in the same way I used to lie in the scorching sun for a whole day at sixteen, or make love without contraception at twenty: without thinking about the consequences."

"No consequences." What a dream! Still, I wish I had not sunbathed for a whole day when I was sixteen, because the burn I received nearly landed me in a hospital. And there was a time in my early thirties when I wished that, unlike Ernaux, I *had* used a condom while making love, because, lo and behold, one of the women I condomlessly made love to, the lovely Norwegian Thorhildur, got pregnant.

Then, when she insisted on having the child against my wishes, I had a near-nervous breakdown.

Recklessly fathering a child I had not wished for made me feel as if my life had gone off its rails. Badly. As soon as I met that child, however—met *my* child, met *our* child—I changed my mind instantly and felt jubilant. I felt grateful to Thorhildur, too, immensely grateful, and recognized that, contrary to how I'd been thinking, my life had actually now gone *onto* its proper rails for the first time. And I whispered a silent thanks to Dame Fortune for my neglecting to use a condom nine months earlier.

The Dame just keeps revising our wishes for us.

Once I asked a German rock star friend of mine named Udo if he would have chosen to be German if he had the choice. "Only," he replied, "if I could be a *German Jew*." I would not have been able to ask the author Robert Graves the same question, because late in his life, Graves is said to have decided to stop speaking to everyone, including his loved ones. Apparently he felt he'd said enough. Before falling silent, however, Graves told a journalist that he wished he could have been a Hungarian. "They've always brought me good luck," he said, "and have more poets to the square mile than any other nation in Europe." Graves added that Hungarians "originally came from Babylon, from which they were expelled. They retained, however, their extraordinary fineness of thought."

If Dame Fortune were to ask me which tribe I wish I could belong to, I'm not sure how I would answer her. Hungarian? Quite possibly—to paraphrase the Irish expression, "Hungary must be heaven because my wife comes from there." How about American, the nationality of my birth? Not necessarily, because I agree with the writer G. K. Chesterton who said, "To say 'My country, right or wrong' is like saying, 'My mother, drunk or sober.'" Maybe I would indeed choose to be American, after all—it's "the Devil I know." But there's no doubt that the title of a certain blues song written by the guitarist Michael Bloomfield—perhaps the only blues song with such a title—applies to me: "I'm Glad I'm Jewish."

Did the writer Ludwig Borne feel the same way? He wrote that "Some reproach me with being a Jew, others pardon me, still others praise me for it. But all are thinking about it." As for outright anti-Semitism, no one described it better than another Jewish author, Isaac Babel, who called it "the socialism of idiots."

I wish that my father had said to me when I was five what the Baal Shem Tov's father told him at the same age: "Listen, one of the Innocent Souls of Heaven lives in you, even though you may seem in the world's eyes a poor shack for the Soul's dwelling. Use your specialness well and do not fear the Enemy." As it was, I had to make do with my father's talk about less lofty stuff, such as sports, politics, his rascally gambling pals Gerson Barondez and Norman Norman, and his adventures in the United States Army during World War II. Bernie Lippman had dreamed of becoming a fighter pilot but he washed out of flight school by crashing his aircraft during training, so he wound up serving as a radar operator on bomber planes, guarding our Eastern Seaboard. He felt grateful that he hadn't gotten stationed in Europe or Asia. He felt even more grateful that he wasn't the gunner on his bomber raids, because the gunner had the lowest life expectancy of any member of a bomber's flight crew.

Bernie Lippman's Army stories, I admit, were pretty good, particularly the one about how he got so drunk at a party that he leaned over his top bunk in his bedroom and vomited right onto the guy who was seated on the lower bunk kissing a girl. Now that I think of it, I'm glad that my father told me this story when I was five instead of telling me any Baal Shem Tov stuff about "Innocent Souls and Enemies."

Although not "fearing the Enemy," or fearing anything too much, does have its importance. As my favorite medieval Zen master, Ikkyu Sojun, the so-called "Crazy Cloud," boasted, "Even if I go to Hell, I'll find a way to enjoy it." Ikkyu could back up such badass talk, even during a brief ferry ride. While on deck, he encountered a hostile priest, and the priest summoned a fire demon to intimidate Ikkyu. But instead of cowering, my man simply approached that demon with a yawn, lifted his robe, and pissed on it until the demon sizzled and melted out of existence.

Problem solved: the miraculous demon didn't stand a chance against what Ikkyu called "the miracle issuing out of my own body." (Could peeing on ninjas be the best way to combat them? We'd have to catch them first…)

Still on the fear theme, another Hasidic rabbi, Nachman of Breslov, said, "The whole world is a very narrow bridge, and the main thing is to not be frightened at all." This advice echoes the first of three rules that Laurie Anderson has said she and her rock artist husband Lou Reed lived by: "Don't be afraid of anyone." ("Now," added Anderson, "can you imagine living your life afraid of no one?") (Their other rules were "Get a really big bullshit detector and learn how to use it" and "Be really, really tender.") As for the fear, can I settle for just a little *less* of it? Or at least a little less of fear's first cousin, worry?

"You're such a worrywart," my mother used to complain to me when I was a child. I'm still the same. Yet I *have* come to recognize what every schoolchild knows: that worry is usually a mistake. As the poet, duelist, and spy Francisco de Quevedo once observed, "Where there is less fear, there is less danger." "Healthy concern" is cool, but how futile and damaging our fretting is with things we can't do anything about. Which is practically everything apart from our own thoughts, actions, and reactions. Actually, our inability to do much might even be a blessing—as the singer Willie Nelson once announced, "Fortunately, we're not in control."

When a Frenchman in a Paris *bistro* overheard my friend David Amram complaining about the state of the American government, the Frenchman sidled over to David and said, "You're right to worry and feel angry, *monsieur*, but politics all over the world have been a dreadful mess for the past three thousand years—so don't forget, in the midst of your worry and anger, to *enjoy your meal*." The philosopher George Santayana probably enjoyed his own meals thusly. About politics, he wrote, "I know nothing; I live in the Eternal."

Speaking of eternity, I wish I could hop back in time in order to behold the look on the rock artist David Bowie's face early in his career when he walked into his dressing room in a nightclub and found that the only toilet available to him was a sink. Bowie complained, but the club's manager snapped at him, "If it was good enough for Shirley Bassey, it's good enough for you." Likewise, I wish I could have seen the look on Bowie's fellow rock artist Jimi Hendrix's face early in his career when he walked into his dressing room in a nightclub and found an enormous tub of dead fish there. Hendrix inquired about this oddity, and the club manager informed him, "Your opening act is a troop of trained seals."

This manager was breaking the first rule of vaudeville, which is never to put the seals on first. With the stage made slippery by those seals' movements, performers tend to slide around, perhaps even crashing into the master of ceremonies and knocking said MC into the orchestra pit. *Life's Rich Pageant Department, Showbiz Section.*

I can change a diaper, but I wish I could pitch manure, set a broken bone, program a computer, fix a malfunctioning automobile engine, cook a proper meal, paint a house, figure out my income tax, perform CPR, repair a toilet the way a French ex-girlfriend of mine did once while I watched, and survive without tools or clothes or sustenance out in the wild. How can I call myself anything but a man-child if I lack such basic adult skills? Alas, not even the deity in the Book of Revelation can scare me out of being a pussyfooting commitment-phobic taker of half measures when he says, "*If you are neither hot nor cold, I shall spew you forth from my mouth.*"

Such a deity can't frighten me out of quitting some enterprises, either. I feel faint when I remember all the achievements I dreamed of doing but didn't finish, or even start. In many cases, other people ended up doing them instead—or else my ideas went to the "*airy limbo*" Billy Collins wrote about, that "*home to lost epics, / unremembered names, / and fugitive dreams…*"

How much better my pussyfooting life would be if I could emulate my penniless immigrant grandfather David Fennel. With his ingenuity, his hard work, and his devoted and equally hard-working wife Lily, Dave built a damn-good business. Most importantly, my grandfather was the "Never say die" type and would have appreciated the Lebanese proverb which goes, "The one who is not dead still has a chance." In fact, Dave Fennel's motto, often repeated in his Yiddish-accented English, was "Go *foidah.*" Easier said than done, Grandpa! Yet it helps, I've found, to remind myself that many problems have a solution which, if you can patiently and diligently seek to find it, will leave your whole situation better off than it had been before the problem arose. In addition, it helps to distinguish between "bad problems" and "good problems," and to recall that every bad problem could always be worse. *And* to repeat after Kinky Friedman: "Falling on your face is still moving forward."

My favorite way to solve problems is by using the "Change Your Reality" intellectual *jiu-jitsu* referred to by Albert Einstein when he said, "No worthy problem is ever solved in the plane of its original conception." Wittgenstein was getting there, too, with his suggestion that "The solution to a problem lies in living in a way that makes the problem disappear." One example of this *jiu-jitsu* appears in Sophie Hannah's poem "If People Disapprove of You," where she wrote, "*Make being disapproved of your hobby. / Make being disapproved of your aim. / Devise new ways of scoring points / In the Being Disapproved Of Game.*"

All you need for this brand of *jiu-jitsu* is a vigorous imagination. "When we were evacuated during the war," Yoko Ono said while reminiscing about her childhood, "my brother was really unhappy and depressed and really hungry, because we did not have very much food. So I said, 'OK, let's make a menu together. What kind of dinner would you like?' And he said, 'Ice cream.' So I said, 'Good, let's imagine our ice cream dinner.' And we did, and he started to look happy. So I realized even then that just through imagining, we can be happy...We had our conceptual dinner, and this is maybe my first piece of art."

Which reminds me of a certain German prisoner of war described by the author Albert Camus, a man who would have made Camus's exemplar Sisyphus smile. This POW lieutenant suffered terribly in a Soviet prison camp but, wrote Camus, "constructed for himself a silent piano with wooden keys. In the most abject misery, perpetually surrounded by a ragged mob, he composed a strange music audible to him alone."

I wish I could hear that music. I wish I could taste Yoko Ono's ice cream dinner. Most of all, I wish I could make a hobby out of being disapproved of.

By the way, an online "Wishing Tree for Yoko Ono" compiled wishes sent by fans to the artist to commemorate her birthdays. What a very Yoko work of art! She has said, "As a child in Japan, I used to go to a temple and write out a wish on a piece of thin paper and tie it around a tree. Trees in temple courtyards were always filled with people's 'wish knots,' which looked like white flowers blooming from afar."

Trees figure in Yoko's song "It's Gonna Rain," which features my favorite lyric penned by her, a little paean to taking the long view: "*You say life is a bowl of cherries. / You give me a bowl of piss. / That piss will grow into trees one day. / I'm getting my cherries anyway.*"

The wish I wound up putting on Yoko's wishing tree was, "I wish that Yoko's remark 'You change the world by changing yourself' could matter more." Yet I liked someone else's wish better: "I wish for love to know that it's stronger than fear."

Let's make as though it's "Arbor Day" for a wee bit longer. You can't find a better living symbol of the universe than the tree, which grows from the singularity of one seed into earthy roots of matter and airy branches of spirit. I wish I could be less self-conscious about hugging trees, because I find this a meaningful activity. (Don't hug every specimen you meet, though—some, like the Ordeal Tree of Madagascar, the Poison Tree of Guiana, and the Nox Vomica Tree of Java, can prove fatal to human beings.)

With trees, I wish I could be as thoughtful as my wife Berta is. During a recent hike we took together through a forest of coastal sequoia trees in Northern California, I kept wishing I could converse with these enormous thousand-year-old beauties whom John Muir called "the greatest of living things." Inspiring my wish to have a powwow with them was a passage in Thomas Pynchon's novel *Vineland*. The passage concerns an infant girl being driven by her father and his friends past a similar forest in northern California. The girl is crying her heart out until she stops abruptly and begins to listen carefully, patiently, to something that the redwoods are telling her. Then, in a calm, adult-sounding voice, she responds to what they've apparently said, speaking in words which make zero sense to the grown-ups with her but no doubt make good sense to those redwoods.

Perhaps this child was coming to know the truth of what the author Hermann Hesse meant when he said, "Whoever has learned to listen to trees no longer wants to be a tree. He wants to be nothing but what he is." Which brings us back to the theme of being disapproved of but not caring.

I wish that Karl Marx had been a brother to Groucho, Harpo, Chico, Zeppo, and Gummo. If Karl had been one of the Marx Brothers, think of how different world history might have been! We might have seen a less savage and more fun twentieth century. Then again, according to Dame Fortune's "Law of Unintended Consequences," which is perhaps her strangest invention, the opposite might have been the case.

The Dame's law is the reason why I do not wish to enjoy the powers of invulnerability, immortality, or even invisibility. Too much can go wrong in spite of what seems so right. Get a load of Fredric Brown's story mosaic "Three Lost Discoveries." In the mosaic's first section, an American man makes himself invulnerable to all *external* physical harm, including a hydrogen bomb. Alas, that bomb's detonation knocks him into outer space, where he runs out of air and suffers the *internal* physical harm of suffocation. Talk about being careful what you wish for!

The second section of Brown's story is just as grisly. A Soviet man becomes immortal but falls into a coma, and when his doctors finally grasp the financial toll that their maintaining the comatose man's life will take on the state, they simply bury him alive.

The third section of "Three Lost Discoveries" concerns an English career criminal who finds that he can make himself ninja-grade invisible. Exulting in this new power, he pays a late-night visit to an Ottoman sultan's harem, where he plans to rape the sleeping women. Being foolish, he's forgotten that the power of invisibility doesn't matter in pitch darkness, so an especially keen-eared eunuch catches and beheads him.

My guess is that the Marx Brothers, including perhaps Karl, would enjoy being sultans with a harem at their disposal. As Lou Reed sings, "*Those were different times.*" I've never met any sultans, and don't wish to, but I do have a cousin who was a most favored member of a harem in Brunei during the nineties. She later published a superb memoir about the experience. Does my cousin wish she'd never wound up there? Or is she glad that she did because she got a great book out of it?

I wish that my palms didn't sweat whenever I speak with someone I want to impress (a sexy person, a hip-seeming person, or a potential employer) because there's usually that awful moment when we shake hands and the person tries not to look disgusted as they brush their own palms against their thigh, wiping away my sweat. Why are my hands so moist? Maybe, as was the case with the humorist S. J. Perelman's own hands, "They've been insufficiently osculated."

In the *Egyptian Book of the Dead*, the sun god Ra announces, "*I have created the other gods from my sweat, and the people from the tears of my eye.*" Could I will my sweat not to be the ordinary stuff but rather something Ra-like, an *elixir vitae* that features magic powers? Not likely. But if I could, I wish I'd be able to lay these sweaty hands of mine on the physically deformed people I've encountered in my life and heal them. I'm remembering in particular a lovely young woman

I made love with for the first time on a Miami Beach hotel balcony as the sun rose over the Atlantic and I realized that her entire body, every inch of skin, was covered by the purplish discoloration known as a "wine stain." What Mikhail Gorbachev bore on his forehead, this woman bore simply everywhere, and so—as she told me later, over breakfast—she had to spend every morning applying pancake make-up on her face and the rest of her exposed skin in order to make her skin look normal. My admiration isn't worth much, of course, yet I wish this young woman could know how much I admire her for her resiliency and courage.

If reincarnation is a real thing, which I strongly suspect it is not—everybody seems to have in a past life been either Cleopatra or the person having sex with her—I wish that lost loved ones could find each other again the way the carnival performer Mr. Electrico found a dead friend inside the twelve-year-old future author Ray Bradbury.

"All of a sudden," Bradbury wrote of their encounter, "he leaned over and said, 'I'm glad you're back in my life.' I said, 'What do you mean? I don't know you.' He said, 'You were my best friend outside of Paris in 1918. You were wounded in the Ardennes and you died in my arms there. I'm glad you're back in the world. You have a different face, a different name, but the soul shining out of your face is the same as my friend. Welcome back.'"

My fellow wisher, may you find your own Mr. Electrico. May your Mr. Electrico find you. Then may you "welcome each other back."

"*Vivu! Revu! Amu!*" is Esperanto for "Live! Dream! Love!" I wish I could speak this lovely language, just as I wish I had a collection of vintage Esperanto-themed merchandise, including the liqueur Esperantine. I'm glad that the Jewish socialist Ludovik Zamenhof idealistically created a universal tongue, however flawed and unpopular Esperanto is. Keeping this language talk going, I'm also glad that I happen to know that the word "*pelinti*" is used in Ghana to connote when you move hot food around inside your mouth, and that the word in Arabic for the amount of water you can scoop up in your hand is "*gurfa*," and that the French word for the scent of perfume that lingers in a room after the perfumed person has left it is "*sillage*."

Unfortunately, aside from knowing these party-trick words

and speaking some French, foreign languages are, as the expression goes, "Greek to me." James Joyce learned Norwegian so he could read Ibsen, yet my mind is such Swiss cheese that I can barely retain enough words in Hungarian to have a rudimentary conversation with my in-laws. At least I'm not as arrogant as Mark Twain, who with typical irony wrote, "In Paris they simply opened their eyes and stared when we spoke to them in French. We never did succeed in making those idiots understand their own language." Anyway, I wish that those neural implants you find in science fiction books and films ("*Plug In And Speak Basque Instantly*!") were currently available to buy. If I had no other choice, I'd even hold my nose and order them from Amazon.

Next, there's my native tongue to consider. I wish that my favorite little-employed English words, both formal (e.g., *micturate, louche, plangent*) and slang (e.g., *keister*), were not likely doomed to disappear from common usage before the middle of this century. Also, I wish I knew English language grammar and vocabulary better. Who can grasp the difference between "I wish I may" and "I wish I might"? Who knows what the words "quiddity" and "inchoate" mean? Not me. Despite calling myself a pro in the writing game, I'm too lazy to look any of that stuff up.

I wish that people, present company included, did not feel so ashamed about the facts that we all micturate, defecate, break wind, and masturbate. Maybe we need a new Diogenes. He was the madcap ancient Greek philosopher who "interfered with himself," which is my favorite euphemism for self-pleasuring, on the steps of the Parthenon while requesting that everyone who performs the same acts privately would join in it with him as a public show of honesty.

Diogenes, I should add, is the same fellow who said that he wished we could satisfy our hunger as easily—by rubbing our stomachs, for instance—as we masturbatorily satisfy our lust. I wonder what he would have thought of an English mother of three, Julie Amiri, who claimed that the mere experience of being arrested by police aroused her so much that she experienced orgasms. During a shoplifting spree that Amiri went on between 1985 and 1993, she got busted, and thereby "got off," fifty-three times. No convictions, either.

I wish I could find myself a literary mentor, or at least a professional peer against whom I could bounce my ideas, because the filmmaker Warren Beatty is right to believe that creative tension, such as daily arguing with as many different people as possible, is a key to making good art. A good life, as well. My own sole encounter with Beatty featured no arguments, although when I mentioned that my wife Berta was Hungarian and asked him if he'd ever been to Hungary, Beatty said, "Never mind about Hungary. Tell me more about your wife." This quip reminded me of what Mae West once told a cowboy who was six-feet-and-seven-inches tall: "Never mind the six feet, let's talk about the seven inches."

Although I've lacked literary mentors, Berta has been an excellent first reader for me and given me splendid feedback. I've also been inspired by this credo of the poet William Carlos Williams: "I'll write whatever I damn please, whenever I damn please, and it'll be good if the authentic spirit of change is on it." At the same time, I wouldn't mind being like G. K. Chesterton, about whom an Italian server in a restaurant said, "He sit and laugh. And then he write. And then he laugh at what he write."

"Talking is searching," according to the novelist Koos van Zomeren, "while writing is finding." Maybe. There are certainly times when I wish I could find myself writing more lucrative, or at least more popular, books. Why not an airport bookstore bestseller? Easily satisfied, I'll settle for one good limerick. The best I've come up with in this form is "*There once was a man who ate knishes / And wrote a list filled with his wishes / He wished for a meal / To make gourmets just squeal / But all he got were rotting fishes on dirty dishes.*"

Maybe I should stick with *haiku*. The first of these fun little Japanese poems that I penned—"*Ga-ga-ga-ga-ga- / Ga-ga-ga-ga-ga-ga-ga- / Ga-ry. What's* your *name*?"—still makes me laugh. But no Italian server is ever around to hear my laughter.

If the Gnostic tradition is correct in asserting that we don't *invent* anything, just remember it, then I wish I could remember a lot more than I currently do. When I'm repeating an anecdote to friends, I'll often realize with horror that I've already told them this story a few weeks ago. My sole consolation here is what the poet Allen Tate said when he heard from a reader that his newest poem resembled one of his previous ones: "It had damn well better."

At age sixty, I do seem to be more frequently sipping from the River Lethe, those waters of forgetfulness. As Billy Collins has characterized it, "*One by one, the memories you used to harbor / Decided to retire to the southern hemisphere of the brain / To a little fishing village where there are no phones.*" My forgetfulness grew most concerning one morning last week when I walked past SoHo Court, an apartment building at 301 East Houston Street in Manhattan. On noticing the building, I started wishing I could remember a person who'd lived there in the late nineties. You'd think I *would* remember this resident, because we had a casual romantic relationship for eight months or so. But I do not.

I do remember how I would wait in the lobby of the building until my lover buzzed me up to her apartment. I remember how that place looked, too, and remember watching movies with her on her VCR. I remember we had fun together. I know I liked her a lot. But liking her a lot has proved no match for my memory loss. Her name, her personality, her fashion sense, her face, and all her other physical characteristics really are a total blank. So cue the pop song "I'll Never Forget What's-Her-Name," and also cue these words by Mark Twain: "When I was younger I could remember anything, whether it happened or not; but I am getting old, and soon I shall remember only the latter."

Here's the dilemma: although most or even all of our memories remain stored inside our brains, the trick is retrieval. My belief that we never completely lose our memories stems from a visit that my mother and I made to Stonehenge when I was a boy in the early seventies. Thirty years later, I returned to Stonehenge alone. On arrival, I thought about an ancient giant in Jez Butterworth's play *Jerusalem*. This giant claims he built Stonehenge himself and declares, "Well, whatever's coming, this is one beautiful morning."

Anyway, as an adult returned to Stonehenge, I remembered nothing about my previous visit. Nothing at all—until, as I turned to leave the site, the fading summer evening light struck my eyes and suddenly there I was again, a kid walking between these standing stones with my mother. My childhood memory of Stonehenge had just been unmistakably restored to me. This memory had been filed away among my brain cells down all the years, only waiting for the right trigger to call it back.

On one hand, I wish that the SoHo Court woman whom I dated but forgot likewise has no memory of me now. This would be only fair. On the other hand, I wish that she *does* remember me, at least a little, so that the pleasure and affection I once felt can have a home of sorts for a little longer. A mnemonic home that could rival, in its own way, the brick-and-mortar structure that still stands at 301 East Houston Street.

To grow forgetful with grace, not to resist aging but to grudgingly embrace it—because it is here to stay—seems to me the ticket to serenity. I don't possess this ticket yet. Or else I did have the ticket and hid it somewhere safe, hoping not to lose it. And now I have forgotten where that hiding place is.

Speaking of hiding places, I wish I knew where Tolstoy's "Green Stick" is located. The story goes that when the Russian author was a boy, his older brother told him that there was a green stick buried in the woods of their family estate and if Tolstoy could find this stick, he would learn the secret of life. When the author was a very old man, he asked to be buried near the general vicinity of that Green Stick.

I'm sorry that I will probably never find it myself, but perhaps I will someday encounter something else that's green—the horn-headed and foliage-faced "Green Man" of pagan European legend. The Green Man would have so much to teach me. As a "chorus of living wood" tells a human character in Richard Powers's novel *The Overstory*, "If your mind were only a slightly greener thing, we'd drown you in meaning." Maybe the Green Man would even be so kind as to identify for me those three gorgeous fluorescent green birds who flew past me in strict formation when I had a typically enriching talk with my Uncle Wolf outside his home one evening last winter.

I wish, while I'm at it, that the Green Man would teach me the names of *all* the birds and trees and plants and other living creatures I encounter—all the rocks, too—so that I can better know this world I live in *and* impress people with whom I happen to be hiking in nature. I also wish the Green Man would teach me how to track animals through the wilderness. This is not only to help me someday in our possible post-apocalyptic dystopian hellscape future but also because I like something the theorist Carlo Ginzburg has suggested. What he suggested was that animal tracking was the primordial origin of stories. It's all about reaching a destination via clues along the way.

Ginzburg also presents a cool take on falling in love, by the way. He labels love "the overestimation of the marginal differences" between potential lovers. Which means that love can be another clue-navigated journey.

Not to be confused with the Green Man is the "Green Sufi" of ancient Delhi legend. Supposedly the grandson of Noah's son Shem, this Islamic do-gooder acquired his name because wherever he knelt to pray, vegetation instantly grew. How can you not admire someone who hung out with Gilgamesh, brought Alexander the Great to the Well of Immortality (although Alex's boldness failed him there, circumscribing his greatness), and taught Moses to be patient? (Patience is a lesson I wouldn't mind learning myself. When a Chinese diplomat was asked recently about the global effects of the French Revolution of 1789, he said, "It's still a little too soon to say.")

I wish I knew the proper rites and invocations to summon the Green Sufi, because it is said that whenever he arrives by water, standing on the back of a humongous fish, he will spark enlightenment while protecting you from all manner of harm, including headaches. The only catch is that to receive such benefits you must be "pure of heart." There's my next wish accounted for. But what if the Green Sufi is unavailable? Then there are other means of attaining enlightenment, means such as hanging yourself upside-down in a well for forty days, eating nothing but snakes or scorpions, and prancing around the Himalayan snows covered with nothing but ashes.

Fortunately, spiritual awakening need not be such a big deal. I'd settle for how one Zen scholar described it: "ordinary everyday experience, except about two inches off the ground." Even so, the context, as always, counts for a lot. According to the humorist Jack Handey, "If you ever reach total enlightenment while drinking a beer, I bet it makes the beer shoot out of your nose."

Forget juggling, or eating fire, or riding a unicycle—I wish I could master the skills of a pickpocket so that I'd be able to do what a leader in this field, Apollo Robbins, claims he's doing, which is "challenging people's maps of reality." Perhaps I could attain my skills by studying at the fabled School of the Seven Bells in Colombia, where students are trained to pick a person's coat clean without triggering the bells placed inside each pocket. As a Seven Bells graduate, I would be able to, like Robbins, secretly swipe a stranger's cell phone and replace it with a drumstick of fried chicken, then transfer the stranger's driver's license into the sealed bag of candy in his wife's handbag.

Would I be tempted to keep what I steal from my marks? Maybe. But I'd probably be tempted to eat that fried chicken, too, if I didn't permit that stranger to keep it. The truth is, I've maintained a strict anti-theft policy for myself ever since the day in my early thirties when my Uncle Wolf visited my apartment and asked about a towel in my bathroom which bore the monogram "*Chateau Marmont*."

"That's the name of the hotel I took the towel from," I told him blithely.

I don't know how I expected Wolf to react, but I did not expect him to give me a pitying look and saying, "So you're a thief."

Which drew an uncomfortable little laugh from me. "What do you mean? I needed a towel to wrap my wet bathing suit in before I checked out of the place, so I brought it along."

"Do you plan to return it to the hotel?"

"Why would I?"

"Then I was right," he said. "You're a thief, nothing but a common thief."

"Chill out, Wolf. Everybody swipes towels from hotels. They don't even charge you for it. Or maybe they do, but so what? Call it a souvenir! Anyway, what's done is done. If you want, I won't 'borrow' any more hotel towels, okay?"

"And that makes you less of a thief?"

I waved a hand in the air dismissively and changed the subject. Still, Wolf's accusation had drawn blood from my superego. Forever desiring his approval, I now felt like mud mixed with rotten Brie cheese. I vowed to hide from him during his future visits all my other purloined hotel towels. Plus hotel bathrobes and hotel ashtrays. And I am hereby making this vow to Dame Fortune: Until this world comes crashing down with planet-wide catastrophes and all hell breaks loose and chaos reigns supreme, I will take nothing that does not belong to me. Still, once the crap *does* hit the fan and I find it necessary to steal stuff to keep me and my loved ones alive, I'll be a most *uncommon* thief. A thief with zero conscience. A thief even capable of snatching the last drumstick of fried chicken from the hand of a small child.

Oh, and if no chicken is available, I'll gobble down this wish list itself, page by page, wish by wish.

In one of my favorite film comedies, *Bedazzled*, Lucifer admits to feeling creatively spent: "I thought up the seven deadly sins in one afternoon. The only thing I've come up with recently is advertising." I wish that the Devil had not invented advertising because even as a kid, I knew enough to change the channel on my TV set whenever commercials started up. Yet I wish TV commercials could positively influence my way of thinking the way a distinctive one did in 1968, when I was five years old and watching *Mr. Ed*, or *Speed Racer*, or *Lost in Space*.

In the commercial that interrupted my program, two gleaming black limousines converge from separate directions on a mountaintop, and out of each limo steps a well-dressed elderly man. The first fellow removes his coat and rolls up his shirtsleeves. The second man likewise takes off his jacket but keeps his sleeves buttoned. Then an attendant shouts, "*Go*," and the old men begin to brawl. Or at least they do an elders version of brawling, with their arms locking around each other's torsos. Soon they tumble to the ground, going down together, yet they continue to wrestle in the dust, huffing and puffing and hurting each other as vigorously yet as awkwardly as my parents sometimes tangled with their fists and their fingernails in front of me when I was a child.

And while the old men keep tussling, a severe-sounding female voiceover says, "*Wouldn't this be a beautiful world if our leaders settled their differences all by themselves and left the rest of us out of it? This public service announcement is brought to you by the Get The U.S. Out Of Vietnam Committee.*"

Health Improvement Department: If only a jumbo Chicago-style deep-dish margherita pizza pie were more nutritious and less fattening than a head of romaine lettuce! Recognizing that this wish might be beyond even Dame Fortune's powers, I'm hoping that I can discover the patience to be a "Fletcherist," improving my health by chewing each mouthful of the food I eat thirty-two times before swallowing. I'll be better off, too, if I could remember to sip every morning the sarsaparilla-flavored Mother Siegel's Longevity Syrup. Its key ingredients are Iron Jelloids and Owsbridge's Lung Tonic and its label promises to cure "*The Cramp, the Stitch, / the Squirt, the Itch, / The Gout, the Stone, the Pox, / The Mulligrab, the Bonny Scrubs, and all Pandora's Box.*"

Word of mouth has it that Mother Siegel's syrup also treats scurvy, scabies, even cat scratch fever. For the best effect, I'm considering supplementing my daily dose by pouring down my hatch some fresh gladiator blood, which was a cherished pick-me-up in ancient Rome, and the aphrodisiacal goat soup from Jamaica known as "Mannish Water."

Follow the bouncing ball, my fellow wisher: "*Boys and girls together, / Me and Mamie O'Rourke, / We tripped the light fantastic / On the sidewalks of New York.*" Good old "Fun City," as they used to call it! It's been my home, more often than not, since I was nineteen years old, but I wish I could appreciate it the way a keen tourist would. Or the way that the corrupt politico Boss Tweed did when he said he'd rather be a lamppost in New York than the mayor of Philadelphia. Alas, "Baghdad on the Hudson," which was the author O. Henry's name for it, feels as exotic to me now as water does to a mackerel. I pass through the place every day like a self-absorbed or otherwise preoccupied blind man. Better to be like the artist Joseph Cornell, who was always reporting to his friends his latest homely New York City discoveries. Apparently, they couldn't resist hearing news like, "At the 28th Street IRT station there's a gum machine with a broken mirror that's really beautiful."

To me, and to many other Americans, the heart of "the city" is Times Square, and I wish that I'd been born not in a New Jersey hospital but, like the singer Tom Waits, on the backseat of a New York taxicab. Then, instead of crying, I would have jammed a cigar into my brand-new mouth and barked at the cabbie, "Times Square, bud—*and step on it.*"

Sometimes, only sometimes, I wish that Times Square could again be colorfully edgy the way it was in the seventies. Back then my mother and my grandmother Lily and I would leave our beige Buick station wagon at a parking garage near Port Authority, enthused about *Amadeus* or *A Chorus Line* or whatever Broadway matinee for which we had tickets. Unfortunately, to reach our theater, we had to walk down the grotesque human gauntlet of Forty-Second Street, or "Forty Deuce," as I learned to refer to it decades later, when it had finally been pacified.

On "the Deuce," the sidewalk on the south side was always crowded with prostitutes, pimps, drug dealers, itinerant lunatics, flea circus impresarios, and uniformed policemen who ignored all the "riff-raff," as my mother called them. Perhaps "the heat," which was my favorite term for cops because it sounds more ominous than "the fuzz," were there to prevent nothing except for blatant acts of violence. The police presence certainly did little to allay my fears of the riff-raff. And yet I simultaneously perceived the whole thing as a kind of carnival, a more compelling one than the amusement park I'd been to near my suburban hometown. And a far more compelling carnival than whatever Broadway musical we were heading over to watch.

"Grass, coke, acid, speed, smack," a spidery man wearing mirrored shades murmured one day to my grandmother, who kept hobbling along, oblivious to what he meant.

"She doesn't want that *trash*, you *pusher*, you!" my mother shouted at Mirror Shades, spittle spraying from her mouth. Taking no offense, he merely turned and made his pitch to the next pedestrian of any age, gender, appearance.

"Hey, honey, you looking for a date?" a bone-thin hooker in lime-and-purple-colored hot pants said to me.

"No, he *isn't*, you *hussy*, you," my mother shouted back. "He's only nine!"

The hooker guffawed at this. Most of the riff-raff had a good laugh at my mother those afternoons, and their laughter angered me. Esther Lippman was my protector, after all, my avenging angel! By the time I'd turned eleven, however, I found her protection embarrassing, because the riff-raff weren't just laughing at her, they were laughing at me and at my grandmother, too. And by the time I'd turned fourteen I began visiting Forty Deuce with my school friends. Clutching dollar bills in our sweaty hands, we were there to take up the riff-raff on their offers of drugs. (The softer ones, I mean—the hard stuff, not to mention the sex stuff, still frightened us too much.) The carnival was still open for business, and now I wanted a part of it. To hang out for a spell with the exotic denizens of Forty Deuce was the closest thing I knew of to running away with the circus.

When I began to write this wish list, the working title was "A Wish List for Dame Fortune." Then it was "Won't That Be a Happy Time?" But it could have been, echoing the artist Barbara Kruger, "I Shop, Therefore I Am," or "I Shop, Therefore I Hoard," or "I Need, Therefore

I Shop," or "I Love, Therefore I Need," or "I Am, Therefore I Hate," or "I Die, Therefore I Was." I wish that more works of art had titles as punchy as that of Philip K. Dick's novel *The Man Whose Teeth Were All Exactly Alike*. Or of Nik Cohn's novel *"I Am Still The Greatest," Says Johnny Angelo*. Or of the horror film *Die Nude For Satan*. (If I do ultimately "die nude," may it not be "for Satan." Or "for" anyone but myself or a close loved one.)

The more specific a title, the better—there's quite a difference between Duke Ellington's "Take the A Train" and "Take A Train." Sam Peckinpah's film *Bring Me The Head of Alfredo Garcia* is plenty specific, as are Duke Ellington's composition "T. G. T. T." ("Too Good to Title") and Thelonius Monk's number "Jackie-ing." Speaking of Monk, did an artist ever have such a beautiful name? It's a poem in two words. And was a title ever as exciting as that of D. H. Lawrence's poetry collection *Look! We Have Come Through!* or as inspiring as that of Djivan Gasparian's album *I Will Not Be Sad In This World*?

How about Allen Ginsberg's poem "Wichita Vortex Sutra"? Those three words each sound great, and sound great together. Also notable is the title "Golf Your Way to Sexual Fulfilment," which appears in Gilbert Sorrentino's novel *Mulligan Stew*. And let's hear it for my friend Landy's uncle, who was a notorious counterfeiter and called his memoir "I Made It Myself."

Staying with non-fiction, I especially admire the title Leo Bersani gave to his essay "Is Your Rectum A Grave?" I'm also fond of Raymond Smullyan's *What is the Title of this Book?* and Stewart Home's *69 Things To Do With A Dead Princess* as well as *My Lead Dog Was A Lesbian*, which is how a dog-sledder chose to call his memoir. I wonder how it would be to live, even for one night, according to how the actor Lee Grant entitled her own memoir: *I Said Yes to Everything*. I smile every time I think of the title of another actor's memoir, that of my friend Bulle Ogier: *I Forgot*. But the memoir title that I savor most comes from yet another female actor, Jennette McCurdy. She chose to call the story of her life *I'm Glad My Mom Died*.

The author Martin Amis wasn't always tops with his titles, but he did see things straight, unfavorably comparing human existence to fiction. He called our lives "thinly plotted, largely theme-less, sentimental, and ineluctably trite. The dialogue is poor, or at least violently uneven. The twists are either predictable or sensationalist. And it's always the same beginning and the same ending."

I'll begin my response to Amis's observation by considering beginnings. We can agree, I'm sure, on how important the opening shot of a film or the opening line of a drama or a work of fiction is. The starter I most wish I'd written myself is the first sentence—actually, the first part of the first sentence—of Gunter Grass's *The Tin Drum*: "Granted, I am the inmate of an insane asylum, but..." I also cherish "I'm wearing a diaper. Right now," which is how Jerry Stahl kicks off his memoir *Permanent Midnight*. Or consider a story by John Collier in which a new patient enters a dentist's office and says, "Rip 'em all out." The dentist protests, saying that the patient's teeth look perfectly good. "So," says the patient, "is my money." This is a tale I wish to keep reading.

Now for endings. More than a century before Amis put pen to paper, Schopenhauer wrote that each individual human life can be read like a novel. Yet we must not forget, he cautioned, that our fully delineated plotlines, themes, characters, and so forth, can be discerned only once we're on the cusp of dying. Accordingly, it's my wish that, when it's my own turn to lose the spark, time will halt and I'll get to read the novel of my life. Here's wishing, too, that the ending is a happy one, given the circumstances. Nevertheless, I believe that the best ending of a novel, or any story, is one that's not only *inevitable* but also *surprising*. Like an O. Henry climax that's been tickled by the Hand of Fate.

Unfortunately, most of the stories I know of fall short in both of those regards. I wish I could compose a story's ending that's as sublimely comic as the climax of Terry Southern's novel *Candy*. And I wish I could break readers' hearts with my writing as effectively as Bohumil Hrabal does with the final words of his novella *Too Loud A Solitude*, those last words being "'*ILONKA*.' Yes, that was her name." According to my friend Andres, the best way for an author to conclude his work is with the phrase "So there!" Me, I'm partial to how Alasdair Gray placed a large hand-drawn "GOODBYE" on the last page of each of his books. Yet no one has topped Richard Brautigan. He promised early in the text of his novel *Trout Fishing in America* to conclude matters with the word "mayonnaise" and, many pages later, kept that promise. Here's a promise of my own: This wish list will *not* end with the word "ninjas."

One final word about the aforementioned Czech author Hrabal: Although he was an animal lover, he was not shy about using his pets for mischievous purposes. He once hid his dog in a Prague alley—"and," he said, "when pedestrians walked by, I ran out and shouted in horror, 'Save yourselves! Nero broke his chain!' And the people ran off, and when they turned around and looked from a distance, a shivering Miniature Dachshund stepped out."

Tragically, Hrabal's love of animals was the death of him, and I wish that he did not feel much fear when he died. Having opened the high window of his apartment to feed some pigeons, he wound up leaning out a little too far. Compare this fate to the more spectacular one experienced by Hrabal's fellow novelist Yukio Mishima. Having raised and trained a private militia to overthrow Japan's post-war government and restore the emperor to full power, Mishima led a raid on a military base, and when the raid failed, he disemboweled himself in an act of ritual suicide. What a way to go! Hrabal's own end was far less exciting. It was much kinder, however. Not to mention more poetic.

FOUR. IMPLACABLE WISHES

How many sunsets have I witnessed in my lifetime? How many times have I coughed? Scratched my ear? Said "I love you"? Said "I wish"? How many times have I declined to write down a good idea because I figured I'd remember it and then promptly forgot it? How many footsteps have I taken, and where have they led me? I wish I could learn the answers to these questions. The footsteps, for example: Would seeing where I've walked disturb me? Would being reminded where I *haven't* walked disturb me? Which would disturb me more?

Walking! I wish I could do it tall, do it proud. I wish I could walk like a panther while walking on the moon. I wish I could walk right back to you or, if you deserve the Nancy Sinatra boots treatment, walk right *over* you. I wish that, clad in a deep-sea diving suit, I could walk on the Pacific floor, left alone by barracudas, jellyfish, and killer squids, until I arrive at some glass-domed sunken civilization, an Atlantis or Lemuria or Mu, where I would be welcomed. Whether underwater or otherwise, I wish I could walk a mile in your shoes. Or at least take a load off my feet while you walk that mile in mine.

"People either feel they can fly or fear they will stumble," said the author Jean Toomer. "Rarely do we sense our ability to walk firm on earth." I wish I could sense that ability and use it more, because I've walked my way out of plenty of emotional catastrophes, most of which were self-inflicted or purely imaginary. And I wish that, while strolling about, I would have fewer specific destinations in mind. I've long been intrigued by the "*flaneur*" mentioned by Baudelaire, this figure being an idle chap who saunters around cityscapes simply for the pleasure of observation and surprise adventures. The Situationist group meaningfully called taking such a destination-free stroll a "*derive*," which means "to drift."

Other footloose souls have recommended "constrained walks." Such walks include strolling in the shape of a word or a symbol, gallivanting in a straight line (intervening buildings be damned), traipsing in such a way as to avoid all security cameras, and being a "*robinsonner*," which is someone who remains in one physical spot yet mentally travels everywhere. Even short walks are better than none; the humorist Evar Evans notes that walking is not a lost art because "one must, by some means, get to the garage."

"Your body is made out of clay," wrote the poet John O'Donohue, "so your body is actually a miniature landscape that has got up from the earth and is now walking..." With this notion fixed in my mind, the least I can wish to do while sashaying through a city or a forest or anywhere in between is to remember to look up rather than down or straight ahead. Everything above your usual eyeline—unusual architectural details, the intricately dappled canopy of trees—tends to be of interest, if only because they're rarely viewed. You can even lose yourself in the unrelenting blue of the bowl of sky if you find yourself, willingly or not, striding through a desert.

Is music, as some say, what language would be if it could? Yes? Then what is silence? Whatever it is, "Silence is so accurate," according to the painter Mark Rothko. I wish I could embrace silence more than I do, following the Arabic advice to "Only speak when your words are better than your silence." For his part, the guru Ram Dass said, "When you know how to listen to people, everyone is the guru." (Then again, he also said, "If you think you're enlightened, go spend a week with your family.")

I wish that I'd asked lost loved ones more questions about their lives while they were still living. Alas, my yen to tell stories to people usually supersedes my yen to hear new ones from them. I can never abide "uncomfortable silences," either, and rarely feel at ease with extremely laconic people, even when they do deign to say something.

Silence was perhaps not so accurate when Rothko had something else to say: "Looking is not as simple as it looks." This calls to mind what Mark Twain observed about Wagner's music, which was, "It's not as bad as it sounds." Twain had a thing about operas; after attending one, he remarked, "I haven't heard anything like that since the orphanage burned down."

Understatements, by the way, are the next best thing to silence. When someone asks the character Jeeves in a P. G. Wodehouse novel if he was "in the First World War," Jeeves's response is, "I dabbled in it to a certain extent." I like this statement nearly as much as that of a real-life English officer who was asked what combat had been like during the so-called "Great War." "Awful!" explained this officer. "The *noise*! And the *people*!"

"He has Van Gogh's ear for music," the filmmaker Billy Wilder said about someone. Oh, how upsetting I found the story of that Dutch painter's self-mutilation during my childhood! I wish that, just when I was recovering from my terror about Van Gogh, my mother had not showed me a newspaper article about the then-current Getty kidnapping. The kidnappers had cut off their young victim's ear and then mailed it to his family.

"Don't you ever talk to strangers," the overprotective Esther Lippman used to bellow at me, "because they'll turn out to be sexed-up, money-hungry freaks high on that *pot* stuff who'll kidnap you and touch your *too-too* and cut off your *ear* like they did with that poor Getty boy and then they'll mail it to me and I'll have to *look* at it," she explained. So back into ear-terror mode I went, imagining one of my ears being chopped off, severed from the rest of me forever.

My mother's kidnapping warning hummed in my head twenty-five years later on a humid night in San Jose, the capital of Costa Rica. I was seated in the backseat of a speeding taxi with Katia, an appealing local woman with dark red hair whom I'd met in the city's most verdant park two hours after arriving in town from the States. Her hair color, Katia had explained in fractured English, was thanks to her maternal grandfather, who'd come from Belfast. After we'd spoken for a while in the park, we began to kiss, and then she agreed to my proposal for us to go "have a drink" at my hotel. Katia even used her cell phone to summon us a taxi. The only problem was, the taxi didn't seem to be heading to my hotel now. And when I spoke up about this, all Katia said was, "*Si, si,* hotel!"

"But my hotel is in the center of town. *Hotel es centro de ciudad.* And this"—I stabbed a finger anxiously out the window at the rough neighborhood looming around us—"this is the outskirts, no?"

Katia grinned at me, apparently oblivious to any problem. "*Si*, hotel soon!"

Was she pretending she didn't understand me? Was she in league with the taxi driver? In other words, had my mother been prescient with her worries? Was I the new Getty boy? Was I being *kidnapped?* Were they going to *cut my ear off*?

I began to think so, and panicked. How to escape? Leap from the moving taxi? Assuming it didn't cripple me, such a leap would still be futile, because these outskirts looked terrifying. *They'd probably cook and eat a tourist here, or eat me raw*—so I thought in my fevered state. Even if I survived the locals, how would I find my way to my hotel? Ultimately, I clammed up and just sat with my eyes pressed shut, waiting grimly and praying for rescue by Dame Fortune as we drove on through the scary Central American night.

After fifteen barely bearable minutes, the taxi rolled into a huge yet poorly lit parking lot which was ringed by dozens of one-storey buildings. Each one had alternating front doors and garages, and each one was shut, with no lights burning and no people to be seen.

"Oh *fuck*," I said. "What *is* this?"

"Hotel!" Katia announced.

In front of one garage, the taxi rolled to a stop. Katia asked me to pay the cabbie, which I did, not thinking clearly, because why else would I pay for my own kidnapping? After we climbed out, the cab sped back into the heart of the endless shantytown. Taking my hand, Katia led me to the nearest door and knocked twice.

"Listen to me," I said, attempting to put some menace in my voice. "I don't know what you're up to, but my government will make you suffer for what you and your friends do to me. The FBI will come down here and—"

Katia was too busy listening at the door to pay attention to my rant. Finally, someone drummed fingernails on the inside of that door and murmured, "*Bueno*." Which was Katia's cue to push open the door and motion for me to follow her in. I refused, having at last summoned up some courage. No, I wouldn't go quietly, wouldn't go without a struggle. Still, from where I stood now, I could see inside the flat, and what I saw there confounded me. Since when did kidnap dens come furnished with Jacuzzis? With mirrored walls and mirrored ceilings? With zebra-patterned comforters draped on round beds? Round (it turned out) *waterbeds*?

"What *is* this?" I said.

"*Estoy* hotel. *Hotel Paraiso*!"

"Hotel what? Hotel Paradise?"

"*Si*!"

"So it's a *sex* place? A sex *hotel?*"

"*Si, por sexo...*If we have *sexo* in your hotel, they think I *puta*, a girl for money, *puta* for tourists, and I no *puta*. I very nice girl, I polite person. In your hotel, I lose my name. *Pero* this place. Nobody see us here. *Privado.*"

"Remarkable," I said. From Hell to Paradise—to *Paraiso*—in one comfortable brief threshold-crossing. Just detour past Purgatory! "And I was thinking that you meant me *harm*!" I had to laugh. "So, like, many people come here?"

"Come here to *Hotel Paraiso? Si*, all of San Jose come!" By now she'd started unbuttoning her blue jeans. "When someone want *sexo privado*, when they not married, or when they married to someone else..."

"I understand," I said, breathless with relief. And with both of my ears intact.

May my ears *remain* intact. And may my vision stay good, too. In fact, I wish that some mad scientist would invent a special pair of eyeglasses I could wear when I'm in a crowd. A jam-packed downtown 6 train hurtling to the Brooklyn Bridge station, for instance. These glasses would not look flashy, unlike the specially made pair I already have, a pair with one red lens and one blue lens. ("Are those 3-D?" strangers often ask, and "no," I answer with a straight face, "they're 5-D.") However unobtrusive my new glasses may look, though, obtrusive is exactly what they'll be, since they will allow me to focus on each of my fellow passengers and read a brief biography about them that lists their principal likes and dislikes, fears and hopes, highest highs and lowest lows.

Talk about a compelling way to pass the time! Each mundane subway ride would provide me the chance to page through this *Who's Who in Humanity*. Yet I would not do it to feel like Dame Fortune. No, I'd do it simply because, as you've learned by now, I *love* stories, and what are strangers in a crowd if not unique story-bearers?

Supposedly, Freud's early colleague Alfred Adler would ask his patients during their first session of psychoanalysis, "What would you do if you were cured?" Then, on hearing their response, Adler would say, "Well, go and do *that*, then!" Bully for Herr Doktor Adler, yet I, for one, would have needed to consult with him for *decades*, which is why I wish I were more of a go-getter, the "can-do" type who would come zipping out of a shrink's office, prepared to follow their advice, and not require a second session. This type of person probably relies a lot on the psychological defense of denial, whose patron saint is Homer Simpson. When his wife comes to him with a big shared concern, Homer blithely responds, "That's a problem for *Future Homer*. Man, I don't envy that guy!"

The truth is, I have mixed feelings about psychotherapy. On one hand, I wish that I, and everyone else, could have been assigned our own therapists at the time of birth. (Have you noticed that whoever says they don't need any psychotherapy probably needs it even more than the rest of us do?) On the other hand, therapists tend to be just like the rest of us—except *even more* fucked-up.

"Be you you," my dear friend Thorhildur has ungrammatically but sagely counseled me. She's in good company with this wish. Proving that effective wisdom can be found in the most banal of places, even a crassly commercial one, a nineties-era Tanqueray billboard in Times Square showed a guy getting his palm read by a fortuneteller with this inscription: "*In his next life, Mr. Jenkins wants to come back as...Mr. Jenkins.*" Which calls to mind Captain Beefheart's advice to "Always be yourself"—although Beefheart characteristically added "*unless* you can be a unicorn. Then, be a unicorn." I'm also reminded here of a verse from Steve Goodman's great wishing song "Eight Ball Blues": "*I wish I was an Opry star, or had me a PhD. / I wish I had the common sense to be satisfied with me.*"

As I mentioned in my wish involving hipness, the yearning to embrace one's personal identity, no matter what the costs, remains among the deepest and dearest on many people's wish lists, mine included. If only we didn't feel such a need to be liked, respected, admired, lusted after, and loved. Can you imagine the multimedia artist Brian Eno covering "Eight Ball Blues?" I can't. But Eno wrote in his diary, "People who don't seem to care whether or not they're liked are nearly always in some way likeable."

Did Eno ever hear the tale about Rabbi Zsuya? When he lived, a few hundred years ago, Zsuya kept trying to be as perfect as Moses was. But then the Rabbi wised up, and he told his disciples, "When I get to the coming world, God will not ask me, 'Why were you not more like Moses?' No, what God will ask me is, 'Why were you not more like *Zsuya*?'"

Easier said than done, Rabbi. I hope it won't take a medical catastrophe for me to get with Zusya's program, because I often think of a hospital-bound character in Denis Johnson's novel *Jesus' Son*, a terribly palsied man who drools and jerks around in a wheelchair, oblivious to everyone and everything around him. About this tragic figure, Johnson writes, "No more pretending for him! He was completely and openly a mess. Meanwhile, the rest of us go on trying to fool each other."

Congratulations to those of you who, against the odds, do manage to "stop pretending," own what a mess you are, and fully live your personal truth. Yet be aware that your struggle *still* isn't finished. Why not? Because Dame Fortune often seems to bestow extra-credit points on those of us who can not only *be* ourselves but who then go on to *transcend* ourselves. You're not just "*you*," you're a tiny part of nature, part of life's probably indifferent (yet perhaps not) rich pageant. To poets, philosophers, and saints, according to the philosopher Ralph Waldo Emerson, "All things are friendly and sacred, all events profitable, all days holy, all men divine." So let's all try to "Say yes," as Emerson's brother-in-wisdom Nietzsche suggests, "not only to ourselves but to all of existence. For nothing is isolated, neither in ourselves nor in things."

Which returns us to the ancient Chinese notion of the "red thread" from a previous wish of mine. As far as I know, Rabbi Zsuya did not know about the red thread, but he might have approved of it. So, perhaps, would Dame Fortune. Next time I see her in a dream, I'll ask her if it's so.

I wish that, borrowing an idea from G. K. Chesterton, I could make my home "allegoric" by inscribing ancient sayings on even the most ordinary objects. Accordingly, my hairbrushes would bear the phrase "Even the hairs of your head are all numbered" and the message engraved on my front lawn's sundial would say, "I COUNT ONLY SUNNY HOURS." (Never mind the Scottish folks who typically respond to sunshiny days by grousing, "Och, now we'll have to pay for this.") Meanwhile, I wish I could think of a cool inscription to engrave on the front door of my home. I could steal the motto that medieval Paris chose for itself, which was "*fluctuat nec mergitur*," or "floating, not sinking." I could filch an anonymous one that goes, "*Good luck and bad luck, / Make no ado. /*

Both will pass, / As will you." Or I could lift the one that Nietzsche chose for himself: "I live in my own place, have never copied nobody even half, and at any master who lacks the grace to laugh at himself, I laugh." The problem is that with such thefts, I could not rightly claim that I "have never copied nobody even half."

Another home decorating-related ambition of mine is to sink a wishing well in my backyard, but not for making wishes. Rather, I'd install a little elevator inside the well so that I can descend to its depths when this gumball planet finally freaks me out too much. Then I would be able to hide out down there, with my body curled into the fetal position and my left thumb jammed deep inside my mouth.

Still at home, I wish that my toilet could have an alternate flush function which could turn the thing into a time machine. I wouldn't mind getting a glimpse of the future, but having read Olaf Stapledon's remarkable novels *Last and First Men* and *Star Maker*, which recount in detail the history of the next million or so years, I know how freaky the future will almost certainly be. Scary freaky. Then again, as the rock band Hawkwind sing, "It is the business of the future to be dangerous." And as the writer Loren Eiseley writes, "Let the storms blow through the streets of cities; the root is safe, the many-faced animal of which we are one flashing and evanescent facet will not pass with us. When the last seared hand has flung the last grenade, an older version of that hand will be stroking a clinging youngster hidden in its fur, high up under some autumn moon." So sentient life will begin again—"but in a different way."

Given a time travel choice, I'd rather get whooshed into the past. So instead of sitting around on my toilet while reading British music magazines and doing "what no one else can do for me" (which is my favorite description of defecation, straight out of the pages of *Don Quixote*), I can watch Miguel Cervantes write his masterpiece, or accompany the Lakotas when they come storming on horseback into the Black Hills of South Dakota, intent on claiming those hills as their spiritual homeland.

Most of all, I wish I could behold the moment when the world's first named author, a high priestess called Enheduanna who lived two thousand years before Greece's golden age, decided to press her reed stylus into a tablet of clay in order to compose in cuneiform a saga about herself entitled "The Exaltation of Inanna." Who wouldn't flush to witness that?

For more better living through technology, I wish that the microwave oven in my kitchen had a button which would allow me to stick my head inside and converse with the character Father Zosima from *The Brothers Karamazov*. Zosima's my choice because I suspect that his serenity and kindheartedness would significantly cure whatever anguished feelings can cause a suicidal person to put their head in an oven. And if Zosima can't aid me, then I wish that the character of elderly Maude in the film *Harold and Maude* could materialize instead of Zosima inside that oven. My hope is that she would console me the way she does her young lover Harold, saying, "A lot of people enjoy being dead. But they're not dead really. They're just backing away from life. So reach out, take a chance—get hurt, even. But play as well as you can. Go, team, go! Gimme an L, gimme an I, gimme a V, gimme an E! L-I-V-E, *LIVE*!...Otherwise, you've got nothing to talk about in the locker room."

Given how pitch-dark this world's darkness often is, I wish I could have Maude's cheerful soul. What a beautiful thing to possess and be known for. Perhaps positive-minded people are genetically so inclined, hence have done nothing to earn their good cheer. Or perhaps their lives have glittered with such entitlement or good fortune that we might long to *kvetch* at their advantages. It doesn't matter. Someone's upbeat spirit, whatever its origin, serves as an example to the rest of us that human existence need not destroy someone. Which is why I like the bumper sticker I once saw on the fender of a sparkly green Subaru sedan: "JOY CAN BE SUBVERSIVE."

The ancient Egyptian tome *The Wisdom of Ptahhotep* says, "Joy is the sign of deep waters." Of calm waters, too. Few Americans have known what "a hard battle" life can be, but the abolitionist and feminist Sojourner Truth said that "If we laugh and sing a little as we fight the good fight of freedom, it makes it all go easier. I will not allow my life's light to be determined by the darkness around me."

One of the most ebullient people I've met is the eternally playful novelist Tom Robbins. During a lecture he gave in New York City in the early years of this century, Robbins memorably said, "There are only two mantras: *yum* and *yuck*. Mine is *yum*." Drawing on Tibetan "crazy wisdom," he said he "insists on joy in spite of everything… All depression has its roots in self-pity, and all self-pity is rooted in people taking themselves too seriously." Being serious is important sometimes, sure—but being *too* serious?

Putting his fiction where his mouth is, Robbins invented a magical incantation, "*erleichda*," for his novel *Jitterbug Perfume*. At the novel's end, we learn that the incantation means, simply yet profoundly, "Lighten up." Which reminds me of the jazz giant John Coltrane, who said, "I don't make a habit of wishing for what I don't have, but I wish I had a lighter nature." I'm also reminded of G. K. Chesterton, who observed that "Satan fell by force of gravity" while "Angels fly because they take themselves lightly." This must be what the Zen scholar Alan Watts meant when he said, "All the best angels wear their haloes jauntily, over one ear."

It all boils down to expectations, and keeping them low, and not attaching to outcomes. This is what the sage Krishnamurti meant when he announced that the secret of his perpetual state of happiness was, "I don't mind what happens." La Rochefoucauld rang the same bell when he wrote, "Little minds are too much hurt by little things; great minds see these things, too, but are not hurt by them." And if we can not just detach from outcomes but *embrace* them, even if they're bummers, all the better! Nietzsche called such an embrace "*amor fati*," or "loving your fate." This is what the title of a Kevin Ayers record album, *Whatevershebringswesing*, was getting at. Ditto the title of a Kenneth Patchen book of poems: "Hallelujah, Anyway." And ditto another bumper sticker I've seen, also on a Subaru. "AVOID UNNECESSARY SUFFERING." Find the difference, suggests this bumper sticker, between genuine pain and neurotic self-indulgence, then banish the latter as vigorously as possible.

Let me circle back to the lecture I heard Tom Robbins give in New York City. After the novelist finished speaking, I joined the line of people wishing for him to autograph copies of his latest book. Once we were face to face, I told Robbins how much I'd enjoyed his lecture, and then I made a special request, saying, "I'm afraid I'm going to forget your overall message once I get back to my ordinary life. So could you please sum it all up in one sentence and write that down in my book instead of just 'Best wishes' or something like that?"

In retrospect, this was a pretty intrepid thing for me to ask the scribe. Yet he didn't seem to mind at all. Gazing down at the book I'd handed him, Robbins set to work right away, scribbling across the top of the title page. Then he handed my book back to me.

"IT'S *ALL* A JOKE" was the inscription.

Years later, I came across a similar quote from Thomas Bernard, who was a very different novelist from Robbins, and a very different kind of "Tom." Bernhard said, "It's all ridiculous when one thinks of death." True enough, but that's less comprehensive than what Robbins penned to me, because one need not think of death to laugh at life. I certainly wasn't thinking of death when I first read Robbins's inscription in my book and instantly, loudly, and wholeheartedly laughed out loud.

Welcome to this wish list's *"Laugh Kills Lonesome" Department*, which is named after Charlie Russell's cowboy painting. I wish I could regularly laugh in my daily life the way I laughed with my Uncle Wolf in 1984 when he took me to see Michael Frayn's classic stage farce *Noises Off* at its premiere on Broadway. Not knowing when we entered the theater what to expect, we soon found ourselves falling out of our seats and gasping for air due to successive paroxysms of laughter, while all around us, our fellow audience members suffered from the same condition. Was this what the great playwright George Bernard Shaw meant by the term "universal laughter?" Probably not. But laughing this way with a loved one while sharing the feeling with nearby strangers—few moments in my life have topped the experience.

Coming close to it was the time when my mother and adolescent me went together to watch a matinee of the movie *Jaws*. During a suspenseful sequence, some poor fellow in the audience accidentally dropped his loose change on the cinema's concrete floor. He must have been reaching for something in his pocket and those coins came tumbling out. But *so many* coins there were! Dozens of them, it sounded like, and the guy who'd spilled them hollered a plaintive "Oh, *shit*," which triggered laughter in the entire audience. Being the subject of ridicule further angered the coin-dropper, so he yelled at all of us, "*Fuck you*," which, of course, cracked up everyone even more.

Now here's the part I find puzzling yet also funniest: the coin dropper soon proceeded to drop even *more* coins on the ground, dozens more. Perhaps as the man was bending over to retrieve the original dropped coins, new ones spilled out of his pocket. At any rate, the sound of that metallic cacophony brought all of us to an absolute roar. Forget *Jaws—this* was the day's best entertainment. Only now, decades later, does it occur to me to feel sorry for the poor guy rather than to continue to chortle at the memory.

What is the greatest laughter captured *on* film? It's probably the collective guffawing at the end of *It's A Mad, Mad, Mad, Mad World.* Once Ethel Merman slips on a banana peel, even the severely depressed Spencer Tracy finds a reason to smile at the sight, then to chuckle, and finally to let loose. Speaking of bananas, a young screenwriter once asked Charlie Chaplin how to best make that old banana peel gag funny onscreen. Chaplin's advice was to show a person approaching the peel, then the peel itself, then the person and the peel *together*—and then show the person stepping over the peel and tumbling into an open manhole.

Since I've mentioned banana peels, I'll need to quote the filmmaker Nora Ephron: "When you slip on a banana peel, people laugh at you. When you tell people you slipped on a banana peel, it's your laugh." And since I've mentioned Chaplin, I should announce how much I wish I had cooked up a plot twist in the Don DeLillo novel *Running Dog*, where all the characters are seeking a purported sex tape starring Adolf Hitler and his wife Eva Braun. What's the twist? Once the tape is found, it turns out to be not pornographic at all but a brief film clip of *der Führer* dressed up as Chaplin's Little Tramp and entertaining his officers' children in the bunker where they're living at war's end. Hitler, as one of his intimates said, "had a *wonderful* sense of humor." I don't find that funny. But how meaningful it is to laugh even in the absence of reasons to! Wrote Rumi, "*It is the rookies who laugh only when they win.*"

Beware, however—nine out of ten doctors agree that too much laughter can kill us. So I wish I could find something funny enough to make me laugh safely for, say, nine or ten minutes. This is because a scientific study has found that such behavior will burn fifty calories and I'm unlikely to lose those calories for myself by exercise (too painful yet simultaneously too boring) or by diet, about which Mark Twain advised us to simply eat whatever we want and then let the foodstuffs fight it out for themselves inside our stomachs. I find this advice funny—but not funny enough to trigger those ten to fifteen minutes of laughter.

Perhaps I should have been born one year earlier than I was and raised in Tanzania, where a "laughter epidemic" began with three children in 1962. Having worked as a volunteer teacher in Tanzania, I heard a lot of glorious children's laughter, but no epidemic of it. Back in '62, that contagion of guffaws spread to one thousand people, and only ended eighteen months later, right in time for my actual birth at a hospital in New Jersey. My mother nearly died during the birth process, hence it was no laughing matter. Still, I wish I had been born laughing instead of crying.

"When I'm bored," said Oscar Wilde, "I pick up a good novel, sit by the fireplace, and watch the fire." My apologies if this wish list bores you, my fellow wisher. "Reality," according to Jorge Luis Borges, "is under no obligation to be interesting," and being easily bored by boredom since childhood, I wish that that obligation *did* apply to reality, despite the fact that "interesting" can also mean "catastrophic." Anyway, the composer John Cage may have been correct when he declared, "If something is boring after two minutes, try it for four. If still boring, try it for eight, sixteen, thirty-two minutes and so on. Eventually one discovers that it's not boring at all."

My wife combats boredom by "looking out of her head," as she puts it. Another boredom-busting technique comes courtesy of Satchel Paige, who remarked, "Sometimes I sit and think, and other times I just sit." What does it say about me that I find "just sitting" so difficult? I remember the first time I watched someone behaving in this fashion. One afternoon during my junior year of college, I returned to my dormitory room and found my roommate Andres lying fully clothed on his bed and staring blankly at the ceiling.

"Why aren't you *doing* something?" I said.

He shrugged his shoulders. "I'm just relaxing."

"What are you thinking about?"

"Nothing. That's what relaxing is. Turn off your mind and float downstream..."

"Good point," I said. Quoting the Beatles will always get you far where I'm concerned. "But aren't you bored?"

Andres laughed at this. "When it comes to relaxing," he said, "boredom is besides the point."

The seventeenth-century Catholic mystic Jeanne Guyon believed that we can best commune with God by behaving like a potted plant on someone's windowsill, doing nothing but soaking in the rays of the sun. To be a plant, even more than being an animal, human or otherwise, means slipping the often-onerous bonds of subjective perception. How about transforming into a mushroom for a day? I have a complicated relationship with fungi. On one hand, I enjoy the taste of most mushrooms and enjoy, also, the high from the so-called "magic" variety of them. On the other hand, I never take a bite of one without worrying that it's a Fiber Head, a Death Cap, a Destroying Angel, or another of the poisonous sort of fungi. I've harbored this fear since reading John Lanchester's *The Debt to Pleasure*, the world's only cookbook which doubles as a murder handbook. (It also mentions an ancient recipe for human brains garnished with rose petals.)

Being a lethal mushroom is safer than *eating* one, I figure, so I'm forging ahead here and officially wishing that Dame Fortune would arrange it with Robigus, the Roman god of fungus, to permit me a single-day-long live-in mushroom experience. Imagine having the ability to taste stuff with your whole body! And to turn a tiny fragment of yourself into numberless interconnected other selves! And to save the rest of the planet's life-forms with your regular behavior! What's not to like?

I wish I could remember jokes I've heard so I can repeat them to others. The only two jokes firmly lodged in my brainpan both involve doctors and masturbation. In the first of these, a woman with a terrible headache visits her doctor, who asks her if she masturbates. When the woman says, "Uh…yeah," the doctor declares, "*Fantastic*, isn't it?" In the second joke, a man visits his doctor for his annual checkup. "You're going to need to stop masturbating," the doctor tells him. "Why?" the man asks. "Because," says the doctor, "I'm about to start examining you."

Recently, I heard a new joke that might stick. After freeing a genie from a dusty lamp and receiving a wish, a man asks that his penis "reach right down to the floor," and the genie obliges the man—by cutting his legs off at the thighs. As an illustration of the maxim "be careful what you wish for," this joke is certainly more succinct than "Appointment in Samarra," my favorite ancient fable, the one that features a king, his gardener, and the Angel of Death, alias old Stretchfoot, the Killer of Kicks. The "reach right down to the floor" joke is also more succinct than the one in which a fisherman out at sea wishes his friends could be there with him. A genie agrees to makes it happen and *presto*, all those friends materialize in the boat, which causes the vessel to sink and drown everyone.

"I get that you're capable of delivering these unpleasant surprise endings," I say to Dame Fortune in a dream. As always, she's standing in the shadows, with her face obscured by a dark veil. "But *why*?"

The Dame's resulting laughter has a peculiar ring to it. She says, "Ever occur to you that you stop being happy as soon as you wish you could be happier, kiddo?"

"Sure. But what about when someone's just wishing for something relatively humble? Good health, say, or long life?"

"Ever occur to you that your moods change far more frequently than your fortunes, kiddo? Maybe the very *act* of wishing is your problem."

"Fair enough. But what kind of existence would we be left with if we stopped wishing? Isn't the act of wishing one of those elements that separate us from other mammals—although they surely wouldn't turn down good health and long life themselves if they could make a conscious choice about it?"

Thanks to this question of mine, Dame Fortune has her biggest laugh of my dream. But all she says is, "The dice are always rolling."

As a kid, I enjoyed playing team sports in school, especially the brutal game of bombardment, otherwise known as dodgeball. An avid collector of professional baseball trading cards, I remember my unbridled joy when I serendipitously acquired the valuable "Roberto Clemente" card. (Clemente had perished in a plane crash just a month before.) And I spent a big part of my childhood in arenas and stadiums watching baseball, football, basketball, soccer (with Pele!), *jai alai*, and hockey games with my father, who was a sports fanatic.

Even before I reached adulthood, my enthusiasm for playing sports as well as following them had faded, and I began to feel embarrassed about this waning interest. Why? Because not to know or care who's playing in this year's Super Bowl seems to put you outside modern society. "In Texas," according to Kinky Friedman, "if you like girls more than football, it means you're gay." To some extent, and not just in this area, all of these United States of ours have become Texas.

Despite my sports apathy, I wish I had the nerve to do like Ken Kesey and loudly cheer for *both* teams at public games. And I do like to recall, and wish I could relive, my most thrilling sports-related experience. It occurred on the night of a Rangers game in Madison Square Garden in 1971. As usual, the game kicked off with the National Anthem, performed by some *mezzo-soprano* from the Metropolitan Opera. The entire crowd stood, and many fans, including my father and I, put our hands on our hearts. But when the soprano began to sing, a tousle-haired drunk in the row in front of us began to shout such foul-mouthed verbal abuse about the woman and her physical appearance that most of the fans in our vicinity looked shocked. I was the most shocked of all.

"Can't someone *do* something?" I whispered to my father, frightened that the drunk would finish with the soprano and then turn his bizarre ire against us.

Bernie Lippman shrugged his shoulders. "It's hockey, pal," he said. "Rougher crowd than Yankees fans."

The drunk's abuse of the soprano continued until the end of her performance. She was too far away to have heard him, but his attack, the savagery of it, and its sheer animal excitement, too, were etched on my memory. Life, I realized, could turn brutal anywhere—even in the comfortable seats of the Garden. Here in New York City, we were now living a dangerous life, and this felt privately exciting for me.

"Let's hope this ruckus is the worst thing to happen tonight," my father said.

A good wish—but it wasn't granted. After the game (the Rangers lost), we walked to the parking lot where we'd left Bernie Lippman's green Eldorado. It was a short walk from the Garden, only four or five blocks, and when we arrived, we found a crowd of angry people gathered around the lot, which stood empty. Not a single car was there. This parking business had been a scam. After the crooks who ran it had collected all the Rangers' fans' car keys and told the fans, "You pay later," they'd stolen every vehicle. Was it Kinky Friedman who said, "An optimist is a man who can hand his car over to a parking lot attendant without looking back"?

Once we figured out what had happened—*our car is gone forever!*—Bernie Lippman started shouting curse words. His tirade wasn't as prolonged or as loud or as creative as that drunk's railing against the mezzo soprano had been, and eventually my father calmed down. (When the poet-singer Leonard Cohen said, "There is only one achievement, and that's the acceptance of your lot," he should have included *parking* lots.) In a taxi on the way home that night, Bernie Lippman was even able to laugh about our situation. But again, I felt shocked, both by the theft and by my father's extreme initial reaction. And again, I will admit, I felt excited, because we really *were* living a dangerous life.

Society to Prevent Whining Department: "We are born crying, live complaining, and die disappointed." In saying this, a fellow named Thomas Fuller was demonstrating his own tendency to complain. I'm a best-in-show complainer myself, and constantly need to remind myself of a minor character in Tibor Fischer's novel *Under The Frog*. Whenever people complain about their lives to this character, a Hungarian ex-soldier, his only response is, "What will you do about it?" How does the author explain the ex-soldier's perpetual calm? "He had returned from his three years at the Russian front with one important souvenir: the inability to get worked up about things that weren't three years at the Russian front."

Another good reminder for bitching-and-moaning me is a Hasidic story about a certain unhappy farmer. This farmer visits his rabbi to lament that he has to live in a shotgun shack with his wife, his mother-in-law, and eight children. Such noise, such high stress, such a stench! The rabbi's suggestion is to bring the farmer's goat into the shack to also live there. The farmer doubts the sagacity of this, but figures that the rabbi must know his job, so he does as he's advised. Keeping the goat inside only his home makes matters worse, of course, so in time the farmer returns to his rabbi to complain even more urgently. The rabbi's advice: "Bring your chickens into the shack to live there, too."

Reluctantly, the farmer follows the new advice—and regrets it immediately. His shack has become stinky bedlam. Hence, the next time he visits the rabbi he announces that he's going insane. To which the rabbi replies, "I understand. Now remove the goat and all the chickens from your home." Gladly, the farmer does so, and sure enough, a few days later, he returns to the rabbi and reports that his shack has never been "so spacious, pleasant and peaceful. Smells better, too!"

I wish that one of my favorite singer-songwriters, Sam Baker, had not been terribly injured in a train bombing in Peru by the terrorist group Shining Path. I'm grateful that the leader of Shining Path, a blood-soaked monster, was ultimately captured by the Peruvian military and imprisoned for the rest of his life. Still, I wish I could accept bummer trips as stoically as that terrorist leader seemed to when he got busted and simply shrugged his shoulders and said, "My turn to lose." Perhaps he would have agreed with the actor Robert Mitchum, who said in one of his movies, "You can't win—you can only lose more slowly."

The above sentiment connects with another wish I've been nursing for a while: to better follow the ancient Stoic recipe for happiness, as stated by the philosopher Epictetus: "Do not seek to have everything happen as you wish, but wish for everything to happen as it actually does happen." Epictetus's colleagues called the resulting tranquility *ataraxia*, a sweet name for a sweet condition, while the Navajo have *hozjo*, which is how they refer to the harmony you feel with your surroundings and situation.

When the Stoic-philosophy-loving Admiral James Stockdale ran for Vice President in 1988, my friends and I mocked his goofy TV appearances. I regretted this mockery once I learned that Admiral Stockdale had been a fighter pilot who'd endured daily physical torture over many years while a prisoner of war in Vietnam. I admired Stockdale even more once I learned that, when he'd been shot down over Vietnam in the mid-sixties, the sentence he muttered to himself as he parachuted to the waiting enemy was "I'm leaving the world of technology and entering the world of Epictetus." This world is ready to admit us at every moment, so when the shit comes raining down, all you can do (and sure, this is another "easier said than done" deal, but it's still the best option) is to shrug your shoulders and embody the quality of "*menefreghismo*," which is the refreshing Italian word which means "not giving a single fuck." Just put on your "game face" and do your best to get through it all. Not around it, or over it, but *through* it.

When a travelling salesman rings a suburban home's doorbell one afternoon, the door swings open to reveal a ten-year-old boy wearing nothing except his mother's brassiere and garter belt. "Are your parents home?" stammers the shocked salesman, and the boy replies, "What do *you* think?" (My wife has suggested an alternate punch line: To the question "Are your parents home?," the boy replies, "Who do you think dressed me like this?")

Fashion! I wish I had a better sense of it, if only because my friend Lorraine says that strangers judge us on what we're wearing as much as they do on any other factor. Unlikely to become a new Beau Brummell, I at least wish that I wouldn't feel so embarrassed when I don a shirt with old food stains on it and my wife says, "There are a lot of stories appearing there." I also wish I could feel more comfortable splurging on true quality rather than searching for discounts, sale prices, "good deals." When asked what he was thinking when his spacecraft was about to launch, the astronaut John Glenn said, "I was thinking that there were twenty thousand parts in this rocket and each was made by the lowest bidder." My friend David K.'s father put it more snappily: "Buy cheap, get cheap."

Finally, lest I get too hung up on material possessions, I wish someone would remind me of what happened when Captain Beefheart met Duke Ellington. Observed Beefheart, "He had on this watch that must've cost eighty thousand dollars, with diamonds all over it, but he had so much class he made it look like a Timex." (The Duke's parting words to the Captain were "Keep your top happy," which might have been connected to Oscar Wilde's advice to a youth who believed that in life one must "begin at the bottom": "No," said Wilde, "begin at the top and sit on it.")

In this material world, I also wish I'd be continually reminded of how elderly Maude in *Harold And Maude* behaves when young Harold gives her a pricy ring. While sitting beside a bay at night, Maude reads aloud the words engraved on the ring: "*Harold loves Maude.*" Beaming at the gift, Maude says, "And *Maude* loves *Harold*. This is the nicest present that I've received in years." Then she hurls the ring into the water. And when Harold gapes at her, astonished, she explains to him, "So I'll *always* know where it is."

One of my loveliest childhood memories is of the time when my mother and my Uncle Wolf brought me to see *Two by Two*, the Broadway musical starring Danny Kaye. This actor had already touched me in the film musical *Hans Christian Anderson* when he sang the ballad "No Two People Have Ever Been So In Love," which was the first inkling pre-pubescent me had of how blissful romance would someday feel. Anyway, *Two by Two* featured Kaye as Noah, getting together his Ark, and decades later, I thought of him when I came upon a *Far Side* cartoon. It depicts a dozen different beasts gathered on the Ark around the slaughtered corpse of a horned animal, with Noah scolding them, "Well, so much for the unicorns…but from now on, all carnivores will be confined to 'C' deck.")

Two By Two hooked me on the theater, and I'd listen with excitement as Wolf recounted to me the great shows he'd seen when he was a young man and believed that Broadway would always be this good: the original productions of *Death of A Salesman*, *The Glass Menagerie*, and *A Streetcar Named Desire*. When I was a young man myself, I got to catch plenty of good stuff on Broadway. Still, I most wish I'd seen the *Harold and Maude* musical with its score composed by my friend David Amram, although this show was apparently so bad that one critic wrote, "The major mistake the producers of *Harold and Maude* made in tonight's opening on Broadway was to have my seat facing the stage." (Don't worry, David found that line funny and simply went on whistling as he worked.)

Another show I wish I'd seen was a late-nineties New York City production of *Hamlet* which was not part of "Shakespeare in the Park" but something called "Shakespeare in the *Parking Lot*." True to its name, this no-frills *Hamlet* was staged on a vacant Lower East Side lot while the audience stood around watching as the actors strutted their stuff. According to my friend Rex, who was there one night, a teenaged kid with a blank face rode up on his skateboard during the last few minutes of the play and took a look at all the "dead" bodies that were the result of *Hamlet*'s bloody climax.

"What the fuck happened here?" the kid asked Rex.

"Well," said Rex mischievously, keeping his face as dead-serious as the kid's, "that young guy over there tried to poison his stepfather, because his stepfather had previously poisoned his father, but then the young guy's mother drank the poison by mistake, so the young guy got even angrier and stabbed his stepfather, but then he got stabbed himself during a sword fight with that other guy who had a beef with him because the young guy had stabbed the other guy's own father *plus* drove his sister so insane that she drowned herself, but the other guy got stabbed by the young guy before the young guy died, so now the other guy is dead, too, and, uh…the rest is silence."

Upon hearing this, the kid's face remained expressionless. Then, in an utterly earnest voice, he asked, "Somebody call the cops yet?"

I wish I didn't feel compelled to snobbishly poo-poo escapist movies, books, music, especially when I recall a statement by the poet John Ashbery: "I am aware of the pejorative associations of the word 'escapist,' but I insist that we need all the escapism we can get and even that isn't going to be enough."

Since we're on the subject of "escaping," let me roll out my latest wish, which is to emulate my childhood hero Harry Houdini. I don't want to be a secret agent, as my biographer friend Ratso alleges Houdini was during World War I, but a world-renowned escape artist, which was of course Houdini's day job. (Fun fact: I've actually met three different men nicknamed Ratso, and the Ratso I know best is friendly with the other two. A rostrum of Ratsos!)

If I could be an escape artist in the Houdini line, I would be able to walk through brick walls, survive falling from bridges while handcuffed inside a packing crate, and get out of various tight spots. These spots would include a mailbag, a padlocked metal boiler, a giant milk can, a giant paper envelope, a straitjacket (while I'm suspended upside-down by a crane), a prison cell (while I'm naked), and a Chinese Water Torture Cell (while I'm naked *and* upside-down).

Here's the beauty part: unlike Houdini, I won't need to rely on well-practiced physical skills or clever tricks to achieve my escapes. Nope—I will actually dematerialize and then rematerialize whenever I pass through brick walls or perform my other marvels. Needless to say, I will require Dame Fortune's kind assistance in managing this trick; to grant my wish, she'll need to repeal a few choice laws of physics.

As to whether I *deserve* the Dame's assistance, well, this leads me to yet another wish: to "deserve" whatever I get in life. As a child, I used to focus a lot on life's unfairness, which must have made Dame Fortune say, "Pshaw." But is she such a good judge of our "just deserts," or "just *desserts*," depending on how sweet our teeth are?

When I think of what someone "deserves," I usually go no further than Bruce Jay Friedman, the author who crafted my favorite literary blurb. When a friend of Friedman's, another writer, asked him to say something positive about this friend's latest novel, Friedman found himself in a quandary. He hated the book and didn't want to lie by saying he liked it, yet he didn't want to upset his friend by revealing his unvarnished opinion, either. So the blurb he submitted was intellectual escape artistry *par excellence*. What Friedman wrote was, "This novel gives me more pleasure than I deserve."

Speaking of pleasure, the singer Waylon Jennings once calmed down a friend of his, a violent homophobe, by saying, "Aw, come on, hoss. We all just grab onto something warm and worry about the details later." Something warm, indeed! I wish I was more sexually intrepid, hence able to live out my most off-the-charts-vivid fantasies. "Try everything once," as the English adage has it, "except for incest and folk dancing."

If, for instance, the title character of the folk ballad "Peggy-O" is half as pretty as the tune's chord change in the second line of each verse, then I'd wish I could meet Peg and make merry with her the way the song's Sweet William wishes to do. (I'm assuming that my wife would grant me a "hall pass," of course.) The same sort of wish goes for Little Delia in the Blind Willie McTell song about her, and goes double for the "gal" in the tune "Coffee Grows On Wild Oak Trees," a gal who's "*gone, gone, gone, / she's gone to come no more / so I bid her my last farewell*."

My musical romance wish list goes on and on. Highly placed there is "Skip-A-Long Sam" from the Donovan song, although I'm not quite clear on which gender Sam is. Todd Rundgren's "Marlene," Nick Lowe's "Marie Provost," and the Pixies' "Velouria" have pride of place, too. Most of all, I'd like to frolic with the "Griselda" of a song by the Holy Modal Rounders. Like that tune's narrator, I would gladly "*slip into the woods in the dark of the night / callin' to the moon up yonder, / "O Lady Moon, won't you shine your silver light / and lead me to my Griselda*?""

In the film *Citizen Kane* a minor character speaks of having once glimpsed on a New Jersey ferry a girl who wore a white dress and carried a white parasol. "I only saw her for one second," he explains, "and she didn't see me at all. But I'll bet a month hasn't gone by since that I haven't thought of that girl." Ferrying through my own life have been dozens of barely glimpsed actual strangers I still think about longingly. The most recent of these was a blond woman who went skipping alone through the midnight daylight of summertime Reykjavik.

Perhaps the stranger I remember most fondly was a congenial Serbian-born brunette who was working in a Lower Manhattan hotel lobby when I met her last summer. Admiring her charms, wistful me wished I was young again and still enjoyed the energy and the willpower and the patience to try to woo her. Yet a different me, weary me, recalled how stressful such wooing usually felt. So weary me was now relieved that I've aged out of the process and could appreciate the Serbian's youth and beauty and congeniality from an objective remove. *Especially* her congeniality, because that bright virtue seems to contain an unspoken message to me. This message was, "You're over there on one side of Romance Road, mister, and I'm here on the other side, and we'll remain apart forever, but if you had been younger or I had been older, perhaps we could have met in the middle and cooked up some F-U-N together."

I wish I had access to the memories, impulses, and fixations that my subconscious mind has repressed. Imagine how different a person would be if all their dark stuff could pulsate right there on the surface! Naturally enough, such madness has gotten buried away for good reason, but only after it's resurrected into consciousness can a person say that he or she is truly psychologically whole.

No, I don't buy this horse dung, either. Consider it another item to file under the command to "be careful what you wish for," because mere minutes after my psychologically suppressed materials come swarming back, I'm certain that I'd wind up committing suicide. Or homicide. Or at least land myself in jail for mail fraud.

Jail! I've already briefly wound up there a few times during my early years. The Santa Barbara County lock-up was one of them. One night in the early eighties, a highway patrolman pulled me over for drunk driving while I was in my rental car on the freeway north of that lovely Californian city. I protested to him that I'd only had one beer, and indeed, I passed his Breathalyzer test with the proverbial flying colors. I even did fairly well at another of his demands, which was to recite the alphabet backwards while standing on one foot, although this took me some time because I had to sing the alphabet song in my mind to come up with each letter.

Perhaps frustrated at my success with his sobriety tests, the cop began acting rough with me, so I mouthed off to him. As a hotheaded kid, I hadn't learned to accede to power whenever it has me in its grip. The upshot was that the patrolman charged me with "resisting arrest" and hauled me to the police station, where, in a bare gray photo booth, a technician took my mugshots. I only got a quick peek at these photos—frontal and profile, like on TV—before the technician dropped them into my arrest file and whisked the file away.

Who knows if this file still exists? I certainly have not seen my mugshots in any "Most Wanted" poster on a post office wall. Still, I wish I had access to those mugshots, because they seemed at the time to be the single best photographs anyone had ever made of me. Perhaps we never look so attractive as we do when we're scared shitless.

Why was I so frightened? The thuggish other cellmates with whom I was sharing the drunk tank, for starters. All night long, I sat with my back against a cinder-block wall and kept my eyes fixed on my new neighbors, ready to be attacked at any moment. I also struggled with my need to use the seatless toilet in the center of the room. But what truly preoccupied me was the prospect that the specter of my dead mother would come zooming through the precinct house, zero in on me, and screech, "You see? *This* is what you get for being fresh with police officers. Didn't I teach you to salute them whenever you see them? You're darn tootin'! And *this* is what you get for drinking beer and running around with riff-raff and chasing after dirty hussies. *Shiksas*, even! I *knew* you'd wind up in trouble, you bad boy, you! What a *problem child* you are! You'll be lucky if they don't give you the *electric chair*!"

Generally speaking, I tend to sympathize more with overly cautious people than I do with the not-cautious-enough. Excessive caution seems uncool, yes, but Dame Fortune often throws surprising whammies at us, and I hate death.

Or do I? Maybe not entirely, since the song "(Don't Fear) The Reaper" has always struck me as strangely seductive. It's akin to a verbal beckoning, as if old Stretchfoot, that Executioner of Exhilaration, was whispering to me, "You're weary, aren't you, terribly weary, so why not just close your eyes and rest?" Does this mean I have a death wish? I *have* identified in myself an intractable doom-curiosity if not a doom-eagerness, accompanied by a touch of mild sadism, which clashes with my self-conception as a life lover. But aren't self-conceptions usually complicated matters? "Whirl is king," wrote the ancient Greek playwright Aristophanes, identifying our inner states as well as what goes on outside us. And Dame Fortune is of course the Queen of Whirl, as well as the Queen of Trickery and of Paradox.

Welcome back to this wish list's recurring "*Shake Hands With Stretchfoot*" *Department*. If you choose to agree with the aphorist

Malcolm de Chazal that death is "the bowel movement of the soul evacuating the body by intense pressure on the spiritual anus," then, by all means, suit yourself. (Chazal also compared "breasts restrained by a brassiere" to "two tennis balls expelled by the ribcage that fall back into the net at each stroke.") I prefer to reflect on the title of the composer Ryuichi Sakamoto's memoir *How Many More Times Will I Watch the Full Moon Rise?* Perishing right before his memoir was published, Sakamoto received his answer.

Another question is whether Sakamoto got to view a "green flash" during one of those sunsets. I saw one myself once over the Pacific at Santa Monica right after visiting the art studio of my friend Bob Neuwirth, and I whispered a thanks to Dame Fortune, because witnessing a brief burst of greenness as the sun sets had been a long-time wish of mine. Another such wish has been to consider each new day my last, thereby foregoing mundane pursuits, dampening excessive yearnings, and ignoring needless worries. Better yet, I've wished that I could regard myself as "already dead," that old Samurai prescription, which would mean that everything starting right now is a bonus. Pure gravy. (Careful how you *carpe-diem*, though. When my wife and I first met, she noticed the skull-and-crossbones ring I wear as a *memento mori*, a reminder of death, and she found it so cheesy that she nearly refused to speak with me.)

My friend Tom has told me that he plans to elude death when it arrives by telling old Stretchfoot, that Murderer of Mirth, "Sorry, I can't go along with you today—I left my passport in my sock drawer." I'll probably be even less keen on accepting when it's my own time to "saddle up the palomino," as the cowboys say, and "beat it on down the line." Who wants to have the world spin on without us? That would leave us with the ultimate case of "FOMO," the dreaded fear of missing out. (If only I could be better at summoning up "JOMO," the *joy* of missing out, as well as turning all paranoia into "pronoia," which is the belief that people, particularly ninjas, are secretly conspiring to do us good rather than harm.)

The Roman emperor Marcus Aurelius compared our lives to roles in stage plays, with some of these roles lasting for only three acts while others get to go the full five-act distance. Our greatest philosopher king's point is that those three-act roles can be just as meaningfully complete as longer ones. Try as I do to live by this, I find it too daunting, because I know that, should I myself wind up only being a three- or four-act person myself, I'll long to keep acting, however amateurishly, all the way to the final curtain. And Montaigne is even less helpful than Marcus Aurelius with Montaigne's remark that "If you have drawn any profit from your life, you have had enough of it. Make way for others, just as others made way for you. Go on your path satisfied."

Let's discuss Jeff Bridges's character in the movie *Fearless*. He's an airline passenger who's panicking as his plane goes down, freaking out like everyone else around him, but then something cool happens. He simply releases his fear, lets go of everything, and embraces the imminent pain and extinction. Soon, exuding a calm presence in the midst of cabin-wide hysterics, he spots a nearby child who's travelling alone, and with his newfound state of serenity, the Bridges character is able to comfort that child with all the strength of his serenity. And then, delicious irony, guess which two of the passengers are among the few plane crash survivors?

I like a remark my Uncle Wolf has made: "When death comes to each of us, it will come as a friend." In this vein, the filmmaker and stage director Mike Nichols said when he was mortally ill that he was "making friends with death." Not a surprising endeavor for him, either, since Nichols's lifelong motto was, "Cheer up, life isn't everything." And when he was asked what happens to us when we die, Nichols said, "We wake up in our dreams." Which reminds me of the poet Walt Whitman's remark that "Death is different from what anyone supposes—and luckier."

It's always fruitful to listen to Whitman. He attended Edgar Allan Poe's funeral, after all, and once amiably locked eyes with Abraham Lincoln, and had a snowy bushy beard that was, according to his fellow poet Federico Garcia Lorca, "full of butterflies." But what did Whitman mean by calling death lucky? I'm not sure, but perhaps one lucky method of "catching a cab," as my friend Bob Neuwirth referred to dying, would be to emulate the idealistic International Brigade in the Spanish Civil War. Those soldiers supposedly marched into battle singing "Life Is Just a Bowl of Cherries."

Or perhaps Thomas Pynchon is correct that each of us should strive to die "a *weird* death." We could follow the Zen teacher Teng Yinfeng, who asked his students if anyone they knew had died upside down. On learning that no one had, this teacher stood on his head and promptly caught that metaphorical cab. Do the Guinness Book of World Records people know about this death? And when Teng Yinfeng tumbled over, did Dame Fortune finally step out of the shadows, elbow old Stretchfoot aside, lift her veil, and reveal her true face to the dead man, saying, "This is no dream—you're wide awake"?

"Away with the fairies" is the charming English expression for someone who, like me, is usually daydreaming. I wish that whiling away hours hanging out with those fairies could be a literal experience—just as long as I don't encounter the rogue fairy who cheats at a card game in Flann O'Brien's novel *At Swim Two-Birds.* When another player catches this n'er-do-well marking his cards and threatens him with public exposure of his cheating, the fairy panics and pleads for mercy, saying that the news of his dishonesty "would kill my mother."

On reading this line, I laughed almost as loudly as I laughed when I gobbled down the final chapter of Terry Southern's *The Magic Christian* and the first chapter of William Kotzwinkle's *The Fan Man.* Those are the two funniest novels I know. Southern's plutocrat trickster protagonist Guy Grand ("Grand's the name, easy-green's the game…Play along?") and Kotzwinkle's daffy hippie burnout Horse Badorties ("I just woke up, man. Horse Badorties just woke up and is crawling around in the sea of abominated filthiness, man, which he calls home")—these are the kind of "fairies" I'd most want to be "away with."

We all know that the ancient Greeks urged us to "know ourselves," and I used to wish for such self-knowledge, but now I'm wavering about it. Didn't Oscar Wilde say that "Only the shallow know themselves"? Besides, I suspect that the psychoanalyst Adam Phillips is onto something when he says that we need to be "cured" of self-knowledge—cured, that is, of our wish to know ourselves in a "coherent, narrative way." Adds Phillips, "We've all got about ten different formulas about who we are, what we like, the kind of people we like, all that stuff… You can only recover your appetite, and appetites, if you allow yourself to be unknown to yourself." A remark which he supplements by quoting the poet Randall Jarrett: "The ways we miss our lives are life."

Some people believe that our truest relationships are with our siblings. Being an only child, I wouldn't know if this is so. Early on in life, I wished I had a brother or sister, if only to share my woes and confirm their reality, but this wish screeched to a halt the day when a sixth-grade classmate told me the reason he was always so sleepy. It was because his older brother woke him up for school each morning by punching him in the face. "Rise and shine," indeed! Nowadays, I take pride in being an only child and consider all other only children my spiritual siblings. Still, I wish I'd had an imaginary friend during my early years, a non-face-punching pal visible to me alone, and during this past year I've started wishing I had a *doppelganger*, an exact and up-to-date double of myself. Not the willfully mysteriously, barely-glimpsed-in-the-shadows kind of double, but a chummy *doppelganger* I can meet for coffee. We'll greet each other with the phrase, "What's the word, Thunderbird?," then amiably discuss the details of the life we've shared since birth. For instance: "Remember Heather?"

"Oh, man, we really blew it with her on that first date. How could we have been so stupid?"

"Tell me about it…"

"I don't need to."

"No," laughing, "you don't. And doesn't *that*, given how we have no siblings, feel so good?"

Opposites may attract, but they don't adhere, and having a doppelgänger is the ultimate expression of the Taoist maxim "Like goes with like." The painter Robert Henri said that "There is nothing more important than having a frank talk with yourself." Henri was worth listening to—he also said that the way he painted was "like a man going over the top of a hill, singing."

The only problem with doppelgangers is if they presage your own fate. It is said that the prophet Zoroaster met his own image while walking through a garden just before old Stretchfoot, that Doomer of Deity Proclaimers, showed up to spoil the day. Zoroaster's murder, let me note, is depicted in Gore Vidal's novel *Creation*, where the protagonist, a Persian diplomat, gets to meet Socrates, Lao Tsu, and the Buddha as well as Zoroaster, because all of these historical sages lived within a century of each other. Makes you wonder about your own contemporaries, doesn't it?

I've long been curious about physical hazards, but I've never sought them out. Tie myself to a tree during a hurricane just to feel its force? No, thanks. What if the tree gets uprooted and blows away? I don't wish to experience any major earthquake, either, having been shaken up enough by two minor ones. And I'm really hoping that my corpse won't suffer the rumored fate of a favorite rock star of mine. When the Northridge quake opened a fissure in the floor of the funeral home where he lay in his coffin, that coffin tumbled into that fissure, so the poor man got buried unceremoniously. And far, far more than a mere "six feet under."

What is hazard-curious me actually willing to try? The stuff Mark Twain was talking about when he said, "Thunder is good, thunder is impressive; but it is lightning that does the work." Just as there are guilty pleasures, there are "guilty wishes," the kind you know you will probably regret indulging but do indulge, anyway. Indeed, this wish list runneth over with such wishes. And one of them is my wish to be struck by lightning.

What a thrill getting lightning'ed would be, provided—and this proviso is *crucial*—you survive it without any lasting harm. After being zapped, you might experience your mind and body quite differently. Hell, you might even be able to suddenly, inexplicably speak a new foreign language! Swahili, for example. (The Swahili word for "hello," *jambo*, is my favorite word in any tongue I know of.) Also, adding "lightning survivor, able and eager to tell the tale" would certainly make a good addition to your life-experience resume.

Finally, getting a taste of a lightning bolt or two might imbue you with superpowers not unlike how my favorite comic book superheroes acquired theirs. Then again, a US Park Ranger named Roy C. Sullivan got lightning-struck *seven* times over three decades and didn't seem to learn any lessons, much less get super-powerful. Unless luck itself was his superpower.

I'm particularly interested in the phenomenon of ball lightning. This interest was stoked when a tall redhaired Dutch flight attendant told me that she'd witnessed a crackling football-sized sphere of the stuff go soaring down the center of a commercial aircraft's cabin during take-off. My fascination with ball lightning deepened when a short redhaired Californian forest ranger (not Roy C. Sullivan) told me that when he was a boy and eating breakfast with his family, a ball of lightning entered their open kitchen window and bounced around from surface to surface ("Everybody hit the deck," said the ranger) until it finally left the kitchen by a different open window.

Make no mistake—I realize that I'm literally "playing with fire" with my lightning wish. Thanks to the few times I've gotten mildly electrocuted—at age six, for example, when even-more-stupid-than-I-am-now me touched the metal prongs of a lamp's plug as I inserted it into a wall socket—I understood that electrocution could truly put paid to me. Still, it's an experience like no other, a kind of adventure that can teach us crucial facts about our bodies and our world. Provided, again, that we come through it unscathed. As the singer of the rock band Grand Funk Railroad said at a concert where he got some serious shocks from a live microphone, "I know it's a hell of a rush, but I *can't* take *too many*!"

In lieu of getting struck by lightning, I wish I could be combustively transformed in the sense of the fourteenth-century Christian monk Abbot Joseph. Asked how to live by one of his fellow Desert Fathers, Abbot Joseph said, "Why not be totally changed into fire?" How would such a metamorphosis happen? Perhaps via something discussed in this dialogue between the protagonist of the seventies TV series *The Mary Tyler Moore* show and her colleague Ted, a ham-actor anchorman. When Mary complains that her life is dull and wonders how she can change it, Ted says, "I know exactly what's wrong with your life! You wake up. You eat breakfast. You drive to work. You say hello to your friends. You work at your job. You go to lunch. You work some more. You say goodbye to your friends. You drive home. You have dinner. You sit down. You watch television. You read a magazine. And you go to sleep. Am I right?"

Mary nods her head eagerly. He's nailed it!

So Ted continues: "You want to change your life completely, this is what you've gotta do, starting tomorrow. *WAKE UP! EAT YOUR BREAKFAST! DRIVE TO WORK! SAY HELLO TO YOUR FRIENDS! WORK AT YOUR JOB! GO TO LUNCH! WORK SOME MORE! SAY GOODBYE TO YOUR FRIENDS! DRIVE HOME! HAVE DINNER! SIT DOWN! WATCH TELEVISION! READ A MAGAZINE! AND GO...TO...SLEEP!*"

Here's some more blues-beating advice, this time from my octogenarian hippie friend Gypsy Boots, who along with his compadre Eden Ahbez and their fellow "Nature Boys" and "Nature Girls" was the world's first hippie. "Whenever you get depressed," Gypsy used to tell me, "just take an *enema*, or take a *hike*!" Having known Gypsy from my childhood until my middle years, when Gypsy died at age eighty-eight, I do not doubt that he was serious about both anti-blues strategies, although I wish I'd thought to ask Gypsy during our last conversation which kind of enema he recommended.

"We're all stupid," the author Nick Tosches wrote. "The trick is to never allow ourselves to be blinded to that by what little wisdom we have." Nevertheless, ignorance can indeed be bliss, or even something better, since fools in their fashion can be wise. Owing to his placement at the start of the Tarot card deck, the Fool figure is positioned to wander his way past all the other denizens of the Major Arcana.

Montaigne said that we are made as much to be laughed at as we are to laugh. So have a laugh on him. And on *me*, as well, because, unlike Montaigne, I've always been a fool myself—and most likely always will be. But I wish I could be the kind of "holy fool" that my pal Gypsy was. Or, failing that, I wish I could at least meet more of such people. I know where to find them, too. They're living in Chelm, the Eastern European *shtetl* populated exclusively by fools. Their folly is exemplary—to brighten dark nights, for example, they try to catch a full moon's light in a bucket, then wonder why this doesn't work.

Fortunately, living among the fools in Chelm are seven wise men. Unfortunately, the wise men's suggestions tend to be wasted due to how foolishly the local fools make use of them.

In psychoanalysis, according to the philosopher Theodor Adorno, only the exaggerations are true. I don't know if this is so, but my friend John Perry Barlow used to say that the least interesting, and usually the least *important*, thing about a good story is whether or not it actually happened. The author Grace Paley said, "Any story told twice is fiction." Probably true. Even so, I wish I could confirm the veracity of a tale I once heard from a New York City taxi driver. The man was gruff, with close-cropped gray hair and a dirty pullover, and merely answered "Europe" when I asked him where he was from.

"Okay, but which *part* of Europe?" I said.

He waved a hairy hand in the air and told me, in an accent I couldn't place, "I come from Europe, okay? Just Europe. Leave it at that."

His reticence didn't stop there. I asked him some other questions about himself, yet the only one he seemed eager to answer was about how long he had been driving a taxi.

"Twenty-eight years, I drive. Fifteen years here, thirteen in Europe. But my father, he was taxi driver also until he have his problem, and many times when I was child, I sit in taxi with him."

I said, "Since you won't tell me what country you come from, I don't suppose you'll tell me what 'problem' stopped your father from driving?"

"No, I tell you," said Drupka Kemeny, which, according to the ID certificate posted on the back of his seat's headrest, was the man's name. "My father, his problem was because of fortune teller. One day my father met this fortune teller in the train station in our town. She wore fur coat, he said, and she spoke to him. Maybe he pay her for to tell him about his future, or she did this for no price. I do not know it. But she says to him, 'Beware of trucks.'"

"*Trucks*?"

"Yes. She says a truck will make the death of him, and he believed this. He did not ask a question of it, no." Drupka Kemeny waved his hairy hand again. "And from this day, you see, my father, he *changed*. From this day to the end, he is afraid of trucks. *Very* afraid. When he was driving his taxi, he stay away from all the trucks on the road, stay away so much, avoid trucks on the road so much, and when he walks on the sidewalk, he keeps his body very close to the buildings. He is afraid a truck would come down the street—"

I nodded my head. "The driver would lose control, yeah, and the truck would squash him." By now we were approaching my home, and I hoped Drupka Kemeny would finish his story before we arrived. "Go on, please."

"My mother," said Drupka Kemeny, "she speak to my father. She say to him, 'This is stupid, do you see how stupid this is?' My uncle Henk, he say the same words. Stupid! But my father was stubborn, he will not listen to them, and one day while he was walking on our street, my father is killed."

"Oh. I'm sorry."

"It is a metal object killing him, something that fall down on his head. I was not where he was killed, I was in my school, but the people who see it, they tell us if he is not so close to the buildings while he walks, this object will go past him, will not do the harm."

"So a truck *didn't* kill him."

"Yes, it is truck," said Drupka Kemeny. "The metal object *is* a truck, a metal toy truck. A toy that a young boy let go of by an accident from his window."

Wow, I thought. *Good story*. But was it true? By now we had turned onto my street. Home was in sight, and I had one more question for Drupka Kemeny: "So are you scared of trucks yourself? I mean, when you drive your cab?"

"No," he said, "I am not my father. Also, I speak with three fortune tellers, three different ones, and each of the fortune tellers says to me the same thing about me."

"Which is what?"

He laughed a bitter laugh. "They say when I am old, I will get drunk and drown in my bathtub."

The aphorist Baltasar de Gracian likened human life to gambling with cards. Both are games of chance, after all, and to improve your chances of winning, Gracian makes some obvious yet potent suggestions: play the hand you're dealt, place bets only when the time is ripe, test the waters before getting in too deep, and get out while the getting is good.

Chances are, wise Steve Goodman understood all of this, and the title of his great wishing song "Eight Ball Blues" grabbed me even before I heard the music, because my birthday falls on the eighth day of the eighth month and eight has long been my favorite number. (Accordingly, I'm happy to know that an avant-garde composer named Count Scelsi, not to mention assorted Pythagoreans, have also considered the numeral eight a big deal.) Please note that I call it my "favorite" number instead of my "lucky" number because I refuse to assume good luck will always, or ever, adhere to me. Sure, we need to make assumptions such as that the sun will rise this morning, or that our flight will land safely in Sioux City. Still, I wish we wouldn't make *so many* assumptions, or make them so carelessly. After all, "If you want to make Dame Fortune laugh," the old homily goes, "tell the Dame your plans."

Need some evidence? Consider the accidentally uxoricidal author William Burroughs and a sea captain he met in Algiers in 1960. This captain boasted that he had not had an accident in twenty-three years. His ship sank later that day, taking his life as well as the lives of everyone else on board. (Beware more than any other number the number twenty-three, say the religious group the Discordians. On the other hand, rumor has it that Tom Robbins stayed in bed each morning until he heard this numeral spoken on the radio.)

Closer to home, I once met an aging sandy-haired surfer in Big Sur. "Call me 'Lucky,'" he'd told me when we were introduced.

"For real?" I said. "Don't you worry that having a nickname like that is, you know, tempting fate?"

"Nah," he said. "I *am* lucky. Always. So why shouldn't I be known for that?"

"Okay," I said, thinking that maybe some people are like dice, as Yehuda Amichai writes, that "*keep landing on the lucky side.*" A year later, though, a mutual friend told me that Lucky was now locked up in a federal penitentiary, doing a thirty-year sentence. Perhaps, instead of boasting, Lucky should have gone riding on a municipal bus that appears in Salman Rushdie's novel *Midnight's Children.* On the front of this bus is a sign reading "GOD WILLING," while on the rear a sign reads, "THANK GOD." We need not believe in God, or gods, or Dame Fortune, to appreciate those signs. Or to hear any divine laughter.

Still feeling lucky? I know a man whom Germans would call an "*Unglucksrabe*," a "*bad* luck raven," a jinx. Whenever I hung out with this bringer of misfortune, I got into some sort of trouble, although he has done quite well for himself. So in his own life he was apparently a *Gluckskind*, a child of good luck. I wish I was superstitious enough to believe in such matters, and to utilize good-luck charms like the Hebrew *chai* amulet, the Arabic Eye of Fatima, the Japanese *daruma* doll, the ancient Egyptian hieroglyph called *nefer*, the Zimbabwean *nyami-nyami* (a manifestation of their river god Zambezi), the Maori jade *hei-tiki*, anything else made of jade (if you're Chinese), the five-bats-in-a-circle talisman called a *weefuh* (also if you're Chinese), "buckeye" horse chestnuts (if you're from the American South), anything turquoise (if you're Persian or Navajo), a fetus's amniotic sac (if you're a sailor), Virginia fairy crosses, fallen eyelashes, pennies minted in leap years, lodestones, four-leaf clovers, rabbit's feet, salt to throw over your shoulder, wood to knock on, dried chicken "wishbones" to pull apart, plus anything colored blue.

To further improve my fortune, I would like to spend time with and be kind to spiders, frogs, caterpillars, beetles, elephants, seabirds, and white hens. I could say "abracadabra" when it seems appropriate, and consider thirteen my lucky number. If I do go down this route, however, I'll need to remember the aphorist La Rochefoucauld's observation that we need greater abilities to bear good fortune than to bear the bad.

I wish I could have consulted the Oracle at Delphi in ancient Greece, if only so I could observe what exactly was going on there. Better yet would be to rebuild that fabled Oracle in my basement. Easy access! I also wish I could have been initiated into the Mysteries of Eleusis, and could glimpse in a wooden bowl of water Dame Fortune's plans for me, and even, like the Etruscans, learn about my tomorrows from the entrails of animals and the flights of birds.

As for modern forms of divination, I've been fascinated by the *I Ching* and Tarot cards since I was seven and browsed through books about them in my childhood's unofficial second home, the local Brentano's Bookstore. For a while I was even keen on "chaos magic," with its imagistic "sigils" that you compose out of written wishes and then "charge" by masturbating while staring at them. Astrology has likewise been an interest, only much less so, because we cannot choose what zodiac sign we're born under. I'm not thrilled about being a Rabbit in the Chinese system, either, although my wife and I once did spend an evening saving the life of a bunny we encountered under slightly strange circumstances.

Much as I wish the fortune-telling tools of Tarot cards and the *I Ching* would prove accurate, in my opinion they're not going to. The philosopher Walter Benjamin probably got it right by saying, "He who asks fortune tellers the future unwittingly forfeits an inner intimation of coming events that is one thousand times more exact than anything the fortunetellers may say." In my view, the best divination tools of all are fortune cookies. I've thought so since the night when I ate at a Chicago Chinese restaurant with a girlfriend while pondering whether to break up with her or not and cracked open a cookie to find this message: "*You love her as much as you can, but you do not love them enough.*"

Just last night, as a matter of fact, I dreamed that I was discussing fortune cookies with Dame Fortune. I don't know how our dream-selves got onto this subject, but I told her that my favorite Lawrence Ferlinghetti poem begins with the line "*Fortune / has its cookies to give out.*" She told me that her favorite fortune in a cookie is "Disregard all previous fortunes." Then I told the Dame that the first cookie message I ever received was at a restaurant called Fong's Garden in my hometown. This message read, "*If your wishes are not extravagant, those wishes shall be granted.*"

Adjusting the dark veil that obscured her face, the Dame said, "How old were you when you got that message?"

"Six or seven."

"Well, since childhood is about wishing big, you probably didn't appreciate those words."

"True. Still, I appreciate that fortune cookie message better now."

"In that case," said the Dame, "you must realize that it should have read, *amor fati*-style, *If you don't* need *your wishes to be granted—if you can gracefully accept or even embrace them not being granted—then there's a better chance that they will be granted.*"

"Er…I guess that's true."

She patted my right cheek gently with her rough-skinned left hand. "Try fitting *that* mouthful inside a cookie."

The punk rocker Keith Morris said about his dead friend, fellow punk rocker Jeffrey Lee Pierce, "I was shocked that Jeffrey died but at some point we're going to hook back up and set a garbage can on fire and roll it down the biggest hill we can find so that it crashes into the West Hollywood Sheriff's Department."

"Wish You Were Here" is the title of a progressive rock song, which Morris and Pierce probably hated. Still, whenever I hear it, I wish my phone would ring and when I answer it I would hear the *heh-heh* laugh of my late friend Bob Neuwirth before he asks, in his lovably yammering voice, "Hey, Gary, what's happening?" I'll know it's Bob even before I take the call because I never erase the names and numbers of my dead loved ones in my address book. I call their answering machines sometimes just to hear them delivering their outgoing messages. And I keep and listen to all the voicemails they left me. Not that I believe in overindulging in the mourning process; the author Henry David Thoreau was right in asking, "What right have I to grieve, who have not ceased to wonder? Only Nature has a right to grieve perpetually, for she only is innocent."

The afterlife! Is it for real? Although John Prine makes the possibility of it sound delightful in his great wishing song "When I Get To Heaven," singing, "*I'm gonna smoke a cigarette that's nine miles long*," I'm unable to give much credence to the concept of any bonus existence. No souped-up telephone service appears to reach the Other Shore, and that boat sailing across the River Styx most likely brings you one way. Nevertheless, if Dame Fortune ever offers me to reunite me with a single lost loved one, it would certainly be my mother.

"Your *mother*?" I can imagine your response, my fellow wisher, to this latest wish of mine. "Throughout this wish list you've been complaining about your mother! Isn't she the person you've most wanted to *get away from* while she was alive?"

You're absolutely right. And isn't it remarkable how a loved one's sins against you get dulled in your memory after they've "bit the big bagel," as my late friend Harry Crews used to refer to mortality? I remember every one of Esther Lippman's vices, but the older I get, the more I cherish her virtues.

For her part, my mother would surely welcome a post-death reunion with me. Even when she was alive, she was regularly announcing that I would need to live my entire future life at home with her. Before death put an end to her scheme, she'd even been planning to move to my university to share lodging with me in my dormitory room.

"*Then*," she crisply explained, "on weekends we'll come back to our house so you can do your schoolwork and not get tempted by any whore coeds or get beaten up by any campus bullies or get forced by local pushers to take drugs like that 'pot stuff.' Enough of that pot and you'll turn hophead and I'll have to ship you to the Betty Ford Clinic and you'll need methadone to get off it!"

My shock at this parental plan, followed quickly by my outrage at it, flew off the charts. I knew that the artist Joseph Cornell had cohabitated his whole life with his mother, but she wasn't Esther Lippman. In a foamy-mouthed fury, I shouted at her, "And I suppose you'll live with me at the Betty Ford Clinic, too, right?"

"Of *course* I will! They're not keeping us apart!"

By the time I was of high school age, I was well underway with my rebellion against my mother. Today I'm happy that I refused to submit meekly to her domination. Still, our hourly shouting matches proved to be traumatizing for both of us, and left a lot of property damage in our wake. I actually punched through two walls, and any time she was enraged with me, she would tear up all my precious books and break my even more precious record albums over her knee.

"Had she lived longer," my Uncle Wolf, Esther Lippman's only sibling, once told me, "one of you, mother or son, would have killed the other." A decade later, he amended his statement to, "Had she lived longer, she would have driven you so insane, that you would have started smoking pot as an escape, then started using heroin, and would have eventually overdosed, immediately after which your mother would have killed herself."

Now, missing my mother in spite of all my lingering anger, I long to see her again. The reunion I'm wishing for would echo the last scene of *Sid And Nancy*. This is the movie about Sid Vicious and Nancy Spungeon, the punk rock couple whose love affair ended when Sid supposedly murdered Nancy in their room at the Chelsea Hotel. (My filmmaker friend Poppy was friendly with both Vicious and the *kitschy* crooner Liberace. Talk about running the show business gamut!)

Instead of realistically depicting Vicious's death by heroin overdose, Cox in his movie shows the punk rock icon Sid dancing with some kids outside a pizzeria in the urban wastes of New Jersey. Then a yellow Checker Taxi comes rolling up and Nancy, who's already dead, smiles radiantly at Sid from the rear window. He smiles back, he climbs inside, they kiss in the backseat, and off drives the taxi drives, Styx-bound.

In my own death scene, I'll be dancing with those same kids outside the same pizzeria when a bell will ring, the lights will dim, and my mother will appear alongside me in our beige Buick station wagon. Cue the Rolling Stones singing, "*Have you seen your mother, baby, motoring in from the shadows*?" From the driver's seat Esther Lippman will smile at me just as radiantly as Nancy smiled at Sid. Then she'll roll down her window and say, "Time's up. You had your fun, sweetheart. I never approved of that kind of fun, you know, but my hands were tied. Now say goodbye to this gumball planet. Let's go, climb in."

And off we'll go, together again, with all her sins (and mine too?) completely—no, make that *mostly*—forgiven.

How many readers of this wish list should I wish for? The French author Henri Michaux said, "A man who has only one reader is not a writer. A man who has two readers is not a writer, either. But a man who has *three* readers, *that* man is really a writer." A different French wordsmith, Andre Gide, said that with each book a writer publishes he should lose the admirers he gained with his previous book. Which leads naturally to Nietzsche's remark that "So long as people praise you, you can be sure that you are not yet on your own true path but on someone else's."

Me, I wish I could be as high-minded as Nietzsche or Gide, but what I really wish for are *legions* of readers—as long as none of them ever learn my home address or unwritten intimate details about my life. Let's deny them access to my personal possessions, too. Fans can be fanatics, as was demonstrated by the avid appreciators of the nineteenth-century ballerina Marie Taglioni, who bought, cooked, and then ate Taglioni's ballet shoes. Nearly as perverse were the bobbysoxers who worshipped the young Frank Sinatra. "Girls hid in his dressing rooms, in his hotel rooms, in the trunk of his car," wrote a Sinatra biographer. "When it snowed, girls fought over his footprints, which some took home and stored in their refrigerators."

"I Wish He Were Me" is the title of a song written about my rock star friend Benny Pompa, singer of the smash hit "Rock and Roll Hernia," which concerns an adverse medical effect of rocking and rolling too energetically. For a long time I too wished I were Benny, as well as other charismatic famous artists, despite my recognizing their manifold personal flaws. I didn't want minor-league fame, either. I longed to be a household name, an international superstar, worthy of a long listing in *Who's Who in America*. Only with such celebrity did I feel I would be getting my genes' worth out of life.

Sure, your privacy would be out the window, but couldn't fame be managed? After all, David Bowie kept fans at bay by pretending to be a Greek tourist, a ruse he supported by carrying with him an Athens newspaper and acting as though he spoke no English. More absurdly, the rock artist George Harrison turned down autograph hounds with the enigmatic explanation, "Sorry, it's Thursday." (Interestingly, Harrison died on a Thursday, and soon afterward, the satirical newspaper *The Onion* published the headline "RINGO NEXT.")

By the time I reached forty, I had encountered the writer John Updike's famous remark that fame is "a mask that eats into the face," and I came to recognize how corrosive such a condition would be for a psyche like mine. So now I wished only for a well-known writer's fame, the kind where you can get a notable table in a fine restaurant yet not be forced to endure fans constantly approaching that table or gawking at you. And at fifty, I'd jettisoned all dreams of glory, no longer craving any fame whatsoever. Anyway, hasn't social media made us all, at least potentially, known to strangers? And isn't this what celebrity is, however you define "known?" As it is, I'm wondering which evil ninjas are currently reviewing my social media posts, my photos, my likes, my dislikes, my current whereabouts. What mischief could these ninjas create, not just in cyberspace, but in "IRL," aka "meatspace?"

Being famous can cause mental problems apart from paranoia. Enhanced narcissism, for starters. As every schoolkid knows, celebrities tend to be just like "regular" people are—except they're usually even *more* fucked-up. Look no further than the tales of Belle Poitrine which she recounted to Patrick Dennis in the most titanic celebrity memoir ever penned, *Little Me*. (Poitrine regularly invoked Dame Fortune in her *meisterwerk*, referring to her as "Dame Chance.")

Another drawback is how fame can rob life of its quotidian magic. I'm thinking of the child film star Shirley Temple, who said she stopped believing in Santa Claus when her mother took her to meet him in a department store and Santa asked the girl for her autograph. Then there's how addictive a dose of fame can be—and how painful is the withdrawal process. Here's a story an acquaintance told me:

In the late seventies, I worked at a revival house cinema in Manhattan, a place where film lovers could watch old movies on a big screen. Such places are gone now, except in Paris, and we're the poorer for it. The famous Hollywood actor Gig Young used to come into our theater whenever one of his films was showing. "Mr. Young," as we called him, was in his sixties then, long past his time of popularity, and after each screening, he and his younger wife would hang out in the lobby, waiting to be recognized by his fans who'd just watched his younger self onscreen. Mr. Young was always friendly to everyone, including those of us who worked at the cinema. Still, I found it a bit pathetic, watching how hungry he was to be acknowledged.

As time passed, the situation became sadder still. Mr. Young's appearance got unkempt, with his hair uncombed and his blazers not so clean. He was just as friendly as ever, but we wondered if he was drunk, or at least really underslept, and soon he was wearing the same blazer each time he came in. It had food stains on it. And his wife stopped showing up with him. 'Poor man,' we thought, although none of us who worked at the theater laughed at him. We were fervent film fans ourselves. Then, one morning while I was walking to work, I picked up a newspaper and saw Mr. Young's photo in it. It was a photo from his heyday, not from his years as—well, how can you avoid the word "has-

been?" And the article that accompanied the photo said that Mr. Young had committed a murder-suicide. He'd shot his wife to death, then turned the gun on himself.

Because hydrofoils and hovercrafts are not equipped to cross oceans, commuter trains are my favorite method of long-distance travel. During my thirties, I often made Amtrak journeys from coast to coast. Not in boxcars, fortunately, but not always in cozy sleeper compartments, either. I loved the pure unstructured time you had on trains, plus unexpected opportunities for hilarity or erotic pleasure with fellow passengers. Steve Goodman's song "City Of New Orleans" was usually the soundtrack for my journeys by rail, even though I never rode south alongside the Mississippi. That tune is not the best one Goodman wrote, by the way. His best number is either "My Old Man," whose last stanza never fails to make me weep, or "You Never Even Call Me By My Name," whose bridge in the David Allan Coe version never fails to make me jump from joy. But "City Of New Orleans" is the greatest train song in the American songbook, and if "Dinah" doesn't like my saying so, then she can just keep blowing her horn.

Many years ago, I got to know the essayist Edward Hoagland, who was close to blind at the time, and now whenever I reread his great essay on aging, it makes me wish I could again be a rider on a train "gone five hundred miles when the day is done." Focusing on trains, Hoagland wrote of "ambling down the corridors toward the bubble car to chum with strangers while the scenery rises and falls," and, like him, I'd "rejoice in gazing out, crossing a continent with the random souls chance has thrown my way."

How happy I'd be to have Hoagland and Goodman's ghost as my fellow passengers. The ghost of Yehuda Amichai would be welcome, as well; in one of his poems, he wrote, "*A man's soul is like / A train schedule / A precise and detailed schedule / Of trains that will never run again.*"

In Paris one evening I met my favorite Icelandic visual artist, Erro, and asked him if he would share any advice for me about making collages. "Scissors and glue" was all he said. Even more disappointing to me was the novelist Don DeLillo's offered wisdom about writing fiction: "You'll keep improving," he said, "if you just stay alive and keep at it, so guard your health." Decades after this exchange with DeLillo, I bumped into him again and asked if he still endorsed his basic "Guard your health" regime. "Sure," said the novelist. "It's worked for me!"

Another item about the artist Erro: I sometimes wish I could emulate his father, another artist, who supposedly travelled constantly around Iceland, stopping only in the many villages where he had a spouse as well as children with this spouse. What a circuit to continually traverse! The senior Erro didn't have access to a train, either—he probably went on foot.

Travel! I'm sure you've heard that our scientists, possibly not mad, have been proposing that this universe is actually a multiverse, with an infinite number of different realities. Should we freak out at this theory? Not according to Walt Whitman, who wrote, "Let your soul stand cool and composed before a million universes." With my spirit braced by these words, I wish I could sign up for a multiverse Grand Tour in order to find out what the Dame Fortunes are like in those other realms. What are the alternate Gary Lippmans like? Do they make more or less wishes than I do? And do the alternate Dame Fortunes grant those wishes more or less frequently?

The ideal vehicle for such a metaphysical journey, I believe, would be the kind of hop on / hop off buses that operate in most major cities. Nothing screams *tourist* as blatantly as these buses do, and I'm sure that if my friends ever spotted me riding in one—cruising through Vienna, for example—I'd blanche with embarrassment. Nevertheless, I've always found these rides to be the best method available for discovering a new place. I like the freedom to leave and return whenever you wish to. And let the driver worry about traffic, not me! Hence my new wish is to be able to charter one of these tourist buses to transport me and my hand-picked other passengers all over creation.

We'd begin by crossing each continent and ocean (our bus will convert into a boat) while our onboard guide reels off fact after fact about whatever locale we're cruising past. Our journeys will make those of Marco Polo and the twelfth-century Jewish traveler Benjamin of Tudela seem like cozy jitney rides to the Hamptons. (Believe it or not, my friend Gary—one of a few Garys I know—once brought Captain Beefheart to the Hampy Hamps by way of that jitney.)

Needless to say, our great challenge on our global hop on / hop off tour will come when we hear the enthralling song of the mythological Sirens on Mediterranean shores. Each Siren will resemble the saucily grinning blonde on the cover of that Roxy Music album, the blonde with the seaweed hairdo, and each will sing with the compelling voice of Janis Joplin. Could any of us resist their song?

Speaking of Janis, I wish I could have gotten to hang out with her. Friends of mine who knew her say she was a terrific person, not merely a terrific artist. I love that she helped to arrange and pay for a headstone to be placed on Bessie Smith's grave in Pennsylvania. ("*Got the world in a jug,*" Bessie sang, "*got the stopper in my hand.*") Even more, I love that Janis said she'd "rather not sing than not be able to sing *loud.*"

I wish I could sing half as well as Bessie and Janis did. Maybe my singing voice could even break dishes, shatter Champagne glasses, and knock down the walls of condemned buildings faster than any wrecking ball. But I'd settle for the ability to feel confident about singing in public. Such singing has been a problem for eager amateur Caruso me since the ill-fated day in 1974 when an older kid with an Afro told me that I should never sing out loud in the presence of people because, he said, "You'll look like an idiot as well as sound like one." Sure enough, I now feel too self-conscious to openly release the song in my heart when I'm around others. What a shame that, whether bursting with joy or sadness, I keep my trap shut.

Mary Oliver wouldn't stifle the song in her heart. In a poem, Oliver wrote, "*I believe in kindness. Also in mischief. Also in / singing, especially when singing is not necessarily / prescribed.*" The rock artist Nick Cave certainly never keeps his mouth shut. In a letter not to God but to a fan, Cave wrote, "We are obligated to make our best attempts to become the thing we wish to be, otherwise we forever remain the sorry consorts of our own defeat."

Finally, there's the matter of listening to what's being sung. Here's an encore by Mary Oliver: "*Imagine how the lily.../ would sing to you if it could sing, / if you would pause to hear it. / And how are you so certain anyway that it doesn't sing?*"

I wish I could be like The Watcher, my favorite bald superhero (probably the *only* bald superhero), and get to observe the Big Bang as well as all the stuff that followed from it and all the even more astounding stuff, if any, that preceded it. This way, I could be privy to the grandest secrets of existence. Early on, this didn't seem like such a far-fetched objective because my mother would tell me that, if I was a "good boy" and obeyed everything she commanded me to do, I might grow up to be the Hebrew Messiah. As I grew older, I longed instead to be one of the *Lamed Vov*, the thirty-six righteous people whose existence, according to Judaic legend, keeps the world worthy of spinning onward. And sometimes I still wish I could be "the light of this world"—not the one Jesus spoke about or the one Ernest Hemingway wrote about but the one that the blind bluesman Reverend Gary Davis sang about. Being this light, I figure, will at least make me, in Hunter S. Thompson's words, "just sick enough to be totally confident."

As with being famous, I've now given up on becoming any world-light or Messiah; I gave up on being a "good boy," too, once puberty hit. More importantly, I'm no longer counting on getting clued in to any cosmic secrets, such as "Why is there something instead of nothing?" The physicists' solution—"Out of nothingness arose a quantum fluctuation"—doesn't get non-physicist me very far. We've learned that mortal minds simply aren't equipped to grasp concepts like infinity and eternity. And maybe it's for the best that our biggest questions receive zero answers. As a graffito I once glimpsed on a New Orleans storefront asked, "WHY SHOULD MYSTERY GIVE ITS LIFE FOR US?" (In suspiciously similar handwriting directly below this graffito was a different one that stated, "CLIFF SLEPT WITH MY MOM.")

Let's "let the mysteries be," yes. Still, I wish that those physicists would at least solve in my lifetime a few of the specific scientific riddles which I'm curious about. Dark matter and dark energy are just for starters. I suspect that, with Dame Fortune making enough time and resources available, we will ultimately uncover those answers. After all, Einstein himself quipped that "The eternal mystery of the world is its comprehensibility." (In this spirit, he refused to believe that God "plays dice" with the universe.) Perhaps we'll even learn that, as some theorists suspect, the laws of physics evolve as eons pass, and even compete with each other as they do. Or perhaps our very act of observing the universe changes it, affecting not just the future but likewise the past. Try to wrapping your noggin around that last part, fellow wisher.

Our biggest challenge is our own all-too-human nature. As one of my casual observations about existence, which I call Lippy Laws, has it, "We all wish for technology to keep improving—and, for better and worse, technology *does* keep improving. By the same token, we all wish for human nature to keep improving—and, for better and for worse, human nature does *not* improve." The scientist E. O. Wilson has written, "The real problem with humanity is that we have godlike technology, medieval institutions, and Paleolithic emotions." About those emotions, H.G. Wells said, "If you make men sufficiently angry or fearful, the hot red eyes of cavemen will glare out at you." Which implies that a few wrong human behaviors, backed by powerful enough technological doodads, can hurtle us back to the Stone Age—and may Dame Fortune have mercy on any of the "lucky" survivors. Will human civilization collapse before any scientific riddles get solved? Before our technology gets much better, too? Would even a new Einstein be able to forestall our planetary extinction?

Faced with that extinction, I wish it could be our emotions that are godlike. Then everything else would fall into place, and we'd be like a phenomenon which Tom Robbins once described: "A blue dolphin leaping out of a sink of dirty dishes."

I wish I had known all of my grandparents better, especially the grandfather who died when I was three, the other grandfather who died when I was ten, and the grandmother who died when I was fifteen. By all accounts, they were fantastic people. My paternal grandmother Lulu certainly was, and I'm glad that I got to know her well. One of my happiest memories of Lulu took place during a mid-nineties night when, in her small sixteenth-floor apartment on Miami Beach, she astounded me by saying, "Your grandfather and I once went to a Beatles concert."

"Wait," I said. "*What*?"

She nodded her head. "It was in the ballroom at the Diplomat Hotel here in town. We got the tickets for the concert from the hotel manager because we were long-time guests there. All these teenaged girls kept crying their eyes out and begging us to give them our tickets, and oh, we felt such pity for those girls…But your grandfather was curious about what all this Beatles hullabaloo was about, so we said, 'We're sorry, girls,' and we went inside."

Lulu was one hundred years old when she told me this, and although her mind seemed as clear to me as ever, I didn't believe her claim. Still, I wish I had not disputed it with her, because I did dispute it, gently, *diplomatically* (in the spirit of the hotel's name), saying,

"Grandma, I think you might have seen a *different* pop group's concert there, not the Beatles."

"Why not the Beatles, darling?"

"Well, because I'm a pretty big Beatles fan and I'm positive that they never played any hotels, especially not in Miami Beach. In their heyday, they played sports arenas, you know? And stadiums. *Not* hotel ballrooms."

Lulu said, "I know you're always right, dear. I never doubt a word you say." Which was a familiar assertion from my supremely affectionate grandparent. Once when I'd asked her playfully, "Would you still love me if I robbed a bank?," Lulu smiled and said, "Of course I would, darling—I'd just say that you really needed the money," and when I'd followed this up by asking, "Would you still love me if I murdered someone?," she kept smiling and said, "Of course I would, darling—I'd just say that they did you dirt and deserved what they got." Now, tonight, in the same spirit, she seemed to be agreeing with me about the Beatles, assuring me she would never doubt my word.

"Thanks, Grandma."

"*But*," she added, just as sweetly, "in *this* case, I know what I know. It really *was* those Beatles boys who your grandfather and I saw singing their loud songs at the Diplomat."

I was surprised by Lulu's certainty, and ready to keep pushing back against it, but now the TV program we'd gathered together to watch in her apartment was about to begin. It was the first episode of the *Anthology* documentary series about the Beatles, which is what had prompted Lulu to make her statement about them in the first place. She harbored no current interest in the Beatles, but she was happy to watch anything I wanted while I was visiting her apartment. As long as I didn't turn down the reheated leftovers she offered me and the cherry Jell-O she always had on hand, I was welcome to do whatever I wanted during a visit with Lulu.

(Another word about her apartment. As small as it was, it did have a balcony with a panoramic view of the Atlantic, and one night I began to walk out onto that balcony only to find, just before I tumbled sixteen storeys to my doom, that there had been construction work done on Lulu's building and the balcony had recently been removed. Sheared off completely! In the nick of time, I leaped back into the apartment with a gasp, and then I croaked to Lulu, my whole body shaking, "Jesus, Grandma, what happened to your balcony?"

Fortunately, she hadn't witnessed my near-death experience—with her back turned, she'd been busy preparing my cherry Jell-O—so Lulu merely said, as placidly as ever, "Oh, I forgot to tell you, darling. They took my balcony away. Don't go out there.")

By the time the *Anthology* episode reached the point in the Beatles' saga when the group first appeared on *The Ed Sullivan Show*, I'd gotten so involved in it that my grandmother's mistaken belief that she'd attended a Fab Four concert at the Diplomat Hotel had vanished from my mind. This belief of hers came rushing back to me, though, as soon as the documentary's narrator said, "For their second appearance on the Sullivan show, the Beatles were filmed at a concert in the ballroom of Miami Beach's Diplomat Hotel."

"You see?" Lulu said, turning to me and smiling a gentle, most *diplomatic*, smile as I stared at her, speechless. "We should have given those poor crying girls our tickets, after all. That loud music and all that screaming were so terrible that your grandfather and I walked out of the ballroom after five minutes."

RANDOM WISHES DIRECTED TO DAME FORTUNE AT 4:22 A.M. WHILE SUFFERING FROM A TYPICAL BOUT OF INSOMNIA:

* I wish I knew how to play the card game Solitaire so that I could pass my insomnia-strafed "white nights" this way, although my Uncle Wolf tells me that whenever he feels an out-of-the-blue compulsion to play Solitaire, someone he cares about usually dies unexpectedly within forty-eight hours.

* If I ever have a sudden heart attack, I wish I could respond to it the way the rock'n'roll guitarist Dick Dale responded to his. He grabbed all the workout weights he had within reach and started to pump that iron like crazy, Dale's rationale being, I suppose, to symbolically inform old Stretchfoot, that Gut-Twister of Guitarists, "If you're gonna take me, you're gonna take me swearing at the world."

* My favorite philanthropic organization is the Make-A-Wish Foundation, which strives to fulfill the wishes of seriously ill children. While volunteering one evening for a distant offshoot of Make-A-Wish, I found myself dining at a theme restaurant, the theme being professional wrestling. There I ordered the "house specialty," *Risotto Fromage*, which turned out be a bowl of plain rice covered by five

squares of un-melted American cheese. I wish that this cheese had been fresh. It wasn't. I was ill for days.

* Let me reiterate: I wish that flying drones did not exist. Why? Because one sunny afternoon at a park near my home, some unseen operator of a drone caused that accursed thing to keep divebombing me, sometimes nearly striking my head. Within minutes, I was gonzo with rage, running around trying to catch the drone and smash it to pieces. Then to find and strangle to death the operator.

* Describing his experience of being tossed around a mosh pit, the rocker Jarvis Cocker writes, "It was like treading water in an extremely stormy sea that smelled of B.O." I wish I hadn't wasted so much time worrying about how fetid my own body odor and breath might seemed to other people—as if smelly me had any choice but to be my purely mammalian self.

* Sometimes we know the effects we're causing in the world, as when Jorge Luis Borges scooped up a handful of sand near the Sphinx, walked a few steps, then dropped the sand in a new spot and announced, "I am modifying the Sahara." Most of the time, however, we're clueless as to what our actions may entail. It's as though we skim stones on the surface of a lake but we can't see the ripples. And I wish that, if only more often than we do now, we could see those ripples.

* "The border between the real and the unreal is not fixed, but just marks the last place where rival gangs of shamans fought each other to a standstill." I wish I'd concocted this sentence, but the novelist Robert Anton Wilson got there first. "Torn animals were removed at sunset from that smile," Randall Jarrell's physical description of Mary McCarthy, is another sentence I wish I'd written. So is Barry Hannah's "I want to sleep in her uterus with my foot hanging out." And so is P. G. Wodehouse's "Uncle Tom always looked a bit like a Pterodactyl with a secret sorrow."

* I wish I could remember that the sooner and more enthusiastically someone tells you they love you before they've really gotten to know you, the sooner and more enthusiastically they will ditch you. Without a goodbye, most likely, and perhaps even hauling with them some of your belongings.

* In my life I've said so many idiotic things to the wrong people, things that I passionately wish I could take back. But none of these abysmal remarks rival what my nineteen-year-old self told Richard Allard, the PTSD-suffering Vietnam combat veteran who was my

Literature professor at university: "I wish I could go to war, just to find out what sort of stuff I'm made of and also to someday have great material to write about." Allard, who'd been quite friendly toward me until this moment, was never friendly again.

* I wish I were better at keeping secrets. I've ruined more than one friend's surprise birthday party with my babbling, and you won't need to torture me to get me to spill any beans. In this I'm like Clive James, who wrote, "A scream from the other side of a closed door is usually enough to convince me." Then again, James and I aren't the only citizens with loose lips—as Mick Herron writes in one of his Slough House spy novels, "First rule of Spook Street: Secrets don't stay secret."

* I wish it was still safe to hitchhike on North American roads, because I enjoyed doing it in my youth, and never got asked for "ass, gas, or grass," either, although one driver with mutton-chop whiskers put his meaty hand on my thigh while I sat beside him. Out I jumped at the next red traffic light. These days, with both the hitchers and the drivers who stop for them likely to be psychopaths, I wouldn't even feel safe accepting a ride from, or offering a ride to, *myself.*

* Of course, no one's fingerprints are like anyone else's. But I wish that mine would consist not of random patterns but ten detailed images of the over-popular yet nevertheless poignant Andrew Wyeth painting *Christina's World*. That painting reminds me of my mother. I wish that she had permitted me during my childhood to set up an ant farm or grow a Venus flytrap. She did allow me to order "sea monkeys," but they looked nothing like how they were advertised.

* Insects! I wish that instead of mostly ignoring them I could be, like the poet Charles Simic, "curious about these little creatures going their merry way, taking care of business…Flies are neurotic, moths are crazy, but for serenity you can't beat a butterfly." As for the cockroaches who infested his New York City apartment, Simic said, "They were the only visitors I had all day. I was brought up to be polite to strangers and help old ladies across the street, so I'd stop whatever I was doing and inquire about these roaches' health."

* I wish that my thoughts could have more gray about them. Isn't black-and-white too restrictive, and usually so boring? I also wish that many of my thoughts weren't so high-minded. As the above-mentioned Charles Simic wrote, "A 'truth' detached and purified of the pleasures of ordinary life is not worth a damn...Every grand theory

and noble sentiment ought to be first tested in the kitchen—and then in bed, of course."

* "*Friday I'm in love.*" What the Cure sing on their album *Wish* applies to me. The rest of the week, though, I'm amazed at how complicated romantic love is and wish I could avoid the anger, jealousy, envy, and regret that come part-and-parcel with the moon-in-June stuff. At least I'm not as bad off as the narrator in the Clovers' song "Love Potion Number Nine," the guy who admits he's *"a flop with chicks / I've been this way since 1956.*" Since 1956! Still, I sure wish I had that potion he gets ahold of.

* In a Borgesian mood again, I wish that if I ever find myself lost in a labyrinth, I'll be able to wander calmly through it until I find the exit. Or could pretend that the labyrinth does not exist until the local king's young daughter arrives to assist me. Or could mentally will those walls to dematerialize so that I can proceed in a straight line back to the world. Or could have access to the magical map that Rabbi Nachman spoke of, one which shows the world as it is now, has been, and will be. With no detail, no matter how infinitesimal, left out.

* While my wife, our friend Tamara, a safari guide, and I were driving around Tanzania's Serengeti Plain, we inadvertently parked our Range Rover between a female elephant and her babies. I wish we hadn't, because we barely survived that maddened mama's charge at us. Never underestimate the ferocity of a mother who's defending her young. Or even her not-so-young. As the singer Hank Williams once said, "There ain't nobody I'd rather have alongside me in a fight than my mama with a broken bottle in her hand."

* I wish that I could take a free-of-charge holiday in Kublai Khan's stately pleasure dome. The fabled Fortunate Islands, the Flower-Fruit Mountain, the High Pure Realm, and the Mills Hotel would be good vacation options, too. But best of all would be the Shangri La in James Hilton's novel *Lost Horizon*, although at Shangri La I probably wouldn't want to mix with some of my fellow vacationers, because one of them might be the title character of another Hilton novel, *Goodbye, Mr. Chips*. Since Chips's one "flashing chance at bliss" got tragically cut off by a flick of Dame Fortune's wrist, I know that if I took even one glance at him, I'd feel sad in the midst of all that splendor.

* I wish I could be brave enough to spend a night sleeping on my dead relative's graves in their cemetery in New Jersey. I'd require the same bravery to spend a night at the rather creepy Gustave Moreau

Museum in Paris, or hanging out in David Lynch's quintessentially creepy American small town of Twin Peaks. Speaking of America, I wish our Constitution could be amended to get rid of the Electoral College. I'd like to amend it to abolish lots of other stuff, too. Maybe, since I'm not a politician, I can get all the abolition work done by being like the Paiute shaman who invented the ghost dance. I wouldn't make white people wither away, but I'd certainly temper their bad behavior while bringing the buffalos back to the plains. And while making our Constitution positively *swing*.

* I wish I hadn't slept late yesterday morning because while I dozed, I had a nightmare about Mr. Ravoon. Remember the black-clad, eye-patch-wearing, *Who's Who in America*-reading old man I used to see around New York and Paris? My nightmare was a scary dramatization of this verse by Paul Dehn about Mr. Ravoon's original female counterpart: "*I hauled in the line, and I took my first look / At the half-eaten horror that hung from the hook / I had dragged from the depths of the limpid lagoon / The luminous body of MRS. RAVOON!*"

* I wish people would stop using the expression "It's all good" when what they actually mean is, "It sucks but I'm going to openly pretend it doesn't." I wish people would stop saying, "Everything happens for a reason." And I wish that whenever people say, "You only live once," someone would pipe up to quote the critic Seymour Krim, who said, "One life was never quite enough for what I had in mind."

FIVE. IMPLAUSIBLE WISHES

I wish never to undergo any of what the novelist John Fowles calls the "class of experiences we should all have had before death if we wish to claim to have lived fully." Among these experiences are being caught in bed with someone else's spouse, seeing a ghost, killing another human being, realizing you're not alone in a house where you'd previously believed you were, and feeling certain that you're about to drown. The last experience is one that, thanks to a riptide at Australia's Bondi Beach, I've experienced myself.

"If there is magic on this planet, it is contained in water," said Loren Eisley, whose epitaph reads, "We loved the earth but could not stay." (A good pairing with that epitaph is the author Rabindranath Tagore's remark that "We live in this world when we love it.") Did water invent living beings as a means of transporting itself from one location to another? Whether it did or not, I wish I could be like Oenethea, the sorceress in Federico Fellini's film *Satyricon* who is able to turn a stone into water.

Another of my water wishes is to enjoy daily access to an Olympic-sized swimming pool. I promise you, as I once needed to promise my mother, that I won't swim for at least one hour after eating a full meal. Esther Lippman promoted the "don't swim for an hour after eating" policy because when she was a child, she had to flee from a Catskills Mountain hotel pool after a boy who'd eaten too much spaghetti at lunch began to vomit up that spaghetti, still undigested, into the water right near her. When my son was himself a kid, I repeated my mother's story to him but gave it a new ending, a twist in which the spaghetti kept pouring out of the vomiting boy's mouth and eventually filled the entire pool, then the entire hotel, and finally the entire Catskills, pasta-packing every valley.

I've loved to swim since the day I first learned how to at my day camp. I knew that day to avoid an older boy, a known bully who would grab all the kids who hadn't had any swimming lessons yet and toss them into the pool in order to rescue them and make himself look heroic. In the book *The Upstairs Delicatessen*, the critic Dwight Garner quotes Iris Murdoch, who once quipped, "Swimming, like dying, seems to solve all problems, yet you remain alive." All of the day camp bully's victims remained alive, I'm glad to report.

As for the title of Garner's book, it comes from another critic, the just-mentioned Seymour Krim—Krim again!—who referred to his memory as "that profuse upstairs delicatessen of mine." Which presumably stocked spaghetti. (And pizza, too? Jim Dodge says, "The mind is a pizza with the works," then adds, "I wouldn't mind a pizza with the works.")

I wish I could again visit the most beautiful waterfalls I've seen: the *Cataratas del Iguazu* in Argentina, which I think about when I'm trying to pee. I'd also like to see again Iceland's walk-behind-the-water *Seljalandsfoss*, where I had an epiphany about my then-newborn son, and Niagara Falls, despite Oscar Wilde having called it "a vast unnecessary amount of water going the wrong way and then falling over unnecessary rocks." (He added that the sight of these falls for a bride on her honeymoon makes for "one of the earliest, if not the keenest, disappointments in American married life.") I even wish I could put my face once more in the downpouring waters of a Catskills swimming hole's baby waterfall, although the last time I did this, I lost my favorite prescription sunglasses. Returning a week later to retrieve them with a scuba mask proved futile. I should have heeded my friend Bob Neuwirth, who had told me, "Forget about those shades, man. Some raccoon is cavorting through the woods wearing them."

Most of all, I wish I could bottle the powerfully nostalgic sensation I get whenever I lower my naked body into a piping hot bath in a pitch-dark room. Every time I do this (or almost every—the water temperature has to be just right), I'm catapulted for a second or two back to my teenage years when I would perform this same bathtub procedure in my home. The nostalgia never lasts longer than that second or two because as soon as my body gets adjusted to the heat, I'm returned to the here and now. Still, a hot bath in a lightless room is the most efficient form of time travel I know. As a teenager again, I've got all of my adult life still before me, and I'm free to make different choices about how to live it. Choices which, because "*Hope springs eternal in the human breast / We never* are, but *are always* to be *blessed*," might turn out better than the choices I actually went with.

May I gush some more about water? I wish I could be swimming naked in the Caribbean the way I did one night when I was young and blissfully not alone. It wasn't a mermaid with me that night, but it might as well have been. I have a separate wish about mermaids, wishing that I had been able to spot one off the shore of Key West when I was living there in 1991 and trying to emulate the cracked-up protagonist of Thomas McGuane's novel *Panama*. While in the so-called "Conch Republic," I wrote my first, still-unpublished book, which I should send to Burlington, Vermont's Brautigan Library. Named for the novelist Richard Brautigan, this library only stores and respectfully displays manuscripts that have been rejected by publishers and never appeared in print.

When I was staying in Key West, I also piloted a rented bicycle around at night with my crime author friend John and hung out with the crazy local hero Captain Tony Tarracino. As far as I know, he bears no relation to Captain Beefheart.

I first met Tony—smuggler, rum runner, fishing boat impresario, and unofficial "mayor" of Key West—in the saloon he owned. Like many popular eccentrics in American communities, Tony ended up running for election as the town's actual mayor, yet unlike most of those eccentrics, this cat won. I learned about his victory when I picked up a *Chicago Tribune* right after I took the Illinois Bar Exam, and eager to celebrate his victory with Tony, I hightailed it down to Key West as soon as I could. I visited the good Captain in his municipal office, where we smoked a joint together. I don't much like grass, but how could I refuse the opportunity to take drugs with a sitting mayor? (The only other cool politician I've met was a former mayor of Albuquerque, who picked me up in the taxi he'd started driving after his retirement from public life.)

Captain Tony was four decades older than I was, but we'd both spent time growing up in the New Jersey port city of Elizabeth, which Tony fled from when he ran afoul of a local mobster. Key West seemed as far as Tony could get from Jersey, so he settled there, and his lifelong motto was "All you need in this life are a great ego and a tremendous sex drive. Brains don't mean a shit." I always assumed that this notion was original to Tony, and definitive. But recently I came across a remark by Diogenes which goes "I wish I could have a drop of luck rather than a bottle of brains"—and I understood that Tony forgot to mention that all-important good fortune.

Do mermaids bring such luck with them? I'm not sure, but had I indeed spotted a mermaid off the coast of Key West, I would have leaped off my bike and run into the sea, where the mermaid would teach me how to breathe underwater. Maybe she would sing to me my favorite sea shanty, "The Wild Goose," or even the single best pop song ever written about Davy Jones's Locker, the Chills' "Submarine Bells," which contains the concluding benediction "*Deep and dark my submarine bells groan in greens and grays. / Mine would chime a thousand times to make you feel okay...kay...kay...*okay." Then, all our sea songs sung, my wished-for mermaid and I would swim off together and come ashore in Havana, where we'd dry our naked bodies on top of the Malecon seawall and wave to all the locals driving by in their well-maintained fifties-vintage jalopies.

From Havana, we'll swim due north, where we'll make land again at Asbury Park. I spent some happy hours there in "Little Eden" as a child. While cruising around in a candy-apple fuel-injected ragtop Superfly Terraplane loaned to us by my friend Stevie, the mermaid and I will scarf down a saltwater taffy dinner, play miniature golf, get our fortunes read by Madame Marie, and neck under the boardwalk. Then, because mermaids feel "nature's call" like any living creature, we'll pretend to be guests at the Berkeley Carteret Hotel so we can use the lobby's rest rooms.

Still treading water in this Department, here's another couplet from Steve Goodman's great wishing song "Eight Bar Blues": "*Well, I wish I had me a sailing ship that would take me over the sea. / I wish I could talk you into coming home with me.*" Me, I'm not much of a sailor, but I've certainly spent a lot of time trying to "talk people into coming home with me." I wish I could get some of that time back. The people I was trying to seduce probably share this wish.

One more word about sailing. I don't much care for the name "Hugh Williams," yet the next time I'm about to take a sea cruise near the northern coast of Wales, I wish I could close my eyes and automatically legally change my name to "Hugh Williams." Then, once I'm back on dry land, I wish I could close my eyes again and automatically legally change my name back *from* Hugh Williams. Why "Hugh Williams?" Because the sole survivor in each of three historical shipwrecks which took place in that region—in 1664, 1785, and 1860—was named Hugh Williams.

This phenomenon is not merely a Welsh thing, either. In an 1820 boating accident on the Thames, the sole survivor was named Hugh Williams. And in the sinking of a coal barge near Leeds around the same time, *two* men survived, one being a man whose name was Hugh Williams, and the other, his uncle, also bearing the name Hugh Williams.

I wish I hadn't eaten so many "Scotch eggs" in local pubs when I lived in London, "the Smoke," during the eighties. I knew that these boiled eggs wrapped in sausage meat, covered with breadcrumbs, then deep-fried were not healthy for me, but they were just too damn good, and now I fear that if I'm ever stricken by a mysterious illness, an expert will scrutinize my medical chart and inquire, "By any chance did you ever happen to eat something called Scotch eggs in London pubs forty years ago?"

"I'm not crazy about reality," wisecracked Groucho Marx, "but it's still the only place to get a decent meal." The question is, what kind of meal? "Eat food," suggests the writer Michael Pollan. "Not too much. Mostly plants." Sage counsel, this. But I've already made wishes about eating for good health. Time now to wish to eat for pleasure. So may Dame Fortune permit me to take my meals in the style of the bluesman John Lee Hooker. According to a friend of Hooker's, "He always had two gorgeous ladies to the left, two gorgeous ladies to the right. On one side, they're feeding him Junior Mints, and the other side, they're feeding him fish and chips."

Another one of my observations about existence, my Lippy Laws, states, "May we always be as easily contented as our prehistoric ancestors, who believed they'd had a good day if a) they got enough to eat, and b) they didn't get eaten." In spite of this notion, I'm a picky eater, and wish I were more adventurous with what I put into my mouth. One night my wife ate fried grasshoppers and worms at a night market in Bangkok, but I refused to follow her example. I'd had enough exotic cuisine when I sampled a bit of seal meat during a visit to Greenland decades earlier. That meat was just as chewy and as salty as I expected.

Other foods I can't stand to eat are cucumbers, olives, and tomatoes, the last of which I call "the Devil's testicles." (Strangely enough, I like tomato sauce just fine, but the thought of consuming tomato soup, tomato juice, ketchup, and tomatoes themselves make me want to retch.) Green peas are a special case. Although I've never consciously tried them and suspect that they're tasteless, I give green peas a wide berth for some reason I can't fathom. "The Devil's pimples," I call them. Perhaps my green pea aversion has to do with my first job. When I was five years old, my grandfather stood me on a crate before a wooden table in a stock room of the supermarket he owned and then instructed me to "shell" pea-pods for an hour while he spoke with my mother about her ongoing savage custody war with my father.

Yet another of my Lippy Laws is, "We're only two weeks' worth of missed meals away from savagery." So I suppose if I'm really up against it I'll force myself to eat anything—even human flesh, though I'll be sure to ask for Tabasco sauce. Hungry enough, I'll even eat squirrel meat if I have to, fur and bones included, bearing in mind what my friend Harry Crews said about such a meal, which he was forced to consume during his childhood in the Depression-era swamps of Georgia: "Squirrel tastes just like...*chicken*."

Oh, and if I'm ever forced to eat alligator meat, scales and bones included, I'll try to believe what my friend Bob Neuwirth said about consuming such a meal, which he ate once with friends in a Louisiana bayou: "Alligator tastes just like...*dinosaur*."

Which rockets us back to our prehistoric ancestors. Well, almost. The fact that dinosaurs and human beings have never co-existed on this gumball planet disappointed me when I learned it in grammar school, since I'd been wishing even then that I could ride on the back of a Pterodactyl.

I wish I knew what happened to Hog, the bearded old ski bum I met one night in Aspen in the winter of 1983. I guess you could say we "met cute." Hog walked into the men's room at the dance hall Little Nell's where I was currently vomiting into a urinal. (At a nearby restaurant an hour earlier, I had accepted a challenge from friends and eaten nearly the entire Triple Jumbo Hamburger Special.) Unlike the other strangers in that crowded men's room, all of whom understandably turned away from me in revulsion, Hog simply burst into a beery cackle and shouted, "Looks like you ate the *whole horse*, son!" Which amused me enough to buy Hog a shot of George Dickel whiskey. "*Water's for flowers*," goes their promotional jingle, which Hog gladly quoted for me, "*and Dickel's for drinkin'.*"

Feeling much better, but automatically hungry again after vomiting, I came to enjoy Hog's raucous company at Little Nell's. I didn't expect to ever see him again, although he said he drank at this bar every night. But then I did encounter him again. It was the next afternoon at the top of Aspen Mountain, which a thick fog had enveloped. Unable to see my gloved hands in front of my numb cold face, much less my skis on the patch of ground before me, I was afraid of skiing, and so I hung back and wondered how long this "white-out" would last for. Which is when Hog came whizzing off the ski-lift—I recognized his hearty cackle—and slid up right beside me.

Given the impossible visibility, I'm not sure he recognized his drinking buddy from the previous night. But he recognized *someone* standing beside him, and this was enough for him to mutter in my direction, "Might as well be *snow blind* in this soup, huh?"

"When do you think it will lift?" I asked, too concerned about freezing to death on this mountaintop to remind him who I was.

"Fuck knows," said Hog. "Anyhow, this is gonna be *fun*."

"Fun? You mean you're going to *ski* now? *What if...*"

"Son," he said, "do you expect to live forever? 'Shut up and die like an aviator,' that's my favorite saying!"

Then, without another word, he launched himself into the vast blank whiteness. As I listened to the whoosh of his skis as well as his louder-than-ever cackle, I admired his courage, and thought of a quip by Aspen local Hunter S. Thompson: "When the going gets weird, the weird turn pro." Hog's laugh went on for three or four seconds, but suddenly, jarringly, horribly, turned into a scream. The kind of scream emitted by someone who's just encountered big trouble. An abyss, for example.

The white-out lasted another hour before it lifted, and I worried about Hog the whole time. Frozen from my hat to my boots, I skied straight down to the bottom of the mountain and frantically told the ski patrol there about Hog. I hadn't seen him, not a trace of him, on my way down. I didn't see him at Little Nell's that night, either, or any other night that week. Had Hog skied straight into the bony waiting arms of old Stretchfoot, that Assassin of Athleticism? Or was Hog merely playing a prank on me, as my wife believes? I'd be a fool to discount her view, since, whenever we disagree, she turns out to be correct ninety-eight percent of the time while I'm correct only one percent of the time. (Neither of us is correct one percent of the time.)

And I can't even enjoy the one percent of the time when I'm correct because when I gloat about it to Berta, she says, "Now you know how *I* feel ninety-eight percent of the time."

"Famous last words," my mother used to say whenever I made a promise she didn't expect me to keep. Her phrase stuck in my mind, and now I take it literally, wishing that, right before I die, I'll be comfortable and conscious enough to utter some meaningful final statement, something along the lines of James Bond's ironic last words in an Ian Fleming novel: "Tell Mother I was game." Or Colette's even better "*Watch this.*" If I'm in particularly fine fettle when I glimpse my own end in sight, perhaps I can write a "death poem" the way Zen masters like to do: "*This must be / my birthday there / in paradise*" (Joseki), "*Bury me when I die / beneath a wine-barrel / in a tavern. / With luck / the cask will leak*" (Moriya Sen'An), and "*Empty-handed I entered the world / Barefoot I leave it. / My coming, my going—/ Two simple happenings / That got entangled*" (Kozan Ichikyu).

Given a choice, I do wish that my last words would become famous, yet what if I'm not sufficiently conscious before my death to be able to utter any words? Or maybe my last words might be gibberish, the detritus of a scrambled mind on the ultimate brink. Or maybe I'll have something meaningful to impart but my voice will no longer be strong enough to convey anything audible. Or maybe I'll have meaningful and perfectly audible last remarks to make but I'll be dying alone and these remarks will not reach any other ears. In which case, merely *thinking* my famous last words will have to do.

The fear of ambush by bandits at a crossroads has lessened since "the olden days," as we used to call them in the olden days. But being chronically indecisive, I still find crossroads spooky, and also wish I could always know without hesitation which way to go when I arrive at them, whether they're geographical or only metaphorical. I've tried invoking Dame Fortune as well as the Roman goddess Diana, or "Trivia" ("Three Roads"), the patroness of wild things on earth. Alas, I've read that Diana in her day job is Hecate, the world's cruelest sorceress, which might explain why my indecision at all the crossroads I've come to has only increased as I've gotten older. Could it be, as Jim Dodge says, that "The crucial decisions are always too close to call"?

One solution for indecision comes from Luke Rhinehart's novel *The Dice Man*. Rhinehart advises us to roll a pair of dice and commit yourself to follow whatever the dice instruct you to do. My own version of this is also to flip a coin, but *not* to follow its result. Rather, you should make note of your internal reaction at the precise moment when you see whether heads or tails have come up. Now you know what you *really* want, and can act accordingly.

Perhaps, to make matters more interesting, you can use the beautifully decaying dice I've seen displayed at the Museum of Jurassic Technology. Those dice, like all dice, are always rolling. And if dice are unavailable, consider employing the Theory of Sinistrality which you'll find set forth in the novel *The End of the Road* by John Barth. According to this theory, one should always, *always*, no matter what, go to the left at a crossroads. Go left and never again feel indecisive about which direction to take.

As I recall, Barth proposes other theories in his novel. When trying to choose between objects, for example, pick the one whose name comes first alphabetically, and when trying to favor one event over the other, go with the one which popped up first in time. Barth developed still another theory that he told me about himself when I met the author in a Chicago bookstore in the late eighties. He said that a story, any story, needs at least three characters. "Less than three," he stressed, "won't be sufficient."

"So two's not enough company?" I said to him.

Barth shook his bald head. "Three is the least acceptable crowd." He did not elaborate on his rule. Yet I thought of it decades later when I read some advice from a different writer, Kevin Kelly: "Whenever there is an argument between two sides, find the third side."

During my conversation with Barth, his baldness reminded me of how fervently I wish that I myself had not gone bald. My wish became still more fervent after I heard a view expressed by the character Danny the Dealer in the film *Withnail and I*. Danny says, "All hairdressers are in the employment of the government. Hair are your aerials. They pick up signals from the cosmos and transmit them directly into your brain. This is the reason all baldheaded men are uptight."

Feeling downhearted thanks to Danny, I wish I could finally figure out whom I should thank for my hair loss. People say that one's mother's father is responsible, but my maternal grandfather had a full head of curly hair until his heart exploded when he walked into the ballroom of the Waldorf Astoria for a supermarket industry event, whereas my paternal grandfather went bald long before his own damaged heart took him down.

A toupee might solve my problem, but it would only create worse ones, and I've never forgotten an anecdote I've heard about a famous American crooner. A lifelong rug-wearer, he stepped naked from his home shower one day only to find that his young daughter had accidentally walked into his bathroom. Screaming in surprise and embarrassment, he reached with his hands not to cover his bare groin but his bald head.

For my final wish in the tonsorial realm, may anyone who mocks me for my baldness remember the Bible's Second Book of Kings, where a band of thugs mockingly shouted "Hey, baldie" at the hairless prophet Elisha. My fellow baldie "held his mud," so to speak, in the face of all that abuse. Then two female bears happened to emerge from a nearby forest and thoroughly mauled those assholes who'd been crass enough to employ baldness as an insult.

The best definition of pop music comes from the songsmith Yip Harburg, who quipped, "Words make you think thoughts. Music makes you feel a feeling. But a song makes you feel a thought." I wish I could live in the world soundtracked by my favorite tunes. There's the music itself, for one thing: the deepest sense of satisfaction I tend to feel is when I'm hearing a gorgeous melody for the first few times. Comprehending what a singer is singing about is rarely important for me. I speak no Portuguese yet love Jorge Ben Jor's "Pais Tropical," Caetano Veloso's "O Leozinho," Elis Regina's "Aguas de Marco," and Chico Buarque's "La Banda" as much as I would if I were a native Brazilian, just as I treasure the songs of Serge Gainsbourg, especially the randy "Les Succettes," while only understanding a *soupcon* of Gainsbourg's French.

That said, understanding a pop song's lyrics does add a whole other dimension. When they're good, lyrics provide just enough piquant details for you to briefly occupy an intriguing alternate reality. Listen to Camper Van Beethoven's "Eye of Fatima, Part One," for instance. Wouldn't it be fun to hang out with this song's "*cowboys on acid*" in a "*government experiment*" where they "*drive like hell*" and "*eat up some wide-open spaces like it was a cruise on the Nile*"? And don't forget the cowboys' two bottles of tequila stashed in their motel room, not to mention the two cats, the broom, and the fifteen bindles of cocaine tied up in a sack. With a party like that, it's no wonder that the lyric's protagonist tells his "*eighteen-year-old angel*" who's "*all dressed in black*" to "*take the hands off the clock, we're gonna be here awhile.*"

Be cautious, however—too many details in a pop tune might cause you to feel overly hemmed in. And the world evoked by such a song shouldn't seem *too* chaotic: Bob Dylan's "Absolutely Sweet Marie" is a far better number than Al Stewart's "Year of the Cat," but I'd prefer to hang out with Stewart's patchouli-soaked enchantress "*who comes out of the sun in a silk dress running like a watercolor in the rain*" rather than with Dylan's "*railroad men who just drink up your blood like wine.*" Nothing paradisiacal about *those* guys. Even cowboys on acid would know to give such men a wide berth.

I wish I could have wandered around Germany's "Congress of Christs" in 1930, which must have been quite a scene. With Hitler's nascent popularity for some reason encouraging many local madmen to declare that each of them was, in fact, Jesus, the followers they attracted decided to settle the matter of who was the true son of God. They did so by organizing a reckoning that took place one summer night in a meadow in Thuringia. Reading about the Christ Congress, my first thought is, *When Noel Coward sang, "I Went to A Marvelous Party," he wasn't referring to anything like* this.

"You must have known the actual Jesus," I say to Dame Fortune in a dream. "What was he like?"

"He was an outstanding athlete."

"He *what*?"

"You know," says the Dame, changing the subject, "I've been to some marvelous parties myself, places 'where the action is.' One was the party Marina Abramovich organized at the Sundance Film Festival. Being an ace performance artist, she had one rule for her guests: absolutely no talking. Anyone who spoke to anyone else would be commanded by security guards, silently yet firmly, to leave the premises. Fascinating stuff. Imagine how 'loud' all the hand gestures and facial expressions seemed."

"Sort of like a Bar Mitzvah reception for a ninja!"

From behind the dark veil that obscures her face, Dame Fortune smiles at my remark. She says, "Abramovich doesn't always encourage silence, you know—she once exhorted throngs of Norwegians in an Oslo park to shriek their guts out in a tribute to their homeboy, Edvard Munch, and his painting *The Scream*."

Now I'm smiling, and I tell the Dame that I wish that I myself had invented that idea as well as Abramovitch's silent party concept. "*And* I wish," I say, "that I could live my entire life, not just my party-planning, in aesthetically challenging and stimulating ways."

The Dame nods her head. "The ancient Roman Terence famously said, 'Nothing human is alien to me'—so why not go to some invented extremes in order to find out what being 'human' can entail?"

"Right! Why not approach each day the way a performance artist would? And if I temporarily run out of enriching ideas for how to pass my time, I suppose I can fall back on the work of some of Abramovich's fellow performance artists. I'm extremely nearsighted, so why not go out on the town without my glasses or contact lenses, as Laurie Anderson used to do, just to see how fuzzy this life looks without 20/20 vision? Or why not set up a roadblock to stop a municipal bus on its route, force all the passengers to disembark, then ask each of them what their birthday is and wish them well before allowing them to resume their journey, as the novelist Philippe Soupault once did in Paris?"

"Or why not," says the Dame, riffing with me, "carry around with you a pair of scissors which you will use to cut a button off the clothing of everyone you met, as a poet, another Frenchie named Jacques Rigault, did in order to create his own idiosyncratic 'art collection'?"

"I haven't heard about him."

"No?" says the Dame. "Well, Rigault was quite a guy, and another great athlete, like Jesus—although he took his life at age thirty, soon after he'd written, 'There's no reason to live, but there's no reason to die, either. The only way we can still show our contempt for life is to accept it. Life is not worth the bother of leaving it.'"

"What made Rigault change his mind on this matter?"

The Dame shakes her head. "Better you should ask what happened to his 'art collection.'"

"Okay, I will. Are all those buttons still gathered together in one spot? Or have they been scattered to the four winds?"

But I wake up before the Dame can answer.

I wish I weren't so addicted to caffeine—especially when I think about a laboratory experiment in which scientists used an eye-dropper to dose spiders with different consciousness-altering substances. Once those spiders got good and stoned, scientists compared the webs they wove. The scientists had employed hashish, opiates, cocaine, LSD, amphetamines, barbiturates, even the mild-by-comparison caffeine. Guess which one made for the most messed-up webs?

My second most unpleasant experience with caffeine occurred in early 1983, when my friend Jimbo and I, both of us being newly minted fans of Jack Kerouac's novel *On the Road*, decided to begin our winter vacation by taking a Greyhound bus from New York's Port Authority to Fort Collins, Colorado. By the time our "Hound" was crossing Ohio, we realized what a brutal experience this was going to be. You couldn't call any of my memories of that journey good, but I find myself smiling now at many of them:

Nearly getting arrested in the Des Moines bus depot for brushing our teeth in a water fountain. Gazing entranced at an enormous toppled-over Christmas tree in the center of Omaha. Becoming enraged when our bus driver only realized at the end of the Nebraska leg of our trip that he'd forgotten to pick up some cargo at the beginning of the Nebraska leg, so he had to drive all the way back to fetch it, meaning we were forced to be transported across that state three times nearly nonstop. The other passengers, even more outraged than we were, hurled their hot dog wrappers and empty soda cans at the driver as he drove, but he hunkered down at the wheel, ignored the abuse, and got on with his job. In retrospect, I admire his humble nobility.

While wandering around Cheyenne, Jimbo and I noticed that almost every retail store appeared to sell either martial arts supplies or lingerie. Great shopping for sex-mad ninjas, obviously. Even more memorable than this weird capitalistic tableau was the cup of coffee I bought out of a vending machine in Cheyenne's bus station. One sip and I spat it all over my friend Jimbo. He was unpleasantly surprised by this reaction, but he forgave me in time. While I helped clean him up, I thought, *I wish to never put anything in my mouth that tastes a fraction of how disgusting this coffee tastes.*

I didn't know that I would taste something worse—far, far worse—two years later at a truck stop in Claude, Texas. But that's a tale for a different time.

Can I support the democratic system in these United States of ours yet still wish that I could secretly possess more than one vote for my preferred pollical candidates? I started making this paradoxical wish when a woman I met in Orlando in 2004 informed me that she loved John Kerry's policies and hated George W. Bush's policies but would be voting for Bush, anyway, because, she said, "Kerry is so ugly and I know I couldn't bear to see his face on my TV screen for the next however-many years."

During half a dozen election cycles, I have volunteered for my preferred presidential campaigns by working with their phone banks, calling up random citizens to persuade them to vote the way I planned to vote. In effect, I was no better than a telemarketer, and felt guilty about this because, like many of you, I hate telemarketers with a passion. (Most of the telephonic salespeople are robots now, but whenever a live person used to call me, I would tell them, "Hey, you must've made an error, this isn't a regular number but a phone sex line, though no problem, I'll give you a freebie anyway, so listen, I'm naked right now. What are *you* wearing?")

The worst political phone bank experience I had was in the autumn of 2020, when I called people and tried to cajole them into voting my way. There were a few positive responses, not least one woman who said, "I've been offering blowjobs to every Republican man I know, trying to get them to change their votes."

"Whoa," I said. "Are you for real?"

"Yup. A damn good blowjob, *to finish*, if they agree to switch sides."

"Amazing! Any takers yet?"

"Just my dentist. I think his hygienist in the other room figured out what was happening. That guy is *not* quiet."

I said, "And you trust your dentist to honor his promise?"

"Oh, yeah," said the woman. "That *hygienist*, on the other hand—I'm a little worried she's gonna squeal to my fiancé next time he's in there to get his teeth cleaned."

My amusement with this conversation took me a long way, yet the truth is that most of the calls I made were bummers. A woman named Perfidia kept shouting at me, "A thousand times the Trump!" A laughing man claimed that Kamala Harris owed him fourteen dollars because the previous week he'd loaned her that money for a lap dance at a striptease bar near his house. And another guy declared himself "as stoned as a rock, too stoned to vote." When I told him, "You can pull the lever if you're on drugs, you know," the stoner just guffawed and said, "Dude, even if I *were* on the natch, I'd be too lazy to get off this sofa. This sofa is my *starship*. I'm one hundred percent wasted potential."

Most bizarre of all was a man who told me that he hated all Republicans, then added, "And you know who the *worst* Republican in history is, right?"

"Who?" I said. "Reagan?"

"Worse than Reagan."

"Nixon!"

"*Much* worse than Nixon."

"Then who? Who's the worst Republican?"

With genuine vehemence in his voice, the man said, "That cocksucker *Lincoln*."

"Lincoln?" I said, truly startled.

"That's right. Lincoln, the railroad lawyer. You know how many farmers he kicked off their land? Do your research!"

"But Lincoln freed the slaves, right? Shouldn't he get credit for that?"

"Someone *else* would have freed them eventually."

"Okay. And the Civil War, Lincoln *did* win it, right?"

"Wrong! *His generals* won it."

"And the Emancipation Proclama—"

"Rhetoric. Empty rhetoric. Trust me, Lincoln was a *prick*."

Apart from phone-banking, I've attended my fair share of political rallies and protest marches, but I wish I had gone to more, because I believe in the value of showing up for whatever you feel strongly about—win, lose, or draw. I also believe in being creative about how you protest. At a rally against the presidency of a certain Texan frat boy we all remember, I walked around with a homemade sign that read, "I LIKE BUSH—BUT THEN AGAIN, I LIKE HEMORRHOIDS." Having infiltrated a Halloween gathering for the campaign of W.'s father decades earlier, I brandished a pro-Bush sign until I got right in front of the candidate at his podium, at which point I dropped that sign and held up a different one, my *actual* sign, which featured the Halloween themed message "BUSH, YOU *GHOUL*."

Sometimes the display of a political message can go too far. In DC to protest the inauguration of the younger Bush, I noticed a goateed man waving around a professionally printed banner that read, "KILL W." Astonished at the foolhardiness of this, I pulled my cell phone from my pocket and primed the camera, ready to snap a photo of the banner. But the banner-waver was gone. Had he gotten swallowed up by the vast crowd? Or was he spirited away by a team of ninja-like Feds who'd spotted him at the same time I had?

The older I get, the less brave I am about demonstrating for a cause, no matter how passionately I feel about it. In part this is due to an anti-terrorism rally I attended in Paris, where some of my fellow protesters were not protesters at all but troublemakers who attacked me and tried to steal my backpack. Then there was a different time in Paris where I wasn't involved in any "*manifestation*" at all. My seven-year-old son and I had come up the escalator at the Port Royal Metro station and stepped out onto Boulevard Montparnasse, only to find that the big roadway straight ahead of us was eerily empty. No cars, no pedestrians, and no sounds of either. A quick glance to my right, however, and I beheld an anxiously hushed gathering of dozens of fully-armed anti-riot police officers. A quick glance to my left and I beheld an equally anxious silent gathering of hundreds of unarmed protesters, who looked ready to charge the cops.

It was the proverbial calm before the deluge, and this deluge promised to be a humdinger. While I was unaware of what the protesters were protesting that day, I figured out fast that my son and I had arrived right in time to be caught in the middle of a violent clash. Perverse me would have enjoyed finding a safe spot from which to witness the cataclysm, but parental me was now in charge, so I grabbed my son's hand and shouted, "*Run like the devil*!" We'd only gotten to half a block away, at the top of rue d'Assas, when we could hear a great roar and then the fighting.

I wish I could remember every gesture, facial expression, old Hungarian saying, and funny observation that make my wife my wife, plus every contour of her body, and every contour of her spirit. I want to remember all of this so that if Berta leaves me for someone else, or if she leaves me not for someone else but just to be rid of me, or if she doesn't want to leave me but is nevertheless parted from me by Dame

Fortune, then I'll be able to carry around in my mind a replica of her which is close enough to the original that she will appear to remain by my side for as long as the Dame will allow.

For another wish concerning my wife, I would have liked that when she was a girl, she had practiced an ancient Halloween custom of lighting two candles while standing before a mirror and eating an apple. According to this custom, such behavior would have led Berta to behold in the mirror the ghostly image of me, her future husband, gazing back at her. I wish that this custom would have been available to me, too, so that I could have glimpsed Berta's face decades before I met her. And I wish that at our wedding in Manhattan's City Hall, on the wonderfully named "Avenue of the Strongest," we had skipped the boring vows and instead joined our fortunes together in Romany style: by peeing together into a wooden bowl. Since City Hall almost certainly does not provide such bowls, we would have brought our own.

I used to wish I could have been "on the bus," the bus called "Further" which announced that it bore a "WEIRD LOAD," when Neal Cassady drove Ken Kesey and his Merry Pranksters in Further across this nation in 1964. Now, however, I'd prefer to have been a passenger riding a different bus twenty years earlier, the bus in which Samuel Beckett drove the teenaged future wrestler Andre the Giant to school.

Back to Kesey. I like that his little grandchild said when he died, "But now who will teach us how to hypnotize the chickens?" Yet I've always wondered what Kesey meant when he kept invoking the Biblical phrase "sparks fly upward" toward the end of his too-short life. Our mutual friend M. G. told me, "That sparks stuff was probably just something he thought sounded cool." (Prankster credo: "Never trust a Prankster.") Still, because I admire Kesey—he was one of the two or three most charismatic people I've ever met—I want to believe that the phrase had some significance, even profundity.

Then again, maybe I'm confusing charisma with the presence of wisdom. Not for the first time.

Another Kesey-related wish of mine is that he had been wrong when he kept invoking another Prankster credo, "Nothing lasts." Fortunately, I'm now a wee bit more comfortable with impermanence than I used to be. Emerson believed that "Everything looks permanent until its secret is known," and in *Forever Chang-*

es, which is the title of my favorite album by the rock group Love, the word "forever" is meant to be a noun and the word "changes" a verb. This is because the singer's girlfriend had complained when he broke up with her, "But you said you'd love me forever," and he replied, "Forever changes."

How about another example of accepting impermanence? In his novel *Beautiful Losers*, Leonard Cohen, who was himself a kind of merry prankster, wrote, "I change I am the same I change I am the same I change I am the same..." Cohen called those words "the greatest prayer ever learned, the truest of the sacred formulas." Bear in mind, though, that he was given to making such lofty pronouncements. When the dance craze "the Twist" became popular in the early sixties, he called it "the greatest ritual since circumcision."

I wish I knew what Cohen meant when he would go to dine at Moishe's, his favorite steakhouse in Montreal, and always tell the host there, who had the same first name, "They're never going to get us, Leonard." Did Cohen mean that "they," the non-Leonards of the world, would never "get," that is, *understand*, these two Leonards? Or did Cohen mean that they'd never "get," as in *catch*, these two Leonards?

They, they, they! I wish I could identify the mysterious "they" sung about by Tammy Wynette in the KLF song which goes, "*They're justified and they're ancient / And they like to roam the land / They're justified and they're ancient / And they drive an ice cream van.*" Could "they" be those pesky ninjas? Also, I wish I knew for certain who, which "*they*," shot JFK. I used to date a woman who claimed that she and her Cuban ex-boyfriend had met at a Thanksgiving dinner the notorious "shooter on the grassy knoll," a man whose crime was openly known to all his neighbors in Miami's Little Havana.

Actually, having studied the matter a bit, I've come to believe that Oswald acting alone was just as likely a possibility as the involvement of a secret many-tentacled cabal. Take the matter of Oswald's FBI file in Dallas. It went missing right after the assassination, which seems sinister, sure, until you learn that the reason it went missing was because Oswald's case officer panicked—he'd previously deemed Oswald harmless—and burned the thing. Doesn't some hapless dude trying to cover his ass in order to save his career seem more likely than any shadowy conspiracy?

"They," all the rumored cabals, certainly beset us at every turn these days. A taxi driver in Boca Raton has informed me that clouds are made in factories, mountains are the stumps of ancient trees, and the people responsible for cooking up those clouds and cutting down those trees are politicians who are reptiles disguised as human beings. "Against a diseased imagination," wrote Mark Twain, "demonstration goes for nothing." For his part, the US Senator Daniel Moynihan said that "Everyone is entitled to his own opinion but not his own facts." Will this Moynihan quote turn out to be the death knell for our democracy? For sure there's little sense of a shared truth anymore, no bedrock platform for agreement, and without that platform, it all just reduces down to who has more weapons and the willingness to use them. I wish this situation could be turned around, but when did the ugly gunk ever get crammed back into Pandora's Box once that box got opened?

I wish that Charles Portis's *Masters of Atlantis* would be required reading in all high schools. This comic novel portrays just how absurd most conspiracy theories (and organized religion doctrines) are. And I wish everyone would employ "Occam's Razor" when they're trying to solve factual problems. This Razor, which is the observation made by the medieval theologian William of Occam that "Entities should not be needlessly multiplied," basically translates as "Always choose the simplest explanation to what baffles you, unless there's a strong reason to do otherwise." Imagine how fewer false conspiracy theories we'd have clunking around if we all used Occam's Razor. We'd certainly have less "true believers," those scary fanatics who are always off on Grail quests. "And these quests," according to Mick Herron, "tend to get fuelled by the blood of anyone who happens to get in their way." (Herron also notes that "With the internet, you can have a paranoid fantasy at breakfast and a cult following by teatime.")

People, it seems to me, are simply too flawed to bring off complex clandestine secret projects, much less to keep them secret, although a big subset of our citizens believe in those projects because they're too wonder-starved, or gullible, or complexity-seeking, or afraid of pure hazard, to do otherwise. Better to focus on how the obvious perpetrators (plutocrats, mostly, and the government institutions who love those plutocrats' monetary donations) are ripping us off more or less in plain sight.

Ultimately, perhaps, it's best to believe in as little as possible. The way Oscar Wilde views it, "A truth ceases to be true when more than one person believes in it." And the way the author Evan S. Connell, Jr., views it, "To believe is to live by error; each hill unfolds some further valley." But would Brother Occam have agreed with Connell? According to his Razor, the number of valleys must be finite.

One of the most remarkable people I've ever met is the Benedictine monk Brother David Steindl-Rast, who eloquently espouses the practice of "gratefulness." I try to feel grateful for everything, including the afternoon on Kuai when a rainbow slowly constructed itself before my eyes and a different afternoon, this time in West Hollywood, when I stood outside an ice cream shop called "Double Rainbow" and glimpsed overhead an actual double rainbow. I'm glad that I haven't "stepped on a rainbow," which is Kinky Friedman's term for dying. But I wish I could take a toboggan journey on a rainbow and find that waiting beside the pot of gold at its end will be Brother David, who'll say, "Now wasn't that one hell of a ride?"

Related to the rainbow connections is my wish that I would more frequently stop and enjoy good weather as well as my wish to appreciate thunderstorms as much as my wife does. This way, I could sincerely mean it when I sing along with the Motown song "I Wish It Would Rain." And while enjoying a storm with Berta, I would like to say to her what the photographer Ansel Adams told a friend about a thundercloud he watched one day: "I wish it had moved over Tahoe and let loose on you; I could wish you nothing finer."

Nothing finer, unless we can toss a rainbow or two into the mix.

"I Wish It Could Be Christmas Every Day" is the title of a glam-rock song. I much prefer a different glam song, the Mott the Hoople ballad entitled "I Wish I Was Your Mother." Now *there's* a sentiment I appreciate—"*...because then I could have seen you, could have been you as a child.*" The Mott number also features one of pop music's best titles, rivalled only by Mudhoney's "Touch Me I'm Sick."

Another wishing song I love is the Dubliners weeper "I Wish I Was In Carrickfergus." Not to be undone is Rod Stewart, who sings "I Wish I Was Home," by which he probably means Beverly Hills instead of London. Yet the geographical title that's closest to my heart is that of the Tom Waits weeper "I Wish I Was In New Orleans." My friend Roy took the words out of my mouth when he wrote, "Every time I go to New Orleans, I am startled by something." Even the local statuary, perhaps? I wish that the New Orleans city officials who righteously removed the statue of General Robert E. Lee in Lee Circle would have taken my friend Huy's advice and kept intact the name of that city circle by subsequently placing there a statue of the martial artist *Bruce* Lee. Also, isn't it about time that we replace "The Star-Spangled Banner" as our national anthem with George Clinton's Funkadelic song "One Nation Under A Groove"? Wishful thinking, to be sure. But that's my favorite kind of thinking.

W. C. Fields said, "Start every day with a smile and get it over with." Far less cynical than Fields, I begin my days by gazing up at the photograph of myself that I've glued on the ceiling above my bed. It's there so that the first thing I can exclaim is, "*You again*!" Other people's morning rituals sound even more enticing. Eager to emulate G. K. Chesterton, I wish I owned a colored pencil long enough to allow me to loll around in bed and draw on said ceiling. Perhaps, too, I could bang a gong or wear my grandfather's Shriner fez as I rise and shine. Certainly while making coffee in my kitchen, I'll abide by the sign I placed there, a sign I filched once from a New York City sex club, a sign that reads, "PLEASE COVER YOUR LOWER TORSO NEAR THE FOOD BAR."

I like that the great American clown Wavy Gravy prays each morning to "be the best Wavy Gravy I can muster." I like that the poet Paul Valery woke at dawn each day and immediately jotted down whatever came to mind, *bon mots* such as "The universe is a blot on the perfection of non-existence." In his old age, the painter Hokusai drew lions every morning, believing that this activity would lengthen his life. He also signed all his letters with a quickly drawn perfect circle, making a neat contrast with Jean Cocteau, who signed his with his first name and a star. Nevertheless, Cocteau would probably have agreed with Hokusai when he asked, "What could be more serious than laughing when things go wrong?"

For his own awakening ritual, the father of Grace Paley advised her to place her hands on her chest, as if cupping her heart, and then to speak to that organ. "Say anything," he advised, "but be respectful...Maybe say, 'Heart, little Heart, beat softly but never forget your job, the blood.' You can whisper also, 'Remember, remember.'"

As for the master cellist Pablo Casals, he would leave bed and go straight to his piano, where he would play Bach preludes and fugues. At age ninety-three, he said of this morning ritual, "It is a sort of benediction on the house" which "fills me with awareness of the wonder of life, with the feeling of the incredible marvel of being human."

Before she gave up music, my mother had been a master pianist, specializing not in Bach but in Debussy and Ravel. How different would her life have been, and how different mine would have been, if, instead of singing "Rise and Shine" to serenade me out of bed each morning, Esther Lippman had made peace with her long-unplayed piano and sat down at it first thing each morning? Perhaps she would have played "Pavane for A Dead Princess," or "Clair de Lune," or, most appropriately, the Bach number "Sleepers Awake."

"Start a huge, foolish project, like Noah did. It makes absolutely no difference what people think of you." I wish I could remember this advice from Rumi whenever people insult me. Or merely when they fail to return my phone calls, text messages, or emails. Despite my advanced age, I still find it a challenge to extinguish childish thoughts of "getting even" with people who've done me wrong; my first impulse is always to turn the Furies loose on my enemies. Big enemies, or just the guy who cut the refreshments line at a sports stadium recently and yelled "Fuck you" at me when I told him, "Nobody loves a cutter." As a punk rock homily has it, "We were not born with enough middle fingers."

I justify my vengeful impulses by recalling a magazine essay I read once (not in *Soldier of Fortune*, either, but in *The New Yorker*) which argued that a deep hunger for revenge may be coded into the human psyche. Coded or not, we do always have a choice about how to respond to provocation. An author named Violet Weingarten penned a couplet I find helpful to ponder whenever someone has wronged me: "*Is life too short to be taking shit / or is life too short to be minding it?*"

While this question suggests no definite answer, our response necessarily depends upon who we are—and the specific context and details concerning the shit that's been "done" to us. Sometimes we shouldn't take that shit, no, and other times we shouldn't mind it. It's up to each of us. Yet perhaps a higher-level approach to the matter, one proposed by my Uncle Wolf, is to refuse to automatically perceive "shit" as shit. As Janwillem van de Wetering writes in his Amsterdam

Cops novel *The Blond Baboon*, "Calamities are only calamities if you define them as such; in reality, there are only events and all events can be useful."

Whether you're with Wolf and van den Wetering on this or not, everyone should agree that throwing a hissy fit is always bad news. Why? Because the pleasurable release we feel at the instant we explode in rage usually functions in direct proportion to the damage we're doing to ourselves and, oh yeah, to others. As Wolf has told me more than once, losing one's temper means automatically losing whatever conflict we're engaged in. "The more like a child the other person behaves," he concludes, "the more like an adult *you* should act."

Following my uncle's suggestion, I've decided to renounce most of my "graveyard grudges," my wishes for payback against my few enemies. Why? Well, payback can be hazardous. For one thing, evil wishes can have a boomerang effect—*honi soit* and all that. Take a look at Susan Mary Aristides, who married into the Dridbrakos crime family in Greece and became their ferociously violent chief enforcer. One day while Ms. Aristides was seated in her car with a homemade bomb that she intended to use to kill some rogue Dridbrakos soldiers, her Rottweiler accidentally sat on the device and detonated it, blowing both human and canine to atoms. Either Aristides loved that pooch too much to leave him home while she went on her assassination run, or she couldn't find a dog sitter. In any event, it's always the little things you don't count on that screw you up, isn't it? A tired canine ass, for instance.

Another reason to eschew seeking vengeance is that it's emotionally healthier. As Mark Twain pithily put it, "Anger is an acid that can do more harm to the vessel in which it is stored than to anything on which it is poured." Which invites us to consider the subject of forgiveness. Doesn't the poet David Whyte make a smart point when he says, "To forgive is to assume a larger identity than the person who was first hurt"?

I wish I could assume that larger identity and thereby remember that everyone has their cross to bear. Some drag it along with them, while others pay servants to carry it on their behalf. Some hide it, while others are only too eager to perversely show off their cross. But do not doubt that in the end everybody will feel a cross's weight. And for those fortunate few who do not bear such a burden right now, rest assured that their cross is currently being hammered together in Dame Fortune's great karmic workshop. Or is already being delivered.

Speaking of crosses, the Gnostics believed that a holy figure named Simon the Divine Syrian willed himself to resemble Jesus and then took Jesus's place when it was crucifixion time. I wish that someone, anyone, would be willing to perform a similar charitable act on my behalf. Incidentally, finding the exact spot of Golgotha, or Calvary—the so-called "Skull" where Jesus was crucified—became a low-grade obsession for me two decades ago when I visited Jerusalem. One afternoon, I stood looking across a ravine at a skull-shaped cliff and felt a pang, thinking, This *was where it was when it happened.* But I wish I knew for sure.

I also wish that we could know who Jesus's father was. His genetic father, I mean. Perhaps the legend I've read about, the one in which a Roman legionnaire whose nickname was "*Pantera*," or the Panther, impregnated Mary, whose actual name was Miriam, was true. If so, how did the legionnaire get his nickname? Did he rape Miriam? I'd prefer to believe they were in love but then the Panther got posted somewhere else in the empire and so was unable to remain with her and their half-Roman child. Whatever the story was, did Miriam bear any hard feelings toward the Panther? And did Jesus?

Which brings us around again to forgiveness. Let's consider the related matter of *self*-forgiveness. When someone asked the theater director Harold Clurman, "What do you do when you've done something unforgivable?" he smartly replied, "Forgive myself." "YOUR INNER CRITIC IS A BIG JERK," according to a graffito I saw in a toilet stall in Austin, Texas, while cognitive therapists encourage us to "Dare to be average." Meanwhile, Japanese people recommend that we learn the concept of "*wabi sabi*," which entails not only accepting but *valorizing* imperfections. I like how they will declare out loud the word "*Shimata*," meaning "I have made a mistake," whenever they do so. I sure wish I had me some of that *wabi sabi* and *shimata* stuff. Just as I wish I could be less of a perfectionist in many areas of my life.

Don't get me wrong, there are ample reasons to expect a lot from yourself. Of all people, it was the big-time hedonist Baudelaire who quipped, "Work is less boring than amusing oneself," while the composer Igor Stravinsky observed that "Inspiration is like a baby—you have to sit it on the pot every morning." (Two months after I passed this Stravinsky quotation on to my rock star friend Benny Pompa, I heard Benny repeat it during a radio interview, claiming he'd made it up himself. Which taught me to expect less of him.) Finally, there has been no greater hymn to industriousness than the essayist Thomas Carlyle's call to "Produce! Produce!...Out with it, then. Up, up! Whatsoever thy hand findeth to do, do it with thy whole might. Work while it is called Today; for the night cometh, wherein no man can work."

With night indeed descending, I can make the argument that "playing," or "not working too hard," are better strategies for fulfillment than "producing, producing, producing." Not everything worth doing is worth doing right—or doing twice, or practicing beforehand, or even finishing once you've started. "If at first you don't succeed," said the poet Ogden Nash, "the hell with it." What sheer relief to feel entitled to an indolent life. According to the comedian Steven Wright, "Hard work pays off in the future. Laziness pays off now." In the end, let's give the last word, or the last few words, to the psychoanalyst D. W. Winnicott, who spoke of the virtues of the "good enough mother." Beautiful words those are, too, for what could be more perfect than fully accepting—and not merely accepting but embracing—our averageness, our failures, our being merely "good enough"?

I wish I could deem myself good enough. Alas, I'm not willing to work hard enough to do that.

SIX. IMPRACTICAL WISHES

One day in the eighties, a dog ran past the writer Lucy Sante in Manhattan's East Village. This dog had a dollar bill in its mouth and was followed seconds later by "a fat man (who) came puffing by in hot pursuit." During this decade, I lived on Manhattan's Upper East Side, but I wish I'd lived in the East Village instead, because to listen to Sante, it was a realm of cool enchantments. Squalid enchantments, but enchantments nevertheless.

Sante lived among armed militants, teenaged stereo thieves, purveyors of "jazz cigarettes," a woman who resembled Billie Holiday, and a "celebrated peddler called John the Communist." No such citizens lived on the Upper East Side during the eighties. And I certainly never witnessed there a sight like what Sante witnessed in the East Village when everyone who walked past her, "every man, woman, and child, was wearing an identical Kenny Rogers T-shirt." "Few of them," added Sante, "would have figured among the singer's target audience." She suspected that these shirts were all purloined from the same source and widely distributed. My own guess is that a case of mass Kenny Rogers hysteria had broken out that day. Perhaps great throngs continue to worship the corny, white-bearded crooner even now.

Welcome to Bohemia. It's the floating-around place where, as the novelist Herbert Gold says, people are "stubbornly devoted to demonstrating that life really is what good sense tells us it is not." The only time I ever lived in a hipster hotspot, a place where cultural energies were at maximum overdrive, was in the early nineties, when I lived in Miami's South Beach. Surrounded by young fashion models and the middle-aged Eurotrash hustlers who loved them as well as old Jewish people who sat playing gin rummy on the patios of their beautifully decaying Art Deco hotels, I knew I wasn't on the boring Upper East Side anymore.

The actor Mickey Rourke lived in South Beach then, and so did Gianni Versace, and every day I'd rub shoulders with Cuban *santeria* practitioners, exotic Latin American tourists, and boxer friends at the Fifth Street Gym, where I worked out. (While sparring I tried to honor the advice of Jack Handey, who urged boxers "not to let the other guy's glove touch your lips, because you don't know where that glove has been.") Near the gym was an eccentric art gallery owned by my lawyer friend Sergio. Showing there were singular local artists like Ras Kimmy, Cesar the Brazilian hippie, and Billy Contino. The last was a leonine fellow who told me one day that no one would be allowed to call him "Billy" anymore. From this moment onward, he insisted, people must address him as nothing but "Contino."

Unfortunately, given how pretentious he was, I never thought to tell Contino the world's shortest joke, which is "Pretentious? *Moi*?" And, unfortunately, every time I saw this name-wisher at a bar called "Don't Say Sandwich To Me," I'd call him "Billy" by mistake, which made him increasingly angry. "There's no *Billy* anymore," he'd say. "I wish you'd stop *forgetting*, man—there's just *Contino*. Get it?"

As fun as South Beach was, I wish I could have lived in other, even cooler hotspots. In this, I'm emulating my friend Bob Neuwirth, who'd been part of, and was usually at the *center* of, every international Bohemian scene from the late fifties onward. Or so I thought. Turns out that no one's ever completely satisfied. One afternoon at Souen, the health food restaurant in the West Village where Bob and I used to have lunch, I asked him if there was any hip scene that he'd missed. I expected this boss king of groovers to answer in the negative. But what Bob said, after considering my question, said, "Yes. One. Beirut in the early sixties."

"*Beirut*?"

"Yeah. I really wish I could have hung out there then. I hear it was *fantastic*."

I know that a life full of surprises tends to be richer than one that isn't. And I know that the best approach as to lemons, those unpleasant surprises, is to lemonade-ize them. Still, I wish that the kidney stone I began to call "Stanley" had not showed up inside me one afternoon last year and ultimately needed to be removed by a very intimate brand of surgery. Forget lemonade—not even morphine could abate the agony that Stanley caused me for a few weeks there. And forget about the title of the Country-and-Western song "I'd Rather Pass a Kidney Stone Than Another Night With You"—my pain made me crawl across the Emergency Room floor and beg the doctor who finally agreed to see me for a better drug than the Big M. Damn his eyes for replying, "After today you'll have to make due with Tylenol—any opioid would constipate you." As if pain-riddled me, the me in Stanley's grip, could give a shit about constipation!

At least the morphine he gave me furnished some good reveries. While a TV in my hospital room improbably played the 1940s noir film *Laura*, I imagined bribing some acupuncturist to poke his needle far into my belly, spear Stanley with it, and then offer that stone to me in the clear light of the treatment room. After which, I'd go home and use Stanley as a ping pong ball the next time my wife and I play table tennis. Or I'd put my kidney stone up for sale online but list Stanley at a price that no oligarch could afford. Or I'd buy myself a jug of some drug even better than morphine, an elixir marked as "the milk of Heaven," then dip Stanley into it and suck on him as if he, like our planet, were a gumball.

A milk of Heaven gumball will be especially helpful if a new and maybe larger kidney stone begins to form in my belly. This time it'll be a she, I feel certain. I've already chosen a name for her.

The irresistibly titled "John Wayne Is Big Leggy" may not be a wishing song, but it's piquant for me, all the same, because the first time I recognized how tall a human being could be (and how short I was by comparison) happened when I was eight years old and met that "big leggy" mythic cowboy actor himself. As I gazed up at "the Duke's" toupee-topped block of a head, I said, being an ass-kisser even then, "Mr. Wayne, on behalf of the American public, I'd like to thank you for the many years of entertainment you've given us." I didn't know yet what a right-wing fanatic he was; all I was thinking about, apart from the fact that I was meeting my first celebrity, was how gigantic he was.

I never wished I could be taller than I did one night in Toronto when my wife and I strolled past a store called "A Small Man's World." The place sold clothes, according to their sign, "FOR GUYS WHO ARE 5'8" AND UNDER." Because I'm 5'8" myself (actually, 5'7", but of course I round up), I felt poorly treated by the store's mission. Why couldn't "A Small Man's World" sell clothes for "GUYS WHO ARE 5'7" AND UNDER?," thus making my height average?

"At least," said Berta, witnessing my glumness and trying to cheer me up, "you're the tallest man in this Small Man's World."

How tall do I wish I were? Let's say six feet and two inches. My friend Ray is that height and seems to bear it well, although Ray and I hung out once with a guy who was 6' 8", and afterward Ray told me that his neck felt sore because he was not accustomed to looking up at people while speaking. Incidentally, the first night I met Ray, back in 1997, he told me that he'd been friendly with Joe Strummer, the lead vocalist of the Clash.

"I *love* the Clash," I said. "Been into them ever since the day when I was fifteen and put their song 'Janie Jones' on my turntable and immediately started bopping. I even went to see their film *Rude Boy* the second or third day it was screening in New York in 1980."

Ray smiled. "Did you like *Rude Boy*?"

"You *bet* I did. The only problem was that movie focused way too much on the Clash's roadie, whatever his name was. Who gave a fuck about some pimply, gawky *oaf*? What a waste of celluloid that dipshit roadie was responsible for!"

By now Ray's smile had turned into laughter, which puzzled me until I finally grasped why this man had looked slightly familiar to me when we were introduced. "Oh, *no*," I said.

"Oh, *yes*, mate."

Fortunately, this former Clash roadie I had just unknowingly insulted did not take offense at me. Tall as he was, and muscular, as well, Ray could have smooshed me like a ladybug—although, as every schoolchild knows, Dame Fortune frowns on those who smoosh ladybugs. They're for appreciating, and making wishes, not for smooshing.

Whenever I listen and dance to "Naughty Boy" by Pan Ron and "Have You Seen My Love?" by Ros Serey Sothea and so many other supremely joyful Cambodian pop songs from fifty years ago, I wish I could travel back in time to 1975 and somehow rescue these artists and their comrades from the Khmer Rouge. That beastly regime slaughtered them all. An entire young and talented generation was gone at once in a genocide. It should go without saying that I wish I could rescue from death all genocide victims—past, present, and future.

But let's stick with popular music, and journey to a night during the late sixties at "Steve Paul's The Scene" nightclub in New York City. While Jimi Hendrix was doing an after-hours jam, Jim Morrison ran onstage to drunkenly and annoyingly goof around with Jimi. Which led Janis Joplin, who had also been sitting in the audience and felt outraged by Morrison's behavior, to run onstage and defend the guitarist. (I know this is how it occurred because my friends Danny and Maureen were each in the audience that night and separately reported the same tale to me.) Because she was as drunk as Morrison was, Janis whomped him on the head with her bottle of Southern Comfort, so he turned his violent attention toward her, and then the three of them, Joplin, Morrison, and Hendrix, wound up rolling around on the stage in a three-way wrestling match.

The public inebriation of artists is, of course, run-of-the-mill. As Ken Kesey noted, "When the king asked Mozart why he drank so much, Wolfgang said, 'King, rock'n'roll is hot, dry work.'" But the image of that writhing pile of rock musicians haunts me because all three of them, Joplin, Morrison, and Hendrix, would die young within a few years of that night.

I would have saved them if I could have, would have prevented their fatal drug overdoses, just as I wish I could have prevented Buddy Bolden from going insane. And prevented Robert Johnson from sipping at that poisoned whiskey bottle in the Three Forks roadhouse. And prevented Hank Williams from climbing into the back seat of his Cadillac. And prevented Buddy Holly, the Big Bopper, and Richie Valens from boarding their little airplane. And prevented Patsy Cline from boarding that other plane. And prevented Eddie Cochran from "catching that cab." And prevented Sam Cooke from tussling with that female motel manager who had a shotgun. And prevented those gangsters from beating up Bobby Fuller and then force-feeding him a canister's worth of gasoline. (Unlike in Fuller's song "I Fought The Law," this time Johnny Law failed to win.) And prevented Brian Jones from diving into that swimming pool ("No Stones without Jones," my friend Maria says). And prevented Gram Parsons from checking in as a guest at the Joshua Tree Inn. And prevented Elvis Presley from sitting on that fancy toilet seat. And prevented Elliott Smith from picking up that kitchen knife. And prevented Brian Wilson, Syd Barrett, and Skip Spence from taking too much LSD. And saved Sinead O'Connor from the hellhound on her trail.

Hell, I even wish I could have saved the very first rock star, ancient Greece's lyre-shredding Orpheus, from getting torn to pieces by the very first rock music fans. At least Orpheus's severed head ended up dispending useful wisdom and the gods transformed his lyre into a constellation.

What a heartbreak, a cliché but nevertheless a heartbreak, that these artists never got to live full lives. And how heartbreaking it is to think of all the music they never got to make. Music we never got to hear. I met a lovely elderly woman once, and only later did I learn that she was Kurt Cobain's mother. For her sake as well as her son's sake, and for all of ours, I wish I could have saved that young man, too.

The poet Juan Ramon Jimenez wrote of his beloved donkey, "Every so often Platero stops eating and looks at me. Every so often I stop reading and look at Platero." This is how it is with me and my dog Rosalita—except that I stop reading and look at her more often than she stops eating and looks at me. How I wish that Rosalita could understand what my wife and I are saying to her. Not the usual endearments, which Rosalita can already probably figure out from our body language, facial expressions, and murmurs of "Good girl" and "That's right" and "Drop it," but the more complicated and important stuff, like "The reason we had to get your stomach pumped at the veterinary hospital in the middle of the night was because chocolate is dangerous to your health and when you ate the Hershey Bar that I accidentally left in my unzipped-up backpack we were worried about you."

At the same time, I wonder if Rosalita harbors a similar communication wish herself—if she has complicated, critical information she needs to share with us, information she's forced to convey with only barks and growls and whimpers that give us no sense of what thoughts are buzzing on inside her small skull. Perhaps she'd say something useful, as does the canine in a Grateful Dead song: "*I ran into Charley Phogg. / He blacked my eye and he kicked my dog. / My dog, he turned to me, and he said: / 'Let's head back to Tennessee, Jed.'*"

Or perhaps if Rosalita could speak, she would describe how she feels by quoting Robert Mitchum's metaphor about his career in Hollywood: "I'm a tall dog on a short leash. The leash is long enough to let me up the wall, but if I try to jump off to the other side, I'm hanged."

Here come a pair of wild geese waddling across my lawn. Last night a local fox snatched away two of their young, cute tiny goslings which these parents had nurtured and protected for two weeks. What are the adult geese thinking this morning, now that their offspring are gone forever? Is it grief, or just a vague sense of loss, or something less than either? And will whatever they're feeling fade before tomorrow, fade to the point where there's no memory at all? Are these speculations germane, or are geese thoughts so alien from our own thoughts that our language can't begin to approach what's going on in their minds?

I'm not the only one with such questions. A child named Nancy asks God in a letter, "Do animals use you or is there someone else for them?" I don't know, but I wish that we could remember that each individual non-human creature has its own personal nature if not its own personality. Also, as the writer Margaret Renkl points out, "Many of the qualities that we think of as uniquely human aren't unique to us at all. Crows play in the snow. Honeybees exhibit empathy, even to bees that belong to a different colony. Elephants call one another by name. (So do dolphins and bats and who knows how many others.) More than 1500 different species of animals engage in same-sex sexuality. Cows enjoy music. A dog that I know of watches musicals on television."

Maybe Renkl wishes, as I do, that Dame Fortune would persuade Merlin, from T. H. White's novel *The Sword in the Stone*, to do to us what that world-class mage did to Arthur, the boy with Camelot in his future. That is, to transplant our consciousness into that of different animals. How fascinating would it be to spend an hour, or even a few minutes, inhabiting the mind and body of a different mammal! My dog Rosalita, for instance, or a fish, or a reptile, or, let's go for broke here, a flower or a tree? What would it be like to perceive the world—*temporarily*, let me stress (if I can't return to my own consciousness and body with a vivid memory of it all, then let's strike out this wish)—the way a different living being does?

If Merlin is unavailable, ditto Dame Fortune, then I suppose I could transform into an animal by getting proactive and making myself a werewolf, or a were-goose, or a were-fox. The problem is that the traditional methods for changing into such creatures are not available to me. I'm not "the seventh son of a seventh son," for example. And even if they were available, most of them sound distasteful. I'd rather not wear a creature's pelt, or get bitten by an already existing shape-shifter, or drink a perfect stranger's blood.

Another potential problem: Because nature is inevitably "red in tooth and claw," I might be forced to be a predator, something like a goblin shark, which can knock out cold its prey with a lightning-quick jaw-thrust, or a spinner shark, which twirls around inside schools of fish, biting continually as it moves. Thanks, but no thanks. I'd prefer to have a cushy ride as an animal. Perhaps I can travel back to ancient Egypt and spend some hours as Petsuchos, the living crocodile who embodied the crocodile god Sobek. Until its death, when it got embalmed, mummified, and replaced by a different member of its species, Petsuchos was given some seriously divine treatment, getting fed and played with and dressed up more than any other being in Egypt except for Pharaoh.

As the joke goes, I wish I could track down the people who invented sex and ask them what they're working on now. It still amazes me how even the most enlightened of human beings are still essentially enslaved to their libidos, though less so as they age. *The Dhammapada* tell us, "People are prey to desire only because they do not see things as they are," while G. K. Chesterton has his own wisdom to offer, saying, "The moment we have snapped the spell of conventional beauty, there are a million beautiful faces waiting for us everywhere, just as there are a million beautiful souls."

Let's talk about sex. I wish that my libido had not been so significantly influenced by furtive pubescent peeks at copies of *Playboy* and *Penthouse* magazines. The first thing I did after my prudish and puritanical mother died was pay for subscriptions to both. Only decades later did I fully grasp how the unrealistic presentations of those centerfolds had skewed my sense of female attractiveness. Some label sex as "the repetitive act that never feels repetitive," although the filmmaker Elaine May might have differed—she supposedly swore off sex with the explanation of "I already did that." (One strange night early in this century, some friends and I accompanied May and her filmmaker boyfriend Stanley Donen to a striptease club in Manhattan, where I bought lap dances for Donen while May chatted with the strippers. What events led us to a striptease club? That's a tale for a different time.)

Please note that I do not wish to follow Bob Dylan's lead when he sings, "*Feel like falling in love with the first woman I meet / Putting her in a wheelbarrow and wheeling her down the street*." Even if I wished so, the woman would have to consent to being wheeled, of course—and be willing to let us switch places, too. The one time a woman playfully pushed me around in a wheelbarrow (in fact, it was a shopping cart),

I cherished the experience even after she lost control of the cart and I rolled, helpless, into traffic on Miami Beach's Ocean Drive, gritting my teeth as I gazed wild-eyed at an oncoming sports car.

Brian Eno has asked, "Do all men leave this life feeling they've seen nowhere near enough nude people, played with far too few private parts…and generally not fulfilled their once extremely promising sexperimental destiny?" Probably so, and this observation likely applies to women even more than men. (Karl Kraus aphorized that "Female desire is to male desire as the epic is to the epigram," while Linda Gail Lewis sang, "*Dear, I swear I'll love you until the very end / But I don't plan on sticking around if it's just to be your friend.*") In this vein, I wish I could convince myself that loneliness is preferable to conducting a romance with the wrong person. Think of the lovers in A. R. Ammons' poem "Their Sex Life," the entire text of which is "*One failure on / Top of another.*"

Fortunately, avoiding venomous people in all kinds of relationships, not just the romantic sort, has seemed to have gotten easier for me as I've grown older. But maybe wisdom mostly derives from becoming observant enough over time to recognize recurring patterns and then to consciously avoid the negative ones.

Here she is again, turning up where I least expect her. This time she's in "Fortuna Court," a tiny square in my wife's Hungarian hometown of Veszprem. The so-called "City of the Queens" is not a remote locale—Iggy Pop recently played a steamer of a rock concert nearby—but I'm still surprised to bump into the queenly Dame Fortune in Veszprem in the form of a larger-than-life sized bronze statue holding in her left hand an open shell. I stand in front of the statue, straining to glimpse what's inside that shell, and once I recognize what it is, I have to laugh. It's neither the scales of justice nor the Wheel of Fortune. No, it's a miniature reproduction of Dame Fortune herself. A reproduction, that is, of this very statue. And the left hand of the reproduction of the statue is no doubt clutching an even smaller-scale reproduction of the Dame, so it's down to the quantum level she goes. Which suggests *what*? That one scrap of fortune is contained within another, and this in turn is contained within another?

One of my favorite outdoor stone sculptures is located atop a hip-high garden wall in the same Hungarian city. Resting on the back of a supine lion is a boy who clutches a cell phone and peers at it intently. The boy looks cozy yet I wish I could shout into his unhearing ears, "Dude, put down that gizmo! You're lying on a lion's back! Isn't that cooler than anything your phone can show you?"

Reclining on a big cat's back reminds me of the time I was speaking on the phone with my friend Harry Crews. He was old and ailing by then, but he had a new girlfriend who was younger than he was. As we spoke, Harry was watching her take a shower and reporting to me how much the sight of it excited him—how gorgeously the water went cascading down the curves and planes and extrusions of his lover's body. What a triumph for Harry, although a credo of his was, "Survival is triumph enough."

"Well," I said to my friend, "*ride the tiger*!" I use this expression as a response to anyone who reports that Dame Fortune has bestowed upon them a welcome new blessing.

"Oh, *yeah*," said Harry in his thick Georgia accent which got brewed in the Okefenokee Swamp. "I'm gonna dig my fingernails deep in that tiger's smelly pelt, I'm gonna hold on like a rodeo champ, and *nothing* that sumbitch does is gonna buck me off its back. I got that tiger by the *tail*, blood, I got that tiger in my *tank*..."

Remembering how Harry elaborated on my advice to "Ride the tiger" makes me wish he was still among us. And I wish that I could ride an actual tiger, provided that Harry would be there with me on that tiger's back, seated in front so I could hang onto him while he hangs onto the tiger and we have ourselves one last adventure together.

Who hasn't at some time wished to "run away with the circus"? Tom Robbins famously wrote, "It's never too late to have a happy childhood." Grandma Moses said, "I had always wanted to paint but I just didn't have the time until I was seventy-six." And may I never grow too old to be creative, to have a happy childhood, and even to join a carnival. If I do join one, I wish I could be like Mr. Electrico, whose meetings with the twelve-year-old Ray Bradbury are recounted by the author during an interview. According to Bradbury's description of Mr. Electrico's circus act, the performer sat in an electric chair with a sword. Then, said Bradbury, Mr. Electrico "touched everyone in the front row, boys and girls, men and women, with the electricity that sizzled from the sword. When he came to me, he touched me on the brow, and on the nose, and on the chin, and he said to me, in a whisper, '*Live forever*.' And I decided to."

Elsewhere in my wish list, I've mentioned my desire to be struck by lightning, provided that no harm comes to me with the lightning strike. If I could be Mr. Electrico's heir, this would be even better. Pretty fantastic, too, would be the ability to eat fire, swallow swords, and possess the multiple carnival skills of one Melvin Burkhart, who died at age ninety-four in 2001. Burkhart's skills were varied. Billed as "The Human Blockhead," he could sustain deep icepick stabs in his skull without flinching. Billed as "The Anatomical Wonder," he could inflate each of his lungs separately. And billed as "The Two-Faced Man," Burkhart could frown with half of his face and smile with the other half. Most of all, I wish I could do that two-faced thing. I wouldn't need to join a circus to find it handy.

In "The Straight Life," a lovely wishing song, the Walter Mitty-esque narrator is eager to "leave the straight life behind" and live out his bohemian fantasies. (What is the character Walter Mitty in James Thurber's famous short story, by the way, if not the Great American Daydream Believer, which also sort of makes him the Great American Wisher?) The composer of "The Straight Life" is Sonny Curtis, a guitar-slinging West Texan running buddy of Buddy Holly. Would you believe that Curtis also wrote such radically different pop numbers as the aforementioned outlaw anthem "I Fought the Law" and the theme song to TV's *The Mary Tyler Moore Show*, "Love Is All Around"? The latter song never fails to remind me of my mother, a woman as beautiful as Moore who, before Dame Fortune turned against her, "*could turn the world on with her smile*."

Prolific as all-get-out, Curtis even wrote a silly tune called "Holiday For Clowns," which ought to be the theme song for my acquaintance Wavy Gravy, the great American clown who calls laughter "the valve on the pressure cooker of life...Either you laugh at stuff or you're going to end up with your beans on the ceiling." Another renowned clown I have known is Slava Polunin, a Russian who puts on a fabulous "Snow Show" and has founded an "Academy of Fools." Polunin likes to say, "Fantasy is only a premonition of reality—dreams are meant to come true." Dame Fortune is unlikely to agree with this notion, but Polunin might not believe in her, or at least not consider her necessary to make his wishes happen.

All clowning aside, my latest wish is an odd one. I wish that Sonny Curtis would have composed not only "I Fought the Law" and his other hits but also all the other pop songs I hold closest to my heart. Why this wish? Because I'm thinking how neat it would be if one person who's already created such diverse material could stretch out even more, penning so many other top tunes.

Better yet, let's make this magically prolific genius songwriter not Mr. Curtis but Kirsty MacColl, another great artist who, unlike Curtis, died young. (She'd been diving around a reef near Cozumel when a Mexican oligarch's illegally speeding powerboat ran her over, killing her instantly. Justice for Kirsty!)

According to my wish, then, it was Kirsty MacColl who wrote Jerome Kern's "The Way You Look Tonight," Donovan's "The Love Song," Kate and Anna McGarrigle's "Complainte Pour Ste. Catherine," Jimmy Van Heusen's "Moonlight Becomes You," Spirit's "Morning Will Come," Damien Rice's "Older Chests," Love's "Between Clark and Hillsdale," the Wrens' "Ex-Girl Collector," Rodgers and Hart's "You Are Too Beautiful," Joni Mitchell's "Both Sides, Now," the Geraldine Fibber's "California Tuffy," Toots and the Maytals' "Sweet and Dandy," "Craise Finton Kirk" by the Bee Gees, "Wedding Bell Blues" by Laura Nyro, "Poor Boy (The Greenwood)" by ELO, Cole Porter's "You're the Top," Aretha Franklin's "I Say a Little Prayer," "Madame George" by Van Morrison, "The Tuba Song" by Michael Friedman, Fairport Convention's "End of a Holiday," Moby Grape's "805," Rickie Lee Jones's "Stewart's Coat," the Left Banke's "Walk Away Renee," "Daydream Believer" by John Stewart, "Pile ou Face" by Corynne Charby, Zumpano's "Momentum," "Pamela Brown" by Tom T. Hall, "Taking Up Space" by the Cavedogs, Bruce Springsteen's "For You," "Diamond Meadows" by T. Rex, the Carpenters' "Top of the World," "Saying Goodbye" by The Muffs, "Graduation Day" by the Beach Boys, "Give Us Bubblewrap" by Half Man Half Biscuit, 10,000 Maniacs' "Arbor Day," "The Girl I Can't Forget" by Fountains of Wayne, "I'm Sticking With You" by the Velvet Underground, the Nitty Gritty Dirt Band's "Collegiana," "I Don't Wanna Die" by Jeff Rosenstock, and Henry Mancini and Johnny Mercer's "Moon River."

The last ballad on this song list never fails to remind me, once again, of my mother. If only Dame Fortune could have been kinder to

Esther Lippman by giving her a "Huckleberry friend" or by giving her a peek, just a peek, at that "rainbow's end." Then again, maybe, as the light dimmed all around Esther, the Dame did step out of the shadows to provide that friend. Maybe she'd provided that peek, too.

In the third grade, I was my class's spelling bee champion, but the following year I was undone by misspelling the word "subpoena." (Owing to my parents' then-raging custody war over me, I knew how to spell "affidavit" and other legal terms, but not the "s" word.) I wish my reign as champ never ended. What I really wish, though, is that I had not accepted a challenge from Philip, our class bully, hours after my defeat.

"Bet you can't spell my name," he shouted.

"Easy," I said. "F-I-L-I-P."

The mocking laughter followed me home. Which was not unfamiliar, because back in my school days, I got bullied a bit. At the same time, however, I bullied some of my classmates, so I guess you can say that I saw "both sides of the Jordan River." Fortunately, I no longer wish, at least not daily, to take revenge on my bullies. I do wish I could apologize to those classmates whom I bullied, although I fear that before I get to do so, they will take *their* revenge on *me*.

The older I get, the more I hate bullies—and what are tyrants, whether political, theocratic, or corporate, if not bullies on a grand scale? Those petty brats with their oversized cruelties, as well as their like-minded followers, have been making chopped-meat of this gumball planet for too long. What a tongue-lashing I wish I could give the world's current despots! Maybe I'd box their ears, too, and pluck their suspenders like rubber bands, and kick a groin or two. Tellingly, however, I was once seated on an airplane next to France's boss Fascist Marine Le Pen, and instead of saying a single rude word to her, I felt relieved when I was able to change my seat to somewhere else in the cabin. So much for bully-beater me.

With bullies in charge, as the novelist Philip Roth observed about nations behind "the Iron Curtain," "Nothing goes and everything matters." I wish that everything could "go" *and* everything would matter—but I guess we're not wired that way. What's more, Roth adds that in democratic societies, "Everything goes and nothing matters," which is, of course, another bummer.

I never imagined until recently that Fascism might find a home in these United States of ours. We've "lived so well so long," as a famous American singer once sang to a melody I considered his finest achievement until I learned he'd filched it from a traditional hymn. Living so well, and for so long—but Dame Fortune's wheel spins every which way, which means that a Fascist regime might indeed take power in this nation. If so, time to remember the words of the arch-Taoist Chuang Tzu: "When the world has Tao, the sage thrives, and when the world loses Tao, the sage survives." In a Fascist America, I have no doubt that plenty of our citizens will sign up to participate in goon squads, just as I have no doubt that many citizens secretly, or not-so-secretly, enjoy being ruled, dominated, bullied. And if our own Fascist regime dispatches a new Gestapo crew, or a team of pesky ninjas, to arrest me, my wish is to make my escape in time. Or to at least put up enough of a fight to take a few of those bad guys with me to oblivion.

What if "fight or flight" isn't possible, though? What if they'll have me cornered? In that case, I wish that when the baddies show up on my doorstep, I can direct ridicule in their direction, pointing my finger in their beady-eyed faces and laughing scornfully, because Mark Twain was right that "Against the assault of laughter, nothing can stand."

And if open ridicule is not achievable? Then subtle ridicule will have to suffice, and I'll receive a goon squad the way Ethiopians say we should treat "great leaders"—with a deep bow and a silent fart. During the Nazi occupation of Paris, the Jewish writer Max Jacob greeted his own bully-boy antagonists in similar-spirited fashion—with a big smile, as if their harsh commands "were no more than meaningless small talk." Jacob voiced a pun for the Gestapo, too, that they didn't understand. He told them, "*J'ai ta peau*," which was French slang for "Your ass is mine." Futile words, of course. Still, accompanied by that smile of Jacob's, he symbolically made it happen.

I wish I could have inherited "Bernie Zen," which is what I playfully called my father Bernie Lippman's easygoing-to-the-point-of-Buddhist-serenity nature. Except for his mother Lulu and my father-in-law Istvan, Bernie was the least upsettable person I've known. One example of Bernie Zen stemmed from the entire day and night I kept trying and failing to reach my grandmother Lulu on the landline in her apartment on Miami Beach. Because she was one hundred years old, lived alone, and rarely left her home or owned an answering machine or cell phone, I feared the worst. But when I phoned my father to say, "Grandma's not *answering*," he refused to share my panic.

"Maybe she just accidentally turned off her phone's ringing device," said Bernie Lippman.

"Has she done that before, Dad?"

"Not that I know of."

"Does her phone even *have* a ringing device that she could have accidentally turned off?"

"Not that I know of."

"Then this is *crazy*! We have to call 911! She might be lying there, *hurt*, and need our help!"

"Or the phone ringer just might be off. Give it another day."

Reluctantly, I did, although I spent that whole day questioning whether my father's Bernie Zen was such a good thing, after all. The next morning, frantic by now, I called Lulu's number again. It kept ringing. Five more phone calls throughout the day. Still no answer. By nightfall, my worry had reached epic heights. *One more try*, I decided, *then I contact the police*. She answered her phone on the third ring.

"Grandma!" I shouted into my receiver. "Oh, my God—are you *okay*?"

"Of course I'm okay, darling. How are you?"

"How am *I*? I've been frightened *sick* about you! Why haven't you picked up your phone the past two days?"

"Oh, were you calling? I'm sorry I didn't answer. I accidentally turned off the ringer device on my telephone. You weren't worried, were you, darling?"

I'd forgotten that Lulu had her own Zen spirit, with her life-long mottos being "Think pink" and "Cool it." In fact, my father must have inherited his Zen from her. Recognizing how much time and energy I'd wasted in freaking out, I vowed to strive to be Zen-like myself. Alas, such serenity was sorely needed during a few of my interactions with Bernie Lippman. The two people he married, my mother and my stepmother, each in her own way had a personality that was extremely, shall we say, *difficult*, so in the heat of one of my rare arguments with Bernie Lippman, I lashed out at him, saying, "You know, Dad, I owe *ninety percent* of my emotional problems to your *bad taste in women*."

As calm as ever, my father took no offense to this insult. In fact, he chuckled at it, patted my knee, and said, "Good one, Gar." Which was precisely the reaction I *did not* wish to elicit with my insult. I'd yearned to get his goat and instead received a compliment.

At the time, we were road-tripping from New Jersey to South Florida, with Bernie at the wheel and me beside him. Our argument had started one gray morning in South Carolina and followed us into a truck stop restaurant in northern Georgia, where the PA system blared truck driver-themed songs. (My friend Jeremy had not yet taught me to savor "rig rock" anthems such as "Six Days On The Road.") Bernie Lippman and I intended to have a quick coffee and then get back to our journey. Unfortunately, our entrance got the attention of all the other customers. They were either bikers or truckers, and were all as tattooed, as muscled-up, and (except for most of the women among them) as lavishly bearded as you'd expect. No one in the gloomy place stopped speaking when my father and I walked in, yet many narrowed eyes found us and stayed fixed on us, and you could almost hear these rough customers' thoughts out loud, thoughts which were mostly just one thought, a hostile identification of us as "*Yankee Jews, Yankee Jews, Yankee Jews*."

Given the situation, I was happy to postpone my argument with Bernie until (if) we made it back to our Eldorado parked outside. My father seemed unaware of the potential danger, though, and said, "I don't know why you keep complaining about my wife—she's been a loving stepmother to you."

"Dad," I said, unable to stop myself, although at least I was able to keep my voice low, "if you really believe that, then you're as deaf, dumb, and blind as the character Tommy in the rock opera by the Who."

"Who?"

"Forget it. You know what? I'm finished debating this with you. I'm finished even *talking* with you. We can continue this nonsense on the road later. Let's just be quiet while we're in here, okay?"

"Suit yourself," said my father. But since I get quickly bored if I'm not speaking with someone, reading, or people-watching (and people-watching in this joint would likely get my ass handed to me), I knew I needed some reading material. So I looked around and, *voila*, spotted a gift shop connected to the restaurant. No doubt they would have newspapers for sale. One paper for Bernie, and one for me. Without a word, I got up and kept my eyes down on the dirty linoleum floor as I hurried toward the gift shop. Alas, no newspapers were sold there. No magazines, either—not even *The National Enquirer.*

"We *used* to sell them papers," explained the jowly pink-haired elderly woman in a yellow sundress who was perched at the gift shop's cash register. "Then our distributor man said we have to sell those *porno* magazines here, and I'm a Christian who doesn't trade in any of that porno *trash*. Never did, never *will*—which is what I told that distributor man. *Loudly*. And can you guess how that jackass came back at me? He said, 'If you don't sell my porno here, then I ain't lettin' you sell nothing *else*, neither. No magazines *at all*. No newspapers, *nothing*. Only these here paperbacks that nobody ever wants to buy.' Dust-gatherers, I call them. Might stop selling them soon, too."

"In that case," I said, "I'll buy some paperbacks. Two, at least. Let's take this book of really short stories and, uh, this novel about Sharon Tate."

"Fine by me," said the queen of the truck stop gift shop. "I only take cash."

A minute later, I was walking back through the dining room, my eyes aimed down again as all the bikers and the truckers watched me from their tables. The silent repeated chant of "*Yankee Jew*" trailed me to my table, where Bernie sat sipping his newly arrived cup of black coffee. Black is how I take mine, too, but before I drew a sip from my cup, I placed the dusty Sharon Tate novel in front of my father.

"What's this?" Bernie said.

"That's your new reading material," I said. "I've got my own book here, see?"

"Why are we supposed to *read* now?"

"Because, like I told you before, Dad, our conversation is *over*. I don't have another word to say to you. We're just going to look at our books until we leave here and start driving again."

My father has been gone now for many years, so I cannot ask *why* he reacted to my book agenda the way he did, but I believe what happened was, his Bernie Zen failed him. My presenting him a paperback and announcing that I had unilaterally ended our conversation triggered the man for some reason, making him so angry that he behaved in a simple yet unexpected way. With a surprisingly dead-eyed glare at me, Bernie lifted "his" new paperback with his left hand (like my mother and unlike me, he was a lefty) and simply flung the book over his shoulder, flung it through the air, flung it out of his life.

Flung it, most significantly, toward the table next to ours, where it bounced off of the ham-and-cheese omelet being eaten by a not very large but significantly cruel-looking tattooed bearded muscled-up trucker or biker.

Now the entire room *did* go silent, amazingly silent. Even the waitress, who wore the same kind of sundress as the gift shop cashier, stopped taking someone's breakfast order and turned to watch what would happen next. If it had been a Wild West saloon, the piano player would have abruptly stopped playing and the bartender would have ducked behind the bar. Meanwhile, in the great silence, those mental exclamations of "*Yankee Jew*" became deafening. To *my* ears, at least. My father had blithely returned to his cup of coffee, exuding his personal brand of calm once more. I don't think Bernie realized that he'd disrupted anybody's omelette, much less a scary person's omelette. I do know that if my father *had* realized it, he wouldn't have cared.

Obviously, the last thing I wanted to do now was walk over to the table where the paperback still rested beside the sullied omelette and to apologize to the interrupted eater. I knew I might not survive this procedure. At least not with my nose, teeth, and crucial parts of my skeleton intact. Yet what choice did I have? Raked by the angry glares of everyone present—except for Bernie Lippman, who may or may not have wondered why I was leaving our table again—I summoned up as much of my father's easy-going nature, his Bernie Zen, as I could. Then I stood and began my long journey of a few steps, with my eyes aimed down on the linoleum once more, already phrasing in my mind the profuse apologies I would make. And knowing that these apologies would almost certainly fail to save me.

Another word about Bernie Lippman. Given my antipathy to my stepmother, I wish that, after divorcing his wife Esther, he had married a different woman than the one he did. Or had not remarried at all. Not only was my stepmother regularly hostile toward me, but "Godzilla," as I came to call her—though never to her face, because she would have blown fire at me and singed my eyebrows—was a terrible cook. Why couldn't my father have married "Puff, the Magic Dragon" instead of this one? Worse, my stepmother would always insist that I finish eating her disgusting meals even though her own children, my step-siblings, were not required to finish them. Most painfully for me, this was a policy that my father, who was ever eager to keep the matrimonial beast pacified, was only too willing to support.

One "Meat Loaf Night" stands out in my memory. "You can only join us after your plate is completely clean," announced Godzilla, but I couldn't bear to taste another bite of her rancid food, so I sat staring at it in despair as everyone else left the kitchen to watch *Love, American Style* on the Tube. Could I force myself to vomit? Would this get me a "get out of jail" card? No, it would offend the Dragon still more. I sat alone for a few minutes as the rest of my family laughed at the TV hijinks. Then—*eureka*! Quietly leaving my chair, I tiptoed to the kitchen's trash can, slid the remaining meat loaf inside there, returned to the table with my empty plate, and shouted, "All finished!"

Sure enough, I was immediately invited to the TV room to watch *Love, American Style*, and as I settled back on the sofa there, I felt supremely pleased with myself for having invented such an effective solution to my problem. Alas, my solution had not been effective enough. Clever as I'd been, I had not been clever enough to cover over the meat loaf with paper towels or anything else, so the next time that Godzilla went to deposit something into the garbage, she discovered my ruse. Much screaming at me followed, along with reluctantly harsh words from my father. Back into TV exile I went. And *Love, American Style* had almost ended before I managed to choke down that awful repast.

"Too soon old, too late smart," goes the old expression. This assumes that we ever do get smart; my Uncle Wolf likes to say, "We learn and we learn and we still die as fools." At least I know better now how to dispose of inedible meat loaf.

I wish I possessed a portable library of tastes I could access whenever my mood craves a specific one. Pink Starburst candy is perhaps my favorite thing to put into my mouth; the first time I bit into a cube of the stuff, six-year-old me stood outside the Starlite Pizzeria in my hometown and I thought, *This is the best thing I'll ever taste for the rest of my life*. Another wish concerning taste is that the food would taste better at my hometown's well-named Fortuna Deli. Still, as long as I don't pick up ptomaine poisoning there, I plan to sing the Country-and-Western song "If I Had My Life to Live Over, I'd Live Over A Delicatessen" every time I go through their door. And I'll reflect, too, on the lesson that Warren Zevon says he learned while struggling to face down old Stretchfoot, that Wrecker of Rock Star Revels: "Enjoy every sandwich."

Another portable library I wouldn't mind owning would consist of scents. Patchouli gets a bad rap nowadays, but it would probably be the fragrance I'd access most often. As for the instrument I use to smell with, I wish I had a Grecian nose rather than a pug nose, and I wish I would sneeze less violently than I do. My sneezes, like my snoring, are capable of frightening anyone within earshot.

What about that other sense of ours, the sense of touch? I wish I could have a team of technicians on hand (androids would be acceptable) who will provide me with "touch experiences" whenever I crave them. I could fill this entire wish list with a list of such experiences, but I'll mention only one that is aptly described by the author Diane Ackerman: "the near-orgasmic caravan of pleasure, shiver, pain and relief that we call a back scratch."

Finally, in this wish list's *Sensorium Department*, I wish I could experience synesthesia, the condition in which the stimulation of one sense stimulates another. Why can't I taste the color blue whenever I'm hearing my all-time favorite pop tune "Georgy Girl," the one that my mother and I considered "our song"? And hear the flavor of Starburst and see the fragrance of patchouli while those technicians are scratching my back?

Sticking with human senses, let's listen again to G. K. Chesterton, who said, "There is a law written in the Books of Life, and it's this: if you look at a thing 999 times, you are perfectly safe; if you look at it the 1000th time, you are in frightful danger of seeing it for the first time." I don't know if I can do the thousand times deal, but I wish I could better notice my surroundings. Mark Twain observed that a cauliflower is nothing more than "a cabbage with a college education." Cute. Yet Chesterton might have differed; he wrote that if an imaginative person will "really look at cabbages and cauliflowers, he will feel at once that they are vast and elemental things like the mountains in the clouds."

Many people believe that nothing should be beneath our attention, and that attention may lead to devotion. Perhaps it's even the case, as John O'Donohue has recognized, that "The quality of our looking determines what we come to see. With dulled eyes, we see dull things, but when our eyes are graced with wonder, the world reveals its wonders to us." Accordingly, I plan one day to sit quietly with wax plugs in my ears and observe the silent movie of ordinary sights that continually swirl around me in the most complex and aesthetically pleasing interactions. Viewed from this perspective, Dame Fortune is one hell of a cinematographer. She must have inspired E. M. Cioran to write that "Walking in a forest between two ferns transfigured by autumn—that is a *triumph*. What are ovations and applause beside it?"

On a similar sensory kick, I wish I had the patience to sit quietly with a blindfold over my eyes and listen to the symphony of ordinary everyday sounds that continually surround me in the most complex and aesthetically pleasing interactions. Listened to from this perspective, Dame Fortune is one hell of a composer. She must have inspired Walt Whitman to write, "The bird is singing—the cars are puffing & rattling, & the children of the neighborhood are all outdoors playing—So I have music enough."

The trick is to observe our surroundings without any preconceptions. Georges Perec was practiced at this, and primed especially to notice absence, because when he was a child, his soldier father was killed during World War II and his mother was murdered in a Nazi death camp. Perec made sure to pay careful attention to the small details, too, which is something I wish I was better at. As the Baal Shem Tov said, "Alas, the world is full of enormous lights and mysteries and man shuts them off from himself with one small hand."

The same Baal Shem Tov had another, related, quip of value: "The sky cannot be so huge for us that we miss the lice on a hawk's wing." I remember the autumn afternoon when I encountered a hawk while I was strolling through an open field. This hawk was sitting on wet grass, checking out our surroundings the same as I was. We gazed into one another's eyes for a long minute before I started fiddling with my phone camera, hoping to catch a photo of the hawk, and it decided to fly away. I'd probably annoyed it with my movements. At any rate, I wish I'd have left my camera alone and let my time with the hawk continue. Even so, I believe that—during that long minute, at least—I was looking exactly where I should have been.

Georges Perec was a member of a group I wish I could belong to, the France-based *Oulipo*. Not only did this "Workshop for Potential Literature" give us the most ingenious novel I know of, *Exercises in Style* by Raymond Queneau, the group's founder, but Oulipo encourages its authors to practice intriguing literary constraints. Among these constraints are palindromes, anagrams, acrostics, the "S-7" method of rewriting poems by word substitution, and the "lipogram," which is "a written text deliberately composed of words not having a certain letter."

I wish I had written the world's greatest lipogram, Perec's novel *Le Disparition*, which lacks, from first page to last, the letter "e." As with Perec's dead parents, a big presence turned into an auspicious absence. I also wish that lipograms had been named after me. Not that I'm fond of my surname—it reminds me of a moist herpes-sore-studded lip—and I avoid saying the embarrassing "pee-pee" while spelling "Lippman" aloud. The way I do so is to say "double p," or even "triple p," instead. ("The third 'p' is silent," I explain. Or else "It stands for 'progress.'" You'd be surprised, or maybe not, how many people find nothing grammatically wrong with those three p's.) I've even considered legally changing my name, but mainly to observe the ancient Hebrew tradition of eluding death by taking a different monicker. As if old Stretchfoot, that Nemesis of the Named, would fall for such a stunt!

After Perec's e-less novel, he wrote a short story in which the only vowel he used was, naturally, "e." In his masterpiece, *Life: A User's Manual*, there are plenty of "e's," not to mention a visual artist character whose own masterpiece is a painting "that would reassemble his entire existence: everything his memory had recorded, all the sensations that had swept over him, all his fantasies, his passions, his hates, would be recorded on canvas, a compendium of minute parts of which the sum would be his life." This wish list, it occurs to me, could be my own literary version of such a canvas.

Perec's lifespan, from 1936 to 1982, nearly coincided with that of my mother Esther Lippman, who lived between 1932 and 1981. Another near-contemporary of hers was the Canadian piano prodigy Glenn Gould, whose dates were 1932 to 1982. Now that I've given Perec his due, let me pay homage to Gould with some bespoke wishes:

* On the radio broadcasts the musician made and in the album liner notes he wrote, Gould crafted for himself dozens of alter egos to hide behind—different selves which allowed him to playfully review, and sometimes disparage, his own performances. "American critic Theodore Slutz," "British conductor Sir Nigel Twitt-Thornwaite," and

"German musicologist Karlheinz Klopweisser" were a few of his other selves. Compare Gould here to the Portuguese author Fernando Pessoa and the alternate selves Pessoa dreamt up and set loose in this world to write the books he didn't feel were apt for himself to write. The Portuguese scribe invented more than seventy of these "heteronyms," believing as he did that "We never know self-realization. We are two abysses—a well staring at the sky."

The upshot? I wish I had the imagination to create some alter egos of my own. The closest I've come are the names of two recurring characters in my story collection *We Loved the World But Could Not Stay*. Both "Pryna Pamlig" and "Map Grylapin" are anagrams of my own name.

* Glenn Gould was particular about how he sat at his piano. The instrument had to be set at a specific height, with wooden blocks placed under each of the piano legs, and the only chair the musician would deign to use had to be one built by his father, with Gould's position before the piano needing to be precisely fourteen inches above the ground.

Lately I've been thinking about how I myself tend to sit, and I'm wishing I enjoyed standing as much as I enjoy sitting. The former is more physically and even emotionally healthy, modern science tells us, and French history's lively Madame Sevigny shrewdly told her daughter, "Almost all our ills come from sitting in chairs." Even so, sitting is an underrated pleasure—note the part it plays in the title of the R. L. Burnside album *I Wish I Was in Heaven Sitting Down*. Being in Heaven isn't enough of a big-ticket wish for bluesman Burnside—he also wants to take the load off his feet! All the better if a credentialed reflexologist could materialize each time we sit down and continually massage our feet until we stand up again. Nevertheless, sitting can be physically perilous, as I learned each of the three times in my life when I lowered my bottom onto a chair which immediately collapsed under me. Perhaps I was overweight from all the sitting I'd previously done.

The most memorable of these occasions was at a pizzeria in Paris. After a Romanian waiter showed me and my young son to our table, I took my seat and it promptly crumbled under me like a movie set prop. It was upsetting enough that I hurt my back when I fell, but once the waiter began to chortle at me and failed to help me stand, much less to apologize, I snarled with rage and threw the biggest piece of that broken chair at him. This felt satisfying. I only wish that my son hadn't witnessed my loss of parental self-control.

More than once I've tried writing my books while standing, hoping to get some inspirational *oomph* from the process. Writing in this fashion apparently worked for Hemingway and Nabokov. Each time I tried to follow their example, though, I soon wound up sitting, with a tiny section of my mind wondering as I did so if the seat in my study would fail to support me. If it went to pieces and I went down again, there would be no available scapegoat at whom I could hurl a broken chair part.

* Glenn Gould notoriously hummed while he played the piano, "singing" the notes in order to evoke the music he heard in his head, music that his eighty-eight-keyed instrument could not quite capture. He said that this humming was unconscious and originated with his mother, who taught him to "sing everything you play." It was not just concert audiences who heard Gould doing this, either, because no matter how hard his audio engineers tried, they were unable to wipe the musician's hums, which sounded like groans, from his recordings.

Whenever I listen to one of Gould's albums, those groans remind me of a humid May night in 1978 when my mother and I were at home in our little ranch house in New Jersey. The cancer that would ultimately kill Esther Lippman had only just started causing havoc to her body, but her own mother, my grandmother Lily, was at the Mayo Clinic in Minnesota, recovering from a heart attack. I loved Lily, who was born on the same day I was, fifty-eight years earlier, and I feel guilty now about how I'd treated her. My grandmother's arthritic legs caused her to walk in such a herky-jerky fashion that Esther Lippman and I used to privately mock her, repeating the TV commercial phrase "*Weebles wobble but they don't fall down.*" I wish her spirit would forgive me.

Anyway, that humid night in May of 1978 was a "school night," so a little after eleven p.m., my official bed-time, I switched off *Fernwood 2 Night* on my TV, stopped by my mother's room to hug her and kiss her and say goodnight (we hadn't argued for the past two hours—a near-record for us in those days), and shut my bedroom door. Then I stripped naked (to Esther Lippman's consternation, I refused to wear pajamas) and drifted slowly toward the rounded edge of sleep. I was about to topple over that sweet edge, too, when I heard a voice outside the open window beside my bed. Not a voice, actually—it was more like a groan. I sat up and leaned toward the window, listening carefully.

Because a forest lay just behind our backyard, I figured that this groaning sound belonged to a wounded deer or opossum. Maybe some such creature had crawled out of those black woods and collapsed here on our lawn, awaiting a peaceful death. If this was so, why did the groan seem to originate not from the lawn one story below me but from the space *directly outside my window*?

"Ma!" I shouted. "Come quick, Ma!" The hot breeze blowing in through the open window ruffled the nightgown she always wore. "Outside," I said once she arrived. "*Listen*."

Sure enough, there it was again, higher pitched than a male voice yet lower than a female's. We crowded together, straining our ears and trying to visually scan the darkness of our lawn.

"What a *sound*," my mother said.

"I know. It's freaky!"

She slammed down the window. "Ignore it, sweetheart. Just go to sleep."

Easy for *her* to say. It soon proved so unpleasant with the window closed, so stuffy, that sleep proved impossible. The mysterious groan continued to preoccupy me. I thought I could still hear it, faint yet urgent, seeping in through the pane of glass that separated me from the universe outside. My curiosity grew and grew, and when I opened the window again, unable to resist, the groan was louder than before, and just as harrowing.

"Ma!" I shouted.

Back she came. The groan persisted through the night. Neither of us could manage any sleep, so a little before dawn, we pulled on our bathrobes, armed ourselves with a flashlight as well as a lug-wrench to use as a weapon, then tiptoed outside to investigate. Frightened though we were, we couldn't resist this mystery. It was "the hour of the wolf," the time when prey are drowsy, when predators strike, and as we took our first steps into our backyard, which was still shrouded in darkness, I felt very close to Esther Lippman. We were sharing this dangerous moment together, challenging a force independent of us instead of tangling viciously with each other.

Outside, we saw, and now *heard*, nothing. No groaning phantoms. No hurt critters. Two hours later, right before I left for school, I asked my mother, "Do you think we'll hear that sound again tonight?" I was sitting in our kitchen, drinking a glass of milk, and Esther was about to answer me—probably to say, "Worry about your schoolwork instead of *that*, dear"—when our telephone rang. Glass in hand, I followed her out to the hallway, where she lifted the receiver and said, "Hello?" Then she didn't speak for a moment, but I could tell something was up.

"Who's calling?" I whispered to her.

"Uncle Wolf," she said.

"Oh. Say hi from me."

I took another gulp of milk and turned to go. Then I heard Esther say, "*What?*," sounding rattled, and when I looked at her again, her eyes had become the eyes of a frightened child. "I don't *believe* it," she said. "I don't *believe* it; I don't *believe* it..."

"What's wrong?" I said, now a frightened child myself. "Ma, *what's wrong*?"

"It's Grandma," she said. "Grandma Lily. She had a new heart attack last night. She's *dead*!"

Three years later, Esther Lippman would occupy her own deathbed in a hospital a few miles from our home, and each night when I tried to sleep, I kept expecting to hear that familiar groaning outside my window. I never did. The closest thing I've heard to those frightening sounds have been the groaning that Glenn Gould makes on his recordings. But recently I learned that the banshee, a supernatural being in Irish folklore, can take the form of an old woman who walks under the windows of your house and screeches in order to announce the death of a family member. Or to announce your own impending death.

I recognize that this wish list is not a page-turner, not the kind of literary work you "can't put down," yet I wish it *could* be "unput-downable" in the weird way that the author Flann O'Brien suggested—as a book that heats up in its readers' hands and changes into a glue that can only be removed slowly, "by taking a course of scalding hot baths." Failing that, I wish that this wish list would appear not in book form but in tiny messages delivered by carrier pigeons to each reader, or conveyed by graffiti on the walls of cities worldwide, or else implanted by some present magic or future technology in the dreaming psyches of you, my fellow wisher.

Books! While rewatching the film *When Harry Met Sally* recently, I grinned with surprise when I recognized that an extended scene was set in a most familiar place. It was the upstairs stacks of Manhattan's Coliseum Bookstore on West 57th Street. All the numberless happy hours during the eighties that I spent browsing around that wonderland, dipping into the brains of other people! ("Reading," said Schopenhauer, "is like thinking with someone else's brain.") What's more, the Coliseum seemed to be the epicenter of high-octane energies. One block east of the bookstore, I witnessed a man in a business suit stagger along the sidewalk with a penknife stuck in his back, while a block further I nearly lost my left hand when an elevator in the Art Students League slammed shut on it and came close to severing said hand from my arm.

Browsing through the Coliseum is no longer possible, alas, because the place shut down many years ago. At least it still exists, for now, in my own brain—and, for probably a little longer, in that scene in *When Harry Met Sally*.

Bookstores! I wish that they were as common as banks, souvenir shops, overpriced clothing emporia, and marijuana dispensaries. I wish, too, that electronic books would shrink in sales, thereby restoring to popularity the objects I most cherish: paperbacks and, to a lesser extent, hardcovers. And I wish that instead of dying, I could be transformed into a book. The author E. B. White said, "Books are people, people who managed to stay alive by hiding between the covers of a book," so let me take him literally and have Dame Fortune, or the ancient Greek muse Calliope, grant me a full person-into-book metamorphosis.

Of course, I have some preferences as to which kind of volume I'd become, preferences based on taste, and I'd be fine if I'm written in Latin or Japanese. What good is an afterlife if you can't learn new tricks? Even so, if I'm not allowed to be choosy, any book will do. What matters is that I will remain on a shelf in a bookstore or a library or someone's home until, well, Doomsday. I'd rather that people would read and re-read me a lot, but, again, this might not be my choice to make. Merely hanging out on a bookshelf, sandwiched between two other books, and with my spine facing out to any eyes that might catch sight of my title—this would be enough of a satisfying afterlife.

Then again, the boredom might torment me to the point where Doomsday couldn't come fast enough.

So, instead of becoming a book, maybe I should wish I could spend each day the way the actor Marlon Brando supposedly favored. He would roll out of bed, gather from his personal library a dozen or so volumes he was curious about, then clamber back into bed with that stack and start reading. Or maybe I could emulate the author Raymond Roussel and sit in a car packed to its sunroof with books while a chauffeur motors me around the French countryside and I delve into each. Oh, and if I die while in the middle of reading a book, please pump me full of "resurrectine," the serum Roussel imagined could bring back alive a corpse so it can "act out the most important incident of its life."

Resurrectine prompts several questions. What would that incident be for me? Would it involve reading? And how good of a reader am I, anyway? It was Goethe, no slouch as a person of letters, who said, "Ordinary people don't know how much time and effort it takes to learn how to read. I've spent eighty years at it, and I still can't say that I've reached my goal."

Some final thoughts about reading: I wish I could abide by the author Anatole France's admonition to "never lend books, for no one ever returns them. In fact, the only books I have in my library are books that other folks have lent to me." One of these days, I'm going to purge my own library of the books I've started reading but not enjoyed enough to finish. I like what Witold Gombrowicz wrote in an essay about his novel *Ferdydurke*: "If you wish to let me know that the book pleased you—when you see me, simply touch your right ear. If you touch your left ear, I shall know you didn't like it, and if you touch your nose it will mean that you are not sure…Thus shall we avoid uncomfortable and even ridiculous situations and understand each other in silence."

Unfortunately, Gombrowicz's *Ferdydurke* is one of those novels that I've wanted to love but haven't. *This time will be different*, I think each time I begin to read *Ferdydurke*. It's never different. The same disinterest goes for Julio Cortazar's *Hopscotch*, Walker Percy's *The Moviegoer*, David Foster Wallace's *Infinite Jest*, and Aleksandr Solzhenitsyn's *One Day in the Life of Ivan Denisovich*. It is said that a Russian literary editor was so impressed by Solzhenitsyn's novel that he got out of bed and put on a suit and necktie in order to show proper respect to the book while he finished reading it. I wish I would do the same respectful thing with books I admire, but I hate wearing suits. And I agree with the writer Lin Yutang that "Neckties strangle clear thinking."

I wish that the country roads in Ireland were not so damned narrow, because the week I once spent driving on them reduced me to a gibbering nervous wreck. The left-side driving and endless roundabouts didn't make matters simpler. It figures that my wife Berta, who had just gotten her first driver's license, ended up navigating those roads far more ably than I did with my decades of driving experience. Even more perilous, I've found, is the stretch of Interstate 95 in Florida south of Hypoluxo Road, which is my favorite street name apart from Thomas Pynchon's fictional "Gummo Marx Way." Riding on that highway one day, I passed an empty car totally engulfed in flames. I wish I knew the story behind that sight. And I wish I had a video of the motorcyclist who did a nonstop "wheelie" with his back nearly parallel to the asphalt for more than ten miles.

Most of all, I wish they hadn't torn down the "Dania Beach Hurricane," which for decades loomed over a nondescript stretch of 95 near Fort Lauderdale. No motorist speeding past the Hurricane (or, more likely, sitting in dense traffic beside it) could have failed to notice the enormous honeycomb structure of "Florida's tallest wooden roller-coaster." Rising one hundred feet, spanning more than three thousand feet, and resembling some steampunk fever dream, the Hurricane in its heyday took passengers on two-minute rides that reached speeds upward of fifty miles per hour.

"Hey, I want to try that!" my wife said to me with glee in mid-2010 when we drove south past the Hurricane. We had just started dating, and I'd brought her with me to Florida on one of my regular visits to see local family and friends. "When I was growing up in Hungary," she added, "I loved going on the roller-coaster in Budapest!"

I already knew how adventurous Berta was, and didn't dare to tell her, especially not in these halcyon early days of our relationship, how *unadventurous* I was, especially with roller-coasters. They'd frightened me since the summer day during my childhood when I rode the big coaster at Palisades Park and suffered through every minute of the ride. I vowed afterward "never again," and in subsequent years, I renewed this vow each time I read about a coaster fatality. Usually it was a luckless rider who'd been accidentally hurled from his open-air cart to an unforgiving blacktop below.

"I love roller-coasters, too," I lied to Berta. "We'll try the Hurricane *next* time we're here, okay?" My hope was that she wouldn't remember my promise. To help her not remember, I made a silent note to myself to research alternate driving routes before we came back to Florida, so we wouldn't need to pass by the Hurricane again.

"But why not *this* time?" Berta said. "We aren't in a hurry now, are we?"

I swallowed hard. Because traffic was light, we had plenty of time to spare before meeting up with my friends in Miami. Forcing myself to smile—she didn't know me well enough yet to recognize my repertoire of false facial expressions—I ran through a grim cost-benefit analysis in my mind. On one hand, if I rode the Hurricane with Berta, perhaps I would please her *and* conceal from her my coaster-cowardice. On the other hand, pleasing her and concealing that cowardice wouldn't matter if I lost my life thanks to the Hurricane. (A fatal heart attack was more likely than being flung to my death, I figured). Or what if I became physically ill in front of Berta? Or if I lost control of one of my bodily functions? Or if I started screaming like an infant?

"Please?" said Berta in a sweet tone. Which was all it took for me to decide. No need to further weigh benefits and costs. And so, twenty minutes later, I had parked our car in the Hurricane's lot and paid the admission fee. The fact that we were the only passengers that afternoon didn't soothe me much. Neither did Berta's uncontainable excitement, nor her many questions about the Hurricane, which she directed to the middle-aged Englishman who was operating it. As he got us seated in one of the coaster's rickety open-air carts (Berta, to my silent distress, had insisted that it be the front one), he seemed to recognize how artificial my brave front was.

"You scared?" he asked me.

"Nope," I said. Still, I couldn't resist asking, "*Should* I be?"

"Not at all," said the Englishman. "Just last week a group of elderly people celebrated their birthdays here. A Guinness Book of Records thing. One man was turning ninety, so we had an ambulance standing by, just in case. But everyone did fine."

On hearing this, I found myself relaxing. If a ninety-year-old could do it, then so could I. Even if the ninety-year-old had once been a two-fisted, blood-soaked mercenary (or was not a tough guy at all but was so far gone in his dotage that he didn't realize what this Hurricane ride was about), I now felt sure that I could survive the coaster. Instead of resting easy, though, I foolishly opened my mouth again, asking, "What's the worst part of the ride?"

With a lopsided grin, the Englishman said, "The loop-de-loops. They're murder. You'll be frequently upside down."

I was just beginning to digest this concept (upside down? *frequently*?) when he pulled a big lever and we juddered off into a maelstrom of strong wind, metallic clatter, and gathering speed. Berta laughed joyously while I gazed down in horror at the loose iron safety-bar. On realizing that this flimsy thing could never keep us inside the cart once we went "upside down," I commenced to scream like an infant, bracing myself for the first certain-to-be-fatal "loop-de-loop"...

Which, as it turned out, never came. The Englishman had played a trick on me. The Hurricane had no such loops. Yet by the time our two-minute-ride-that-seemed-like-ten was finished, I wasn't angry at him. In fact, I'd very much enjoyed the ride.

The reason for this enjoyment was a kind of protective mantra I muttered to myself over and over as we approached maximum speed, a phrase I remembered from *Macbeth*: "*Let it come down.*" To my amazement, the mindless, meaningless repetition of these four syllables soon hypnotized me into calmness, then into actual pleasure. If Dame Fortune wanted me to perish, bring it on!

Was this reaction of mine merely bio-chemical, a giddiness from free-flowing adrenaline? I didn't know. Yet by the time our ride ended, I had not just philosophically accepted a death-by-roller-coaster, I'd embraced it.

"I love you," I said to Berta as soon as our ride was over. I'd said this to her before, but never with such intensity. Thanks to my girlfriend, I was now a born-again roller-coaster rider. *Maybe*, I told myself, *we'll even get to celebrate our ninetieth birthdays together on the Hurricane!*

What I hadn't imagined was that two years later, the coaster's owner would shut it down and build a fence around the whole structure to keep out trespassers. During the following four years, the Hurricane took on an increasingly forlorn appearance, with grass growing wild over much of it. If it had looked unearthly before, now it looked all too of-this-world. This vast, ornately designed abandoned wooden thing sitting beside a major highway remained a bizarre sight, but it had become an obvious victim of entropy.

Berta and I got married in 2013. Each time we would drive past the coaster, I expected not to see it anymore, to discover it had been torn down and replaced with something far less extraordinary.

A shopping center, for instance. Eventually, sure enough, I drove alone past the Hurricane in 2016 and found the coaster surrounded by bulldozers. Parts of it had already been demolished, with broken wood piled in heaps, and a large sign placed there by a demolition company read, "WATCH IT COME DOWN." A shopping center would indeed replace the coaster.

As much as I hated to see the sign, I had grown rather comfortable since my one and only Hurricane ride with the metaphorical wisdom of "letting it come down"—letting things in life "come down" if Dame Fortune ordains they must. And I have additional consolation: If it is true that, as the author Ramon Gomez de la Serna put it, "Love is believing you have managed to persuade time not to pass," those thrilling few minutes I spent with Berta on the Hurricane were timeless.

Speaking of "letting it come down," I wish that, whenever I'm facing a truly daunting quandary, I would remind myself of a sunny afternoon in Paris in mid-1997. That afternoon, I was struggling with one of my life's most dire crises. I didn't know how to respond to this crisis at all; each possible action I considered taking seemed likely to spell my destruction. In a near-suicidal funk, I wandered into a bookshop near the Odeon and opened the first paperback my eyes landed on, which was Tibor Fischer's novel *The Thought Gang*, then turned to the last page, where Fischer wrote, "The only good solution to a really difficult problem…is to leave it."

So here was my solution: a decision not to seek a solution! I bought the book, left the bookstore, left Paris, and found, with time, that my crisis had resolved itself without my "doing" anything.

"Leaving it" and "letting it come down" are synonymous with the term "letting go," and all of these phrases make me think of an observation by Henry Miller. "Once you have given up the ghost," Miller wrote, "everything follows with dead certainty, even in the midst of chaos." I wish I were better at "giving up" ghosts, because what makes life "so unbearable," as the Zen teacher Charlotte Joko Beck knew, is our "mistaken belief it can be cured."

I was introduced to the suggestion "let go" by a wise old man named Fogerty the week after my mother died. Fogerty's suggestion is represented in diverse religious texts, including that of Meister Eckhart, who said, "Only those who have dared to let go can dare to re-enter." Consider a drunken lunk who passes out on his front lawn after a two-day drinking spree. When the lunk's children ask their mother if they should carry him inside, the mother says, "Nah, just leave him where Jesus flung him." I imagine Meister Eckhart would have approved of this, maybe even with a chuckle.

A related philosophical concept I wish I could better practice is the Taoist ideal of "*wu wei*." Often described as "non-action," *wu wei* is better, though still inelegantly, called "action for its own sake without any concern about the action's outcome." The concept is also represented in the *Bhagavad Gita*, and many other ancient texts from around the globe, but perhaps nowhere as well as in a particular scene in Ken Kesey's novel *One Flew Over The Cuckoo's Nest*. There, the protagonist McMurphy tries to lift a heavy control panel in the psychiatric hospital where he's imprisoned. He fails, but then mutters words that matter more to me than any he could have spoken if he'd succeeded with his task: "At least I tried." Bonus points if you fail in good spirits. And remember Willie Nelson's words: "You can't lose them all."

For their part, Japanese people like to say, "Fall down seven times, stand up eight." Maybe the best part of this maxim is not the finally standing up, but the suggestion that no fall is permanent except for our last one, when we get knocked down by old Stretchfoot, that Liquidator of Liveliness.

"It all comes down to the glide," surfers say. Not only do I wish I knew how to surf, I wish I could levitate the way I've heard that Muhammad Ali could levitate (although a different source has told me that this levitation was just an optical illusion that trickster Ali knew how to perform). I also wish I could cross an ocean in a bathtub, go over Niagara Falls in a barrel, get shot out of a circus cannon, soar over the flaming statue of a Pterodactyl on Evel Knievel's motorcycle, and go sky-diving, because I know that, if I were able to surmount my fear of those activities and actually coax myself into trying it—jumping out of an airplane, for instance—I'd enjoy the experience. This is assuming, of course, that my parachute opens and I don't get so overwhelmed by the experience of falling through the clouds that I forget to pull my ripcord, which apparently occurs to a significant number of skydivers. (Old joke: The good thing about your parachute not opening is that you've got the rest of your life to solve your dilemma.)

(Not a joke: One how-to manual on the subject, *The Easy Sky Diving Book* from 1977, accidentally printed the instruction "STATE ZIP CODE" when what they meant to print was "PULL RIP CORD." As Oscar Wilde noted, "A poet can survive everything but a misprint.")

Then there are jetpacks. Since my endless hours watching *Lost in Space*, *Land of the Giants*, and other science fiction TV programs when I was a kid, I've always wished I could own one of these gizmos. Zooming through the sky, feeling unafraid of heights because of the raw power supporting me, dropping in on friends (literally), speeding up and slowing down at will, maybe even peeping in some interesting strangers' windows—I don't reckon I would grow weary of such pursuits.

Alas, such gadgets probably won't be commercially available before I die, so my favorite name for an actual rock group, "We Were Promised Jetpacks," succinctly invokes my sense of deflated technological expectation. Here's a substitute wish: to admire the sunburst finish of a day from a Hawaii-bound 747 while I'm riding inside it. Moved by all that natural glory, I'd punch through my cabin window without harming my fist, squeeze my body through the small oval now-empty space, and go bouncing from cloud to cloud as though they're all bloated silver trampolines.

Along with sprinting and the long jump, trampolining is an athletic activity that I used to be good at. I remember when I was six years old and climbed onto a trampoline the first time, frightened that I would propel myself so high that I would crash through the ceiling of the gym in my local YMHA. I'd seen such an accident on my favorite TV show, *Candid Camera*, but, as it happened, there was no need to worry. Within a minute, I got the hang of it and felt proud enough to start showing off for my mother, who was watching from a bird's-eye view on the gym's viewing deck and applauding me with fervor.

This trampoline memory reminds me of an afternoon forty years later, when my own child was six and entered a pie-throwing contest in the parking lot of the Book Soup store in West Hollywood. Before Gideon's turn came, many other children as well as adults had hurled shaving-cream "pies" at a clown who sat ten feet away. Because all of these folks missed the clown, I hoped that my son wouldn't embarrass himself by throwing the pie so wide of the clown's face that people would chortle at the boy. Again, no need to worry: Gideon scored a bull's-eye, filling that gaudy greasepainted face with a splat of shaving cream. Jubilation!

Only a year or two after the pie-throwing contest, on a different vacation, my son and I took a walk near the *fjord* where his grandparents live in a remote mountainous region of Norway. Eventually, we came upon a trampoline at a trailer park, which gave my son his first opportunity to bounce around on one. Soon enough, Gideon was able to break through his fear and started to bounce around and do a flip the way I did them back at the YMHA. Needless to say, I applauded him the way my mother had applauded me, and now Gideon and I were laughing so much and feeling so ecstatic that we might as well have been bouncing together from cloud to cloud in a sunset-splashed sky with our 747 disappearing in the distance, Hawaii be damned. And with no jetpacks necessary.

A child named Jeff in a letter to God writes, "It is great the way you always get the stars in the right places." What if each star represents an ungranted wish, or the residue of a wish that has been granted? Not only am I prone to "wishing upon a star," but I wish I could swing on one and, while I'm at it, bring moonbeams home in a jar. Maybe I could even drop a saddle on Comet Kohoutek and ride that flame-spewing stallion through our solar system while I wave my Stetson at each planet I zing past. (A mnemonic trick for the planets' names which we learned at school was "*M*y *V*ery *E*ager *M*other *J*ust *S*erved *U*s *N*ine *P*izzas." This pizza-bestowing mother differs greatly, I'll wager, from Mother Fist, with those Five Lovely Daughters of hers, as well as from Mother Goddam, which is what the actress Bette Davis encouraged her children to call her. And they all differ from the Mother Luck whom Kris Kristofferson sang about, this Mother being another incarnation of Dame Fortune, whose children, if any, are not known to me.)

While on my comet-borne way, I'll identify the constellations I zoom past, making particular note of Canis Major, with its delightfully named "dog star" Sirius. Perhaps I'll get to witness "attack ships on fire off the shoulder of Orion," "C-beams glittering in the dark near the Tannhauser Gate," and other notable sights from the imaginative galaxy of *Blade Runner*, whose original screenplay was written by my friend Hampton Fancher. (I wish that Hampton had not mocked the title of my first novel, accusing me of "trying too hard" with it, but I reminded him at the time that the novel from which he adapted *Blade Runner* bore the far better title of *Do Androids Dream of Elec-*

tric Sheep?) Finally, while cruising through outer space, I might even get to spot Dame Fortune's visage peeking at me from behind a far-off planet's harvest moon, her dark veil removed at last. She might even be smiling the way the mysterious 113th element in my wish for a Periodic Table dance party smiles…

Back on Earth, I'll reminisce often about my comet ride, how I got to sup on hydrogen and scarf down stardust. Like you, my fellow wisher, I'm made of such material. Didn't Joni Mitchell say as much in a song? Meanwhile, a character in Jim Dodge's novel *Stone Junction* believes each star out there is actually an alchemist's forge, and he grooves to the sight of "so many souls at work." Or could the stars be Dame Fortune's dice, and these dice just keep on rolling?

Anyway, here on this gumball planet, I wish I could be like Oenet-hea, the sorceress in Federico Fellini's film *Satyricon* who is able to snuff out the stars. A great party trick, that. I'll remind myself that one of the loveliest names I know of is that of the Persian prophet Zoroaster, whose name means "stars undiluted." And I'll remember the loveliest fare-thee-well I know of, a salutation that a certain hypnotist said to one of his patients when they parted: "I'll see you in the stars."

When I hear Stevie Wonder sing "*I wish those days could come back once more*," I wish I could relive the day at a California airport when I met Mr. Wonder and told him how much I loved his now-forgotten first hit record "Contract on Love" and he looked surprised and then said, "Oh, man, thank you so much for remembering my song" as if I'd complimented one of his children. Isn't it lovely how much pride some artists take in their work? And how much pleasure they take in it, too? "If it ain't a pleasure, it ain't a poem," said William Carlos Williams. Groucho Marx would have agreed, his own view being, "If you're not having fun, you're doing something wrong."

When a prison production of Samuel Beckett's play *Waiting for Godot* was transferred to a theater in Stockholm, three of the four actors, all of them convicted criminals serving long sentences, escaped before showtime and went on the lam. I wish I could learn why the fourth actor, whose role in the play was as the silent slave "Lucky," did not run away. And I wish I could have witnessed the moment when Beckett was first informed about this occurrence. Apparently, the literary agent who told the esteemed playwright the bad news feared that he would become angry. But what Beckett actually did was grin and tell the agent, "You know, that's the best thing that's ever happened to my play!"

Ah, the art of the insult, and the pithier the better! Said one mid-forties Hollywood wag about the sharp-tongued Hollywood actress Tallulah Bankhead, "A day without seeing Tallulah feels like spending a month in the country." Still, La Bankhead could dish it out, too. When a former lover bumped into her after not seeing her in many years and gave her a hug, she snapped, "I thought I told you to wait in the car." Next time someone puts me down me in such a fashion, I wish I could swing back at them with an insult as effective as, "I'd call you an asshole but you lack the warmth *and* the depth." Or Mae West's "Your mother should have thrown you away and kept the stork." Or G. K. Chesterton not responding after George Bernard Shaw dressed him down in print. Explaining his unwillingness to respond, Chesterton explained, "To a man of Shaw's wit, silence is the one unbearable repartee." He understood that the dogs bark and the caravan moves on.

No one could top Groucho Marx for searing retorts. One time on his live television show *You Bet Your Life*, he asked a woman why she had a dozen children and she said, "Because I'm very fond of my husband," which led Groucho to quip (quite spontaneously, it seems), "I'm very fond of my cigar, too, but I take it out of my mouth sometimes."

I've never been good at thinking up and deploying insults, whether in a heated moment or a playful one. It's an art that even otherwise unsubtle people can sometimes achieve, as when the rock star David Lee Roth explained why critics prefer the music of Elvis Costello to Roth's own music: "It's because they all look like Elvis Costello." I also relish how a rock'n'roll critic compared the sound of the Ramones to "the din of ten thousand toilets in Caracas all flushing at once." Which isn't as direct as how Thomas Carlyle criticized the writer Algernon Charles Swinburne: "A man standing up to his neck in a cesspool—and adding to its contents."

Pick of the litter is the Victorian wag who described Thomas Carlyle's marriage by saying, "How kind of God to have Mr. Carlyle married to Mrs. Carlyle, thereby making two people unhappy instead of four." That wag could have been describing my parents' own union, a union that ended in endless acrimony yet resulted in the wisher whose wish list you're reading.

Youthful me tried to be like the poet Rilke, who said, "*Whenever I saw something that could ring, I rang,*" or like the poet Lord Byron, who said he could not "resist the first night of anything." A longtime wish of mine was never to end up as "a boring old fart." And I'm glad I spent so much of my youth with dangerous people, people like the irrepressible title character of the Dead Milkmen's song "Punk Rock Girl": "*We jumped into a car, away we started rolling / I said, "How much you pay for this?," she said, "Nothing, man, it's stolen.*" I'm glad I lived to tell the tales, too. These tales were wacky but also romantic, just as my favorite thing about the song "Punk Rock Girl" is how the lovers go from wishing to "dress like Minnie Pearl" to wishing, in the last chorus, to have a child together, a child they'll name after the goofy singer Minnie.

But here's the thing: while I'm still happy to meet edgy people, I no longer wish to place myself in the extreme situations we would typically get ourselves into. As I recently wrote in a poem of my own (Rilke and Byron need fear no competition from me), "*Let someone else buy up a shopping mall / For Kansas City Butterball. / Let someone else help Cherry Red / Pop that pink cork on her waterbed. / Let someone else smoke crack for days / And days and days with Ruby Glaze. / Let someone else* menage a quatre */ With Ruby, Cherry, and their rich Dutch brat. / Let someone else run from the shotgun / Of Ruby's husband Tobias Two-Ton.*"

It's not just the people. Even most of my familiar hungers and thirsts and efforts to satisfy those hungers and thirsts simply don't move me now. Who cares whether or not I'm boring? The point is, I've grown *bored*. Of first nights, at least. Besides, those thrills I siphoned out of "drama" were always far outweighed by the emotional toll that the drama took. "Save your drama for your mama," says my tattoo artist friend Jonathan. Maybe he's even inked that phrase into someone's skin. It certainly suits me since my own "mama" was the primary source of my attraction to more drama than was good for me.

What's my latest wish, then? It's for serenity. As I conclude that above-excerpted poem, "*Farewell, best wishes to them all: / Cherry, Ruby, and the K.C. Butterball. / Peaceful's my thing now / I don't crave no more high times.*"

I wish I didn't feel so competitive with everyone I know, including, maybe especially, those I am closest with. When I first heard the writer Gore Vidal's quip "Every time a friend succeeds, I die a little," I felt shocked by his awfulness—until I identified that awfulness in myself, and felt guiltily validated by having the company. Not that I'm proud of my sense of *schadenfreude*. And not that I would go so far as to agree with Confucius, who said, "There is no spectacle more agreeable than to observe a friend fall from a rooftop." In fact, I wish I could more readily experience *freudenfreude*, which is *schadenfreude*'s good-spirited opposite. As Vidal concluded his novel *Myra Breckinridge*, "Happiness, like the proverbial bluebird, is to be found in your own backyard if you just know where to look."

I should mention that much else of what Confucius and Gore Vidal said fails to jibe with me. Vidal's warning to "Never turn down the opportunity to have sex or to appear on television," for instance. Although I do regret having turned down the latter once, I do not regret the few times I turned down the former. On those occasions when I said no to sex, my motivation derived from the novelist Nelson Algren's advice to avoid at all costs playing cards with a man called Doc, eating at a place called Mom's, and sleeping with someone "whose troubles are worse than your own."

Rumor has it that the afore-mentioned Tallulah Bankhead had an affair with her fellow screen actress Greta Garbo. Unlike Bankhead, Garbo left showbiz at her peak. This wasn't because she famously "vished to be alone," it was because, as she told her thespian friend David Niven, "I had made enough faces." Despite my being somewhat extroverted, I more often than not share Garbo's "vish." And I agree with Tom Robbins, who said, "Funny how we think of romance as always involving two, when the romance of solitude can be ever so much more delicious and intense." For S. J. Perelman, happiness need be nothing more than "a brown bag of possessions and a room at the Mills Hotel."

Let lone wolves beware, however: too much solitude can be a bad thing. Hence, I would decline to follow the lead of the English eccentric John Slater, a former Marine commando who lived in a secluded cave. (His wife had said, "It's the cave or me.") He did this after the London Zoo had rejected his offer to spend half his year as a human exhibit in a cage there. At least Slater was not a misanthrope—his personal motto was, "Wag your tail at everyone you meet."

Then there is the pleasure of being alone in a public place, which I wish I could experience more often. Any time I find myself in a New York City subway car with no other passengers—at least none until the next stop—I like to shout, "I am the Duke of Earl, the Duke in my domain," run back and forth, jump up and down, and, to echo that hoary advice, "dance as though no one is watching." Fine, except that whoever is operating that subway car's security camera *is* watching. These days, someone is always watching. Which is one of the reasons why increasingly often you can find me acting like Greta Garbo with her "vish" for solitude.

I wish I would not keep getting nasty cases of "tennis elbow" on my right arm, because each time I go to see a wrist-and-hand doctor to alleviate the problem, I wind up leaving his office with a worse problem. The first time I saw him, he gave me a shot of cortisone in my elbow and sent me on my way, but before I walked out of his waiting room, I noticed an obese elderly woman who was slipping dangerously out of her wheelchair. No one else was there to help her in time, so I ran over to do it. The problem was that as I lifted her, I slipped a disc in my spine. The agony I felt now was worse than my tennis elbow.

"Did you forget something?" the doctor's receptionist asked when I reappeared before her desk.

"No," I said, gasping from the pain, "but I wonder if the doctor could give me *another* cortisone shot. Just now, you see, I injured my lower back."

"I'm sorry," said the receptionist, frowning. "We only treat hands, wrists, and elbows."

Eleven years later, the tennis elbow on my right arm began to act up again, so back to the same specialist I went. He fixed the elbow again with cortisone. On my way out of his office, I stopped to use the restroom, and the heavy door there slammed on my left hand's middle finger, crushing it. The agony I felt now was worse than what my new tennis elbow had been causing. And worse than my lower back pain from eleven years ago.

"Did you forget something?" the doctor's receptionist asked when I reappeared before her desk.

"No," I said, gasping from the pain, "but I wonder if the doctor could give me *another* cortisone shot. You see, I just injured my finger."

"You mean you hurt your finger in a hand doctor's office?" Shaking her head scornfully, the receptionist glanced down at her computer monitor. "Sorry," she said, "we don't have any open appointments until next month."

RANDOM WISHES DIRECTED TO DAME FORTUNE AT 5:18 A.M. WHILE SUFFERING FROM A TYPICAL BOUT OF INSOMNIA:

* Should I read something that might send me back to sleep? Yes, but what? I wish I could sneak a peek at the one-hundred-and-ten plays by Sophocles that were lost forever in the burning of the Library of Alexandria, although the last time I bothered to read one of Sophocles' surviving plays was in high school, so what I might really be wishing for is that the Library had not burned, although I don't spend nearly enough time fretting about the outrageous book burnings and book bans currently happening in my own nation.

* I wish I could extricate myself from boring cocktail conversations as cleverly as the showman P. T. Barnum hurried all the curious customers out of his Hall of Wonders, hence making room for new ones. Barnum posted a sign beside the exit door which read, "THIS WAY TO THE EGRESS." (Isn't the entire universe a gigantic Hall of Wonders? And aren't we all customers who are more or less curious yet avoiding "the egress" the best we can?)

* I wish I knew the story behind the name of an actual punk-rock record company called "You Look Like A Guy I Fucked In Prison." When I learned about this enterprise, I laughed out loud, and my son, who was then six and seated beside me, inquired what I found so funny. So I told him, "I just read about a record company called, 'You Look Like A Guy I *Met* In Prison,'" and the boy laughed even harder than I had.

* I wish I knew if Thucydides was correct that good stories only tend to happen to people who know how to tell about them. And if Tom Robbins is correct that miracles only happen to people who believe in them. And if the poet Rita Dove is correct that "If you feel strange, strange things will happen to you."

* I wish I could conduct my life to the accompaniment of the meltingly melodic pop music of Burt Bacharach and Hal David. Whenever I'm feeling ecstatic, cue the "Casino Royale Theme."

For irony-tinged romantic interludes, let's go with "I'll Never Fall In Love Again." Feeling winsome? "Raindrops Keep Falling On My Head." Then there's onrush of feeling, alternately melancholy and rollicking, that I'd feel whenever I watch and listen to the "South American Getaway" musical sequence in the film *Butch Cassidy and the Sundance Kid.* I also wouldn't mind possessing the character Butch's insouciance. Nor would I mind looking like him.

* In a Tom Stoppard play, a character says, "Happiness is equilibrium. Shift your weight." Lower your standards and expectations, in other words, but not too much. Much of life is about balancing on a fine line—the one, for instance, between taking yourself *too* seriously versus not seriously *enough.* I wish my balance was better—about as good, let's say, as that of a champion tightrope walker. Even the Flying Wallenda who ultimately fell to his death.

* I wish that a message in a bottle would wash up on some seashore while I'm strolling along there. Ideally, the message would bear some relevance to my life, yet I'd be satisfied with a silly riddle such as, "*If Harpo Marx Had Spoken, World War Two Would Not Have Happened.*" If no seashore is available, I'm fine with the kind of message that Leonard Nathan receives in his poem "Bladder Song": "*On a piece of toilet paper / Afloat in the unflushed piss, / The fully printed lips of a woman. / Nathan, cheer up! The sewer / sends you a big red kiss. / Ah, nothing's wasted, if it's human.*"

* Said Jean Prevost, a leader of the French Resistance who was murdered by the Nazis when he was forty-three, "I need three or four cubic feet of new ideas every day, as a steamboat needs coal." I wish I could be that intellectually hungry, and that brave. At the minimum, I'd settle for not feeling the overwhelming urge to punch or kick any inanimate object against which I have accidentally, painfully bumped my head or other body part.

* I wish that Jung was right about synchronicity—that coincidences have a magical origin. But I doubt this is true because I've noticed that these phenomena, "Dame Fortune's practical jokes," occur most often to those folks who just get out of their homes a lot, wander the world, and pay close attention to its random patterns.

* Let me reiterate: I wish that flying drones did not exist. Why? Because one morning outside my tent at a campsite in Tanzania, I was delirious with fever and sitting on my humble "bush toilet" when I suddenly noticed right overhead a drone which was filming me.

The Dutch TV crew who operated this drone later assured me that the situation was accidental and that they would erase the footage. Nevertheless, I've worried ever since then that a video of toilet-straddling me will someday be viewable online. I should have gotten their assurances in writing.

* Listening to Kate Bush's uncanny song "Sat in Your Lap" makes me wish I could have gotten to sit in Leadbelly's lap when I was a child the way my friend Anne did, a wish which inspired me to write this brief poem: "*I threw myself in the lap of the gods / but one of those gods got aroused by my being there / so I jumped back out.*"

* I'm happy to have blue eyes, if only because of how amused I felt when the novelist Norman Mailer, who was notorious for his machismo, told me when I first met him, "You have *such* bright blue eyes." Because his own eyes were bright and blue, was he fishing for a return compliment? Anyway, I'm glad these peepers of mine work properly, although I wish I had 20/20 vision. And I'm too frightened by the popular eye-corrective laser surgeries to see that as an option.

* Abraham Lincoln had respect for the semi-colon, calling it a "useful little chap," but the author Kurt Vonnegut, Jr. hated it, calling it a "transvestite hermaphrodite." I wish I didn't feel a Vonnegut-inspired guilt whenever I use one. A similar guilt plagues me whenever I use the word "suddenly," which my writer friend Dalia hates as much as Vonnegut hates semi-colons. Maybe Vonnegut could have benefited from behaving more like his Uncle Alex. A life insurance salesman, Uncle Alex always made sure to notice when things were going really well, saying out loud to anyone nearby, "If *this* isn't nice, what *is*?"

* I wish I could eat again at Shopsins, the now-gone Greenwich Village restaurant where I lunched regularly in the nineties. Who could resist their Egyptian Risotto Burrito and five hundred other menu items, the insult-dispensing owner-chef named Kenny, his server wife Eve who ate the food off your plate in front of you, a soundtrack that blared Al Jolson music, a set of crackpot unwritten rules for all the customers, and a sign above the kitchen reading, "ALL OUR COOKS WEAR CONDOMS"?

* Some days I wish I could possess a sage's temperament in order to overlook my political differences with certain friends, saying, "Let's just agree to disagree and not let anything ruin our friendship." Other days I wish I could ditch the sagacity and bluntly announce to those friends, "These aren't just political differences between us,

they're differences of core personal *values*, and therefore our friendship is over."

* Wittgenstein said, "The eternal life is given to those who live in the present," and you don't have to be a German philosopher to grasp the perils of straying too often into memories or into anticipations. Of course, the present moment might be just as illusory as any other time, and living in the now isn't exactly easy. We all cling to our yesterdays and tomorrows like shipwreck victims clinging to broken pieces of tinder. But I'm with Wittgenstein, wishing I could simply let go and drown.

* I tend to feel wistful whenever I walk past a mother with her adult son, or parents holding the hands of their young child. These are two sweet situations Dame Fortune denied to me. Yet the older I get, the more my wistfulness comes accompanied by a sense of satisfaction for those mothers and fathers and children. In fact, I wish I could behold such sweet situations daily. Does this mean that—in one zone, at least—I'm growing less narcissistic with age? I hope so. I *wish* so.

* Statistically speaking, many of history's highest-achieving humans never got the chance to exist, because specific sperms did not meet and intermingle with particular eggs. That's just how it is, although I wish I could somehow learn about a few of these phantoms and what their achievements would have been. Talk about hairy "alternative histories!" By comparison, to ask, "What if the Axis won World War Two?" and "What if the Russians landed on the moon first?" is strictly for amateurs.

* I wish I hadn't taken a nap yesterday because while I dozed I had a nightmare about Mr. Ravoon. Remember the black-clad eye patch–wearing *Who's Who in America*-reading old man I used to see around New York and Paris? My nightmare was a scary dramatization of this verse by Paul Dehn about Mr. Ravoon's original female counterpart: "*I stood by the waters so green and so thick / And I stirred at the scum with my old, withered stick / When there rose through the ooze like a monstrous balloon / The bloated cadaver of MRS. RAVOON*!"

* I wish that slightly miserly me would spend money so freely that, as Kevin Kelly says, my "last check should go to the funeral home and bounce." And just before I wind up in any funeral home, I'll probably wish I could "do it all over again," my fellow wisher. If only, as in my favorite Bob Dylan song, so I can "do it all over you."

SEVEN. IMPRUDENT WISHES

In Pieter Brueghel's painting *Netherlands Proverbs*, he depicts a globe hung upside down, which suggests the Dutch expression "*de wereld op zijn kop*," meaning "a world stood on its head." What's more, a fool with a winning hand of playing cards is defecating on that globe in Brueghel's painting, which suggests a more widely used expression: "Dame Fortune favors the stupid."

Perhaps a more useful word than "stupid" is "simple," which reminds me of my wish that, with my writing, at least, I had the "gift of being simple" extolled by the religious group the Shakers. "Just don't get too complicated, Eddie," a character in the movie *The Blue Dahlia* advises. "When a man gets too complicated, he's unhappy. And when he's unhappy, his luck runs out." Oscar Wilde agreed with this sentiment, although the way he stated it was, "Life is not complex. We are complex. Life is simple, and the simple thing is the right thing." As fractals show, the simple can be complex in its own simple way. And visa versa. Which might helpfully describe Dame Fortune's nature.

Speaking for myself, I used to strive so diligently to be a brilliant writer, deploying the most sumptuous syntax, aiming to be fancy, or "*punci-schmunci*," as they say in Hungarian. What turned me around was someone's remark that if you can tell a story in a bar, then you can write it. (Teetotalers like myself can tell them anywhere.) The longer I live, the less I appreciate *punci-schmunci*—in anything. What sealed the deal for me in this realm was the riposte by Hemingway about William Faulkner after Faulkner complained about Hemingway's spare language. "Poor Faulkner," said Hemingway. "Does he really think that big emotions come from big words?" (Still, it was Faulkner and not Hemingway who said that we often love not *because* but *despite*.)

Speaking of elegance, the Talmud says you can learn from a rabbi even by the way he ties his shoes. I wish I could perform everyday tasks such as unlocking a car door, filling a glass with water from a pitcher, and lifting a book from a table with the simple yet elegant attentiveness, precision, and care that my father-in-law uses. Istvan survived many harsh experiences in his life, and every movement made by this strong and kindhearted and handsome old Hungarian man reflects a kind of personal grace. There is a multitude of people whom I admire. I admire Istvan the most.

Forget about that *oonts, oonts, oonts, oonts* techno music—it's rock'n'roll for me, forever and ever, amen. Bruce Springsteen and the E Street Band in 1978, the David Johansen Group in '79, the Clash in '80, Elvis Costello and the Attractions in '81, an unknown combo called the Double-O-Zeros in a near-empty nightclub in '82, REM in a Hardee's fast food joint in '83 (that's a tale for a different time), the Patti Smith Group in 2001, Lydia Lunch (who makes Patti Smith seem like Britney Spears) in 2011, Gogol Bordello in a forest near Lviv, Ukraine, a few months before Covid-19 began spreading—these rock'n'roll concerts that have meant the most to me felt like mass public baptisms. I'm hardly the first fan to make this connection, and yet listening to the music while alone in my bedroom or in my automobile strikes me as even more religious than the public experience. Transported and transformed by what I'm hearing, I feel, well, sort of divine. Like a tiny weak short-lived god but a god, all the same, transcending human cares while dancing goofily between four walls or two car doors.

Is it any wonder that I wish I could be a rock star? The closest I've come to realizing this ambition was singing on a New York City concert stage alongside my rocker friend Willie Nile. An exhilarating experience, you bet, although what I remember best about the number I performed with Willie was some middle-aged bald guy in the audience who slightly resembled me. To my chagrin, he kept pointing my way and laughing scornfully. Was he just a mirage? Or was he a visual projection of my unshakable imposter syndrome, the nagging sense I felt that I didn't belong up there onstage in front of paying customers?

At least no one hurled eggs at me, or more dangerous canned foods, or the "salads and beefsteaks" that audience members threw at Dada poets in early twentieth-century Paris theaters. Not that the Dadaists were deterred by such abuse—their motto, after all, was, "If you must speak of Dada, you must speak of Dada. If you must not speak of Dada, you must still speak of Dada." Which is the rock'n'roll spirit I can channel as a listener and as a spectator but not, alas, as a performer.

There was a time when I wished I could live by the two rules that the writer Brenda Ueland said she tried to live by: "Tell the truth, and don't do anything you don't want to do." Then I wised up. The latter rule is certainly appealing. Who doesn't like to hear the Rabelais prescription "Do what thou wilt shall be the whole of the law"? Unfortunately, this rule is impossible. For example, I tend to say "yes" to social invitations when I really want to say "no," though someone has advised me that we should only say yes when this yes is actually a "Hell, *yeah*" or a brisk Japanese "*hai*!" Perhaps the best "no" to give someone is the hedging phrase "I'd love to, but now is not a good time for me." Which is akin to saying "You may be right" whenever you disagree with someone about something but you don't feel like arguing about it—an argument being perhaps what the other person is truly seeking.

As for Brenda Ueland's other rule, "Tell the truth"—well, I would declare a wish here to be a more truthful person were it not for the fact that I so often find myself wishing that I could be a better liar. And wishing at the same time that I could get better at spotting other people's lies. One thing I know for certain is that whenever a person, a corporation, or any other institution tells you, "We're putting *your* interest before ours," don't believe them. Among the worst offenders in this category are denizens of the Hollywood machine, where, as the old joke has it, "*fuck you*" is pronounced as "*trust me*."

Having mentioned rock'n'roll religiosity, let me identify myself as one of the countless Americans who self-define as "not religious but spiritual," even though there are times when I wish I could be both. Organized religion, in spite of all the catastrophes it causes, does have the virtue of satisfying our need for "fellow feeling" in a community built on shared values and kindness. Thomas Pynchon puts it well: "You may never get to touch the Master, but you can tickle his creatures."

As for that Master, this higher being whom the author Scott Sanders labels "the original conspiracy theory," the philosopher Voltaire said, "God is a comedian playing to an audience too afraid to laugh," but van Gogh went Voltaire one better by declaring, "We must not judge God from this world, which is just a study that didn't come off. It's only a master who could have made such a blunder."

If I were God, or at least had God's omniscience and omnipotence, you'd best believe I'd set this universe right. All those pesky ninjas would go scattering, and Dame Fortune would deign to socialize with me outside my dreams. Do I wish I could actually *be* God, that "which beyond which there is no witcher"? Nope. Too much responsibility, and I already feel guilty and ashamed enough as it is about so many of my behaviors. Still, being one deity among many—one of those in the Hindu pantheon, for example—might be fun. I wouldn't mind being the elephant-headed Ganesha for a day. Like me, he's got a sweet tooth. ("Sure, I'll have the dessert," a friend of mine told the server at a restaurant where we were dining recently. "Let them cut off my foot tomorrow.")

I often wish I could believe in an interventionist deity, if only to bask in the throb of self-acceptance I felt when I encountered this graffito on a building in Brunswick, Georgia: "NEVER ONE TWINGE OF DISAPPOINTMENT IN YOU. YOURS TRULY, GOD." A good deity to follow might be Abraxas, who is mentioned by Hermann Hesse in his novel *Demian*, which was the first work of serious literature I read (unless I count Raymond Chandler's hardboiled books *The Little Sister* and *The Long Goodbye*, which I probably should). According to Hesse, Abraxas is Jehovah and Satan mixed together, both dark and light, so "he does not take exception to any of your thoughts, any of your dreams. But he will abandon you once you become blameless and normal."

Most of all, I wish I could find out for certain whether any deity actually exists. Does our belief in God stem from our earliest fuzzy sense of our parents? They were, after all, gigantic beings who loomed over us, nurturing, protecting, rewarding, and punishing. If this is indeed so, then that atheistic soldier who nevertheless prays to God while in a foxhole is unwittingly begging for his absent mommy to save his ass.

Fortunately, I haven't landed in any foxholes yet, but I've prayed a good deal to my absent mommy (despite remembering this definition of "prayer" in Ambrose Bierce's *Devil's Dictionary*: "To ask that the laws of the universe be annulled in behalf of a single petitioner confessedly unworthy.") When a journalist asked Iggy Pop if he believed in God, Iggy's charming response was, "I believe in *all* gods, just for kicks." Which raises the question of whether Mr. Pop *prays* to any of those gods. Would he consider addressing the delightfully named "Last-Last-First-Father Namandu," for example? Or Dame Fortune? Will Iggy keep believing right up to the brink of *Gotterdammerung*? And will the Dame also get finished off during that "twilight of the gods?"

I wish I knew the answers to all of the above. I probably never will. But Pop's "all gods" belief reminds me of these lines from "Courage," Wilhelm Müller's poem set to music by Franz Schubert: "*When your heart within you breaks, sing serenely and brightly / If no God is here on earth, let's all be* gods *together.*"

I hope the humorist Ivor Cutler was only being ironic when he remarked, "The best thing about being dead is that you no longer have to say, 'I wish I was dead.' The best thing about being alive is you can still say, 'I wish I was dead.'" For all such wishing, Cutler lived into his eighties. As a forlorn teenager, I was *not* being ironic when I would sit on the edge of a tall rock cliff in the forest behind my home and mentally compose a suicide note. This note read, "My parents killed me long ago. What I'm doing today just formally seals the deal."

Despite my lack of irony, I wasn't serious about topping myself; I merely had an acute case of the teenage blues. Still, I spent a few decades continuing to blame Mom and Dad for all my problems. Hadn't they, more than anyone else, shaped who and how I was? I even went to Times Square one night in the late eighties and got a t-shirt printed up for myself which read, "I SURVIVED ESTHER LIPPMAN." ("Surviving" her had always been a more demanding process than "surviving" Bernie Lippman.)

I wish that during my childhood I could have done as Thomas Pynchon recommends and simply viewed my parents as characters in a television sitcom: "Pretend there's a frame around 'em like the Tube," writes Pynchon, "pretend they're a show you're watching." And I wish I could go on blaming Esther and Bernie for my adult problems, because having ever-present scapegoats, even dead ones, certainly streamlines one's life. But blaming your parents for anything is a loser's sport. Far better than laying any blame is to correctly identify how your mother and father's behavior affected you and then note that such past behavior is a stone-cold given, like your height.

One big transformative moment for me arrived when I recognized a gift in my early suffering. I wanted to be a writer, so wasn't this great material? (As my father's poet friend John Ciardi once noted, you don't have to suffer through a war or other adult tragedies such as war in order to become an artist. "Adolescence," wrote Ciardi, "is enough suffering for anyone.") Another transformative moment came when I became a parent myself and, to my dismayed surprise, immediately began fucking up enough in this role that it felt like I'd fucked up everything. I certainly felt parentally impotent. As Adam Phillips writes, "To be a parent is to face how little you can protect your child from. And powerlessness...doesn't tend to bring out the best in people."

Eventually, my recognition of my faulty parenting turned to compassion for myself, since I knew that I was at least doing my level best to parent my son well. And then this self-directed compassion extended to my parents. Weren't they, in spite of all their limitations, some very glaring limitations, nevertheless trying to do their level best with me? They were. So instead of taking that easy route of blaming Esther and Bernie Lippman for having caused my problems, shouldn't I wish instead that I could retroactively somehow send a message to them, a message saying, "I get it now, and I forgive you, and, just as emphatically, I thank you"?

As a father I wish I would be forever able to "parent the child I have," not the child I fear I have, or the child I wish I had, or the child I used to be myself. And how about a bonus wish for all the parents reading this list? To sharpen your sense of the gravity of parenthood, and of life, try to spend some time in a hospital with seriously ill children. *Hopital Necker* in Paris, for example. This program works even better if your own child is a patient there.

Time for me to introduce you to Dr. Michel Zerah. How I wish that Dr. Zerah had not died so young, at age sixty-five, because this French neurosurgeon was a *mensch* of the first order, one who saved the lives of many children. And because he saved the life of my own child, I wish I had told Dr. Zerah more emphatically and more often how grateful I am to him.

In February of 1999, my then-girlfriend Thorhildur and I brought our infant son Gideon to a female doctor near our home in Paris. Gideon seemed to have chronic headaches, so we knew something must be wrong. Still, we were utterly unprepared, and totally poleaxed, when the doctor came rushing back into her office with Gideon's new MRI results and announced, in a newly frantic state, "This child needs emergency brain surgery!"

Parenthood, Thorhildur and I realized, was no longer just fun and games and the frequent need to change a diaper. "But—but—"

we sputtered together while the doctor used her Mont Blanc pen to scribble an address on a pad of paper. Then she told us, "Take your boy to this address, *right now*, or he will die!"

Enter: Dr. Zerah, the top pediatric neurosurgeon at the Hopital Necker. In spite of his formidable reputation, Zerah had a soft voice, owlish spectacles, a crazy Harpo Marx-style mop of silver hair, and an open round face that belied the air of slight sadness that seemed to follow him like a nearly visible cloud. Perhaps this sadness derived from all the children whose lives he had tried to save but could not. While Dr. Zerah explained to us that our son had hydrocephalus, a fluid blockage in his brain caused by a congenital cyst, my mind was reeling, and Thorhildur looked even more shocked and devastated than I felt. But Zerah reassured us that the surgery he would perform a few days later would most likely be successful, successful and without many serious after-effects. The relief we felt surpassed any relief either of us had ever felt before, and enhancing this feeling was Dr. Zerah himself, with his aura of calm authority. The aura suggested to us, *We can trust this man*. Not that we had any other choice.

I remember well the days before and after Gideon's surgery, when our friends Kees, Txiki, and Alosha came to visit us. I would often leave our hospital room to wander alone through the halls of Hopital Necker, heading to the cafeteria or the gift shop. Feeling confident that our son would survive, I sometimes even hummed a jaunty song to myself until I rounded a corner and encountered a young couple who were pushing their own child in a wheelchair. The child's head was shaved, with a terrible scar across the scalp, and he had an awful faraway look in his eyes. So much for my elation. Each time I walked near this family, I would say hello to them but then look away, my eyes welling with tears, and feel ashamed that my apparent current good fortune could not likewise be theirs. Why was my child projected to survive his ordeal intact and this other child possibly would not? What was Dame Fortune's reasoning?

Most vividly of all, I remember the day of Gideon's surgery. As zero hour grew close, Thorhildur and I began to wonder if Dr. Zerah was really the wizard we hoped he was. Or what if he was a wizard, yes, but something went wrong, anyway? Something even his keen owlish eyes had been unable to glimpse in advance?

At zero hour, two orderlies transported Gideon out of his room on his wheeled bed. Our waiting began. Thorhildur and I didn't speak much. We felt too anxious to do anything now but to sit in silence. Not total silence—I was playing soft music on a portable cassette player I'd brought to the room so we could entertain Gideon with children's songs in the days before his surgery. The theme of *The Addams Family* TV show was a particular favorite of his. Unaware of what he was up against at Hopital Necker, he would laugh and clap along as Thorhildur and I sang that tune to him.

About ninety minutes after they took our son to the operating theater, Bill Evans's poignant ballad "Waltz for Debby" began to play on my cassette player. I'd always found endearing this song about an adult's love for his child, a love made bittersweet by his knowledge that she would one day be a child no longer. Halfway through "Waltz for Debby," the door to Gideon's room swung open and the orderlies wheeled our son back into the room. He was unconscious, his tiny head wrapped in bandages, and behind the bed walked Dr. Zerah, who smiled diffidently at us.

"*Ca marche*," he said. *It worked.*

And now Gideon, like the girl in "Waltz for Debby," is an adult, already halfway through his twenties, and Dr. Zerah is gone, dead from cancer, the same illness that killed my mother. Zerah is no longer able to save, or try to save, the children in Paris who need him. He cannot "take his children home," as Uncle John does in that magnificent Grateful Dead song. And even though I thanked Dr. Zerah for what he did for my son and our family, I failed to thank him enough, not nearly enough, and when I think of the doctor now, I feel not only gratitude and regret but also something of his sadness, sadness that surrounds me sometimes like a nearly visible cloud.

I wish that we could know for certain what Jesus looked like. A few historians suspect he was not tall and thin and blond but a short, tubby, full-bearded balding black-haired guy. In other words, he was more cuddly-looking. Another wish of mine is that more people knew that "Jiminy Cricket" is a euphemism for "Jesus Christ," and that the name Jesus went by during his life, the only formal name people called him, was "*Yashua ben Yosef*."

Names, names, names: I wish I could have chosen my own moniker once I grew old enough to make a mature choice, though none could rival "The Big Figure," which is the stage name of the drummer of the rock band Dr. Feelgood. I wish I'd given my son the same opportunity to choose his own name. I wish I hadn't laughed out loud when a woman told me that her actual name was "Tajma Hall." And I wish I could meet some of the imaginary freaks who populate the lyrics of the pop group Steely Dan: Babs and Clean Willie, the Babylon Sisters, Lady Bayside, Razor Boy, Hoops McCann, the Expanding Man, Dave from Acquisitions, Deacon Blues, Daddy G (moonlighting from the Gary "US" Bonds song "Quarter To Three"), and El Supremo, who may be an incarnation of Dame Fortune.

If you agree with the cliché that truth is often more grotesque than fiction, you might prefer these confirmed names of actual persons from times past: Willie the Pleaser, Kidneyfoot Rella, Bang Zang, the Bobbed-Haired Bandit, Sheep Eye, Miff Mole, Mangle Minthorne, Mary Meathouse (not to be confused with Snaggle Mouf Mary or Flamin' Marie), Primrose Goo, Goody Faldo, Andy from the Sixties, Buster Hymen, Good Lord the Lifter, Fate Marable (who gave Louis Armstrong his early gigs), Queen of the Forty Elephants, Stack 'O' Dollars, the medieval religious painter known only as "The Master of the Eleven Thousand Virgins," Teddy Odd Legs, Jennifer 8. Lee, The Devil's Son-In-Law, Charlie Bow Wow, the female Viking named Aud the Deep-Minded, Boo Boo Fortunato, the Mayan being called "Jaguar of Sweet Laughter," and King Loon, alias the Who drummer Keith Moon, but also perhaps an incarnation of the Dame in drag.

Even a single name is capable of telling a story if you set your imagination loose on it. Consider "Thalassa Doxa," the monicker not of a person but of a gargantuan Liberian container ship which I once saw moving by night on the river that runs through Savannah. Or consider the siblings Bugless, Energetic, Euphrates, and Goliath Smith. Names don't reveal everything, however. One of the most fascinating people I've known was named Richard Smith.

If the vaunted technological "singularity" predicted by scientists does indeed arrive soon, I might clamor to have my individual consciousness not flicker out but instead get downloaded into a robot which looks like me, only better, and is immortal, or at least lives as long as energy supplies allow. And the closer I get to death, smelling old Stretchfoot's fetid breath, the stronger this wish may grow. Still, I can't help but wonder why Dame Fortune would allow me to receive this opportunity when none of my already-dead loved ones got to have a crack at it. Isn't my place with them and the rest of humanity as I know it? I already feel guilty as it is that I've outlived my mother by more than four decades. I don't want to become superhuman if the cost is losing my humanity. Too weird. Plus, how comfortable will a titanium body feel?

The truth is, I'm something of a Luddite, prone to singing Lord Byron's verse "*Down with all kings but King Ludd*!" Advanced technology all too often lessens that "sweet mystery of life" sung about by Ruby Levine. Take social media, for instance. Isn't it, to quote Rickie Lee Jones in her song "Livin' It Up," "*more trouble than it's worth*?" Even the Internet itself can be problematic. For decades, I used to scour used bookstores for out-of-print volumes on my biblio-wish list, and this hunt proved fruitless yet fun. Then, as soon as I leaped online for the first time, I discovered a rare book website, and within fifteen minutes I'd purchased every one of those dearly wished-for volumes. My hunt was over. And I felt—well, excited to finally own and read those books, yes, but empty, too. The process had been too easy.

Another invention to gripe about is the cellular telephone. We're all familiar with the horrors of losing them or breaking them or having them inconveniently run out of power or accidentally "butt dialing" the wrong person, which in one case ended a relationship of mine. Worst of all is their alienation effect, what the sociologist Sherry Turkle meant when she said, "Because of our cell phones, we are forever elsewhere." Accordingly, I wish that these things had never been invented. I'm not alone in my sentiment, either—Sigmund Freud hated all telephones. Then again, he also posited that "The fetish is a substitute for the mother's penis" and labelled the United States "a gigantic mistake." He certainly made some triple-X-sized mistakes of his own.

Please note that my gripe with phones does not extend to landlines, and I sometimes miss public payphone booths, which had an innocence about them. When a character in a movie tells W. C. Fields to speak louder, Fields retorts, "If I could speak louder, I wouldn't need a telephone." Which reminds me of the famous piano player who purchased a small portable keyboard and, as he walked home with it, a stranger who recognized him shouted, "Hey, haven't you heard of business cards?"

There was a similar innocence about having to rely on landlines at home, too, although they had their own pitfalls. Throughout my childhood, my mother used a "second line" that she'd installed in order to eavesdrop on my phone conversations with my father. After I hung up from each of these talks, she would scold me viciously for all of the things I had "said wrong"—the things that sounded "too nice" to Bernie Lippman. She wished that I'd spoken to him with the same spitefulness that she did. Of course, I would have spoken in an even kinder way to my father if I had not been aware that Esther Lippman was listening to our every word. In the house I grew up in, my mother's house, the worst sin was for me to actively love my father.

I'm sorry to report that Esther's program of demonization and indoctrination was ultimately somewhat successful. Because of that program, I wound up loving Bernie far less than I would have otherwise. Which is probably why so much of my adult life has been spent in befriending older men whom I find in some way appealing or inspiring. I call these men friends, or big brothers, or mentors, but what they are is surrogate fathers. ("The question for the child," wrote the psychoanalyst Bruno Bettelheim, "is not, 'Do I want to be good?' but 'Whom do I want to be like?'") Unfortunately, I've never dared to tell any of my surrogate fathers how much I care about them. I don't want to scare them away the way my mother hoped I'd help her scare my actual father away. But I wish I could tell them.

I wish I didn't know so many rigid moralizers, the kind who, as Cyril Connolly said of George Orwell, "can't blow their noses without complaining about the state of the handkerchief industry." Many of these types can't stop being hypocritical, either. Someone once said about the writer Arthur Koestler, "As is the case with so many people who boast that they want to save the world, you couldn't trust Koestler alone with your wife." I'm thinking here of a strident anti-war activist I know who was recently exposed as a paid propagandist for Vladimir Putin. And I'm thinking of a self-righteous environmental activist I met once on the shores of a lake in Montana. Not only was he smoking a Camel cigarette, which surprised me—couldn't he treat his body with the same care that he insisted the rest of us show to the planet?—but when he'd had enough of his cancer stick, he openly tossed the butt into the lake. Shocked by this behavior, I politely challenged him on it, and his response was, "Do you have any idea how many other cigarette butts are on the lake bottom?"

In retrospect, I should have identified this fellow as trashy from the get-go, given how prone he was to using New Age jargon. (I once heard him warn a woman that she had "a leak in her aura.") Nevertheless, I wish I'd challenged the cigarette polluter more zealously. And I wish that all our self-professed world-savers would do as much good on the micro level as they do on the macro. Starting with themselves.

Is there life after death? Don't ask me, fellow wisher. Sometimes I'm strictly a rationalist, refusing to believe in anything not verified by science. The only meanings there are in life are what we bring to it. Yet at other times I do feel what the author Reynolds Price has called "a suspicion of the transcendental." And wish I could feel more of it.

Our current metaphysical knowledge is certainly meager. Nietzsche observed that every philosophical statement, no matter how obvious, should have a "Perhaps" or two in there, while the cynical scribe H.L. Mencken quipped, "We are here and it is now. Further than that all human knowledge is moonshine." Even Descartes's immortal maxim "I think, therefore I am" has something wrong with it, so another cynical writer, Ambrose Bierce, improved it as "I *think* that I think, therefore I *think* that I am." Bierce called this new maxim "as close an approach to certainty as any philosopher has yet made." I wish we could all live more in the "perhaps" mode, with less certainty about everything leading perhaps to a more tolerant planet. Alas, we humans seem to crave being sure, to insist on it. We just can't relax with so much uncertainty swirling around us.

"Perhaps" holds most of the cards, yes. Which returns us to the concept of an afterlife. Anyone who claims to *know* what happens to us after we die is mistaken. People may *believe* they know, but beliefs, intuitions, suspicions, are as weightless as hope when it comes to hard cold testable scientific facts. Asked if he believed in ghosts, the author Robertson Davies wrote, "I believe in them the way that Shakespeare believed in them." What I reckon Davies meant is that, although ghosts do not exist, they make for some seriously good stories. This is because they embody (pun intended) how we feel about death: our awe and fear of it, our desire to live beyond it (even if we're just transparent ectoplasm), and our yearning to be reunited with our dead loved ones (even if they're just transparent ectoplasm).

On the subject of "reuniting with our dead loved ones," I have one item to share. While eulogizing his beloved saxophone-playing bandmate Clarence Clemons at Clemons's funeral, my fellow New Jerseyan Bruce Springsteen said, "Clarence doesn't leave our band when *he* dies. He leaves the band when *we* die." With strong enough emotion, those "reunions" need not be in the flesh to be meaningful.

I wish that I'd paid less attention to Lainie, a girl I knew from my summer job at a children's day camp, when I drove past her suburban New Jersey house one summer afternoon when I was seventeen. I drove past Lainie's house because I was in love with her, and wished to see if I could spot her on her lawn as I motored by. I didn't tell my plan to my mother, who was seated beside me in the passenger seat of our beige Buick station wagon. I didn't tell her because my mother had forbidden me from having girlfriends, or even speaking to any girls, until I'd finished graduate school. What harm, I figured, could come from a quick drive-by and peek?

A lot of harm, as it happened. Just as I drove past her house, Lainie stepped out of the front door wearing a pale blue bikini. For a moment there, I couldn't believe my good luck. *Dame Fortune is smiling on me*, I thought. But I took my eyes off the road to gawk at Lainie for too long and, as a result, I crashed our car into a telephone pole. I was brand-new at love then, and equally new at driving, so this crash may have been inevitable.

For a few moments, my mother and I just stared straight ahead at the smoke pouring out from under our extremely crumpled car hood. Once I recovered from my shock, I turned to Esther Lippman, frightened about how bad my punishment would be. Once she recovered from her own shock, I had my answer. She began to scream at me and punch me. This was my answer. And once Lainie recovered from *her* shock—how many people walk out of their front door just in time to witness a car accident in front of their home?—she recognized my station wagon and began to laugh.

Given my humiliation, I wished I could stay in our station wagon, hiding from my beloved as well as from the rest of the car-accident-reality I now lived in. Unfortunately, our vehicle was wrecked, and in the contained space of the front seat, a furious middle-aged woman kept screaming at and punching me. To save my life, or at least to prevent serious injury, I jumped out and took off running at a fast clip down Lainie's street. I should have known that Esther Lippman, despite the cancer that was already devastating her, would follow me out of our car and give chase, intent on doing more screaming and punching. In the meantime, Lainie's laughter hit overdrive as she watched me running down the street with my mother running after me, chasing me all over Lainie's neighborhood.

By the time Esther Lippman finally grew weary of the hot pursuit and limped back to our "totaled" station wagon, my humiliation was complete. So was my sorrow. There would be no chance of me ever driving off into the sunset with Lainie. *My heart will never repair itself*, I thought. I was wrong, of course—my heart would get fixed and then be broken again on many other occasions. I even broke my own heart once, and in seventeen places. But that's a tale for a different time.

With no choice but to trail my mother back to our car—where else was I supposed to go?—I dodged my mother's final half-hearted slaps and mumbled an unbearable hello to Lainie, trying not to ogle her bikini-clad body. She couldn't stop grinning in my face. Then came *further* humiliation: Because we were unable to drive away, we had to ask my beloved if we could step into her house to use her telephone to summon a tow truck. She agreed, but the truck did not arrive for an hour, which made for a supremely awkward visit. And at work the next morning, Lainie made sure to recount the story of my disgrace to all of our colleagues.

As for our station wagon, it took a month for it to be repaired, with these repairs quite costly, yet that vehicle never drove well again. The steering wheel kept tugging to the right, as if it wished to humiliate me again by forcing me to ram into another telephone pole. Or maybe my car had simply developed a taste for pain and yearned for more of it.

When my son was a toddler, I secretly wished that he would stay at age five forever so that he'd never mature enough to look at me with judgmental eyes. I was his hero back then, but I feared that once Gideon started comparing me with other fathers, then with other men, then, eventually, with his own self, he would see his old man as the deeply flawed guy I am.

At the same time, I had a conflicting wish about my five-year-old: that he would grow older overnight so I could experience him right away as an adult, speak with him about adult matters, and interact with him as two peers rather than as adult-to-child. As soon as Gideon hit puberty, however, I realized how wrong this secret wish of mine had been. I missed the innocence of his childhood self and lamented its passing. Anyway, who was I to deny him his normal human growth?

As the cartoonist Lynda Barry points out, if you ask a group of children, "How many of you are serious artists?," every hand will shoot up. Nietzsche's definition of reaching maturity is "to recover the seriousness one has as a child at play." Remembering the Barry and Nietzsche points, I wish I could retrieve my childhood's lack of crushing self-judgment. Oh, to view the world again with a childlike sense of wonder! Mistaking the name "Ella Fitzgerald" as "Ellafitz Gerald" when I was three, for example, I felt amazed at how beautifully weird a person's moniker could be. And I felt even more amazed around the same time when my father explained to me that I would gradually grow up to be an adult. Before then, I'd assumed that children were children and adults were adults and each group always remained this way, as two subspecies of humans with separate fixed places in this existence. And fixed interactions. What an extraordinary opportunity, it now seemed to me, to gradually age and wind up a grown-up myself!

Every so often lately, I find myself wishing that those sub-species *did* stay fixed, with my son still existing on the kids' side of the line. And with *myself* on Gideon's side of the line, as well.

Another Lippy Law of mine is, "Just as 'You can choose your friends, but you cannot choose your family,' you can choose your friends, but you cannot choose the people they marry." Accordingly, I wish I could choose the spouses for my friends. This would give me a lot of work, yes, but I wouldn't have to shudder through certain dinner parties with a smile pasted on my face while I regard those obnoxious wives or husbands instead of doing what I really want to do, which is to scowl or roll my eyes at them. Of course, the spouses probably feel the same way about me.

Actually, I've always enjoyed playing matchmaker. I wish, for example, I could fix up with each other the ex-spouses of my friends Shelly and Mike, because both Shelly and Mike have independently, at great length and in forensic detail described to me what straight-up *psychopaths* those exes were. The idea in putting these two psychopath ex-spouses together is to see if they spark with each other romantically and then to stand back and watch, ideally while munching popcorn, as the fur flies.

The greatest blind date I could wish to set up would introduce Maude, that elderly free spirit of the film *Harold and Maude*, with Martin "Grandpa" Vanderhof from the George S. Kaufman and Moss Hart play *You Can't Take It With You*. Grandpa's the yin to Maude's yang, the yang to her yin, and I'm sure that Maude will start preferring Grandpa to that whippersnapper Harold as soon as she hears Grandpa make his usual remarks, stuff like, "Life is simple and kind of beautiful if you let it come to you. One day it struck me that I wasn't having any fun. So I just relaxed. And I've been a happy man ever since."

To sweeten their blind date further with some serenades, I will hire Ruby Levine, the "sweet mystery of life" street violinist. And I'll make sure to keep far away from Kaufman and Hart's other fine creation, the acerbic-beyond-belief Sheridan Whiteside. (How acerbic was Whiteside? This "Man Who Came To Dinner" tells an intimate, "My great-aunt Jennifer ate a whole box of candy every day of her life. She lived to be one hundred-and-two, and when she had been dead for three days, she looked better than you do now.") I'm sure that Maude and Grandpa and Ruby will know just how to handle the Whiteside beast if he tries to gate-crash their dinner date. And Dostoevsky's Father Zosima, dropping by for a Brandy Alexander, might even soften Whiteside's dark heart.

When I was single, I got fixed up on plenty of my own blind dates, and I wish that most of them could have gone better than they did. A cousin of mine named Sally once urged me to go on a blind date with a woman named Beth who, according to Sally, "looks exactly like Brooke Shields." Interestingly enough, Beth turned out not to resemble Brooke Shields but Cousin Sally herself. Darcy, another woman with whom I got fixed up on a blind date, was, to my considerable surprise when I met her, eight months pregnant. Somehow the mutual friend who'd paired me with Darcy had neglected to mention her condition.

A different amateur-matchmaker friend urged me to meet someone named "Serena Smiley," who never smiled once during our date, while yet another matchmaker urged me to meet a woman named Jilissa who was "a tantric sex instructor with a good heart." Needless to say, I got excited. The problem with Jilissa happened when I went to meet Jilissa at her house for our dinner date and Jilissa's housemate told me, "You missed her by three hours. A pair of cops showed up and arrested her and drove off."

"You're not serious," I said. "Jillisa's inside there, right?"

"Dude, I'm as serious as a heart attack. They didn't handcuff her, though. She went willingly. Lately she's been a people pleaser. Tantra smoothed out her edges."

"What did she do that was illegal?"

"How should I know? Ask Jilissa."

I wish I hadn't inherited my mother's allergy to alcohol. Still, I prefer having inherited this allergy to having instead inherited my father's thirst for liquor. Esther and Bernie Lippman's dissimilar relationships with alcohol are further evidence of how mismatched as a couple they were.

Which brings us to the matter of other recreational drugs. Adventurous me wishes that I'd tried more "*stupefiants*," to use the French term, because I believe that with each new experience you try (the ones you're curious about trying, that is, and not repulsed by), the more you're getting your DNA's worth out of life. Perhaps we're here on this plane of existence to learn lessons, and one way to learn is to have everything which is familiar get *de*familiarized by that good old intoxicating "mischief for your brain," as the poet Edna St. Vincent Millay deliciously called drugs. Recreational drugs have their other practical uses, too; I once met a woman who wore a t-shirt that read, "I CAN EITHER PASS A DRUG TEST *OR ELSE* WORK WELL WITH PEOPLE. I *CAN'T* DO BOTH."

Although I've tried more than a few controlled substances, I have never smoked crack or opium, dropped Quaaludes, or sampled DMT, which seems to lead everyone to hallucinate that they're in the same landscape, a gray mechanical world inhabited by armored gremlins. Nor have I have snorted glue or huffed gasoline or sipped the cocaine wine Mariani or received LSD enemas, and I have never come across the recreational drug on offer by the delightful character Danny the Dealer in the film *Withnail and I*. Brandishing a capsule, Danny says, "Trade: Phenodihydropchloridebenedrex. Street: the Embalmer." This drug, he promises, "will make you think a brain tumor is a birthday present."

In my drinking days I was especially partial to absinthe, the liquid "Green Fairy" which my son's mother Thorhildur and I were drinking the night we first made love. (In my dream that night my mother came to me out of the shadows, wearing a hooded robe and carrying a torch.) My favorite brand of absinthe is home-brewed by my friend Marcella, who also makes her own laudanum as well as a liqueur made of Bosco Chocolate Syrup and hashish. The first time my future wife Berta and I imbibed that latter concoction, we were dancing at a Brooklyn nightclub until Berta froze in place and told me, utterly serious, "My legs have just grown roots into the dance floor."

I've long been curious about doing an *ayahuasca* ceremony with all the fixings, but on the one occasion I was invited to participate in such an experience, my host emailed me a reference to "our Charmin," by which he meant "our Shaman," and I found the toilet paper word-association so off-putting that I cancelled my attendance.

For which high do I have the utmost freak hots? That would be nitrous oxide, about which the poet Robert Southey chirped, "*The air in Heaven must be this wonder-working gas of delight.*" During my university days, someone I knew would illegally purchase a tall cylindrical gleaming silver tank of the stuff every few weeks, and we'd have ourselves a party, ingesting this stuff we called "laughing gas" by fitting empty balloons onto the nozzle and then sucking it all in until the balloon was empty again and we'd collapsed onto the floor of our domitory's common room. After thirty seconds or so, we'd slowly come to, not knowing when it was, or where we were, or even *who* we were. It was temporary amnesia and I loved it. My consciousness was like the Holy Grail and I had discovered it without having to bother making any Grail quest.

Even better were my subsequent nitrous oxide experiences at my dentist's office. You wouldn't think that such a place would adequately tick the "setting" box on the drug user's "set and setting" checklist, but I liked the absurdity of feeling as high as Saturn while being seated with my head tilted backward and a white-coat-clad person jamming gleaming sharp steel instruments into my mouth. I also appreciated the fact that dental office nitrous oxide was cut with enough oxygen so that I wouldn't black out—I could just keep grooving in a steady state of bliss, ice-skating on Saturn's rings, while all that prodding and poking and spraying and rinsing seemed to be occurring to someone else.

Another reason I got off on ingesting "the gas of delight" in my dentist's office is because for many years when I was single I had a dentist who was a beautiful woman in her mid-thirties. She was married, but this did not prevent an erotic element from creeping into my nitrous oxide-propelled stupefaction while in her dental chair. *Please,* I'd goofily pray to Dame Fortune, *make my dentist leave her husband, if only for an afternoon, and climb into the chair with me.* This prayer led me to write a poem, "Heart in Mouth," which ended with the verse "*I'm gonna make love to my dentist according to my chart. / She'll say, 'Inside each smelly mouth is a fragrant heart. / Some hearts get gobbled down by others. My own got gargled by my father and my mother.' / I'm gonna make love to my dentist, and then we'll rinse.*"

Eventually my wish was granted. Not the wish about the dental chair, but the wish that my dentist would leave her husband. A few months after her legal separation, my dentist and I went on a few dinner dates. These were chaste evenings, mostly—all we did was French-kiss. But this kissing has allowed me now to joke to my friends, whenever the subject of good oral hygiene comes up, "My dentist put her tongue in my mouth."

We ended up parting as friends, and she soon married a different suitor, yet I remained my dentist's patient, and kept sampling her nitrous oxide supply during my visits to her office. Even while getting my teeth cleaned, I would trick her into giving me the gas by complaining, "I have such a low tolerance for pain that I need the nitrous oxide jacked up to a setting of at least six or seven." She obliged me. She probably figured that no harm could come of it. Then came the day when harm *did* come of it.

I blame Keith Richards for the brief clinical death I experienced. I also blame this notoriously drug-gobbling Rolling Stone (supposedly, he snorted his cremated father's ashes!) for my premature retirement from receiving nitrous oxide. If it weren't for Keith Richard's influence, I would have happily continued getting high on the glorious gas for as long as I needed dental care. What happened was, the morning before my latest appointment, I was reading a biography of Keith, and I was so amused by the reports of his drug adventures that I decided, *A nitrous oxide setting of six or seven is just for milksops. Today in the dental chair I'm going all the way to* ten. I knew I'd have to be crafty about my goal, knew I needed to wait until my dentist, who was intent on replacing an old filling of mine, was thirty seconds into the process of drilling into my molar. Then I pretended to be in agony, even though I was already approaching Saturn on my ice skates. "*Ow*, this *hurts*," I mumbled.

"It hurts?" said my dentist. "But you're at seven—that's the top end of your usual nitrous setting."

"I don't know what's wrong, but this is *killing me* today!"

"Hmm," she said. "Let's try you at eight."

Eight felt like a profoundly different location in the solar system from seven. My ice-skates were gone, and so was my entire body. I was a planet-hopping pure psyche now, and Uranus was in sight. But as my dentist drilled away it dimly occurred to me that my Keith Richards-inspired objective had not yet been met. I needed to bounce to nine and then to ten. So I did more complaining, lots of eager mumbled complaining, and up to nine my dentist took me.

Pluto, I found out fast, isn't even a planet. It's a garden of celestial delights located in your mouth. Even if my dentist had climbed into my chair and started to French-kiss me again, it would have been nothing compared to the bacchanalian festival currently in progress amid my lips, teeth, and gums. Thanks to the gaseous ambrosia at a nine-and-counting setting, what ordinarily would be pain because of this endless drilling became sheer bliss, the height of dental nirvana...

And "dental nirvana" was my last port of call until two or three minutes later, which was when I returned to consciousness in the same chair, same room, same building. My entire body was drenched with sweat. What's more, my dentist had indeed climbed into my chair with me. At last! But she wasn't there for any erotic enterprise. No, she was giving me the full CPR treatment.

"Your heart stopped," she explained once I got fully conscious. "You weren't breathing. I thought I lost you. You're never using nitrous oxide in my place of business again."

"*And*," my wife informed me after I'd recounted to her my crisis, "you're never reading more of that Keith Richards book, either."

Behind her back, I did pick up the Keith biography one more time, only to find this quotation from the man: "I come from a very tough stock and things that would kill other people don't kill me... The only criteria in any of this game called life is knowing yourself, knowing your own capabilities. The idea that anybody should think they should take on what I do as some sort of recreation or emulation is, like, horrific."

I know when I'm beat. No more nitrous oxide-powered trips around the solar system for me. I'll have to qualify for Heaven before I can breathe the wonder-working gas again. Novocain in my dentist's office will have to suffice. And no more pretending I'm Keith Richards, that bastard, although I still wish I could be him.

During the second month of the Covid-19 pandemic, my wife and I leased for ourselves a small house in upstate New York. Because no one at the time was permitted to physically enter any available rentals, we took the place almost sight unseen, judging it only by photos we found online. The house looked satisfactory to us. But as we discovered when we arrived to move into it, there were a host of problems. Unlike in the photos we'd seen, the place was filthy, with mouse droppings everywhere and a possible black mold problem. The biggest problem, the problem that caused us to get out of our lease, was the big round pile of mammal feces that I came across in the bedroom. Shining a flashlight on the feces, I thought, *No mouse is capable of producing* this *amazing pile.* And I had just started to wonder whether the shit belonged to some human squatter who was living in the house—maybe even a band of ninjas!—*when the pile of shit moved.*

I blinked, not sure my eyes were working right, and I took a step forward, focusing the flashlight on the shit—at which point *it shifted again*, and a portion of the shit rose up and looked at me with two small black eyes. Leaping backward and screaming, I realized that this was not a pile of shit at all, it was a rattlesnake. Who knew that such creatures could be found in New York State? They can. And this rattler was now occupying my new rented home.

I'm aware of how universal and ancient is the worship of serpents. The scholars of myth are welcome to them. Me, I wish to live a totally snake-free life. No other creatures on earth frighten me as much as they do. Instead of enjoying my surroundings whenever I hike somewhere natural, I keep my gaze fixed on the ground, ready to spot any slithering, and all the while I'm imagining the fast, outrageous sting in my calf, the feel of those puncturing teeth, then the panic, and the pulsing pain spreading upward, and finally the paralysis and the rapidly dimming light.

Even when I'm in a confirmed snake-free area, I brood about the stories I've heard about snakes. There was a demolition worker who poked a hole in a dilapidated building's first floor ceiling which caused that ceiling to collapse and shower serpents, dozens of them, on the poor man's head. Then was the herpetologist who told me about a type of black mambo in sub-Saharan Africa which leaps from the ground to bite your throat.

Finally, there was the fer-de-lance I came face-to-face with in a grocery shop in rural Costa Rica. The grocer there kept the venomous snake in a cage for his customers to take a gander at. In a queasy blend of fascination and terror, I did my share of gawking, and after a while, something caused the fer-de-lance to become as unsettled as I felt. It kept repeatedly butting its head against the chicken-wire cage, which fortunately seemed to be strong enough to withstand those hammering headbutts. Or was it? Each time the fer-de-lance darted back and then plunged forward, its head battering the wire, I took a little step back. And when its eyes met mine, I thought I could recognize all the hatred and the rage this creature must have acquired in its captivity. As with Mr. Ravoon, that black-clad, eye-patched old man who used to frighten me, I wish I could feel less snake aversion, could even make friends with these slithering creatures, could caress them and learn their lessons. But such a wish seemed totally unrealistic with the Costa Rican fer-de-lance. It wanted to bite the world, to swallow this planet like a gumball, to demolish reality itself. And it would initiate this grand endeavor by first demolishing snake-fearing me.

The way Mark Twain figured, "There is no sadder sight than a young pessimist, except an old optimist." Speaking for my current self, I veer daily between pessimism and optimism. On one hand, the rewards for being a pessimist are obvious. Either Dame Fortune confirms your prediction about a situation or else the Dame makes your day better than you'd predicted. On the other hand, Jim Dodge sounds persuasive about extreme negative outlooks, calling them "easy, cheap, and ignoble. If you want to refuse the glorious opportunities life offers, fine—shut up and destroy yourself. But don't spit on the gift and extend your destruction to others."

Perhaps a practical middle ground is the best place to situate ourselves. The poet Adrienne Rich recommends that we possess a short-term pessimism and a long-term optimism. Meanwhile, the philosophy team of Adorno and Horkheimer wrote that they do *not* believe that things will turn out right, "but the idea that they *might* turn out right is of decisive importance." Meanwhile, I'd like to shake the hand of whatever genius first proposed that "The pessimist may be right in the end, but the optimist has more fun getting there."

Occupying the middle ground between high hopes and dire expectations can certainly lead to strange weather. Consider "Silberman's Paradox," which states: "If Murphy's Law can go wrong, it will." It might be best never to *count on* an unexpected and impossible-seeming happy ending—but how glorious it is when they appear. And they *do* sometimes appear, because life can turn on a dime, often for the better (a fact which, according to Tom Robbins, makes for a persuasive argument against suicide). Just ask Hunter S. Thompson, who spoke of accidentally tumbling down an elevator shaft and landing in a pool of comely mermaids.

Or ask the ancient Greek artist Apelles, who wanted to reproduce the foam from a horse's mouth in his latest painting. Unable to get it right, he angrily hurled a wet sponge against the canvas. Lo and behold: that sponge serendipitously produced the exact visual effect of foam on that horse's mouth.

Sometimes just a few bars of music and lyrics can provide the miracle. I've never felt my emotional condition change for the better more dramatically than the bleak Chicago dawn in 1987 when I heard Jerry Jeff Walker's song "LA Freeway" play on the radio. If I'd been wearing a mood ring at the time, it would have exploded on my finger, or at least shorted out.

My friend Bob Neuwirth believed in sudden transformations. Though he was supremely realistic about improving your life—he liked to say, "There's nothing you can do that's going to make you feel better. You can only stop doing things that are making you feel bad"—but he also said, "You have to dance to whatever music is currently on the turntable…Accept whatever comes, but always wait for a miracle."

Speaking of miracles, the last time I saw Bob, Santa Monica was suffering from a heat wave, the sunlight was blinding, but on the phone he told me it was okay for me to drop by his art studio and say hello. Bob was seriously ill by then, often relying on the use of a portable oxygen tank, and when I arrived at the studio, I noticed his car in the parking lot. Then I noticed something else—his passenger seat door was wide open and Bob lay halfway hanging out of it, his head bowed.

Uh-oh, I thought, running over. *Looks like he's in trouble.* "Bob," I shouted, already reaching for my cell phone to dial 911, "are you okay?"

What Bob did next struck me as perfectly emblematic of his cool and indomitable self. He slowly raised his head to me, removed the oxygen mask, and with his twinkly eyes and thin-lipped grin, Bob said in his most nonchalant voice, "Just catching some rays, man. *Just catching some rays.*"

I wish I had high fidelity tape recordings of my most rewarding personal conversations—as a veteran Spanish spy nicknamed "King of the Sewers" told a journalist, "There is so much you miss in a conversation if you can't listen to it later. The shades and nuances…the tonality, the timbre of the voice. You can hear when they have doubts about the information they are telling you." I wish I had more photographic records of my life, too, although there have been certain photos I wish I *hadn't* looked at. The autopsy Polaroids of two elderly murder victims which my law professor Lamar offered to show to me, for example. More upsetting than the victims' fatal wounds were the looks of horror on their faces. Viewing the autopsy photos had been for my job—I was helping Lamar defend in court the victims' son, who'd been wrongly accused of their murder. I regret taking that peek, anyway. I also wish I had not witnessed an elderly man in an orange parka jump to his death in front of a 6 train as it roared into Manhattan's 86th Street station. And no, I would not have been tempted to take a photo of that horrible scene.

Asked in an interview, "What makes you a writer?" Martin Amis answered, "You develop an extra sense that partly excludes you from experience. When writers experience things, they're not really experiencing them anything like one hundred percent. They're always holding back and wondering what the significance of it is, or wondering how they'd do it on the page. Always this disinterestedness…as if it really isn't to do with you, a certain cold impartiality."

It goes without saying that I'm nowhere near Amis's class as an author, but I share his impartiality and disinterestedness all too often. And despite my professional pride, I wish I didn't share it. A few friends of mine have been murdered, and as soon as I heard the news of these catastrophes, I began reporting the details to other friends.

Was I psychologically processing my shock, horror, and sadness by making these reports? To some extent, yes. But I was also turning the murders into fresh storytelling material. Turning them, that is, to gossip. Which, of course, betrayed the personhood, the humanity, of each of the victims. Each of my *friends*. Better by far that I would have kept my mouth shut and honored my friends' memories with my silence.

On a lighter photographic note, I wish I could have had a camera with me whenever I chanced to come across highly photographic subjects. A few of such uncaptured images still nag at me as missed artistic opportunities. I also wish that a film crew could follow me around, recording my reactions to whatever bizarre events regularly confront me. Perhaps the crew's movie camera will zoom in for a close-up of my face whenever I say, "What the—?," with a narrative voiceover then intoning, "Now the fun begins." Or "Watch this part carefully." Or "Oh, *no*, Gary, not *that.*" Or "Only minutes later, as we'll see, *all hell shall break loose.*"

A bigger, better wish in the above vein is not to merely to *watch* that footage of my life but to be able to *adjust* it, as in Steve Goodman's semi-wishing song "Video Tape," in which Goodman sings "*When your head hurts the morning after, / Then you could roll it back to late last night. / You could replay all the good parts / And cut out whatever you don't like.*" On second thought, Goodman's idea might not be so wise—I'd spend too much of my life trying to erase and replay minutes, hours, whole days. Still, I'd gladly take the opportunity to wipe clean the Polaroids of those elderly murder victims as well as the image of that subway train-crushed man, thereby restoring to them their lives.

Speaking of "replays," one of the most poignant scenes I've ever watched in the theater was at the end of the play *Madame Melville* by Richard Nelson. Set in Paris in 1966, the story concerns the friendship between an American teenager and an older Parisian woman for whom he develops an unrequited passion. The last time they see each other, Madame Melville is leaving the boy's apartment to go on a romantic date with a new suitor. She asks the boy to zip up the back of her dress, the same request that my mother used to make of me when I was a child. Even then, my mother's request felt, well, not sexual, but *adult*. And Esther Lippman did have a curious thing she would tell me whenever I asked her why she refused to go out on any romantic dates with men. Shaking her head emphatically, she'd say, "Ever since that homewrecker who calls himself your father abandoned us, you're the *only man* for me, hon."

"Yeah," I'd reply, "but my friend Mike's mom is divorced, too, and *she's* always going on dinner dates with different guys."

"Forget it. No more boyfriends. *You're* Mommy's boyfriend now, you're all the man I need. Just being at home with you is better than any dinner dates I could go on with anybody, sweetheart. Besides, Mike's mother is a dirty hussy!"

"What's a hussy?"

"Never mind! Get your mind out of the gutter!"

A slice of my psyche welcomed the "no more boyfriends" response from Esther Lippman, given how much I longed to be the center of "Mommy's" attention. Yet an increasingly growing other psychological slice of myself felt disturbed by what she was saying. If she didn't date any new men, if I was the only "man for her," wouldn't she just keep getting weirder and weirder?

But back to 1966 and the play about the teenaged American boy who loves his Parisian tutor Madame Melville. After he zips her up, she asks about her dress, "Is it smooth? No wrinkles?" Then she finally leaves for her assignation, and the boy turns to the audience, telling them about something he learned about Madame Melville a few years later. She died young of cancer. Silence. And in a sorrowful voice now, he addresses not the audience but the play's director, or perhaps Dame Fortune, that great stage manager in the skies. The boy says, "Wait, wait! Can I see that *again*?"

More silence. Finally, his wish is granted. Instant theatrical replay! Madame Melville rushes back through the door, she gets ready for her date, the boy zips her up, and she asks him of her dress, "Is it smooth? No wrinkles?" Then she's gone once more. Nevertheless, the boy looks grateful for this redo of their last parting. Just as there are times, in spite of everything, when adult me would feel grateful to replay, to redo, to *relive*, any of the moments from my eighteen years with my mother. Zipping up her dress, for instance—if only that.

Unfortunately, I'm still having trouble shaking those autopsy Polaroids out of my head. "America was never innocent," says the crime novelist James Ellroy. "We popped our cherry on the boat over…" I wish it weren't true that violence, as the activist Rap Brown said, "is as American as apple pie"—and I wish that all firearms were illegal in the United States. Just look at how this nation has pumped itself full of these slaughter devices, automatic weapons especially, with mass shootings as well as individual shootings coming at us nearly every minute. If you agree with Brown, and with the author D. H. Lawrence, who said, "The essential American soul is hard, isolate, stoic, and a killer. It has never yet melted," then do you sincerely wish to place dangerous weapons in such dangerous hands?

I confess that I've enjoyed firing various weapons at shooting ranges, but I believe in sensible gun policy, and a solid argument for it was made in a *Simpsons* episode wherein Homer tries to buy a pistol. When the salesman tells him, "There's a five day waiting period," Homer shouts, "Five days? But I'm mad *now*!" If you do insist on getting yourself a handgun, I wish you'll remember the cautionary example of one Simon Dally. This foolish chap kept his pistol on the bedside table next to his telephone, and late one night when he received a phone call, he woke up, groggily reached for the receiver, put it to his ear, and blew a bullet through his brain as he said, "Who's calling?"

As it happens, I am a survivor of a public outbreak of gunfire. This catastrophe took place in Buenos Aires instead of the States, and the two gunmen there fired pistols, not semi-automatics, and they were shooting hot lead at each other instead of at the group of us who were seated near the gunmen at an outdoor café. Still, I knew I was in trouble. Fearing that if I overturned my table and cowered behind it for protection, the way everyone else around me was doing, I'd eventually be finished off by one of the shooters, I decided to instead listen to my instinct and make a run for safety. This meant that I foolishly dashed through the line of fire, hence exposing myself to an errant bullet or a ricochet.

It was the wrong instinct, but, as it turned out, I survived unharmed. The same cannot be said for the shooters. One of them was slain while the other was wounded and crying out for—guess who?—his mother. When I realized I'd come through the shooting unscathed, I felt elated, more alive than I ever had before. Adrenalin can be a powerful intoxicant. I wish I could add a few drops of it to my morning coffee.

Incidentally, I used to joke with people whenever I recounted this anecdote that perhaps one of those Buenos Aires bullets that missed me is even now travelling up the coast of, say, Costa Rica, whizzing along in its own good time. And soon, one overcast spring morning, let's say, this bullet with my name metaphorically carved in it shall at last overtake me, splitting my spine or cracking open my skull. Unfinished business, now finished, and spelling Kaputsville. Hello, Stretchfoot—goodbye, gumball Earth! Still, I don't tell this joke anymore because here in contemporary America, there may well be a different bullet, maybe even many, coming my way. With a lot less far to travel.

Sudden and violent death preoccupies me, as it does so many citizens in our crime-saturated society. Cruelty, according to the Marquis de Sade, who would know, "is the earliest sentiment wrought in us by Nature; the infant breaks his rattle, bites his nurse's tit, strangles his pet bird, long before he has attained the age of reason." How fortunate we are that that age of reason kicks in at all.

"But does reason ever truly kick in?" Dame Fortune says to me in a dream. "You mortals don't seem reasonable to these old eyes of mine."

"Well," I say, "I can only speak for myself, but I wish I'd started to practice *ahimsa*, the reverence for all life and refusal to harm another living creature, a lot sooner than I did, because there were way too many intentionally squashed bugs, swatted flies, and toyed-with spiders (no strangled birds) during the first third of my life."

"I remember," says the Dame. "I was watching you back then, after all. Especially horrendous was the gleeful way in which you used a shovel to chop an earthworm in half when you were four years old. What a heady rush of brute domination you felt!"

I shudder, but then I assure Dame Fortune that now I know better. "I didn't change overnight," I say, "but now I leave those insects alone, and I capture cockroaches when I find them in my home and safely remove them. My inspiration in this is my wife Berta, who goes way out of her way to help creatures in need, repairing damaged spider webs with Scotch tape and rescuing sparrows trapped in empty houses. Another inspiration to me was my reading this quip by Milan Kundera: 'True human goodness, in all its purity and freedom, can come to the fore only when its recipient has no power. Mankind's true moral test… consists of its attitude towards those who are at its mercy: animals.'"

"That's very good," says the Dame.

Encouraged by her approval, I add, "Stated more starkly is this formulation of my own, another of my Lippy Laws: 'You can judge a person's decency by how they behave toward those with less power than they have.'"

The Dame says, "I like Kundera's remark better."

"Fair enough. But my Lippy Law is broader, applying as it does not just to mistreaters of animals but also to snotty restaurant customers who behave obnoxiously to the staff. Although the power differentials, as at restaurants, may only be situational and temporary."

Cocking her veiled head at me, the Dame is quiet for a moment, perhaps reflecting. "Let's stick with animals," she finally says. "Have you heard of the novelist Olga Tokarczuk? Won the Nobel Prize, didn't she? Anyway, Olga says, 'Whenever I come across, say, a rat or a fox and I meet its eyes, I can sense a whole cosmos behind them. To reduce such a being is to deny that this cosmos exists, deny that there's a world inside there we know nothing about.'"

"And worse than denying mammalian integrity," I say, trying to impress the Dame, "our mistreatment of animals does *ourselves* harm. Let me quote Chief Seattle: 'What is man without the beasts? If the beasts were gone, man would die from a great loneliness of spirit.'"

Unfortunately, Dame Fortune is not impressed. Behind the veil, her obscured face seems to frown at me. "You know, you can speak about animal liberation as nobly as you want, but let's not kid ourselves. You're still a meat eater."

I hang my head. "I know this makes me a hypocrite."

"Indeed it does," says the Dame. "And the same reasoning applies to how you and your fellow human being treat this planet here. For all your joking about sucking on it as if it's a gumball, you've made a rank mess of Earth. You treat it just as shabbily as you treat your fellow creatures. Here's Olga T. again: 'Maybe why humans feel so alienated from nature is because we feel the burden of our guilt toward it.'"

"Good one," I say.

"Of course it's a good one," Dame Fortune replies. "Not even *I* have the time to waste on material that's less than good."

I wish it would be possible for me to clamber on top of the Wheel of Fortune—not the wooden one in the camp at the Burning Man Festival where I first met my wife, but the mythical Wheel itself which Dame Fortune is always spinning. Then I'd like to figure out a way to ride that sucker through my hometown, where any residents who remember me will need to jump out of my Wheel's way, muttering to themselves, "*That* guy? *Really*?"

May I elaborate on this wish? Last year Carson City, Nevada celebrated a day in honor of their most famous native citizen, my rock star friend Benny Pompa. Would my own hometown perhaps see fit to commemorate me with an official "Gary Lippman Day?" If it would, my wish is that they will hold no symposia, scavenger hunts, three-legged races, or Hokey-Pokey dance contests. No tours inside my childhood home, either, or public executions of the schoolteachers who bedeviled my early years. (Miss Lee, for example—she who twisted my ear after she caught me cheating on an exam, which I did by writing helpful information on a piece of paper and then gluing this paper to the top of my black Puma sneakers.)

No, let's eschew all the penny-ante celebratory gestures. What I wish for when I'm "king for a day" is that we *go big*. By this, I mean that my hometown's elected officials should make Stagg Field, my grammar school playground, available to me and a team of historians, archaeologists, architects, and stonemasons for a few years before the celebration. Our plan, inspired by my childhood reading of the canary-yellow-covered *Curiosity Book*, is to erect on Stagg Field full-scale reproductions of the Seven Wonders of the Ancient World.

"Gary Lippman Day" will kick off at dawn with me leading celebrants on a stroll through the Hanging Gardens of Babylon, followed by my shimmying up the left leg of the Colossus of Rhodes while everyone cheers. Once I reach the groin area—it would prove too tiring for me to press on all the way to the head—I'll be transferred by crane to the pointed top of Giza's Great Pyramid, where I'll begin my speech to everyone with the puckish announcement "Now that I've gotten your attention, I'd like to say a few words about *Amway*..."

After a lunch break, I'll be buried alive, but immediately revived, in the Mausoleum of Mausolus at Halicarnassus. Then I'll lay supine in the lap of Olympia's Zeus statue, sit with my legs dangling from the Ishtar Gate, and pray not to Artemis but to Dame Fortune at Artemis's Ephesus Temple. Finally, I'll single-handedly work the Lighthouse of Alexandria's jumbo spotlight, shining it straight into everybody's eyes. This is not to blind the people who love me but to dazzle them even more than they've come to expect.

For a bonus, *eighth* wonder—eight being, you may recall, my favorite number—we will conclude the day with me presenting to my hometown a brilliant reproduction of a bronze statue that stood in Antioch in the third century B.C.E. It's a statue of the goddess Fortuna, alias the Dame. And for the grand finale of today's celebration, I will munch on the ears of corn that the goddess clutches in her right hand, these corn-ears symbolizing generosity. Why the corn-munching? Because, for all the grandiosity of Gary Lippman Day, the concept I want to leave everyone with is generosity. Didn't I announce toward the beginning of this wish list that so much of life boils down to kindness?

The beehive-hairdo'ed middle-aged woman who sang the song "Frank Mills" from the musical *Hair* at a café late one night near my college campus—I wish I could find her to say that her rendition of that limpid little ballad was the single most poignant musical performance I've experienced. Clichéd as this sounds, I had the impression while I listened to her that she was truly living the song, every note of it, every syllable.

More than two decades on from the beehive-hairdo'ed woman's performance, my five-year-old son and I would often listen to the *Hair* soundtrack, especially the song "Going Down," which begins with the phrase "*Me and Lucifer, Lucifer and me…*" One afternoon at the Disneyland Park outside Paris, we sat singing that song together, and a wholesome-looking family walked past us just as Gideon and I did the "Lucifer" part. The father gave me a dirty look, clearly disapproving of the kind of "devil music" I was sharing with my child.

Some years later, I got to know Jim Rado, who was the last surviving co-creator of *Hair*, and one evening we crossed paths at a production of his musical in the East Village. It was a singular event, because the entire cast in this version of *Hair* consisted of actors in their late seventies and eighties. In other words, they were the same age that the characters themselves would have been at the time of the performance. And the same age as Rado himself. During the elders-only version of *Hair*, the actor who sang the title song was totally bald, and the cast ran through the dance numbers very gingerly, so that no aged bones would get broken.

At the intermission, I got to speaking with Rado and asked him if he was enjoying the show.

"Very much," he said. "But I keep trying to think of ways I could trim down the first act, because it's too long."

There's a true artist for you. Fifty years after his play reshapes musical theater, he was still trying to figure out how to improve it, still yearning for something closer to perfection. He would have felt right at home in the Louvre with the artist Pierre Bonnard, who got arrested at that museum with his paintbrush and his palette. Bonnard's crime? Retouching one of his old paintings that hung there. I love Bonnard and Jim Rado for how perennially ready they are to transcend their own work, and I wish Rado could have been by my side those decades earlier when the woman with the beehive hairdo so memorably sang "Frank Mills." I wish my son could have been there to hear that, too.

"*I wish I had a pencil-thin moustache*," sings Jimmy Buffett, "*the 'Boston Blackie' kind. / A two-toned Ricky Ricardo jacket / And an autographed picture of Andy Devine*." In the same wishing song, Buffett informs us that he's getting old and no longer wears underwear or goes to church or cuts his hair, yet he "*could still go to movies and see it all there / Just the way that it used to be*." I know the feeling. I love films made in the Silent Era, when Blackie got started, and sometimes wish that sound and color had never arrived in the cinematic universe. I also wish that everyone would go to movie theaters as often as they used to. Like Buffett, I relish the experience of gathering with strangers in a dark room to watch stories projected onto a screen.

Even buying a ticket outside could be fun, despite it not having been fun for a particular ticket-seller one night in the nineties at the subterranean Lincoln Plaza Cinema in Manhattan. Arriving there alone for the last screening of the night, I found the poor ticket-seller fast asleep in her glass booth, with her head resting on her crossed arms. I felt sorry for rousing her, but I really wished to see the movie, a well-regarded import from Norway, so I knocked on the glass and she opened her eyes, and I couldn't help but smile when I told her the movie's title: "*Insomnia*."

I've already mentioned how when I was a child and my mother would bring me to our local cinema, she would haul me out of the place whenever a sex scene got underway. Ethel Lippman, I must add, had another moviegoing quirk which bothered me. She didn't care what time our movie was due to start, so we would show up at any time, usually somewhere in the middle of the story, and once our eyes adjusted to the darkness and we found seats, we would need to try to figure out who was who and what their deal was. Then, when the film ended and the lights came up, we'd hang around until the movie began again and we'd watch it until we got to the scene in the story where we had first entered, at which point we would say to each other, "This is where we came in. Time to leave." And leave we did, standing up and walking out. Our fellow audience members must have figured we didn't like the film.

My divorced father, whenever I saw him on our court-mandated weekly "visitations," would also bring me to movie theaters. Unlike his prudish, puritanical ex-wife, he would let me watch sexy scenes unimpeded. He got us to the cinema at the proper time, too. Sadly, however, the moviegoing experience that I best remember sharing with him was when I was seven and he almost got into a fistfight with another kid's father over a "saved seat." For the first time, I glimpsed a spark of fear in Bernie Lippman's eyes, which was a dispiriting sight for an admiring son to witness.

Considerably older than seven—ninety-four years older, in fact—my grandmother Lulu caused a minor ruckus of her own at a cinema in Miami Beach when I took her there to see a film in the mid-nineties. Remarkably, she wasn't hard of hearing at her age, but she insisted on sitting in the very front row and spoke loudly to me throughout the screening. When another elderly woman who sat in front of us turned around and made a slapping gesture at Lulu and shouted, "Shut up," I got so enraged that I nearly strangled the woman, which would not be a laudable act for me, slaughtering someone else's grandmother. I managed to calm myself. Yet a few minutes later, I got murder-minded all over again when the offender herself began speaking loudly. Oh, the hypocrisy!

For the last film I got to watch with my grandmother, a matinee of *Forrest Gump*, Lulu managed to remain quiet from the beginning to the end. *We've made progress*, I thought. Did she intend to show me that she could hold her tongue through an entire movie? If so, she succeeded. But as soon as the end credits commenced to roll, Lulu turned to me and said, louder than ever, as if she could no longer control herself, "*Some* cast!"

Unlike some of my fellow wishers, I enjoy going to movies alone. (Eating alone in restaurants, too.) In the late eighties, I had an interesting solo moviegoing experience while sitting in the crowded screening room of the *Melkweg*, or "Milky Way," nightclub in Amsterdam. It was three in the morning, and like others in the audience, I was high on hashish-laden "space cakes," so I felt even more absorbed than I otherwise would have felt in the disturbing war film being shown, which was *Platoon*. When the celluloid abruptly broke in the projector, the screen went blank and the small dark auditorium went silent. No one began clapping or booing or shouting, "Hey, *fix the movie*," which they no doubt would have done if they weren't so stoned. Everyone simply sat, feeling cozily enveloped by the silence and the darkness. Actually, the silence and the darkness *became* the movie, and soon I felt a sense of oneness with all of my neighbors, these utter strangers who were sharing this weird experience with me, sharing it in the same place, at the same time, on the same plane of existence, and I wished it could last forever until—minutes later? an hour later?—the projectionist at last fixed the film and we resumed watching *Platoon*.

Some of the happiest times I have spent in movie theaters were when I brought my young son with me to see children's films. Inevitably these experiences reminded me of my childhood moviegoing with my parents, and I thought of my grandmother Lulu, too, because Gideon shared her habit of speaking loudly through each picture. The most memorable time I spent with the boy at a cinema was not in the theater itself, though, but in the facility's restroom, where Gideon at age five was using a urinal for the first time. When I told him, "You're doing a great job," he turned to proudly face me, still in "mid-flow," and urinated up and down the leg of a burly middle-aged man with a pencil-thin moustache who had the misfortune to be standing at the urinal next to Gideon.

Horrified by this accident, I spent the next minute alternating between reassuring my kid that it was okay and apologizing to the victim. Because said victim had been wearing cargo shorts, the urine hit his bare skin, and as I begged for his forgiveness, he just glowered at us, which prompted me to think, *If this guy is angry enough to punch me, I'll let him have one free shot before I start to punch him back.* In retrospect, the whole thing made for a new twist on the meaning of the novelist Fay Weldon's remark, "Before you have children, you can believe you are a nice person. After you have children, you understand how wars start."

In the end, the guy went to the sink, washed off his leg, and left us alone, Gideon got over his guilt, and now the event reminds me of something I'd read by the writer Mark Jacobson, who was at a late-night screening in a Times Square cinema when he heard a stranger yell at someone, "You're *sorry*? You pee on my date, and you say you're *sorry*?"

By the time I turned thirty, I had not peed on someone's date in a cinema—still haven't—but I did once remove all my clothing in a multiplex in Chicago and romp around the place for thirty minutes. I wasn't alone this time, I was with my own date, my then-girlfriend Terri Jo, who was a Finnish-American psychic. The local police consulted her about unsolved crimes, and we ourselves were stalked by an infamous serial killer one night in Lincoln Park. But that's a tale for a different time.

As soon as Terri Jo and I entered the cinema on a late spring evening and found that we were the only customers, we got the idea that other young lovers would have gotten: "Let's make love here, in public!" The fact that the film we'd come to see was titled "Impromptu" seemed to confirm the wisdom of our brainwave, and the risk that the projectionist might observe us, or that other moviegoers might arrive to catch us *in flagrante delicto*, did not sway us from getting to it.

What I remember now even more than our lovemaking is how we danced through the aisles afterward and ran up to the screen, both of us buck-naked, like toddlers who haven't learned about sex yet. The sense of play was everything that night, and fortunately, no one ended up intruding on our revels. We laughed non-stop, then put our clothes back on and went home, having paid no attention to the film we'd paid good money to see. And it occurs to me only now, half a century since those days when my mother used to haul me out of movie theaters during the sex scenes, that my revenge against the unofficial film censor Esther Lippman had at last been achieved.

For our "third-act climax," let's return to the subterranean Lincoln Plaza Cinema where I once reluctantly woke up a sleeping ticket-seller by asking her to sell me a ticket to the Norwegian film *Insomnia*. The next time I went to Lincoln Plaza, I brought with me a Chinese-American journalist named Carol who still spoke with a twang from her native Texas. This time my date and I remained fully clothed in the (crowded) screening room, although the film we saw that night was *Y Tu Mama Tambien*, a Mexican film which remains one of my favorites because it achieves what Tom Robbins says are the four goals of a great narrative: it makes you think, it makes you laugh, it awakens your sense of wonder, and it makes you horny.

The showing of *Y Tu Mama Tambien*, the last for the day, ended after midnight. While the other audience members left the theater, Carol and I remained behind to discuss what we'd just watched. My assumption was that the Lincoln Plaza manager, or at least a janitor, would eventually appear to kick us out, but I was wrong. No one showed up to say, "Sorry, we're closed." Around one in the morning we decided to call it a night. This was another wrong assumption, because our night was far from over at this cinema. When we got to the exit, which led to an escalator that went up to street level, we found that the exit, the only exit in the place, was locked up tight.

Our first reaction was to chuckle. Our next reaction was to yell out for that had-to-be-somewhere manager or janitor, neither of whom answered or revealed themselves. In time, Carol and I set off wandering around the movie theater, searching for another exit to the waiting world. There was none. Our cell phones could not get a signal underground, either, and the sole payphone we could find was, according to a neatly typed sign taped to it, "OUT OF THE ORDER." We searched for any office door behind which a manager or a janitor might be watching TV, or pumping themselves full of drugs or, like that *Insomnia* ticket-seller, fast asleep. No luck. Now we weren't laughing anymore, and Carol had to calm me when I felt a surge of rage and wanted to break into the concession stand, which was also locked up. *They've trapped us underground for the night*, went my reasoning, *so aren't we at least entitled to free food*?

This was not the first time I had felt trapped somewhere, *been* trapped somewhere, and fumed at my plight. A decade earlier, at four a.m. in a Greenwich Village apartment building where I then lived, I had walked into my elevator alone and pressed the button for my floor, the eighth, and felt the familiar upward motion. I was drunk after a night out with friends—perhaps we'd even seen a movie at the subterranean Lincoln Plaza Cinema—and I already had my keys in my hand, ready to collapse into bed, when the elevator lurched to a stop between floors five and six. It bounced a bit, then settled in and wouldn't move.

Again, my first response was to chuckle. Yet pressing the appropriate buttons didn't help. Neither did ringing the alarm bell, because given the late hour, no one heard it, or responded to hearing it. Before I finally got rescued three hours later, I had used my fist to shatter the little glass screen that protected the Elevator Safety certificate, the notice that assured all passengers that this machine was in up-to-date working order. Then, with bloodied knuckles, I pulled the certificate out of its case and tore it to shreds.

A friend of mine has told me that she once survived a commercial plane crash, one in which other passengers perished, yet she boarded a new plane the very next day because, as she said, "I knew that I would fear flying for the rest of my life if I didn't 'get back in the saddle' as soon as possible." I felt the same way about elevators. After my problem, I continued riding them right away, although the possibilities of my being trapped in one again, or of plunging to my doom in an elevator whose cables have snapped, do still occur to me.

What had never occurred to me until my night at the subterranean Lincoln Plaza Cinema with Carol, however, was that I would someday be trapped overnight in a movie theater. I tried to console myself that there were far worse temporary prisons, that come the morning we would surely be liberated, and that I had beside me a serene companion who had reconciled herself to the situation. Unfortunately, I kept stomping around, shouting for help and trying the handles to locked doors, until a nondescript-looking door actually opened. It led to a brightly lit, nondescript-looking hallway.

"What's this corridor all about?" asked Carol.

"Who knows?" I said. "I'm off to find out. You stay back here in case someone shows up."

Into the hallway I plunged, trying each doorknob to each nondescript-looking door I came upon. All were locked, and when I reached the end of the hallway, it branched into two others. A crossroads. Practicing John Barth's "Theory of Sinistrality," which I discussed in an earlier wish on this list, I stomped down the left corridor, where other locked doors presented themselves. Then came further hallways and further locked doors. Before long, I'd stopped observing Barth's sinistrality rule, and the linoleum floor was bare except for the occasional object I had to walk around or step over: a broken chair, a Batman lunchbox, some dental floss. Was there any connection between these objects? In a Kinky Friedman novel, the protagonist discovers in a tenement building's hallway an empty bottle of Scotch and a toppled child's bicycle and concludes, "The kid had good taste in booze but couldn't park his bike too well."

On I walked, down successive hallways, past successive closed doors. Eventually, I recognized that I was now pretty much lost in a nondescript-looking, brightly lit maze, a *labyrinth*, totally unsure how to return to Carol. There was no princess to guide me to an exit—and what if a dank-breathed minotaur waited just around the next corner? Where was my Golem when I needed him? Where were the Green Sufi and Neckcracker Tommy Drake and Richard Stands and, hel-*lo*, Dame Fortune?

Soon enough, I began to panic, shouting, "Help!" To no avail. Perhaps, in a reality slightly different from this one, I'm still lost in that labyrinth, lost until I perish or else lost, like the Wandering Jew, until Jesus comes back. Or perhaps the labyrinth was just an illusion because I actually died in one of those near-death experiences in my past—that gunfight I ran from in Buenos Aires, for instance, or the head-on Mack truck collision which my law school classmate Hepzibah Max had dreamed about.

Fortunately, within fifteen minutes, I was able to find my way out and rejoin Carol, and a few hours later, the tall and gangly movie theater janitor at last showed up. Would you believe that he sported a pencil-thin moustache? Amazed to find us, this janitor was extremely apologetic, sheepishly admitting he'd taken a sleeping pill in his office. He urged us not to fink on him to his boss. And before he freed us into a new day's early light, he explained that the maze I'd been lost in, all those hallways and locked doors, were part of the basement of the enormous apartment complex, also called "Lincoln Plaza," which was linked to the cinema.

I have no idea why an apartment complex, even an enormous one, required so many hallways with so many locked rooms. The subterranean movie theater went out of business several years ago. I don't know what occupies its space now. Nevertheless, my memory of the night we were trapped there remains indelible; I still sometimes shudder to recall how I wandered through that mundane lit-up labyrinth, increasingly desperate as I tried to return to a locked-up cinema. Most of all, I remember how alone I felt, utterly, punishingly alone, with no girlfriend or mother or father or grandmother or young son or even Jimmy Buffett to share this strange, and strangely *cinematic*, experience with me.

Think of every human event that occurred on a single patch of land through the eons. The Lincoln Plaza Cinema, let's say, or the place where I'm standing right now, which is the southeast corner of Third Avenue and 73rd Street in Manhattan. A popular diner is currently located on this spot, but what stood here before? How many people have parted here forever? Cried here? Laughed here? Kissed here? Fought here? Bled here? Perished here? What a movie you could make of the meaningful interactions any given mundane spot has hosted! I wish I could watch such a movie, although I know it would last far longer than my lifetime, even if it were edited to show only the kinetic parts.

I wish I knew more about psychogeography, the pseudo-scientific discipline which posits that the unknown history of the places we inhabit, stop at, or pass by have the power to somehow change us. Would psychogeography help me to find where in Russia the Tolstoy Green Stick is buried? Or the location of the fabled Mills Hotel? Would it explain why certain pockets of San Francisco have always struck me as haunted? Would psychogeography explain why a New Haven dermatologist's office I once walked into overwhelmed me with a sense of evil? Why I felt such a deep sense of serenity at the Sikhs' Golden Temple in Amritsar, India? Or why I kept getting lost while wandering on foot in Venice no matter how diligently I consulted my map? Or why a bearded old blind man seemed so disturbed by my presence when I walked past him on a sidewalk in Helsinki? Had he mistaken me for someone else? Was he just mixed-up? Or had he sensed some terrible element in my character that I'm unaware of, a sense of evil like the one I felt in that dermatologist's office?

The above questions suggest further ones. Could a few square feet of land somehow be aware of our presence? "Is it not possible," asks John O'Donohue, "that a place could have huge affection for those who dwell there? Could it be possible that a landscape might have a deep friendship with you?" Perhaps something even smaller than a landscape is sentient. Saint Benedict said he glanced outside his window and "the whole world appeared to be gathered in one sunbeam."

Now for some wishes about a favorite location of mine. I wish that the next time I stand in front of one of the four stone pillars holding up the archway in front of Grand Central Station's Oyster Bar, I will speak to that pillar and be able to hear a response from my Uncle Wolf, who'll be standing nearby at an opposite pillar.

More than forty years ago, Wolf taught me the secret acoustical trick that happens when two people speak to each other, with their backs turned, by way of the Oyster Bar archway. I was a newly motherless teenager then, and my uncle had adopted me, teaching me all sorts of tricks, secret and otherwise, while bestowing on me a far more mature love than I'd known before. I wished so much to please him, to deserve his love, and to understand him better, which explains why I read the work of his favorite poet, Edna St. Vincent Millay, and listened to the albums of his favorite monologuist, Ruth Draper, and studied the diaries of his favorite historical figure, Samuel Pepys. (I wish Wolf would finally finish writing his decades-in-the-making scholarly book about "Pepys Island.")

In those early days after my mother died, Wolf would take me to restaurants all over Manhattan, including the Oyster Bar, and the archway outside that spot felt as though it belonged to me and my uncle alone. Now, whenever I stroll past there, it's a busy scene, with crowds always gathered at the pillars, enjoying the acoustical trick, whispering by way of the pillars with one another. Our secret is most definitely out. The Oyster Bar archway belongs to everyone.

Maybe someday, however, I'll find a space in front of a pillar that's empty and I'll stand at it and say, "Thank you for saving my life, Wolf." My uncle won't be there, but I'll hear his voice, anyway, and it will answer, "You're welcome, Chief." And then, as if to bless me in parting, he'll say to me the same phrase that Federico Fellini said to my friend Hal Willner after the two men had lunch in Rome around the same time that my uncle first taught me the Oyster Bar's trick: "I leave you to your destiny."

One more wish concerning my Uncle Wolf: I wish that I'd been sitting beside him back in the fifties when he was studying psychology at the University of Chicago with the esteemed professor Bruno Bettelheim. I especially wish I could have been in Bettelheim's lecture hall when the great man became irked by a young female student who sat in the front row knitting a sweater. To demonstrate his annoyance, Bettelheim announced to the class in his strong Viennese accent, "You know, Freud believed that the act of *knitting* was a substitute for *masturbation*."

The knitting student did not look up from her work or react in any other way. Which led Bettelheim to repeat Freud's provocative statement about knitting and masturbation. The student continued knitting, ignoring her professor. So Bettelheim, obviously frustrated, raised his voice to repeat the Freud statement once more, and this time the student looked up at the man, fixed him in her basilisk glare, and said, much to the shock of everyone in that classroom, "Professor, when I knit, I *knit*, and when I masturbate, I *masturbate*."

A Chinese proverb advises us to treat our wishes the way we treat our children. I'm wishing I could do that, and at the same time wishing that my son Gideon would discover the paradise described by an ancient Chinese sage, this paradise being a pulsating circle of matter with a mysterious hole at its center. May Gideon pour some powdered sugar on this glorious doughnut and share it with a chosen intimate and devour that thing in eleven or twelve bites, tops. If such a paradise cannot be located, then I'll stick with the baked goods theme and wish that Gideon could discover in the restroom of a doughnut shop a magic pearl that he can affix to his forehead so it will serve as a useful third eye.

If no magic pearls are available, then I'll be perfectly content if Gideon can "stay alive and smart and figure out the rest," which was the prayer of the early twentieth-century Jewish gangster Arnold Rothstein. And let me wish for my son the occasional sense of pure joy that he felt one marvelous Mardi Gras night in New Orleans.

New Orleans! How about a last visit there? Maybe we could be accompanied by the Reverend Gary Davis, who sang of his wish to find "*a candy man sitting on a candy stand*." Another great Crescent City number is "I Thought I Heard Buddy Bolden Say," and I wish I could have squirmed my way into the raucous audience at a sporting house in early twentieth century Storyville when doomed Buddy ("the blowingest man who ever lived since Gabriel," according to Jelly Roll Morton) performed songs like "Don't Send Me No Roses Cause Shoes Is What I Need," "Your Mammy Don't Wear No Drawers, She Wears Six-Bit Overalls," and "Stick It Where You Stuck It Last Night." Oh, and "Funky Butt." Who cares that the joint might have stunk of "burnt onions and train smoke"? How wonderful to hear jazz, or "*jes' grew*," as Ishmael Reed calls it in his novel *Mumbo Jumbo*, during its earliest days!

New Orleans tends to stir up a lot of wishes. I wish, for example, that I could remember the exact Burgundy Street location of the guest house where my college roommate, Andres, and I stayed in 1984 when we bucked the Spring Break trend of visiting Florida and instead journeyed to the French Quarter. I was twenty, it was my first time sojourning in New Orleans, and I'd never experienced anything so exotic. Every street name in the Quarter was like a one-word poem, or the suggestion of a story, a novel, an epic. By making this nostalgic wish, I suppose I'm mostly wishing I could be twenty again, a new adult but mostly still a child, with a child's notion of everything in life that lay ahead of me. A whole bright new America lay out there to plunder, with my youth never likely to run out. So whenever I'm back in the Quarter now, I wander around on foot alone, searching for that guest house and never finding it.

What I *have* found, while wandering out to the city's Bywater district, was a green Eldorado much like the Eldorado my father used to drive us around in during my childhood. A bumper-sticker on this new vehicle's rear bumper read, "YOUR EGO STORY IS JUST A DAYDREAM." Although I wish these words were not true for me, I know they are; our egos really are stumbling blocks. *Wake up, you*, I sometimes tell myself. According to Jung, "If you're unhappy, then you're too high up in your mind." This notion dovetails with something G. K. Chesterton wrote: "How much larger your life would be if your self could become smaller in it; if you could really look at other men with curiosity and pleasure...You would break out of this tiny and tawdry theater in which your own little plot is always being played, and you would find yourself under a freer sky, in a street full of splendid strangers."

A street like Burgundy, for example.

I wish I had fewer "Little Armageddon Days," as I call them, when Dame Fortune deems that little in my life will go smoothly. And I wish that just once I would be able to observe from morning until night the Georgian tradition of *beboda*, or "Fate Day," which is celebrated every second day of January in that former Soviet republic whose cuisine I learned to love so much during my sole visit to St. Petersburg. On Fate Day, Georgians live their lives in the precise fashion that they want the rest of the year to go. If they wish to make a lot of love in the coming twelve months, for instance, they make sure to make love on January the second. And so forth.

I learned about this *beboda* tradition from a young Georgian painter who'd left her homeland to study art at a university in our American state of Georgia, so she called herself "a double Georgian," which reminds me of a different woman I knew who called herself a "double Indian" because her mother was from New Delhi and her father was of the Nez Perce tribe. Anyway, as soon as I heard about Fate Day, it fired up my imagination, and I vowed to live by it each year. Alas, by the early afternoon of any given January second, Fate Day has already slipped my mind. But the dice go right on rolling.

While I keep blowing it with *beboda*, I don't plan to fall short in celebrating my wife Berta's next birthday. On that morning, I wish we could wake up not just in each other's arms but also having recently starred in each other's dreams. We'll make love. Then, although I'm not much of a cook and Berta doesn't much enjoy eating breakfast, I'll prepare a sumptuous morning meal and serve it to her in bed in our treehouse on the slopes of Mount Kilimanjaro. To complete our morning ritual before going out, we'll separately exercise, although I'll only pretend to do it, which Berta will quickly figure out. As usual.

Our first stop of the day will be nineteenth-century Austria, where Berta's much-admired "Sisi," the free-spirited though ultimately tragic Hapsburg Empress Elisabet, will give us a helpful lecture on nutrition (despite the empress's anorexia). Next, we'll take a hike through our favorite Connecticut forest with our dogs beside us—not only our living Rosalita, but also Egon, Barney, and Roxanne, who are the dogs we've lost.

Appetites whetted, we'll munch on apples from our friend Scott's orchard and take our lunch at a street fair on the Hawaiian island of Kuai, where the *kava kava* will make us so sleepy that we'll need to take a nap in our cabin on a Mississippi riverboat that's floating down the Danube. We'll let our dogs snooze in bed beside us. And to help send Berta into Dreamland, I'll give her the most excellent foot massage, making sure I touch all the therapeutic pressure points.

On rising, I'll boil water to brew Berta's favorite tea. We'll drop in on our favorite orphanage, or "children's village," in Tanzania and our favorite elephant sanctuary in Thailand. Then we'll take the dogs for another walk, this time on a certain road in Bearsville, New York, before we drop in on a soccer match at a stadium in Budapest where we'll be joined by Berta's parents. What a pleasure to watch the great Puskas and his team from 1951 beat the English all over again!

Much of my pleasure, I admit, will come from watching the excitement shining in the eyes of Berta's father Istvan.

Next, a magic carpet ride to the shores of Hungary's Lake Balaton, where Istvan has been fishing the silky waters since he was a boy. He and Berta, my favorite licensed fisherman and fisherwoman, will catch our dinner of carp, pike perch, catfish, and eels before we take a short drive to Berta's hometown of Veszprem for a "*finom*" meal prepared for us by Berta's mother Marike whom I've nicknamed "the Dumpling Queen" because I just can't get enough of her *nokedli*, the distinctive Magyar noodles.

Following dinner, Berta and I will move over to the living room, where we'll dance to Eddie Hinton's song "Shout Bamalama" the way we did at our wedding reception. Then we'll look through photo albums and reminisce about past times, especially the summer day in 2009 when we first met. I had been bartending for a camp at the Burning Man Festival, and Berta came around in a pink tutu and a bikini top made of candy, asking for a shot of whiskey, and before I gave it to her, I suggested that she spin a wheel of fortune my campmates had set up.

With so much left to do, we'll get all dressed up and set out for a big fiesta in Paris. No, make that London! First, there'll be a concert with a long slate of Berta's favorite performers: Jarvis Cocker, Chopin, Dinah Washington, the Bonzo Dog Band, Massive Attack, Laurie Anderson, and the violin wizard Lajko Felix. Rudolf Nureyev will dance during the encore. Then we'll find a nightclub and dance our own asses off until dawn, when the happy howls of wolves will follow us back to our treehouse on Mount Kilimanjaro. We'll make love. Berta's eyelids will flutter when I recite to her a poem by Mario de Andrade, a poem about how I'll travel to England, Italy, everywhere just to "*tell all the women that I don't need them / Because I have you.*"

As Berta dozes off, I'll end the day by whispering to her King Lear's poignant words to his loving daughter Cordelia: "*We two alone will sing like birds i' the cage: / When thou dost ask my blessing, I'll kneel down / And ask of thee forgiveness…*" And in our dreams Dame Fortune will shrug her shoulders, saying, "What the hell," and grant Berta all of her as-yet-ungranted birthday wishes.

I wish that, whenever it's my time to say a "long goodbye"—to a loved friend or relative, to good health, or to life itself—I won't cling too tightly. Better to emulate the character Mitya Weismann in the musical *Follies* by Stephen Sondheim and James Goldman. Based on the entertainment impresario Florenz Ziegfeld, Weismann has been invited to attend a reunion of the pulchritudinous dancers who worked for him decades earlier. Now those dancers and their spouses are middle-aged and having a challenging time with the experience of growing older. One of them asks Weismann, who's already old, if he misses the shows that he used to put on long ago.

"Me?" says Weismann. He shakes his head. "I always know when things are over."

Just in case we've missed the point, Weismann reappears right before the end of the play. As another of his former dancers "gazes fondly" at his soon-to-be-demolished former theater, she turns to him and asks, "Ah, Mitya, don't you hate to see it go?"

Weismann, one of my heroes, remains Weismann. "If nothing else," he says, "I know when things are over."

Step carefully here in our *Senior Citizens Department*, where I agree with Gertrude Stein, who said, "We are always the same age inside." Still, I wish I could live to a ripe old age with most of my physical strength and "with all my f-a-c-u-l-t-i-e-s intact," as the character Esme says in that luminous J. D. Salinger story. I wouldn't mind winding up like my friend James, a motorcycle racer well into his eighties, or like the protagonist of Martin Newell's pop song "Wow! Look At That Old Man." "*Watch him go now*," Newell sings, "*bombing round the town in all kinds of weather / Dressed in skinny jeans and leather*." Yes, that's the kind of old man I want to be, "*rock and rolling when he should be quietly bowling / Speeding on a bicycle with gray hair flying...*"

Throughout this wish list, I have included excerpts from letters that various children wrote to God. I wish I knew what kind of letters to God they would write once they reach old age (assuming, and wishing, that all of them do get to reach old age). Will these elders still maintain wish lists? If so, will their wishes consist mainly of regrets? According to the palliative care health worker Bonnie Ware, the most common regrets of the aged include "I wish I hadn't worked so hard," "I wish I had stayed in touch with my friends," "I wish I had let myself be happier," "I wish I'd had the courage to express my feelings," and "I wish I'd had the courage to live a life true to myself, not the life others expected of me."

Becoming old, according to Edward Hoagland, "involves constructing a new persona, as one did in adolescence." Mirth is important here; as the philosopher George Santayana reminds us, "The old person who will not laugh is a fool." As far as mirth goes, Maude in *Harold and Maude* as well as the Wife of Bath in Chaucer's *Canterbury Tales* are more mirthful than any man, and the most mirthful of all might be the modern-day Wife of Bath in Noel Coward's song "I Went to A Marvelous Party": "*We talked about growing old gracefully / And Elsie, who's seventy-four / Said, "A, it's a question of being sincere / And B, if you're supple you've nothing to fear," / Then she swung upside-down from a glass chandelier / I couldn't have liked it more!*"

A major key to aging vigorously is not to let anything faze you. In 1960 a male resident of the Haslemere Home for the Elderly in Great Yarmouth, England, died of a heart attack when a fellow resident, an eighty-one-year-old woman, performed a public striptease. Three other male patients were treated for shock during this incident, and the following year there were three more deaths from cardiac arrest when another resident, an eighty-seven-year-old, dressed up as the Grim Reaper and waved a scythe at everyone. This led the Haslemere Home to be permanently shut down. Perhaps if the Reaper had been costumed as Dame Fortune instead of the Reaper, that place would still be open for business.

Dare I toss some sexual potency into my wishing pot? I do. If I make it to a rude old age, my wish is to be not just vigorous and mirthful but unquenchably randy, with enough libidinal juice and erectile function to see me through regular steamy interludes. Someone, in other words, of whom the goat god Pan would feel proud.

Which brings us back one more time to my friend Bob Neuwirth. When Bob was near eighty, he and I were checking out an exhibition at the Whitney Museum one afternoon. After catching sight of an alluring woman as she sauntered past us, the two of us watched her until she had gone around a corner. Then Bob turned to me and said, "You know, Gary, I may be too old to cut the mustard, but I can still lick all around inside the jar."

Wow! I thought. *Listen to this old man.*

Let's hear it for the mothers out there! Harry Smith said, "I received my original education in my mother's womb and found that other scholastic organizations were inferior," while according to Donald Winnicott, "Every man or woman who is sane, every man or woman who has the feeling of being a person in the world, and for whom the world means something, every happy person, is in infinite debt to a woman."

In spite of all my complaints about my mother, I'm aware of my great debt to her. Even so, I have one more complaint about her. I wish that Esther Lippman had told me she was dying of cancer when she was in her forties and I was a teenager. Each time she went into the hospital for a mastectomy or a hysterectomy, my mother lied to me, saying, "It's nothing serious, sweetheart, it's just my bad back acting up again, they need to treat me, to put me in traction. Soon I'll be as good as new, *you'll* see."

Observing how ill she looked, I had strong suspicions that this "bad back" business was just a ruse. Yet whenever I'd ask her, "Are you sick with something *else*, Ma? Do you have some life-threatening problem? Do you have, like, *cancer*?" she'd deny it, saying, "Of course not, don't be silly. Like I said, it's this darned bad back of mine. You just focus on your schoolwork and don't worry about me."

"Not worrying me" was the main reason my mother told her lies, I see now. Not worrying me was one of the ways she expressed her love. Also, she truly did want me to focus on my schoolwork and get accepted to a good college, and how could I achieve these plans she had for me if I was worrying day and night? But perhaps something else was going on, too. Perhaps by not admitting her cancer to me or to anyone else she knew except for her brother Wolf, who'd helped to arrange her medical treatment, Esther Lippman could deny to *herself* how seriously ill she was. Could deny, I mean, that she might be facing death. If she pretended to me that she was healthy—healthy, except for her "bad back"—then she could keep the truth at bay even, on occasion, from her own psyche.

During these terrible few years, and for more than a decade after she died, I considered it reprehensible that my mother refused to tell me what she was going through. How dare she go on lying to me! Couldn't she see how frightened I was? Daily, nightly, constantly, I would speculate what could really be wrong with my mother, and I would repeat her falsehoods to myself, trying to summon up reassurance that the "bad back," nothing worse, might indeed be her only problem.

Meanwhile, though, week after week, month after month, the cancer ate Esther Lippman alive, spreading from her breasts to the rest of her body as she stuck to her guns, adamantly refusing to admit her dire condition to me.

"What's wrong with Ma?" I would ask my Uncle Wolf whenever Esther returned to the hospital for more surgery. "She says it's just her bad back, but I think it's something worse..."

Wolf would always sound so mournful when he sighed and fed me the same answer: "I'm sorry, Chief," he'd say. "I wish I could tell you, I really wish I could. But I'm not at liberty to discuss this matter with you. Your mother has asked me not to. She says, 'It's *my* business, no one else's. It's *my* body, it's *my* son.'"

"But—"

"As I said, Chief, I'm so sorry. But I have to respect her wishes."

Toward the end, I started snooping around Esther Lippman's bedroom to find evidence of her mystery ailment, and one afternoon I discovered a brown glass bottle of something called "Laetrile." She'd hidden it in her dresser drawer beneath all her colorful polyester blouses. Laetrile, I knew, was a then-popular quack treatment for cancer, but when I confronted her with it, shaking that brown glass bottle in front of her face, she held my wild gaze and said, "I have no idea what that stuff is."

This denial led to a terrible argument, one that ended with me smashing the medicine bottle against our kitchen wall and my mother sobbing as she crawled around the floor on her hands and knees, picking up her pills and the shards of broken glass. I hated myself for what I had just done. But I hated Esther Lippman, too, for what she was doing to me. Or at least I felt so angry that I confused anger with hatred. She was a dragon, I believed, a dragon bent on destroying me. And I had not yet encountered these words by the poet Rilke: "Perhaps all the dragons in our lives are princesses who are only waiting to see us act, just once, with beauty and courage. Perhaps everything that frightens us is, in its deepest essence, something helpless that wants our love."

As the eighties dawned, my mother's denial about her condition continued. Even when she lay dying on her deathbed in a room at Saint Barnabas Hospital near our home, she told me in a broken voice, "Just my bad back again, dear... *You'll* see, I'll be fine again, in *no* time... You just concentrate on your homework and get ready for college and we'll keep living our happy life together..."

She said these words to me in October of 1981. A few days later she slipped into a coma, a week-long coma that concluded with her death. By the time she'd become comatose, I knew at last what the score was, knew that old Stretchfoot was hovering, and her brother, my Uncle Wolf, was finally able to speak openly with me about her cancer.

Esther's coma did afford me a benefit of sorts. It banished my fear, banished my rage, and freed me to express my love for her. I would whisper in her ear, "I love you from here to the moon and back one hundred million times," the endearment we'd been saying to each other since I was a child. And I softly sang into her ear the title song to the 1966 film *Georgy Girl*, the catchy pop ditty by the New Seekers that had been "our song" since my childhood.

After my mother was gone, I heard "Georgy Girl" playing in Central Park on the children's carousel there and thought of her. Years later, in my early thirties, I finally saw a videocassette of the Lynn Redgrave film in which the song first appeared. And a couple of years after *that*, one rainy night in a Greenwich Village café, I had a meaningful encounter while I sat trying to write a short story about Esther. (Decades later I would publish this story in my book *We Loved the World But Could Not Stay*. The story described a woman who was an alternate-universe incarnation of my mother, a woman who enjoyed all the pleasure, serenity, romantic success, personal independence, good health, long life, and other blessings that Esther Lippman never received from Dame Fortune.)

As for my "meaningful encounter" in the Greenwich Village café, I was deep in writing mode, scribbling my story by hand with my blue gel-ink pen, when a young woman at a nearby table inquired what I was so busy working on. As I looked up from my notebook, annoyed at this interruption, I considered saying, "A suicide note" to shut down any conversation. I had a first draft to finish, after all! But something about this young woman—her sweet open face, perhaps—made me willing to be friendly, so I told her I was writing "a story about my dead mother."

"Oh. Hmm. Got a title yet?" she asked, playing with a strand of her cropped honey-colored hair.

"I do, actually. I plan to call it 'Georgy Ghost.'"

"'Georgy Ghost?'" The young woman looked surprised. "You m like *Georgy Girl*, the movie with Lynn Redgrave?"

"Exactly."

"Wow!"

"Wow what?" I said.

She laughed. "Wow, as in: Lynn Redgrave is my mother!"

It was true. The original "Georgy Girl" had made a Georgy Girl of her own, and now I had met her, and we became friends, Kelly Clark and I, and she has since gone on to make "Georgy children" of her own. On the rainy night we met, we spoke for hours, and Kelly said that she adored the song "Georgy Girl," too, and about a year later, I got to meet Kelly's mother Lynn. The actor was appearing forty streets north of Greenwich Village, starring in a one-woman Broadway play entitled *Shakespeare For My Father*. My favorite part of this play, which Lynn herself had written, was when she recounted to the audience an anecdote about her dad, the distinguished English actor Sir Michael Redgrave.

In Lynn's anecdote, Sir Michael lay on his deathbed in a hospital in London, and because he'd been made delusional by either his medical condition or his medication, the old man mistook the plastic curtain that was drawn across his bed for a velvet curtain in a West End theater. So he said to his two daughters, Lynn and Vanessa, who were seated together beside the bed, "Please ask the stagehand to raise that curtain and let me take a bow for my audience!"

Troubled by this delusion, Vanessa explained to her father that he was *not* onstage at a theater, he was "in hospital," as the Brits say, and he was gravely ill. In other words, she gave her father a gift, the gift of absolute honesty, no matter how painful he might find this honesty. (They don't call it "the brutal truth" for nothing, although I've noticed how often people who favor telling this kind of truth seem to favor the brutality more than they do the truthfulness.)

Maybe Sir Michael appreciated what Vanessa said. Knowing that you're "circling the drain" can certainly be valuable; dispelled illusions and a sense of cold reality do have their benefits, especially for an artist. As soon as Vanessa briefly left the hospital room, however, her sister Lynn took a different tack, one that she believed might be more welcome for her father. Lynn whispered to Sir Michael, "Actually, Dad, it's *true*, you *are* onstage, you've just delivered a magnificent performance, and beyond this velvet curtain here, your audience is applauding."

Lynn, in other words, was giving her father a different kind of than Vanessa gave him: the gift of a comforting illusion. This was der gift to give, Lynn believed, and perhaps better suited for her too, for what do artists like himself do if not conjure illusions?

Artists traffic in truth, yes, but they get there by way of artifice, and Lynn might have been right in believing that artifice was a more appropriate balm for her father on his deathbed than her sister's honesty had been.

Perhaps, I thought as Lynn Redgrave told this story while onstage herself, *a teenaged boy who was frightened to lose his mother likewise needed the comfort of an illusion, the illusion that his mother was suffering from "a bad back." Perhaps he needed that illusion more than he needed the terrible truth.* And from this night on, I started asking myself "Should I behave like Lynn or should I behave like Vanessa?" in situations where speaking honestly to someone may or may not be required.

The play ended. Lynn took her bows, I applauded along with her daughter Kelly. Everyone went home, then time did what time does. It got away from us, and seventeen years after her Broadway performance I watched, Lynn Redgrave died of breast cancer, the same illness that killed Esther Lippman. In the year Lynn died, 2010, my Uncle Wolf and I walked into the bank where I had been renting a safety deposit box. This box contained my mother's wedding ring, her other jewelry, her business documents. Also inside the box was a sealed manila envelope, an envelope on which my mother had scrawled in her left-handed, forward-leaning scrawl "COPY OF ESTHER LIPPMAN'S WILL FOR GARY."

As always when I opened my safety deposit box to retrieve some item, I left the envelope alone, thinking, as always, that I had no need to tear it open. I already kept at home a copy of my mother's will. Yet while I leafed through all the papers today, I had a curious thought, a sort of intuition, and I said it out loud to Wolf: "What if there's *something else* inside the manila envelope? Something, that is, apart from this stated 'COPY OF ESTHER LIPPMAN'S WILL?'" And as we stood together in a tiny office next to the bank vault, with the safety deposit box opened wide and a glorious spring afternoon in progress outside the office's grimy window, Wolf said, "Why don't you open the thing and find out?"

So I did.

My poor mother! She'd assumed that by writing "COPY OF ESTHER LIPPMAN'S WILL FOR GARY" on the outside of this most important missive, she had given me sufficient cause to check inside the envelope as soon as I got my hands on it. What she *should have* done was to add "PLUS SPECIAL MESSAGE" after what she'd scrawled. But she obviously didn't feel that a "PLUS SPECIAL

MESSAGE" was necessary, so the upshot was that I never opened the envelope for thirty years. In fact, I might never have opened it at all had I not had that little hunch, that intuition, and acted on it.

To my amazement, there was indeed something else in the envelope besides the copy of Esther's will. This "special message" was a single sheet of white lined paper, not yet yellowed, on which she'd written a letter. I recognized Esther's handwriting instantly, and as I read it, the song "Georgy Girl" should have started playing over the bank's PA system.

GARY DARLING,

Please forgive me for leaving you! I wanted to tell you how ill I was, but I just couldn't bring myself to do it. Promise me that you won't mourn me for too long. Start today and look ahead to a bright future. Do what will be best for you and enjoy your life. Always remember that I love you very, very much—from here to the moon and back a hundred million times. Please keep well, sweetheart—and in a while smile, live, and be your happy self again.

LOVE AND KISSES,
MOM

EIGHT. A FAREWELL TO WISHING

According to this list's *Wish Quantification Department*, I've been running out of wishes the way Hemingway characterized going broke: "gradually, then suddenly." Just a few more wishes are in the pipeline.

Having visited Stonehenge with Esther Lippman during my childhood, I wish I could go back there, but all by myself this time, with nary a tourist or a tour guide in sight. I would spend a whole night at Stonehenge, enjoying how the sunset and then the subsequent darkness settle around those standing stones. I would sing aloud my favorite wishing songs at bedtime before falling asleep, hiding 'neath the wings of the bluebird as she sings. A red, red robin would sing, as well. And I would dream of riding a Pterodactyl through younger skies, with everyone I've loved doing a *Seventh Seal*-style "Dance of Death" in a playground far below. What a fun Pterodactyl ride this will be!

At dawn I'll wake up, with the sound of my mother singing "Rise and Shine," and for my morning ritual I'll say out loud the words that are uttered by that ancient giant in the play *Jerusalem*, the giant who claims he built Stonehenge: "Well, whatever's coming, this is one beautiful morning."

Maybe this giant can call to our aid the world-saving Golem I've been wishing for. Maybe he can summon Kurt Vonnegut, Jr.'s uncle, too, Uncle Alex who would always say to everyone in his vicinity when he was really enjoying himself, "If *this* isn't nice, what *is*?" Not a bad recognition to have, even if it might fall short of Kurt's favored state in which "Everything is beautiful and nothing hurts."

"It began in mystery," writes Diane Ackerman, "and it will end in mystery, but what a savage and beautiful country lies in between."

Someday, maybe even today, a bell will ring. A banshee will wail. A familiar female voice will whisper the phrase "*sum sine regno*" in my ear. Then, through rapidly dimming light, I'll glimpse Dame Fortune leaning over me. Her veil will be gone, and I'll feel only slightly surprised to discover at last her human incarnation. Turns out that the Dame is the old man I used to see in the libraries of New York and

Paris, the "Mr. Ravoon" with the eye patch and the black clothes and the open volume of *Who's Who in America*. So *he* was a *she*—what a master of disguise! Or maybe gender is beside the point. Anyway, she won't be wearing any eye patch now, and both of her sea-foam-green eyes will be fixed on mine as she shows me her open volume of *Who's Who*. Guess what? I'm not listed in it. Which is okay, because the best wish one can wish is for everything to be just as it already is. This is the Lippy Law to end all Lippy Laws, and you don't have to be a child to write to God about it.

"I'm wide awake now," the Dame will say. "How about you?"

Whatever my answer is, the time has come for me to "saddle up the palomino," to "beat it on down the line," to "light out for the Territory." To either swallow or else to spit out this gumball planet. It's time, in other words, to say goodbye.

I wish you calm waters, fellow wisher. Deep waters, too. And I hope you'll take to heart the words of Vonnegut's Uncle Alex as well as those of Mae West, who said, "You only live once—but if you do it right, once is enough." May we all get to "do it right," with Dame Fortune granting us a maximum of beauty and a minimum of hurt. Beyond that, I leave you to your destiny. Perhaps I'll see you in the stars…

In the meantime, though, the dice keep rolling. Always rolling. And *they're* still standing in the shadows, noting every wish we make: those pesky ninjas.

(ALS ICH KAN)

ACKNOWLEDGEMENTS

For professional support, I warmly thank Tyson Cornell, Hailie Johnson, Delia Bennett, Jennifer Psujek, Mike McNamara, and the other fine folks at Rare Bird.

I'm also immensely grateful to the Internet wizard Fotis Tzanakis, Laura Albert, David Amram, Laurie Anderson, David "Bomba" Baum, John Bliss, Sarah Bloom, Lorraine Bracco, Tamara Braun, David Brendel, Joan Juliet Buck and Nick, Carla Capretto, Chris Cardy, Nathalie Detourne, Barry Ellsworth, Danny Fields, Rosie Flores, Carolyn "MG" Garcia, Bill Glazer and Tom, Juan Guzman, Yasmine Hamdan and Elia Suleiman, Stacy "the Groover" Hoover, Kimberly Huie, Eugene Hutz and Victoria Espinosa, Michael Hyde, Michael and Victoria Imperioli, Heidi James, Charles and Josh Kalish, Dorka Keehn, David Keil, Rick and Beverly Kestenbaum, Simon and Maria Angelica Kirke, Ilene Landress, Jillian Lauren and Scott Shriner, Steven List, Dave Lombardi, Pam Lubell and James Hammond, Lydia Lunch, Paula Madrid, Ann Marlowe, Patricia Marx, Dana McCoy, Sergio, Susana, Sebastian, Santiago, and Sergio Jr. Medina, Jimbo Ospenson and Meryl Perlman, Myra Pasek, Melodie Provenzano and Hans Chew, Matthew Rhys and Keri Russell, Nic Richard and Julie Bonnie, Lou Rittmaster, Alexa Robbins, Yvette Scharf, Susan and Donald Schreiber, Tammy Jo Setner, Jessica and Martin Smith, Jeff Stein and Angela Janklow, Sara Sugarman, Sean Sullivan, Haviva and Joshua Swirsky, Jacques Thelemaque, Maureen and Stevie Van Zandt, Maria Santoro, Lori Santoro and Darryl, Andres Virkus and Margy Rung, Judith Weinstein, Michael Wherly, Jonathan Young and Audrey Grumhaus, as well as my goddaughters Thelma and Lorelye.

Where would I be without Marvin Dunn, Stacey Bell, Eileen Salzig, Brigitte Bako, Bill Ehrlich, L. Gabrielle Penabaz, Larry Kirstein, Arnie Civins, Sean Fellin, Matt Marcello, Dr. Michael Bush, Jack Morer, Antony Wong, Mariela Rosales, Tatiana De Almeida, and the ever-amazing Alan Dreher and Cathy Clarke?

Very much missed are Szombathelyi Istvan, Erik Dreher, Jeremy Tepper, Bobby Neuwirth, Tom Robbins, Richard Smith, Susan Kalish, Alison Bevan, and my uncle Bobby Lippman.

I also miss Frau Elisabeth Schmeding, Madeleine Jensen, Irving Cooperberg, Ole Egset, Harry Crews, Gypsy Boots, John Perry Barlow, Kevin Byrd, Maryellen Cataneo, Ceil and Norman, Ian Cuttler, Gael Greene, Yaakov Gladstone, Wendell Green, Michael Greene, Amie Harwick, Peggy Hitchcock, David Johansen, Mark Kamins, Nina Mattson, Meg Mazursky, Daniel Menaker, T-Shirt Philippe, Lou Reed, Mort Roth, Marla Ruzicka, Sam and Mildred Schreiber, Rona Smith, Scott Sommer, Sam Weiner, Hal Willner, Atman Tom Fronterhouse, and Ida Winston.

Thanks as well to Tatiana Abbey, Masha Alloin, Alosha and Vali, Scott Asen, Barbet Schroeder and Bulle Ogier, Norena Barbella, Paula Batson, Sandrine Bluet, Dan and Beth Bootzin, Richard Bradley, Arthur Cacossa, Lafcadio "Jim" Cass, Vin Cycz, Huy Dao, the Delaney/McCarthy/Collinson trio, Janine DiGiovani, Linda Dinerstein, Gita Drury, Hampton Fancher, Sharyn Felder and Will, Juli Jo Fehrle, Rachel Fox, Ray Gange, Chef Paul Gerard, Boris Grebenschikov, Bobby and Kathy Golden, George Dawes Green and Esther, Adam Grosso, Rajesh Gulab, India Howell, Maite Iracheta, Rickie Lee Jones and Jamie dell'Apa, Danny "Kootch" Kortchmar, Steve Krulwich, Diana Lehr, Jenna Moskowitz, MarieVic, Maria Muldaur, Jenni Muldaur, Mark Murphy, Mitch Myers, Nadine Neema, Willie Nile and Cris, May Pang, Barbara Petratos, Pippin Petty-Schroeppel, Pat Place, Paul Roosin and Sarah, Toni Ross, Derrick Rossi, Eric Sandys, Sammy Semenza, Jonathan Shaw, Dalia Sofer, Jerry Stahl, Jeff Stettin, Supercali, Magic Carla and Alex, Russ Titelman, Holly Troy, Monica Vaughan and Jasvinder, Ali Zacker, George Zaver, Zsofi Tomas, Mimi Roman, Sharon Raider, Courtney Greenhalgh, Michelle Blankenship, Paul Comsuela, Deb Kosakoff, Cait O'Riordan, Warren and Jane Rosen, Elizabeth Kipp-Guisti and Alex and Ibolya Szasz, plus Suzanne, Ben, David, Teddy, Lindsey, Jacki, Beth, and Steven Lippman.

Let me hereby declare my love to Ethel Lippman ("from here to the moon and back 100 million times"), Bernard Lippman (Charlie Samsam says hi), David and Lena (Lily) Fern, my dear Norma Lippman, David and Lena (Lulu) Lippman, my lovely co-parent Ingunn Egset, Szombathelyi Marika, Szilard (Dr. Meyer), Ginger, and Bibi, plus all of my Hungarian relatives and the fabulous fjord-dwelling Bodil and Ols Egse.

Even if I had my pick to parent any child in the universe, I'd go with my son Gabriel Olai Beauregard Egset, whose wit, warmth, resilience, and brilliance "make me feel ten feet tall."

If I owe my sanity—indeed, my existence—to a single person, it's my uncle Dr. William H. Fern, who for five decades has listened to me vent, helped me to "tailor expectations," shared family lessons, imbued me with his courage, served as my greatest teacher, and enhanced the lives of hundreds of other people.

This book would not exist if not for the flower of Veszprem, my wife Szombathelyi Vera Kata, a tender, wise, beautiful, and fun soul who's given me a loving home while helping me to "grow up" and acting as my first and best reader, for which I say "*Szeretlek nagyon big-time*" to you, *Mutyi*...

This book was powered by coffee made by the American café companies Bitty & Beau and Café Joyeux, which employ people with special needs. May they continue to flourish and inspire other businesses to emulate their thoughtful personnel policy.

Finally, the story goes that whenever the journalist Mike Royko gave copies of his books to his research assistants, he signed each volume with the inscription, "You were the best. Don't tell the others." To everyone whose names appear above, you were the best. Don't tell the others. And please don't tell any ninjas.

www.ingramcontent.com/pod-product-compliance
Lightning Source LLC
LaVergne TN
LVHW040846180326
834161LV00001B/43

* 9 7 8 1 6 4 4 2 8 5 1 4 5 *